The
MEASURE
of a LADY

Books by Deeanne Gist

The MEASURE *of a* LADY

A Novel

DEEANNE GIST

BETHANY HOUSE PUBLISHERS

Minneapolis, Minnesota

Published by Bethany House Publishers
11400 Hampshire Avenue South
Bloomington, Minnesota 55438

Bethany House Publishers is a division of
Baker Publishing Group, Grand Rapids, Michigan.

Printed in the United States of America

| Paperback: | ISBN-13: | 978-0-7642-0073-1 | ISBN-10: | 0-7642-0073-9 |
| Hardcover: | ISBN-13: | 978-0-7642-0285-8 | ISBN-10: | 0-7642-0285-5 |

Library of Congress Cataloging-in-Publication Data

Gist, Deeanne.
    The measure of a lady / Deeanne Gist.
       p.   cm.
    ISBN 0-7642-0285-5 (alk. paper) — ISBN 0-7642-0073-9 (pbk.) 1. Brothers and
sisters—Fiction. 2. San Francisco (Calif.)—History—19th century—Fiction. I. Title.

PS3607.I55M43   2006
813'.6—dc22   2006007823

To my parents,
Harold and Veranne Graham,
who have given tirelessly
of their time, their wisdom, and their love.
Thank you so very, very much.
I love you. Dee

DEEANNE GIST has a background in education and journalism. Her credits include *People, Parents, Parenting, Family Fun,* and the *Houston Chronicle.* She has a line of parenting products called I Did It!® Productions and a degree from Texas A&M. She lives with her husband, four teenagers, and two dogs in Houston, Texas, and loves to hear from her readers at her website.

a c k n o w l e d g m e n t s

I cannot seem to complete a manuscript without first visiting the actual locale in which the story takes place. Many thanks to Richard and Linda Alvarez for opening their home to me, for taxiing me around San Francisco and the surrounding area, for giving me the skinny that only the locals are privy to, and for enriching not just this novel but also my life. May God bless you tenfold to how you have blessed me.

My first novel, *A Bride Most Begrudging*, took me three years to write. Once I sold it to Bethany House, I was given one year to finish writing *The Measure of a Lady*. Nothing like a little pressure to send one into a complete panic. My saving grace throughout this project was my critique partner, Meg Moseley, whose input was invaluable. She encouraged me, prompted me, taught me, and prayed for me. I do not know what I would have done without her. Thank you, Meg. I am looking forward to many more years as professional colleagues and dearest friends.

I could not possibly close without thanking my team at Bethany House. What an incredibly talented group of folks they are, not to mention a good deal of fun. Special thanks to David Long for going above and beyond, and to Paul Higdon and his creative team. As far as cover art for books goes, the buck stops with Paul. And you must agree that the cover of *Lady* is one of the most incredible covers of all time. Thank you. I am truly blessed.

Love, Dee

SAN FRANCISCO ◆ *April 1849*

chapter 1

*T*his Street Is Impassable, Not Even Jackassable.

Rachel Van Buren reread the sloppily painted, dripping red letters splattered across the rickety sign. Even as she watched, its supporting post tilted forward, better exposing an endless blanket of mud stretching up behind in and beyond.

Where are the trees, Lord? Why, it's nothing but mud and scrub brush.

With the Pacific at her back and a sea of mud before her, she hadn't even a dry spot to drop the valises she held in each hand.

"What are we going to do?" her sister asked, swiping a strand of golden hair from her face.

"I'm not sure, Lissa."

Her fifteen-year-old sister, fourteen-year-old brother and she were all exhausted from their two-month voyage. And all newly orphaned by the unexpected passing of their father, Jacob Van Buren.

The promise of easy gold in the California territory had seemed like an answer to her father's woes. So, he had scrounged up what little capital they had and bought the family tickets on the *Oregon* with high hopes. Hopes lost in grief and stranding the three of them in a foreign territory with no guardian, no money to speak of, and no means of support.

"We can't go back to the ship," Michael said. "The crew has abandoned us."

Not only the crew, Rachel thought, but their fellow passengers as well. She'd never seen that many men move so fast. Glancing at the now-empty rowboat secured to the rustic wharf, Rachel decided they had no choice but to leave behind their traveling trunks which sat forlornly on the pier like little caskets destined for the graveyard.

Fog whipped in from the waterfront, swirling onward to the slopes of San Francisco peppered with rambling tents and shacks. Twilight had begun its final curtain call, ushering in the deeper shadows of nightfall. One-by-one, lanterns inside the distant canvas dwellings came to light, transforming the hills into fiery nuggets.

Rachel tightened her grip on the leather valises. "I'll tell you what we are going to do, Lissa." She took a deep, fortifying breath. "We're going to get muddy. We're going to get quite muddy."

"But look how steep it is," Lissa said.

Rachel eyed the extreme incline they must traverse to get to what she assumed was the town square. Even if the road were packed hard, it would be a strenuous hike. But soggy mud? Near impossible.

Michael yowled with delight and raced right into the thick of it, slipping, sliding, and coating the bags he carried with the clinging goop. His feet way too big for his scrawny fourteen-year-old body, he landed on his backside before he was even a third of the way up. "Ho, it's slippery, girls. And deep."

He twisted around, flashing them a full-sized grin barely discernible in the fading light. "If you'll wait for me, I'll come back and give you piggybacks."

"What do you think, Lissa?" Rachel asked, quirking a brow.

Lissa worried her bottom lip. "I will if you will."

Rachel hesitated, then shook her head. "No, I think I'll try it on my own."

Her shoulders drooped at this introduction to San Francisco. She had donned her best dress for this momentous occasion, its skirt peeking out from beneath her three-quarter-length coat. She stepped into the murky ankle-deep mess, caking herself with wet, malodorous mud, and trudged up the incline.

Panting from exertion and shivering from the biting wind, she crested the hill and stood with her siblings in mute fascination. But *fascination* didn't cover the half of it. More like consternation. Disbelief. Shock.

Light poured from the open doors of the huge tents that lined San Francisco's plaza, crisscrossing the square like a swath of gingham. Signs tacked to the canvas shacks greeted them with that now familiar red paint, but with unfamiliar words in a variety of languages.

The muddy streets teemed with people. No, not people. *Men.* Oriental men with long braided pigtails. Dark-skinned men with colorful sombreros. Men with so much facial hair one couldn't even begin to guess from whence they came.

And with them a swelling of voices. Yelling. Laughing. Cursing. In more languages then she could count and set to a lively musical score made up of banjos, bugles, fiddles, and jig-time ballads.

This was San Francisco? The Golden Gate? The Mother Lode? *Oh, Papa. You were thinking to strike gold in this mess?*

She placed one foot in front of the other, crossing the plaza, until she stood in front of a wooden building sporting a large projecting verandah and a sign that read "City Hotel."

A huge man weaved into the doorway, blocking the path of light from within, then stumbled into the street. Face first.

"Oh my," Lissa breathed.

The man lay still and unmoving.

"What if he drowns in this muck before he can get up?" Michael whispered.

Handing her valises to him, Rachel moved forward. "Sir? Are you all right?"

No response. She slanted the others a glance. "Maybe we better help him." But before they could, the man rose onto all fours with a roar.

She squeaked and jumped back. The man pushed himself to his feet and stumbled past, never even acknowledging them.

"Oh my," Lissa breathed again.

Rachel smoothed down the front of her coat with her hands. "Stay here. At least until I can be assured that this is a, um, proper hotel."

Michael frowned. "Maybe I better go instead."

She shook her head. "No. I'll go. Besides, I need you to wait here with Lissa."

Mud oozed beneath her skirt, her pantalets, clear up to her shins as she hoisted herself onto the large verandah. The interior could not be determined from the murky view beyond the open doorway. Straightening her coat sleeves, she stomped her feet in an effort to dislodge the clinging mess and proceeded into the City Hotel.

Nothing could have prepared her. Smoke stung her eyes, curses seared her ears, and rancid smells assaulted her nose. She hesitated, trying to adjust, and scanned the room—squinting to see through a haze almost as thick as the mist outside.

The interior was one huge area that functioned as bar, gambling house, and sleeping quarters. With a border of four-tiered bunks running along three of the walls, men alternately read by candlelight, lay asleep in their bunks, or hung off the edges watching card players at the various tables.

To the side was a dressing table and mirror. One man used a hairbrush chained to the mirror rack while another rinsed out a toothbrush and handed it to the next gent waiting in line.

Along the fourth wall ran a plank bar with patrons in suspect condition draped along its edge. Above it, a large ornamental gilt mirror duplicated the scene before her. A chalky white life-size statue of a nude woman caused Rachel's gaze to skitter elsewhere.

Strewn throughout the rest of the room were green baize tables with hoards of tobacco-spitting men, shoulder-to-shoulder, flinging down nuggets and calling out their bets. Some tables offered chairs with respectable looking gentlemen giving the patrons a choice of "the red" or "the black."

Behind one such chair was a dark, beautiful woman. Her full shimmery skirt and bespangled shawl of every color dipped and swelled over voluptuous curves. Leaning over, she whispered something into a gambler's ear, freely exposing her bosom, as there was no boning to her camisole.

Rachel barely swallowed her shock. And that's when she saw it. The cigarette. Plain as day, poised between the woman's rouged pouting lips.

Rachel squeezed the neck of her coat together. Never, ever had she seen a woman smoke before. She didn't even know it was done.

Yet no one seemed shocked. Why, the men at the table looked to be as dignified as any you'd see back in New Jersey, and all were acting as if nothing were out of the ordinary.

A resounding cheer on the opposite side of the room drew her attention. A wall of backs garbed in blue flannel shirts surrounded whatever it was that held their interest. As if drawn by an invisible cord, she moved to the circle and wove through the press of bodies until she could see.

"How much is in the sack, boy?"

"Ten thousand."

"And you wish to stake it on one card?"

"Yes, sir."

The dealer, dressed in a fine dark jacket and matching vest, leaned back in his chair, drawing deeply on his cigar. "Why?"

"I was heading home, sir, and thunk to myself, 'This may be my last chance to play monte. Why not bet it all and go home with pockets not just full, but bulgin'.'"

She held her breath. Surely the dealer would tell him no. The boy's face was as smooth as a baby's. He shouldn't be allowed in here, much less allowed to gamble. And ten thousand—on one card!

"You've been mining quite some time for this?"

"Almost a year."

Not a sound issued forth from this corner of the room. *No. Please, say no.*

The dealer didn't look to be a hardened man, though he was up in years—thirty-five at least. Still, he was clean, combed, and shaven. He would most certainly tell the boy no.

The man's face split with a rakish grin as he clapped his hands together. "Ten thousand it is."

The roar of the crowd was deafening, absorbing her cry of denial. Then silence. Total, complete, and fraught with tension. The dealer turned over a queen of diamonds, then a five of clubs. The boy plopped his heavy leather sack atop the queen.

"Queens?" the dealer asked.

"Queens," the boy replied.

The dealer set the deck of cards face down on the table, then slowly, very slowly, turned over card after card. Eight of spades. Ten of clubs. Ten of hearts. Six of diamonds.

On and on it went until a five of hearts was turned over. The dealer didn't reach for another card but rested his hand on the table, his blue eyes lifting to meet those of the boy.

What has happened? What does it mean? She glanced from one man in the crowd to another, but all were focused on the card. The boy fell back against his chair, his face white.

The dealer reached for the bag, opened it, took out a handful of dust, then let it sift into a small pile in front of the boy. "This should be enough to either get you home or get you started here again. Your drinks are on me tonight."

Johnnie Parker tensed as a low murmur raced through the crowd. Young Rattlesnake was a favorite amongst the miners, but business was business. The five came up in the deck first, and winner takes all.

He carefully tied the leather pouch closed, then allowed his gaze to roam over the other miners. But it wasn't Rattlesnake who held their attention.

"Give him his money back," the woman snapped.

Johnnie was halfway out of his chair before he realized it had been well over a year since he'd stood up for a lady. But lady she was. Standing amongst these disreputable miners in her coat, skirt, and sunbonnet. Caked in mud and looking so blasted pretty he could scarcely catch his breath.

Every eye in the place was on her. Even Rattlesnake appeared to have forgotten he'd just lost his fortune. And the lady? The lady's attention was fully and completely focused on Johnnie.

And she was none too pleased.

"Give it back to him," she repeated.

"I won fair and square."

"He's nothing but a boy."

"He's older than you, I'd wager."

Her back stiffened. "I believe there has been enough wagering for one night." She pulled off her glove, one finger at a time, having no idea, he was sure, how long it had been since these men had seen a female perform such a simple task. "Where's the owner?"

He took a pull on his cigar. "That'd be me." He offered her a slight bow. "Johnnie Parker. At your service."

She pursed her lips. "Tell me, Mr. Parker, do you make a habit of stripping hard-earned fortunes from the hands of babes?"

He narrowed his eyes. "I've stripped no one of anything. I run a clean, honest house here."

"Really? Why, I didn't know there was such a thing as an *honest* gambling house."

"So now you know." He swept her with his gaze. She was of average height, and though her rust-colored coat hid the contours of her shape, he would guess there wasn't much meat on her bones. Her heart-shaped face held high cheekbones, soft-looking lips, and dark brows that arched slightly above coffee-colored eyes. Eyes that simmered with disapproval.

"Is there something I can do for you?" he asked, snuffing out his cigar.

She slapped the glove into her hand. "The sign outside says 'City Hotel.'"

"Yes, it surely does."

"Then where is the registration desk?"

Another murmur from the men. "Well, miss, I've never really needed a desk just to rent out a few bunks."

Her eyes widened. "You've no rooms?"

Flipping his coattails back, he slipped his hands into his pockets. "No. Can't say that I do."

"For heaven's sake. A hotel without rooms." She pulled her glove through her palm then slapped it back again. The simple movement enthralled every man in the hotel.

"I have a room, ma'am," a voice offered. "You can hitch up with me."

Johnnie swung his attention to ol' Harry and scowled, but the words on his lips died as the lady turned fiery red at Harry's proposal. Take the deuce, but he'd forgotten the power of a woman's blush.

"Well. I . . . I . . . oh. Thank you, but I really just wanted to rent a room."

A hundred offers poured forth. She held up her hand for silence. "A *hotel* room." She turned again to him. "Is there a hotel in town that has *rooms* for rent?"

"I'm afraid hotels in San-Fran-cisco only offer bunks, not rooms."

"Then would you be so kind as to direct me to a woman who might put me up for the night?"

He rubbed his jaw. "I'm afraid all the respectable women are up in the mining camps with their husbands."

"You cannot mean to tell me there is not one single church-going woman in this whole entire town?"

"What he says is true, miss," Harry replied. "You're the first sunbonnet us fellers have seen in a month o' Sundays."

She frowned. "Sunbonnet?"

"That's what the boys call the respectable women," Johnnie said. "The, um, other women don't worry overmuch about their skin and, therefore, do not wear sunbonnets."

She hesitated. "I see. Well, then. Where is the church?"

"We don't have one."

"You don't have a church?"

"I'm afraid not. Not the way you mean. Sunday services are held in the old schoolhouse."

She surveyed the bunks along the wall, a slight frown wrinkling her brow.

"What about your shack, Johnnie?" somebody hollered. The rest of the room erupted with approval, and before he knew it, his own patrons were showing her the way to his private quarters behind the hotel.

He needn't have worried, though. She dug in her heels after the first two steps. "Absolutely not."

They all stopped and looked at her expectantly.

"I couldn't. I just . . . couldn't."

"Sure ya could. Cain't she, Johnnie?"

He sauntered forward. "Well, as it happens, Miss . . . ?"

"Van Buren. Rachel Van Buren."

". . . Van Buren, I would be honored to lend you the use of my shanty until you can find other accommodations."

She glanced toward the door, then back at him. "But what about your family?"

He smiled. "I've no family, miss."

"Oh. Then where would you stay?"

"I'm in the process of building a new shack. It's not totally complete, but enough to where I can bed down in it."

She brightened. "Well, then, perhaps I could stay there instead?"

"No."

"I insist."

"And I said no. It's not finished and would not be suitable."

She frowned.

He tried again. "I'd be hung for sure, miss, if I gave you anything but the best. And my shanty is the best place in town."

Nods of approval circulated.

"Sir, surely you understand. I cannot stay in an unmarried man's—No. I'm sorry. If you won't let me stay in the unfinished shack, then I'll just have to find someplace else."

Harry stepped forward. "Where's yer man?"

Shadows swept across her eyes. "My father died of cholera during our passage around the Horn."

"It's right sorry I am about that, ma'am. You married?"

"Um, no, I'm afraid not."

A resounding roar broke forth. Miss Van Buren took an involuntary step back.

Harry scratched his beard. "Well, then, you'd best be stayin' right here. Ain't no man in town you can trust better than this here Johnnie Parker. That is, o' courst, unless you'd be willin' to marry me?"

She swallowed and looked back at Johnnie, for confirmation, he supposed. He offered nothing.

"There just ain't no other place fer a sunbonnet," Harry contin-ued. "No, miss. It's either marry up or stay in Johnnie's shack."

The men rumbled their agreement.

She fingered the buttons of her coat. "I see. Well, then, I suppose, for tonight only." Large brown eyes met his. "You're sure it's ... proper?"

Johnnie bowed. "Absolutely. Right this way."

She shook her head. "I must get my family first."

He stopped midstride. "Family?"

"Yes. My brother and sister. They're right ..." She pointed to the door, and as the men parted for her, he discovered a scrawny boy and a lovely girl standing in his doorway looking tired and lost. "Well, they're right there. Come, Lissa, Michael. I think I've found us a room."

But Michael wasn't listening. Michael had all his attention cen-tered on the nude statue. Fortunately, Miss Van Buren couldn't see over the shoulders of the men to what was distracting him.

"Michael?"

He started, turned completely red, then nearly tripped over him-self in his haste to get to his sister's side.

"Michael, Lissa. This is Mr. Parker. He's the proprietor here and has a, um, shack that will suffice for tonight until another arrange-ment can be worked out."

The children nodded politely. A pair of valises appeared in the clutches of Harry's hands.

"I'll take those, Harry." Johnnie turned to the crowd. "Carry on, everyone. Drinks are on the house tonight."

But the usually uproarious group of miners didn't move. Didn't howl with approval. Instead, they stood solemn and intent while Johnnie guided the sunbonnet woman and her family to his private quarters behind the kitchen.

c h a p t e r 2

he shack had no door. Nothing. Not even a cloth
covering. Steps away from the hotel's threshold
and built with the roughest of planks, the structure listed a bit to the
left.

Rachel missed Lissa's abrupt halt, bumped into her back, then had
her own heels trodden by Michael.

With a flourish of his hand, Mr. Parker indicated entrance into
"the best place in town."

None of them moved.

Glancing from one to the other, he cleared his throat. "Perhaps I
should light a lantern first."

He disappeared through the doorframe, and light spilled forth
almost immediately. She heard the unmistakable sound of objects
being shuffled to and fro before their host reappeared. Again, he indicated entrance. "Please."

She nudged Lissa, and the three of them filed in. Scarcely register-
ing the crackle of the straw-covered floor beneath her feet, she gave
the ten-by-twelve room a quick perusal.

A giant bedstead took up most of the room, so solid and heavy it
must surely have been pieced together at that very spot. A hodge-

podge of materials and old clothing stitched in haphazard fashion formed its tick. No pillows. One small blanket. And a deep indention from where its owner had last slept.

Her gaze shied away and moved to a fireplace built of stones and mud. She'd never seen a chimney finished off inside a room, yet layers of stones, rough sticks, and rude mortar reached clear to the ceiling. The mantel, considered the crowning glory of a parlor back home, was no more than a beam of raw wood covered with strips of ready-made tin cans—cut open and laid flat, labels of their former contents still intact.

Mr. Parker had set their valises beneath a window, or rather, a two-foot hole in the wall. He now grabbed some flint and began to light the pre-laid kindling situated in the fireplace. "The washstand is there in the corner. I'll show Michael where to fetch some fresh water."

Rachel turned to the corner, noting an empty vegetable bowl sitting atop a trunk with a common dining pitcher in place of a ewer. "I see," she murmured.

A warped piece of wood nailed to the wall held an assortment of books. Fashion plates from magazines hung about the room, offering a bit of decoration. Women with impossible waists and miraculous bosoms dominated the collection.

Michael drifted to a little round table flanked by a pair of spindly chairs, a chessboard decorating its top. Picking up a chess piece, he examined it, turned fiery red, then quickly set the piece down.

Mr. Parker chose that moment to finish his task. "Do you play chess, Michael?"

"Um, yes, sir. Um, some. I'm, um, I'm not very good at it, actually."

"Well, we'll have to play us a game."

Michael nodded, looking as if he'd swallowed his tongue.

"If there is nothing else, then, Miss Van Buren, I really need to get back to the hotel."

The fire popped, though its warmth had not yet permeated the shack. Rachel summoned the energy for a polite smile. "Of course.

You've been far too generous already. I don't know what to say nor what we would have done."

He nodded. "Not at all."

"Michael? Why don't you go ahead and have Mr. Parker show you where to fill the ewer." She lifted her brows. "If that is acceptable, that is?"

"Certainly."

Michael grabbed the pitcher and followed Mr. Parker out the doorway, the contrast between brawny man and skinny boy striking Rachel anew and reminding her again her young brother was quite without a father to guide him in his ways.

The unique blend of their voices, one deep, one all over the scale, drifted into oblivion before the sisters turned to each other.

"There's no door and no window covering," Lissa exclaimed. "Whatever are we to do?"

"I guess we'll be safe enough. At least that seemed to be the consensus." Rachel eyed the open doorway and window. "It might be prudent to look for a spare cloth to drape over them, though."

"Was the shack leaning or was it my imagination?"

"Shadows, I think."

"Um." Lissa scrunched up her nose. "The chimney's inside the house."

Rachel looked at the mess of mud and stones. "Well, not entirely. The flue still goes up through the roof, and it looks to be working properly."

"But have you ever?" Lissa moved to the fireplace, examining the tin-covered mantel. "Seems your Mr. Parker is partial to peas."

"He's not my Mr. Parker and it was extremely kind of him to offer up his room."

"Is his family back east?"

She began to unbutton her coat. "He's unmarried."

Lissa blinked. "But look at that bed. Why, all three of us will easily fit on it. Whatever would he need with such a large bed if he hasn't a family?"

Frowning, Rachel studied the mammoth structure. "I'm not really sure, but I'm too tired to think."

She considered the window without panes or drapes, the entry without door or lock. She bit the inside of her cheek. The safety and security of her family now rested on her shoulders. And the best she could do was rely on a total stranger.

———

Something was different. Rachel opened her eyes to sunshine and a room that didn't sway like a ship. All came rushing back. The muddy city, the appalling excuse for a hotel, the rough patrons, the decadent statue, the young boy who lost his fortune, the hotel owner who held it.

A bit confounding, that. A man who would fleece a young boy of gold, yet would give up the use of his home to a pitiful group of orphans.

She noted Michael at some point had moved to sleep by the fireplace, leaving the bed to Lissa and her.

The articles of clothing they'd tied together and draped over the doorway lay in a heap on the floor, as did the ones by the window.

She tucked the covers up about her neck. The cabin looked even more pathetic in the light of day, though the fire chased the chill from the air. Michael must have stoked it then fallen asleep at its hearth.

After putting off the inevitable, she finally edged her feet to the ground, scurried to the washstand, and splashed water onto her face. Its frigid temperature stole her very breath but removed the last vestiges of sleep.

Retrieving her hanky, she patted the water from her cheeks, lips, eyes, and forehead. She still couldn't quite fathom a washstand with no towel, but such was the case.

She glanced at the open entry. Covering it up again would require help, and she hated to wake Michael just yet. Moving to a corner of the room, she managed to put her garments on without exposing anything of importance, all the while cringing at having to once again wear yesterday's mud-caked dress. Slipping out the doorway, she tied her bonnet strings and made her way back to the hotel.

Mr. Parker sat in the small kitchen that separated the hotel proper from the back door. He looked different this morning. A blue flannel shirt, dark cotton trousers, and high boots replaced the fancy attire of last evening. So absorbed was he in his newspaper he didn't appear to have heard her approach.

She allowed herself a precious moment to study the cozy little alcove. It wasn't a conventional kitchen, of course, though cast-iron pots, frying pans, and Dutch ovens lay strewn across the stove. The room—hardly big enough to turn around in—held cheek-by-jowl preserved meats, a bag of beans, a pork barrel, and a heap of clean clothing. The overwhelming odor of what must be coffee assaulted her nose. A far cry from the soothing smell of Papa's brew.

Shoved against the wall, the dining table was nothing more than a semicircular board laid on top of a sea chest, surrounded by three chairs, none of which matched. The top of the table had cleats to hold the dishes so they wouldn't slide off—not because it was a seafaring table, but, she assumed, because the slope of the floor was so terribly uneven.

Mr. Parker, sitting in one of the chairs with a tin mug in one hand and a newspaper in the other, must have sensed her presence. He looked up, stood, and bowed. "Good morning."

"Forgive me. I didn't mean to disturb you."

"Not at all." He folded his paper and snagged another tin cup out of a candle box. Before she could protest, he filled the cup from the coffeepot at his elbow and offered her a seat.

She really needed to secure passage back home, but the man had been more than generous—with her, anyway. So she settled herself down as best she could. "Thank you."

Reaching for a jacket from the heap of clothing on the floor, he shrugged it on and sat down beside her. The wrinkled jacket did little to disguise the breadth of his shoulders and the strength in his arms.

She disliked taking refreshment with a man minus the protection of a chaperone but had been forced to do so since her father's death. And Mr. Parker, with his dark, curly hair and square, angular jaw, exuded a kind of raw masculinity that enthralled and intimidated all at the same time.

She warmed her hands around the perimeter of her cup, her mother's admonitions repeating themselves within her mind.

The man of "perfect manners" is calmly courteous in all circum-stances, reliable as a rock, judicious in every action, dependable in trifles as well as large affairs, full of mercy and kindness, affectionate and lov-ing. His brain must be as fine as his heart.

There had been no such man on the ship . . . after Father died.

Mr. Parker lifted his cup to his lips, swallowing some of its con-tents without ever taking his eyes from hers. "You slept well, I trust?"

"Yes. Thank you. And you?"

"Fine."

Silence. She braved a sip of the black brew. Never had she tasted anything so ghastly. Eyes watering, she swept the room with a glance, looking in vain for evidence of sugar or cream.

She set her cup down. Both started to speak, both stopped, both started again. Mr. Parker indicated her with a nod of his head. "Please."

"I was just saying my family and I will be purchasing tickets for our passage home this morning. So rest assured, you won't be incon-venienced any longer."

"There aren't any ships going out."

"Your pardon?"

"Once the vessels arrive, the crews abandon ship in favor of searching for gold."

She pursed her lips. "And how long does that take? A couple of days?"

He harrumphed. "No, miss. The easy gold is gone. All that's left will require months and months of back-breaking work and, even then, there are no guarantees."

Frowning, she tilted her head. "But the papers back home said one simply needed to go up to the hills, pick the gold out of the streams, and within a few days, a fortune could be accumulated."

"Where's home?"

"Elizabeth, New Jersey."

"And do all the good people of Elizabeth, New Jersey, believe everything they read?"

She stiffened. "President Polk verified the rumors."

"He may have verified the rumors that gold had been discovered.

And, I will admit, that just after the discovery up at Sutter's Mill, the gold lay like pebbles in the stream. But that was the exception, not the rule."

She twirled her hand in the air dismissively. "Well, the availability of gold is neither here nor there. It is the ships that I am interested in, and never have I heard of a port where ships travel in only one direction. Why, it's simply too preposterous to even consider."

He said nothing. Just took a sip of coffee, his light blue eyes, with a knowing look, studying hers.

She recalled the captain urging her to go to shore last night instead of waiting until morning. Because he wasn't sure his crew would return once they reached land.

She swallowed. "Isn't it against the law to abandon ship?"

"It is."

She sat back. "Well, then. The sailors must be arrested and forced back into duty."

"We don't have any officers of the law."

"What? Why not?"

"We're a brand new territory. There are no police, no laws, no jail. Once those men reach the shore, there is no way to get them back."

She fingered the three hundred dollars in the false pocket of her skirt. It was all they had in the world. Father had assumed that money would not be an issue once they arrived. Never had it occurred to them the newspaper reports were false. Nor had they considered the possibility of losing Papa.

She took a deep breath. "But if no ships leave and more arrive— which they most certainly will—the harbor will fill up with ships, one stacked on top of the other."

He nodded. "A rather daunting thought, isn't it?"

She rubbed her forehead. "Well, I will still go down to the docks and see if I can secure passage home. If I cannot, then I will have to find a place to live temporarily until I can figure out what to do."

He said nothing.

"Do you have any idea where I might find a suitable place to lodge?"

"I've been giving it quite a bit of thought, actually." He rested his forearms on the table. "The boardinghouses that come to mind are nothing but a mess of square berths with about six bunks per berth. The area's so confined, they leave just enough room between bunks for a man to stand."

"Perhaps I could rent out an entire berth."

He shook his head. "You would have to pay for all six bunks, which go for about twenty-two dollars each, not to mention the person who sleeps on the floor."

"The bunks are twenty-two dollars a month?"

"A week."

She frowned. "That much?"

"I'm afraid so. You'd have no privacy at all."

"Are there any shacks for rent?"

"Not like mine. Most rag houses are no more than four sides of light lumber topped with a canvas roof. Every time it rains, the whole place gets wet."

"How often does it rain?"

"The entire winter. That's why the streets are so muddy. We're just on the other side of the rainy season, though, so the streets will turn back to dirt in no time."

"Do you know how much these rag houses run?"

He shrugged. "Anywhere from two to three hundred dollars per month would be my guess."

She moistened her lips. "What about real estate?"

He reached for his paper. "I was just looking over that very thing." Folding the paper in half, then in half again, he slid it toward her. "Lots are running about fifteen hundred."

She leaned over the paper, not to look at the prices, but to try and corral her desperation.

"How much money do you have?"

She gasped. "Mr. Parker."

"This is no time to be standing on ceremony, Miss Van Buren. You are what, about twenty years of age?"

She neither confirmed nor denied his estimate, though he was dead on.

"There are upwards of three thousand men in this town," he continued. "With your father gone, you'll need some guidance."

She stiffened. If there was one thing Mama had instilled in her at an early age, it was a distaste for men who automatically assumed a woman had no power within her brain. Though an unpopular view in the East, it was one that had begun to gather momentum amongst the women in Mama's circle.

"And what, sir, makes you my self-appointed guardian?"

He stilled. "Your pardon. I didn't mean to presume." He stood. "If you will excuse me?"

She blanched at his rebuke. Clearly, he'd offered out of kindness, misplaced or not, and she'd responded without thinking. Before she could recover, much less apologize, he had left the room.

Leaving instructions for Michael to look for employment and for Lissa to stay in the shack to receive their trunks as soon as someone could be found to transport them, Rachel headed straight to the wharf. The ship they had arrived on, along with dozens of others, sat silent and empty in the bay.

There would be no vessels leaving San Francisco anytime soon. Former farmers, professionals, and ruffians poured through the streets buying picks, shovels, and pans before heading upriver. Abandoned, their trunks sat on the beach beside a hodgepodge of dilapidated chairs, soiled provisions, and empty liquor bottles. The two partially finished wharves jutted out into the water, pointing to the deserted ships.

Muddy ochre hills dotted the southern and western borders of the village, bare but for low scrub and chaparral, yet protecting the community from the wind whipping off the bay.

Rachel climbed back up the hill. Unpainted shacks and vast numbers of tents dotted the landscape. And at every footfall was a gaming hall. That these saloons were not only open for business at this early hour but bulging with customers produced a great deal of consternation within her.

Their canvas walls shook and swayed as if the tents themselves were intoxicated. One such structure with grimy muslin stretched between its wooden posts sported a sign that read "Boardinghouse, $24 a week".

Approaching the open doorway, she slipped in for a closer look. The smell of cigars, liquor, and unwashed men filled her nostrils. Cards slapped, bottles clinked, men guffawed.

In the corner a fiddler ground out "Old Dan Tucker." Beside him a Spanish-looking woman with unbound curly hair danced to the music, her skirt hiked well above her ankles, displaying bare feet and the absence of pantalets.

Rachel's mouth went dry. Twirling around, she bumped square into a pot-bellied man with shaggy brown hair and an overgrown beard. He grasped her upper arms to keep her from tumbling over, she supposed, then let go as if he'd been singed.

"A sunbonnet woman." It sounded more like a prayer than an observation. He whipped off his hat. "You lost, missus?"

"Miss. And, no, I was looking for room and board but have clearly come to the wrong place."

He grasped her elbow and escorted her out the door. No sooner had they crossed the threshold than he proposed marriage. With her shocked silence came a repeat of his entreaty.

The man topped her by about a half inch, smelled of unspeakable odors, and looked as if his strained suspenders would snap in two at any moment. She couldn't guess at his age, what with his bushy beard and sunburned skin, but his hazel eyes were clear and very serious. In spite of herself, she felt an unexpected softening to such obvious admiration. "Thank you, sir, but no. Right now all I require is a place to board."

"I got that, miss. Say the word and it'll belong to the both of us."

"I'm not in the market for marriage at the moment."

His face filled with alarm. "Every 'spectable woman's in the market for marriage." Leaning over, he spit out a stream of tobacco.

Good heavens. "I'm sorry, truly I am. Now, if you will excuse me?"

He shifted over, then followed her down the walkway, across the street and around the corner. One by one, other miners joined him, and within a block's span, she had an entire entourage trailing her.

The men spoke to each other as if she were not present.

"Look at them slippered footprints. You ever seen such dainty-like prints, Mitch?"

"Cain't say as I have. Where's her pa, you think?"

A third voice chimed in. "Probably up the river and lookin' for the elephant already."

"Naw. I seen this sunbonnet at the City Hotel last night. Her Pa died 'fore he ever hit the shore."

"She's alone? But there ain't no place for sunbonnets to stay. Not that I knows of, anyway."

"Me neither. She'll have to marry one of us."

"I'm the best lookin'. Oughta be me."

A dull pounding began at her temple. A whiff of spirits grazed her nose.

"Cain't be you. You're poor as a church mouse. No, Chauncey's a sight better on the eyes and has a sack full of dust at the tent."

"Not no mores. Spent it on a couple o' them Frenchies in the Plaza last night."

She spun to face them, her skirt flinging out mud like kernels in a corn sheller. "*Gentlemen*. If you please?"

The gathering was even larger than she had supposed. All skidded to a halt, all removed their hats, all presented her with ridiculous smiles.

One brave soul stepped forward. "Marry me, miss?"

"No . . . thank you."

Another knelt, plopping a knee into the mud. "Would you do me the honors?"

She reined in her exasperation. "No. I'm sorry."

His expression fell.

Pulling her gaze from his, she ran it across the assembly. All had the unspoken question on their lips. She wilted a bit before taking a deep breath and squaring her shoulders. "*No.*"

"But without your pa, there just ain't no place for unmarried ladies to stay." This from the young man still kneeling at her feet. "You'll be needin' to double up, miss, and I'm as good a feller as the next."

She closed her eyes, prayed for patience, tried to suppress a spurt of anger toward her late father, and very sweetly but firmly refused once again. Then she resumed her search.

But rather than discouraging the men, her polite refusal seemed to have emboldened them, and they stuck with her, adding steadily to their numbers throughout the afternoon. She decided the proper thing, the only thing, was to pretend they weren't there.

She did find places to stay—for men. But she had seen dog kennels at home that were nicer than the conglomeration of hovels that made up the city of San Francisco, and they certainly were no place for two women and a boy to lodge. Why hadn't the papers warned of these deplorable conditions? What in the world were they to do?

The legitimate boardinghouses overflowed with men on floors, tables, benches, shelves, cots, and bunks, all covered with filth. She found the restaurants much the same but with bad fare worked into the equation. She didn't even bother to ask for prices; she wouldn't have stayed had they been free.

Crammed betwixt and between these coops were more barrooms, saloons, and public houses than a body should ever see. Much to her disgust, gambling clearly dominated the life and soul of the town. Why, at this very moment her devotees were betting on how long she'd last before "marrying up."

And the marriage proposals had continued relentlessly. Surely even Penelope did not have to endure such as this. What she would give for a glimpse of just one other respectable female.

Boards, bushes, and tobacco boxes lay in the street as a makeshift walkway. The sun began to set and the saloons became livelier, causing the size and makeup of her "following" to finally dissipate as the call to gamble lured the men away.

She had only intended to leave Michael and Lissa by themselves for a couple of hours. Concern for how they had managed without her for an entire day quickened her pace.

Barely lifting her skirts, she picked, jumped, strode, and tottered back down Washington Street to the Plaza. The closer she came to the Plaza, the larger and noisier the saloons, until finally she stood across from the hotel. Her stomach growled, her legs ached, her bonnet drooped, and her disposition flagged.

She'd had nothing to eat other than that sip of coffee from this morning. All she wanted was to freshen up in the shanty out back and have a bit of soup, but the crowd of men outside the door covered the huge verandah and spilled over into the muddy street.

She frowned, for though she had discovered the gambling houses stayed busy during the day, she also knew that no one stood idle for very long. Men passed each other, jostled the next one's shoulder, and threw out insults by the minute, but never did they stand still, much less silent.

But still and silent they were until someone shouted, "Here she comes."

Anticipation rippled through the crowd. She tensed. Surely they weren't waiting for her. But no, they didn't turn around—were not, in fact, even aware she stood there. She watched the mass step back as one, as solemn as if someone had died.

It wasn't until Lissa appeared from around the corner of the verandah that all the day's aggravations surged to the fore and grabbed hold of Rachel's very being. How *dare* they subject a girl of her age to such treatment?

With outrage pumping through her blood, Rachel flounced across the street, shoved her way through the throng, and whirled to face them, effectively blocking Lissa from view. "Just what do you think you are doing?"

A sea of men with flannel shirts, topcoats, pea jackets, and even a Mexican blanket stood tongue-tied before her. The sound of a fiddle from one of the neighboring saloons wove through the air.

"Is something amiss?"

She jerked her attention to Mr. Parker as he leaned a shoulder against the doorframe, crossed one ankle over the other, then took a long puff on his cigar. Not even for an instant would she appreciate his cleanliness and freshly shaved face, not so long as he was one of *them*.

"Cannot a lady walk on the street without constantly being accosted by unwelcome attention?"

He blew a steady stream of smoke into the air. "The attention might be unwelcome, but I feel sure it would be respectful."

She narrowed her eyes, fumes from his cigar curling around her.

"Rachel," her sister implored.

She ignored Lissa's plea. The girl was too sympathetic by half.

"I will not have Lissa ogled. She's but a girl."

"I'm fifteen. Sixteen in two months."

"Hush up."

"Rachel?" This from Michael, holding his hat in his hand. Not out of courtesy but out of necessity, for it was filled to brimming with gold.

"Michael! What are you doing with all that?"

"It's ours, Rachel." His eyes shone with pride. "The men paid an ounce of gold just to hear Lissa sing for five minutes time."

Blood drained from Rachel's face then surged back into it. "Give it back. Every last bit of it."

Michael balked. "I can't do that." He frowned, then straightened his shoulders. "I won't do that."

"Oh, yes you will."

Rumbling began amongst the miners.

Mr. Parker stepped forward. "Miss Van Buren, the men become a bit agitated when they don't get what they pay for."

She centered her focus onto him. "I cannot *believe* you would be party to this."

He raised his brows. "I've nothing to do with it. In fact, this clever scheme of your lovely sister's is keeping patrons from my establishment." He gently grasped her elbow. "Now, if you please."

She resisted his tug, but he increased the pressure on her elbow, bending down to whisper in her ear. "The men are intoxicated, they have guns, and, as you know, we are without a single police officer or watchman. You may take your sister to the back in but five minutes time. For now, however, and for the safety of all, you must step back. Please."

This couldn't be happening. What was Lissa thinking? Mama would turn over in her grave were she to witness such impropriety.

Her head light, she allowed him to pull her against the front of the hotel. The cheers of the men made her ears ring as Lissa smiled adoringly at the crowd then began to sing "Now Gently O'er the Moonlit Sea."

It was supposed to be a quartet for female voices, and Lissa had sung it in many a drawing room with other girls her age, but that was different. She had been in the homes of dear family friends, with invited guests.

Rachel scanned the rough crowd, whose expressions would have been comical if the situation had not been so dire. All of them, that is, but one.

He stood on the perimeter of the crowd, calmly watching the scene before him, his speculative gaze roving boldly over Lissa. He looked nothing like the typical miner. This handsome but solemn-faced gambler wore a black frock coat and skintight green checkered trousers.

Goose pimples broke out across Rachel's arms and up her spine. She shivered.

The pressure on her elbow increased for a fleeting moment. "Steady, now, it's almost over."

She barely registered her captor's comment, noting instead, for the first time really, how much Lissa had matured these last few months. Her sister's curves were more those of a woman's, and her height nearly matched Rachel's five-foot-six. Would, perhaps, surpass it soon.

The face beneath the bonnet was such that one would not be able to tell if she were fourteen years or twenty. On top of that, not only did she have all her teeth, but they were straight, pretty, and framed on each side by deep, attractive dimples. Wispy blond curls escaped her bonnet, clinging to her neck and collar.

What was to become of such a beauty when surrounded by decadence? Consternation wrapped its tentacles around Rachel. Her empty stomach clenched. And Lissa's song came to an end.

All remained silent for a mere beat before the men bellowed, whooped, and shot their guns into the air.

Lissa curtsied. Rachel pulled away from Mr. Parker and walked over to Michael, who had been lingering in the shadows. She held out her hands and he obediently gave her the hat full of gold.

Lissa turned.

Rachel moved to the edge of the porch and spun the hat, gold and all, into the crowd.

c h a p t e r **3**

$\mathcal{P}$andemonium broke out as dust and nuggets flew in all directions. Some of the boys dove for the hat and some fell to their knees, scrambling to recover the unexpected gift that plopped into the mud, while others mined the mineral out of each other's hair and clothing.

Johnnie jerked upright, snuffed out his cigar, and tried to prepare himself for just about anything.

"Rachel," Lissa screeched. "What did you do that for?"

Miss Van Buren grabbed the girl's arm and propelled her toward the alley. "Let's go."

Lissa broke free from her sister's grasp. "You had no right."

"You are making a scene. Now come to the back and we will discuss it there."

"I will not. I will stand on this porch and sing the day away, and there is nothing you can do to stop me."

Miss Van Buren leaned close to her sister, whispering furiously. Johnnie could not hear what she said, but Lissa clenched her fists, whirled around, and marched down the alley toward the back of the hotel.

Miss Van Buren shooed Michael in the same direction. He immediately acquiesced.

Then she pinned Johnnie with her gaze. "I need to speak with you."

He glanced at the crowd. It didn't appear any blood would be shed in the scramble to recover the gold. And discretion being the better part of valor, he decided he'd best see what she had to say.

Michael and Lissa were waiting for them when they rounded the corner.

"I cannot believe you just did that," Lissa hissed. "Michael and I earned that gold, not you."

"Tainted money is tainted money, and we'll have nothing to do with it."

"Tainted? I've being singing for people my entire life."

"Go to the shack, where we can discuss this privately. I will be there momentarily. I must first speak with Mr. Parker."

Lissa glanced between the two of them, clearly not wanting to be put off.

"Go on," Miss Van Buren said gently. She looked to Michael. "Escort your sister to the shack, please."

Michael touched Lissa's elbow. She jerked away from him and stormed to the shanty, her brother on her heels.

Miss Van Buren stepped into the kitchen. "Please excuse our little display," she said as Johnnie followed her in.

"No apology necessary."

She took a deep breath. "This town is a disgusting mess."

If she'd been armed, he would have raised his hands up in the air. As it was, he chose to remain silent and see what, exactly, she expected him to do about that.

"The hotels and boardinghouses are uninhabitable. The food is even worse."

Still, he said nothing.

"When was the last time you laundered the bedding in your hotel?"

Frowning, he straightened his spine. "I change out the bedding when necessary."

"How long?"

"I don't know. A while. If you're looking to pick a fight, Miss Van Buren, I believe you have a sister primed and ready."

"How long since the ticks have been beaten clean?"

He didn't dare tell her he had never cleaned the mattresses. No telling what she would do.

She scrunched up her nose when he didn't answer. "And the hotel itself? When was the last time it has been scrubbed top to bottom?"

"The men don't mind it."

"That may be so, but if they had the choice between clean and dirty, I imagine a great many would prefer clean. Might even pay extra for it."

"And your point?"

"When was the last time you had a home-cooked meal?"

He sighed. "If you are on a mission to change the habits of hotel owners by badgering them to death, then you are wasting your breath. Are we finished here?"

She moistened her lips. "I have a proposition for you."

He frowned. "I'm listening."

"I need food, shelter, and income. You need a woman's touch in that hotel of yours. The kitchen is too small to prepare dinner for your patrons, but it is certainly good enough to provide yourself and my family with decent meals. I propose you provide room, board, and pay for me and my family in exchange for home-cooked meals, washed and ironed clothes, and a clean hotel."

"How much pay?"

"Thirty dollars a day."

He lifted his brows. "That's a whole month's wages back home."

"I've been all over this town, Mr. Parker. I know what the going rates are."

"Still, that's two-ten a week."

"One-eighty. We don't work Sundays."

Slipping his hands into his pockets, he rocked on his heels. He couldn't care less about having a clean hotel, but home-cooked meals and a family to share them with? That was something else entirely.

Particularly a family with two sunbonnets. No need for her to know that, however.

"What room, exactly, were you expecting to stay in?" he asked.

"Why, the one we are currently in." She hesitated. "I thought you said last night you were almost through building your new one. And I saw a very nice wooden dwelling just behind the one we are in. I assumed that was the one you were referring to?"

"It was."

"It looked complete to me. Is it not?"

"Not quite."

"Well, that's no problem. Michael can help you finish it. With two of you working, it would be ready in no time and you could live in it."

He rubbed his mouth. The cabin was dried in. It just needed trimming and a bit of furniture. But he'd planned on renting the shanty out, not paying someone to stay in it.

And had she forgotten his place was more than just a hotel? That it was, in fact, a gambling hall? But time and again, he had seen people do things here in California that they never would have done back home.

He considered her as she stood motionless with her head high, back straight. If he said yes, she and her ladylike ways would put a crimp in his daily routine. But if he said no, she would probably go one door down and make the same offer to Ralph. Who would jump at the chance to have a sunbonnet live with him, wash for him, and cook his meals.

By Judas, just having a sunbonnet on his property would most likely double his business.

"All right, Miss Van Buren. We can give it a try, I suppose."

She nodded her head once. "Thank you, Mr. Parker. You won't be sorry."

Rachel tugged loose her bonnet strings, pulled it from her head, and tossed it on the bed. Lissa sat in a chair, legs crossed, foot swinging.

"Have you any idea what you just did out there?" Rachel asked.

"Yes, dear sister. I made it possible for our family to afford food and a place to live. Do you have any idea what *you* just did?"

"As a matter of fact, I do. I reestablished us as ladies worthy of respect in a society without law and church-going women. At least, I hope I did."

"And in the meantime," Lissa asked, "how do you propose we eat?"

Rachel unbuttoned her coat. "We are not destitute and you know it."

"Not yet."

Rachel slipped off her coat, folded it in half, and laid it over the back of a chair. "A lady would rather starve than offer herself up as a public display to an unruly crowd of men. Men who would certainly get the wrong impression and who might very likely come to the conclusion that she was open to all sorts of immoral suggestions."

"I wasn't *displaying* myself, I was singing to them. Much like I did to our friends back home."

"Those are two entirely different things, and well you know it. You had only to paint your face and dress immodestly to proclaim yourself beyond the pale."

"You are being ridiculous."

"I am very serious and hoping they will attribute your little lapse to youthful ignorance. But you and I both know you have been taught how to behave so that you do not invite unwelcome attention. If we are to survive in this degraded town, we must be very circumspect, very careful and above reproach."

"I'll not starve, Rachel."

"Nor will you have to. I have secured a source of income for us."

Lissa's foot stilled. "And just what would that be?"

"Mr. Parker is going to provide us with room, board, and pay to cook his meals, wash his clothes, and clean his hotel."

Lissa leaned back in her chair. "How very circumspect and above reproach of you to find us employment by caring for an unmarried man and working in his saloon."

Rachel stiffened. "It is not a saloon. It is a hotel."

"Do not try and wrap that establishment up in a pretty little bow when you know good and well it is a saloon that serves spirits and caters to gamblers. Renting out bunks and slapping a respectable name on it does not make it any less than what it is."

"We will not be in it while it is open for business. We will do our cleaning between hours. Besides, it is only temporary. At some point, there will be a ship going back east. And rest assured, we will be on it."

Lissa rolled her eyes. "You are simply trading one desperate situation for another. We starve here or we starve back east. What's the difference?"

"The difference is that Elizabeth, New Jersey, is an established, civilized community with churches and women and morals." She held up a hand to stop Lissa's counterpoint. "We will not starve, either. We will save every bit of gold we earn here and use it to set up a home and a respectable livelihood once we return."

"Save our gold? Similar to the gold you just tossed out like so much garbage?"

"It was tainted."

"So is money earned working in a saloon, Rachel. There is absolutely no difference."

"We have been over this already. I am through talking in circles with you."

Lissa's foot began to swing again. "'And thus I clothe my naked villainy with old odd ends stolen out of holy writ; and seem a saint, when most I play the devil.'"

———

The following morning Rachel found Mr. Parker in his usual spot—coffee, newspaper, and all.

He stood.

She hovered in the doorway. "We need to discuss a few things when you have a moment."

"Of course. Won't you join me?"

She stepped into the kitchen. "Actually, I thought I should start breakfast."

"I've been making do with coffee every morning for quite some time. One more morning won't hurt." He poured her a cup of the same and set it in front of a vacant chair.

Settling herself down, she picked up the tin cup. Maybe if she drank it swiftly, it would go down better.

She took a big swig. *Hot.* Slamming the mug down, she pressed a hand to her lips, tossed the brew around in her mouth, and finally swallowed. When she looked up, he offered her a cloth.

She dabbed at her mouth. "It's hot."

"So it is. Are you all right?"

She could barely breathe. "Fine. Thank you."

He leaned back in his chair, took a slow swallow, and stared at her. "So what is it you wanted to talk about?"

"Well, for starters, I need a tour of your storeroom." She folded her hands in her lap. "I also need to know what time you would like your meals served, where your mercantile is, and what kind of budget you would like me to adhere to."

He tugged at a string around his neck and withdrew a key from behind his shirt, then placed it on the table beside her.

"Here is the key to the storeroom. Eight, noon, and five for meals. If you will make a list of sundries, I will pick them up for you. And there is no need to worry over budgets. I can afford whatever you need."

She fingered the key, still warm from lying against his skin.

"Don't lose that," he said.

She slipped it over her head and allowed the piece of metal to shimmy down behind her bodice. It settled inside her corset. His eyes tracked its progress.

"Mr. Johnnie?"

A black man with friendly eyes and hair sprinkled with white stood at the door between the kitchen and the hotel.

Johnnie smiled. "Come in, Soda, and meet the lady I was telling you about. Miss Van Buren, this is Soda. He serves, uh, refreshments to my customers and looks after things when I'm not here."

She nodded. "How do you do?"

"I do jus' fine, miss. Jus' fine." He turned to Johnnie. "Alverson and Canfield are headin' to the mines and wanna settle up."

"Tell them I'll be right there."

"I'll do that. It was nice meetin' ya, miss."

"Nice meeting you, Mr. . . . Soda?"

He bobbed his head and left as quickly as he'd come.

She pushed her chair back.

Johnnie leapt to his feet to assist her. "I have some work to do on another piece of property," he said, "and I would like to take Michael with me. We'll be gone all day."

"Oh. Well, of course. I'll pack you a lunch and then fetch Michael."

———

The boy talked nonstop during their hike to the four acres Johnnie owned on the outskirts of town. He repeated verbatim the heated argument between his sisters and the subsequent dressing down Miss Van Buren had given him.

"She said I should have known better," Michael continued. "And that she can't trust my judgment anymore, that her and Lissa are in danger of lawless men every time they step outside the door, that I did a lousy job of being a protector, and—"

Young Michael's soliloquy came to a sudden halt as they topped the hill. "Thunderation," he said, "would you look at that? I wouldn't have thought a blade of grass could grow here without four posts to hold it up."

Johnnie scanned the once barren sandy spot he had reshaped into gentle hills and covered with native lupine. It wasn't exactly the pastoral greens one would see back home in Connecticut, but it was a start. "It's a long way from completion."

"What do you mean?"

"Well, I plan to convert this into a pleasure ground."

Michael's mouth hung open. "You're building a *park*?"

"No, not a park. Just a quiet place that has something other than sand dunes and scrub oak."

"But, you can't just make something like that. God has to. Shoot,

I haven't seen one single tree since I got here. Never heard of no pleasure grounds without trees."

Johnnie smiled. "The pond's over here. Come on, I'll show you."

He led the boy toward the west side of the property but got no farther than the greenhouse when Michael stopped yet again.

Alone on the crest of a hill, a large glass-encased structure winked in the sunlight.

"What's that?"

"My hothouse."

"Why, it's nicer than any building in all of San Francisco."

"Just about." He turned to go, but the boy climbed up the slope, pushed open the door, and went inside, his lanky form moving down the window-lined aisles.

"What's wrong with your plants?" he asked.

Leaning against the doorframe, Johnnie inhaled the loamy smell of closed-in soil and plants, then sighed. "I don't know. I'm really good at surveying and design, but the only thing I know about trees and shrubs is what I've read. So far, I'm not having much luck."

The boy bent over and stuck his finger into the soil of a struggling *Garrya elliptica*. "Rachel would have a fit if she saw this. Nothing makes her madder than somebody killing their trees."

Johnnie stiffened. "I'm not killing them; they're dying all on their own. I don't know what's wrong with them."

"Rachel would. 'Course, her specialty is bugs, but she knows an awful lot about trees, too. Can't say what she knows about bushes, though."

"Bugs? Her specialty is *bugs?*"

Wiping his finger against his pant leg, Michael walked back out of the greenhouse. "Yeah. But Pa made her leave her collection back home. Said he wasn't carting no trunk full of dead bugs clear around the Horn. She cried for days. We still don't mention it in front of her."

A slow smile tugged at the corners of Johnnie's mouth. He'd not realized the boy had such a dry sense of humor. "Really? Well, what do you know about that? I collect wild beasts. Of course, I had to leave mine back home, too. Took up too much room in the wagon."

Michael looked at him a moment before he let out a bark. "You're fooling me, Mr. Parker. You don't have no wild animal collection." He sobered. "Do you?"

Johnnie pushed himself away from the door. "No more than some female has a collection of dead bugs. Come on, now. I'm paying you to help me bulk up the edges of that pond, not jaw all day."

*R*achel stood just inside the entry of the City Hotel banging on a frying pan with a large metal spoon. "Attention, gentlemen. The City Hotel is now closed. Please gather your things and exit the building in an orderly manner, if you will."

Mr. Parker and Michael had left half an hour earlier or she'd have had them clear the place out. As it was, she had no choice but to do it herself.

There were a few men at the bar and several more circling the gaming tables.

Soda rushed to her. "Now, missy, you cain't jus' be kickin' the boys out like this without no kinda warnin'. Why don't we waits fer Mr. Johnnie to comes back and let him handle the fellers?"

"I haven't time to wait, Mr. Soda. I have a job to do and I intend to do it."

An unkempt man with gray whiskers frowned at her. "I rent this here table from Parker. You cain't jus' up and close down my business."

"Watch yer tone, Lambert," the man beside him said. "That's a sunbonnet yer talkin' to."

Rachel awarded her scruffy defender with a smile.

The man running the table scowled, then moderated his tone. "Does Johnnie know about this, miss?"

"Of course he knows," she replied. "I'm sorry he neglected to tell you, but we'll be closing down every day between breakfast and supper. Now off you go."

She looked at the men, but no one moved. She rapped on the skillet. "You heard me. Time to go."

Those seemed to be the magic words. Within a few minutes, she'd closed the door behind the last customer.

"Come along, Lissa," she called. "All's safe now."

Lissa entered the room, a pouty look about her mouth.

"Mr. Soda," Rachel said, "we are going to need a good deal of water if our efforts are to be fruitful. Would you be so kind as to show Lissa where she could fetch some?"

He swallowed. "Yes, miss. I suppose I could."

"Why do I have to haul the water?" Lissa asked. "Why don't I stay here and you haul the water?"

Rachel took a deep breath. "Mr. Soda, I'd like to introduce you to my sister, Miss Lissa. Lissa, this is Mr. Soda and he is going to show you where to fill the water pails."

Soda nodded his head in acknowledgment and Lissa threw her sister a glare before following him out the back.

Rachel put away the frying pan, slipped on an apron she'd found earlier, and grabbed a gunnysack. She walked back into the hotel only to stop short as she spied a crowd of men jostling for position at the front window.

One tipped his hat. Another waved. And yet another pasted a ridiculous grin onto his bushy face.

Oh, for heaven's sake. Ignoring them, she ripped a hole in the bottom of the sack, walked over to the statue, and pulled the burlap bag over it until the statue's head popped through. There. Much better.

Brushing her hands together, she hauled a tick off the bunk closest to the kitchen.

The front door crashed open. "Here, miss, let me get that fer ya."

She whirled around. A man wearing the customary garb of rolled pantaloons, muddy boots, and an unadorned monkey jacket hurried toward her.

"Good heavens, sir," she said, touching a hand to her throat. "You scared the living daylights out of me barging in that way."

He halted and whipped his hat off. "I'm sorry, miss. It's jus' that I cain't rightly stand around watching you struggle with this here tick when there's a man around to carry it fer ya."

She offered him a soft smile. "It's no trouble, sir. It's my job. But thank you. Now, please, you're keeping me from my work."

He rolled his hat round and round in his hands. "It's right sorry I am to be disturbin' ya, miss. But, I'm not leavin' till ya tell me where it is yer wantin' this here tick."

Sighing, she stepped away from the mattress. "Very well, Mr. . . .?"

"Albert Roberson."

"Mr. Roberson. I'm taking it out back to the line I've rigged up."

Throwing the tick to his shoulder, he glanced at his friends still peering in the window and tossed them a triumphant grin.

Suppressing the urge to roll her eyes, she guided Mr. Roberson to the cord she had tightly stretched between two posts in the yard.

"Careful not to let it drag in the mud, sir. It's a nice sunny day for cleaning, but I don't wish to add to my labors by caking the tick with mud."

"No, miss. I'll be real careful."

He threw the tick over the line, its weight causing the rope to bow some. Thanking him, she walked him back to the front door and closed it firmly behind him. The latch did her no good, for the ring it was to slip over held a padlock that was closed tight. And with no key in sight.

Turning her back on the men, she went to the kitchen and retrieved a coal shovel. After wiping it clean, she set to using it on the tick.

Never had she seen—or smelled—a mattress so filthy. With each whack of the shovel, more dirt and debris poofed out. Stopping to catch her breath, she propped her hands—shovel and all—against her knees.

She mentally counted the number of ticks lining the walls of the hotel and groaned inwardly. How could anyone let his bedding get into such a state?

Straightening, she lifted the shovel again.

Whack. Whack. Whack.

When her arms stung to the point they no longer obeyed her commands, she returned to the kitchen, found a broom, and started knocking away cobwebs and brushing down the plank walls of the hotel.

She wondered where Lissa was and what was taking her so long. She wondered what exactly Michael was helping Mr. Parker with. And she wondered what on earth she would make for supper.

Pausing, she cocked her head, listening. Then, she heard it again. A shuffling. A subdued giggle. A *"shhhhh."*

Rachel moved to the back door, and there stood Lissa, surrounded by a group of miners placing buckets of water next to the shack.

One of the men saw Rachel and nudged his neighbor. Who nudged the man beside him. Like a line of dominoes, one man tapped another until all were aware of her presence.

In their center stood Lissa, eyes defiant and challenging.

Rachel nodded her head. "Gentlemen, thank you for the water. You are excused."

They silently, and somewhat sheepishly, filed down the alley, leaving Lissa and Soda to face her alone. Lissa cocked a brow. Soda wrung his hands.

"Lissa, you will beat that tick hanging on the line behind you until you have knocked every speck of dirt from its stuffings."

"I tried to haul the water, Rachel, but those men would not hear of it. They insisted on doing it for me, and then some. I tried to say no, but they would not let me."

Rachel's gaze wandered to the tick. She swallowed. "Yes. I suppose that's true enough. Still, look at all those buckets. Who do they belong to?"

Lissa shrugged. "I really couldn't tell you."

Rachel then turned her attention to Soda. "Do you have a key to the padlock on the front door?"

"Yes'm."

"Would you please go and lock the front door for me?"

He hesitated. "I don't know, miss. Mr. Johnnie, he hardly ever locks the door."

She held out her palm. "Then give me the key and I'll lock it. I don't wish you to get into any trouble."

He shook his head. "No, miss. I'll lock it, if that's what you want."

She allowed him to pass by her, then reached to the side, picked up the shovel, and walked it out to Lissa. "You've a mattress to beat. And so help me, if I see some man doing it for you, cleaning the ticks will become your sole responsibility and no one else's. Do I make myself clear?"

Lissa jerked the shovel from Rachel's grasp and made her way to the tick.

———

Johnnie frowned and jiggled the door again. Why was the door locked? Where was Soda? His customers?

He pounded on the door. "Soda! Open up."

Seconds later, he heard the lock snap free and the latch release. The door swung open.

"What in the blazes is going on?" Johnnie asked Soda, stepping into the hotel, then coming up short.

The floor gleamed, the bar shone, the tables were dust free, his statue was wearing a burlap sack, and the fourth bunk over was missing its tick.

His gaze reversed its course. His statue was wearing a *burlap sack*?

Michael stepped in beside him, then went back outside and began to swipe the mud from his boots.

Johnnie turned to Soda. "Where are my customers?"

Soda swallowed. "From now on we's closed every day from mornin' to supper so's the ladies can clean up the place."

Lissa shuffled in with a bucket and rag. "Hello, Mr. Parker."

"Lissa."

She moved to the empty bunk and began wiping down its base. Setting his jaw, he made a move toward the kitchen.

Soda reached out a hand, stopping him. "You'd bes' be wipin' off them boots or goin' round the alley. The missy will be givin' you a tongue-lashin' fer shore if'n you walk acrost her floor in them muddy boots."

Her floor?

Johnnie glared at him. "The floor will be a mess the minute the men start piling back in."

Soda stared right back. "She's been workin' mighty hard. I'll not have ya ruinin' her floor."

Johnnie hesitated. "Soda?"

"Yes, Mr. Johnnie?"

"When I return, my Lorenzo Bartolini had better not be wearing a flour sack."

"I'll be glad to return her to her former glory, Mr. Johnnie."

"Thank you." He spun out the door and made his way down the alley. He shook his head, barely suppressing his anger. What could that woman possibly have been thinking?

At the end of the alley, he paused and watched as Rachel swung at a tick with all her might.

Uumph. Up the shovel came. *Whack.*

Uumph . . . whack.

Uumph . . . whack.

Straightening, she leaned the shovel against the post, then braced one hand against it and the other hand on her back.

After a moment, she left the shovel, returned to the tick, and struggled to lift it off the line. All instincts urged him forward, but he checked them. Surely she didn't mean to move that thing all by herself?

Yet that's exactly what she set out to do.

She tugged, inching it off the line bit by bit. Anyone could see she was too weak to handle the mattress alone.

She crouched underneath it, allowing half of it to fall down her back like a cape, then propped her head along the crease in its middle. Lifting her hands up to steady it, she stood, balancing it on her head, and started moving backward.

The other half of the tick slowly followed, and when it finally came free of the line, it fell with a thud against her face and torso, folding over her like an upside-down book trying to slam closed. She staggered.

He jogged toward her. But not soon enough. Like a top that had lost its momentum, she tottered to the ground and hit with a resounding splat. The mattress still sandwiched her inside of it, and mud now caked both it and her.

He smiled at the epithets coming from inside the folded over tick. They were the cleaned up versions of the real ones and were spewing from her mouth with feeling.

Ankles, pantalets, and petticoats peeked out the edges like lettuce and leg o' lamb. She flayed about. He reached down and flipped back the top of the mattress.

She now lay completely flat on the tick. An open-faced sandwich. She squealed.

He bowed and extended a hand. "May I be of service?"

She scrambled off the mattress and turned a gorgeous shade of red.

Any neatness that her serviceable brown dress had held this morning had long since disappeared. One of his aprons drooped down her front, its ties wrapped multiple times around her waist. The hair twist at the back of her head sagged, with one section of silky hair tumbling free across her shoulder.

She lifted her chin. "Good afternoon, Mr. Parker. I didn't realize you were home."

He allowed his smile to widen. "I know."

The blush moved down her neck, but she held firm his gaze. The girl had pluck. He'd give her that.

"Next time you need to move a tick," he said, "just let Soda or me know. We'll be glad to assist you."

She tightened her lips. "I can do it. I just slipped is all. It's my fourth one today and I guess I'm a little tired." She took a deep breath. "Are you hungry? You're a bit low on supplies, so supper will be a simple affair. But it is on the stove when you are ready."

Moving to the nearest post, he undid the rope, stretched it taut, and re-secured it. "You closed down my hotel."

"I forgot to have you do it before you left."

Lifting the tick, he flung it back over the rope and began to roll up his sleeves. "Had you discussed your intentions with me, I would not have let you close it. Do you have any idea how much money you cost me today?"

"I can't very well scrub it down while the men are in there."

Picking up the shovel, he swung it into the tick. Mud flew everywhere.

She gasped and jumped back, but not before the stuff peppered them both.

He swung again. "That may be, but I rent out tables to certain men at certain times of the day. They depend on the money those bring in, as do I." *Wwwwhump.*

"If you will just let that be, I will do it later."

He continued to beat the mud out of the mattress. "You can have the hotel from nine to noon. That should be sufficient."

"But it took me all day just to do the floor and four ticks." She paused. "Three ticks."

He swung. "Nine to noon, Rachel."

"Eight to noon. And I haven't given you leave to call me by my Christian name."

Wwwwhump. "The men stay up almost all night long. They aren't going to rise at eight in the morning. And, please, call me Johnnie."

"You are making a mess. You need to let that mud dry, then beat it."

He glanced at her and swung.

Her lips pursed as if she'd taken a chunk out of a lemon.

Lissa entered the yard and set her bucket down by a dozen others. Where had they found all those buckets?

"Well, Rachel," she said. "How nice to have a *man* do your chores for you."

Johnnie glanced between the two women.

"He is our employer, Lissa. If he wishes to beat his ticks, there is nothing I can do about it."

Wwwwhump.

Lissa raised a brow. "How very convenient for you."

Rachel pulled down the corners of her lips. Lissa strode to the shanty.

Wwwwhump.

"You shrouded my Lorenzo Bartolini with a burlap bag," Johnnie said.

She reluctantly moved her focus back to him. "If you are referring to that vulgar . . . *thing* in there, then you will receive no apology from me."

"It's not a thing, Rachel. It's a piece of art. Sculpted by one of the masters. It came all the way from Italy, and it cost a fortune." He wiped his face against his shoulder. "And you dressed it in a gunny sack. A *gunny sack.*" *Wwwwhump.* "Do not ever do that again."

She crossed her arms.

He swung a few more times. "Michael says you are a tree expert."

Her face softened, just barely. "Hardly an expert. More like a tree lover." She shrugged. "They are one of my passions, though."

He smiled as he recalled Michael's jest about her passion for bugs but refrained from saying anything. He moved to the other side of the tick and swung.

"Well, there is something wrong with the trees on my property. Will you look at them for me?"

She lifted her brows. "I've seen no trees since arriving. Where is your property?"

"Southwest of town."

Wwwwwwwhump.

She glanced to the southwest, interest evident in her expression.

He straightened. "Do you ride, Miss Van Buren?"

She blinked. "Horses?"

He nodded.

"Well, yes." Her eyes widened. "Have you a horse, Mr. Parker?"

Setting the shovel down, he made a formal bow. "Would you kindly accompany me out to my place tomorrow afternoon? I'm afraid I've no carriage to offer, but I've two horses and a hothouse full of trees that desperately need some help."

Her entire countenance lit up. "Oh, tell me you are not jesting."

"Not in the least." He frowned. "Though it may take some doing to find a sidesaddle, but not completely impossible."

She clasped her hands behind her back. "It would be my pleasure to examine your trees."

"Tomorrow's Sunday. Your day off. Are you sure you don't mind?"

"Not at all."

He moved to her. "Show me your hands."

She frowned. "Your pardon?"

He held his hands palm up. "Your hands, Rachel."

She moved her hands in front of her and turned them over so he could see. Red, angry blisters dotted them.

It was all he could do not to cradle them within his. But he didn't dare. "No more beating of ticks until I purchase a baton. Now come inside and let's see if we can find something to put on those."

He indicated that she precede him, then followed her into the kitchen.

c h a p t e r **5**

*J*ohnnie sighed. "Will you *please* sit down? There is not enough room in here for both of us to be at the stove."

"This really isn't necessary," Rachel said. "I can do it."

He narrowed his eyes. "Sit."

She sat, finally. Whiffs of fried pork and boiled beans came from a covered pot at his elbow, teasing his nose and reminding his stomach of its hunger.

He shook some crushed witch hazel out of a tiny bag and seeped it in a small tin of warm water. While waiting for it to take, he lifted the lid from the pork, broke off a large piece, and popped it in his mouth.

"Want some?" he asked around his mouthful.

She shook her head.

He had no doubt that she was hungry. But if she chose stubbornness over sustenance, so be it.

Poking a cloth into a cup, he poured the witch hazel into it, straining out the solid particles, and reached for a bottle of whiskey on the uppermost shelf.

Uncorking the bottle with his teeth, he poured a splash into the cup and hesitated. Best not wash down the pork. He set the bottle back on the shelf.

"If you will just place it here on the table, I will do it," she said.

He put the concoction and a fresh piece of flannel beside her. She dipped the cloth into the cup and touched it to her palm.

Sucking in her breath, she paused. He grabbed her fingers, knelt in front of her and blew on the place the witch hazel burned.

She tugged on her hand. He held it more firmly as he removed the cloth from her other hand and continued to dab on the liquid.

She bit down on her lip, her eyes blinking rapidly.

"Sting?" he asked.

She nodded.

He blew some more. When each blister had been treated, he reached for her other hand.

She hid it beneath the folds of her skirt. "I will do it."

Easily uncovering it, he held firm her wrist and turned it over. "I'm not making an indecent proposal, Rachel. I am putting witch hazel on your cuts."

"It isn't proper," she whispered.

He dipped the cloth into the cup, lifting the corners of his mouth. "Why are you whispering?" he whispered.

She thinned her lips and yanked, ineffectively, against his hold.

He winked and applied the cloth to a particularly raw blister.

She gasped. He blew.

When he finally laid the cloth down, he looked up to find silent tears escaping from the corners of her eyes.

He sat back on his heels. "Ah, Rachel. I'm sorry."

She swiped her face with the back of her hand, smearing the tears across her cheek.

Removing a handkerchief from his pocket, he dabbed at the moisture on her face. She reached up to do it herself, but instead of relinquishing his hold, he moved his hand so that it cradled hers.

She stilled, leveling the full force of her liquid brown eyes on him. He felt their impact clear down to his toes.

"Why didn't you stop when you realized the shovel was blistering your skin?" he asked.

"I had a job to do."

"It could have waited until we had a baton. I don't want you to do something like that again. When you have need of a certain item, just tell me and I will see that you receive it."

Like a puppeteer and a puppet, he guided her hand with his, and together they wiped the tears from her face. He followed each stroke with his gaze, cataloging her prominent cheekbones, the hollows beneath, and the jaw that culminated in a softly rounded chin.

He paused and lifted his thumb, catching her lower lip.

She jerked, shoved back her chair, and surged to her feet.

He stood. Slowly. Not missing the cinched waist and the curves it heightened, though he never allowed his attention to linger. Only to capture. So that later, when he was alone, he could take the images out and examine them in his mind as he longed to do now.

"If you will excuse me?" she asked.

He stepped back.

She all but flew out the back door.

"Is it straight?" Rachel asked, touching the gold brooch pinned to her collar.

"It's drooping a little to the left," Lissa responded. The girl had brightened at the prospect of a day off, giving Rachel a momentary reprieve from her sister's petulance.

Rachel lifted her chin, released the delicate latch, and tried again. They had no mirror, making such simple tasks ten times harder than they had to be.

Lissa finished tying her bonnet, then shooed Rachel's hands away. "No, that's even worse. Let me."

With tongue held between her teeth, Lissa pinned on the piece of jewelry, then leaned back to inspect it. "There."

"Thank you, dear. Michael? Are you about ready?" Rachel reached for her shawl, then turned to find Michael resting his long legs atop a chair, ankles crossed and hands hooked behind his head.

"I've been ready."

She raised one corner of her mouth. "Well, come on, then."

Standing, he grabbed his coat from the back of the chair, shrugged it over his miner's garb, and opened the door for his sisters.

The three of them headed to the square, the girls' muslin delaine dresses collecting brown goo with each step.

Canvas sheds and half-finished buildings with goods stacked in front of them stood on every side of the Plaza. Nestling in the southwest section of the muddy knoll, a forlorn looking schoolhouse had its door thrown open for Sunday services.

Several yards north of the school, a tall flagpole fronted a long one-story adobe building used as the customhouse.

They climbed the stairs of the school and entered the one-room affair. According to Mr. Parker, it had opened a year ago this month, when San Francisco was a quiet little town with a scattering of families and children. But when word came that gold had been discovered, the schoolmaster deserted his post and headed straight for the diggings. The majority of residents evidently did the same.

Dust covered the shelves, the seats, the stove, the teacher's desk. Everything. But the rectangular room's wooden frame sheltered them from the breeze whipping off the ocean; its solid roof, from any weather they might experience.

Wind whistled around the walls and men rose to their feet while the Van Burens silently wove between a row of chairs toward the middle of the room. As they settled, dust motes swirled in the sunlight pouring through the east windows.

A thick film of grime covered the leaded glass, and from her seat Rachel had a muted view of the City Hotel down on the corner. She ran a surreptitious glance throughout the room and spotted Soda, but not Mr. Parker.

A thin ragged man carrying a Bible went to the front. Without an introduction of any kind, he broke into song, wrapping the schoolhouse with "My Faith Looks Up to Thee."

Rachel started slightly upon discovering such a glorious sound could pour forth from such a puny man. He stood straight and tall, his pointy chin bobbing and swaying with every note. Though his worn frock coat looked as if it had been slung across a valet stand rather than a set of shoulders, his booming voice quickly drew a crowd from outside, several of whom added their voices to the Reverend's.

"While life's dark maze I tread,
And griefs around me spread,
Be Thou my guide."

Rachel closed her eyes, absorbing the words as they poured into her heart, then joined her life's blood in transporting them to every vein, vessel, and extremity before returning to her heart, only to be pumped throughout her body again.

The song ended and, for once, all was still.

"Your favorite rule in arithmetic is that of loss and gain," the frail man thundered. "Yet what has a man profited if he shall gain the whole world and lose his own soul?"

The motionless quiet of the crowd drew Rachel's scrutiny. All were men. All were grubby, young, and in their prime. With intensity and intelligence, they had fixed their attention onto the preacher as he offered them more than just words from God's Book; he offered them life.

She returned her focus to the reverend, his impassioned delivery warming her. Washing her. Renewing her.

The benediction drew near and he closed his Bible, tucking it underneath his arm. "There will be divine service here next Sabbath—" he paused, a suggestion of a smile flitting across his face— "if, in the meantime, I hear of no new diggin's."

Rachel's jaw slackened and she almost forgot to bow her head for the closing prayer. After the service, all waited for the preacher to step outside. The men closest to Rachel and Lissa introduced themselves, asking where the girls were from. Fortunately, no one asked for their hand in marriage.

As the crowd dispersed outside, the greater portion headed to Mr. Parker's hotel, the rest to the Bella Union saloon.

Rachel's eyes widened. Surely the gaming establishments were closed on Sundays. But no, a tinkling piano tune picked up where the hymns had left off, wafting from nearby canvas walls and reaching ears that moments before had been receiving the Word of God.

From the school yard, Rachel watched men enter Johnnie's hall with enthusiasm and pouches full of gold, while one stumbled out with an empty bottle of liquor and, most likely, an empty soul to match.

Swallowing her disappointment, she lifted her skirt and moved to greet the preacher. Men bowed and tipped their hats as she and her siblings passed.

"Good morning, Reverend," she offered.

He turned, a smile lighting his face. "Well, now, what have we here?"

"If I may present myself and my family to you, sir?"

"Of course, of course."

She made the proper introductions and spoke of her wish to meet other women in town.

"I'm afraid there aren't any, my dear. Now, I know of a few here and there that have passed through town with their husbands before going up to the mines, but I couldn't tell you where they eventually ended up settling."

Before she could question him further, a stir within the square distracted her. She caught her breath as three ladies in exquisitely made gowns and fashionable headdresses made their way across the Plaza.

Every man they passed bowed and stopped to speak with them in respectful tones. Rachel's heart sang. *Women. Oh, praise be.*

She met Lissa's delighted expression and quickly turned back to Reverend Taylor. "Why, sir, there are some now. Would you be so kind as to introduce us?"

The reverend drew up his lips. "Miss Van Buren, those particular, uh, *ladies,* are not of a, uh, *respectable* nature. I suggest you just head on home."

Rachel blinked and returned her attention to the women in question. Their outdoor gowns were at the very height of fashion, well within the confines of propriety. Skirts and bodices were flounced and trimmed—one with lace, one with velvet, the third with pearls.

Their ensembles were modest and in excellent taste. Their flowered and puffed headdresses came straight from pictures Rachel had seen in *Godey's Lady's Book*.

She could not imagine that the men would treat them with such respect and deference if they were indeed women of ill repute. No, she had seen for herself what those women looked like. Loud colors. Spangled shawls. Loose camisoles.

The reverend must be mistaken. She opened her mouth to say as much when one of the women caught Lissa's eye and thoroughly perused her. Lissa curtsied.

Clearly amused, the woman raised an eyebrow and whispered something to her friends. The group turned toward the two sisters.

Rachel felt her back straighten. The calculated and proprietary gleam incorporated into the women's eyes set her heart to pounding.

"Lissa," she said quietly. "Come."

Lissa didn't move, clearly captivated with the fetching picture the finely attired women made.

Rachel touched her arm. "Come on. We must depart from here."

Lissa turned. "But look at them. Why, they look as if they came straight from the tea parlors of home."

Rachel threaded her fingers through Lissa's.

The reverend cleared his throat. "That is one thing you must become used to here in California. Dress does not make the man— or woman. Lawyers, doctors, and scoundrels alike dress exactly the same and share the same ambitions. You'll find that women who dress so fine are not often of the churchgoing sort."

"But why?" Lissa asked.

He smiled gently. "Because God-fearing women haven't the time to dress in such a fine manner, my dear. They are too busy feeding their families and attending to their duties at home."

———

Swinging down from his horse, Johnnie felt conspicuous in his go-to-meeting clothes. Why hadn't he simply worn his cotton trousers and flannel shirt?

He had no desire to pursue a permanent relationship with a woman, but he had missed the companionship of a female who was interested in something other than how much gold she could lift from his pockets.

Of course, all sunbonnets wanted marriage. So he'd have to tread very, very lightly and make sure she understood their relationship was strictly business.

He needed someone to save his trees. They'd cost a cock and a hen to import, and watching them die gave him such a feeling of impotence. He had to do something. Even if it meant employing Rachel's help.

He wrapped his mustang's and the mare's reins around the hitching pole and headed down the alley. He'd scoured the city for a sidesaddle, paid a ridiculous amount for it, then told Adams down at the livery to have his horses ready for a Sunday outing.

Johnnie reached the door Michael had installed on the shanty and paused. What if she was wearing a calico? What if he stood here in his courting clothes and she stood in there dressed for outdoor labor? What if she *didn't* have on a calico? What if she wore *her* courting clothes?

He needed to run over to his cabin and put on his flannels. What was he thinking to wear such a getup when the last thing he wanted to do was go courting?

But it had been as natural as breathing. When you picked up a lady on a Sunday afternoon, you wore your Sunday clothes. The thought held him paralyzed a second too long, and Michael opened the door.

"Mr. Parker? What are you standing out there for?" he asked. "Did you have something for me to do?"

"Uh, no. Nothing today, Michael, thanks. Is your sister home?"

"Which one?"

"Miss Van Buren."

Michael smiled.

Johnnie relaxed his shoulders. "The elder, please."

Michael stepped back. "Come on in."

Johnnie crossed the threshold.

"Rachel, it's Mr. Parker. I'm going outside."

The boy slammed out the door, leaving Johnnie high and dry.

She was standing by the fireplace, wearing some green thing with a pouffy skirt, a waist so small he could encircle it with one hand, and tucks going all across the bodice in such a way that he could hardly pull his gaze up where it belonged.

But direct it he did, and when it connected with hers, breathing grew difficult. Her cheeks glowed, her lips parted, and those blasted tucks on her bodice moved upward with every breath she took.

Say something. "You ready, then?"

She jerked. "Yes. Of course. Well." She turned to her sister. "You'll be all right, Lissa?"

Lissa sat at the table, a book in her hands, legs crossed, one foot swinging. She gave him a knowing look. "Guess I will. Sure you don't need a chaperone?"

Rachel frowned, fingering the brooch at her neck. He could see Rachel thought that just maybe she did.

"I've only two horses," he said. "We'll be fine. But if you like, I can have Michael walk up to the place. He knows where it is."

Rachel's expression smoothed. "Yes. Let's. That would be . . . good. Very good."

She picked up a cloth-covered basket and he opened the door then looked back at Lissa.

Lissa waggled two fingers. "Have fun."

———

Michael had stopped to admire the horses. He now held the mare's head and the food basket while Johnnie grasped Rachel's waist and lifted her into the saddle. Yards of green cloth bunched against his chest and the horse's rust-colored hide. A whiff of vanilla replaced the musky smell of animal for barely a moment.

Rachel hooked her right knee over the saddletree, arranging her skirt and petticoats down her mount's left side.

He swallowed. The fabric outlined her unbelievably long legs. He'd have to lengthen the stirrup.

He hesitated, eyeing the piles of green fabric and the long, long legs between him and the stirrup bar. Taking a deep breath, he placed a hand against the saddle flap and rode it up to the stirrup bar, hidden beneath Rachel's dress, petticoats, and thigh. He heard her quick intake of breath as she moved her leg so that it rode just inches from his hand without making contact.

"I need you to walk up to my place on Market Street, Michael," he said, careful to keep his voice level.

Michael pulled back from nuzzling the horse's head. "What for?"

"Your sister is uncomfortable being out there alone."

"Alone? Aren't you going?"

Grasping the buckle, Johnnie pulled it down and away from the saddle until he could easily reach it. He released the breath he'd been holding and pushed Rachel's skirt to the side. Her leg settled back against the horse.

"Yes, I'm going," he replied.

"Then why do I need to go?"

Lengthening the leather, Johnnie wove it through the buckle, then impaled the boy with a stare. "Your sister wants you to go, so you go."

Michael looked every bit the fourteen-year-old when he turned pleading eyes to his sister. "Oh, come on, Rache. It's Sunday and I was just going to, well, do nothing. I've toted and lifted and dug and nearly killed myself these last couple of days. Please don't make me go all the way out there. He just wants you to look at his trees. What do you need me for?"

Leaning forward, Michael unknowingly played his trump. "Besides, if I go out there with you, then Lissa would be all alone. You don't want that, do you?"

Johnnie jerked the strap, testing it.

Rachel sighed. "No, of course not. You're right. I'll be fine. You have fun. But do keep an eye out for Lissa."

Michael released the horse and reached up to give his sister's hand a squeeze. "Thanks, Rache. I will." Making good his escape, he set the basket on the porch and ran back down the alley.

Wrapping a fist around the strap, Johnnie's hand retraced its route against the saddle's flap, sliding the buckle back up. Rachel adjusted her leg.

He tried to concentrate on the suppleness of the saddle's leather but instead felt heat emanating through the yards and yards of pliant cotton wrapped around young, firm limbs.

His nostrils flared and he once again captured the faintest scent of vanilla. His hand accidentally skimmed her knee. She jumped.

He secured the buckle, quickly slid his hand free, and looked up at her. "You don't have to go."

Confusion played across her features. "No, my brother said your trees are in a bad way. And I really do want to see them." She smoothed her hand down her skirt, straightening out the places he'd crumpled and bunched up. "You'll, uh, conduct yourself with propriety?"

This woman was a sunbonnet. The very last thing he wanted was a shotgun wedding. Or a lynching. "You have my word."

Her foot rooted around for the stirrup but couldn't find it. Reaching for the metal triangle, he held it with one hand, grasped the delicately shod heel of her lace-up boot with the other, and guided it home.

"Are your hands all right?" he asked. "I mean, will it hurt to guide the reins?"

"They're much better today." She flexed them within her gloves. "I'll be fine."

Without another word or glance, he handed her the reins, grabbed the basket, mounted his stallion, and squeezed its flanks. "Here we go, fella."

chapter 6

Rachel luxuriated in having a horse beneath her once again. Its rocking rhythm, its earthy smell, the shaking of its head filled her with pleasure.

The fog that had cloaked the area at dawn had lifted to reveal a sunny day and the onset of spring. A slight breeze rippled across her skirt like waves, cascading down to her white petticoat frothing at the edge. She surveyed the town that had no trees. No songbirds. No women.

Only hills, mud, and men. But soon she would see some trees. Sick trees, but trees nonetheless. She could hardly wait.

She peeked at the man riding beside her. What a paradox he was. Miner's garb in the morning while he read his newspaper. Gambler's garb in the evenings when his saloon was at its busiest. And fashionable gentleman's clothing when escorting a lady on a Sunday afternoon.

She had no business going with him and certainly not alone. But the temptation to ride and tend to fledgling trees overpowered all else. How could she possibly resist?

She couldn't. But she must resist the man.

She shifted her weight, readjusting her position on the horse, as her mind began to convict her of the numerous compromises she'd already made. His beating of the mattress for her. His ministrations with the witch hazel. His sun-darkened hand disappearing while adjusting her stirrup, grazing through the fabric places no man had touched before.

Goose pimples raced across her arms, her mother's voice ringing inside her head.

A girl of good breeding has always sufficient force of character to steer clear of such difficulties. She ran a hand up the back of her neck, smoothing her hair. She must strive to do better.

Bending down, she patted her mare's long cinnamon-colored neck. "What's my horse's name?"

Mr. Parker looked at her horse, then at her, humor brightening his eyes. "Sweet Lips."

Her mouth parted. "That is not amusing."

"Be that as it may, it's her name."

She glanced at the mare, appalled. "You must change it. It is simply not to be tolerated."

He quirked a brow. "If it's a good enough name for George Washington's dog, I think it will do just fine for my mare."

Her spine straightened. "President Washington did *not* have a dog named Sweet Lips."

"Oh yes. Yes, he did."

She drew her mouth down into a frown. "I don't believe you. But even if that were true, I could not possibly call her such."

Johnnie said nothing but instead took in the sight she made sitting atop the well-trained mustang. She handled the animal with ease and proficiency, her feminine geegaws the only splash of color for miles around. If the wind blew just right, he could pick up the hint of vanilla he'd come to associate with her.

No harm in looking. Smelling. Maybe even touching. But no tasting. No, sir. No tasting whatsoever.

"What's your horse's name?" she asked.

"J.B."

Worrying her lip, she eyed his mount. "What does that stand for?"

"Jim Beam."

"You gave your horse a first and last name?"

"I guess I did."

"Well, at least it is a good, respectable name."

He smiled.

"Perhaps I should call mine by her initials, too. S.L."

"You just do that." Touching his heels to his mount, he picked up the pace. They were almost there. He wanted to be in front where he could see her reaction when his property came into view.

The horses' hooves squelched through the mud keeping cadence with each other. Johnnie crested the hill and pulled J.B. up. Rachel immediately slowed, her eyes widening as she took in the mounds and hillocks he'd shaped with his own hands.

"Oh, Johnnie. Is this your place?"

She'd used his forename but didn't seem to have realized it. Nor did she appear to want an answer. For she rode right down into the property, onto the lupine, unhooked her leg, and slid to the ground. He didn't miss the glimpse of ankle her descent afforded before the purple blooms swallowed the sight. She dropped to her knees, skirts billowing out around her.

She fingered the prolific green leaves, peeking under several. Looking for . . . bugs?

Standing, she bent over one of the tall showy blooms, inhaling, then reached for Sweet Lips's reins. The breeze pushed against her fancy bonnet as she pulled the sorrel close and whispered something to her.

Sweet Lips perked her ears, then snorted, generating a delighted laugh from Rachel. The sound hit him square between the eyes. He stilled, not daring to breathe lest he miss it should it happen again.

But she turned and led the animal further onto the property with one hand, lightly brushing the hip-high foliage with her other. He swung down from the saddle and followed, J.B. at his side.

She easily tracked down the hothouse. Dropping the mare's reins, she moved to the entrance and paused, her hand atop the door latch. She slid her eyes closed. A child savoring a package.

Blast it. He just wanted her to fix his trees. "It's open," he barked.

She started, turning those incredible brown eyes to him. "Oh. I forgot you were here."

Yeah. Well. Wish he could say the same.

She pushed up the latch and swung open the door. He followed close behind, catching the door before it slammed shut. Moist heat. Earthy smells. Pitiful looking trees.

"What have you been doing to these trees?"

After securing the latch, he leaned back against the door and crossed his arms. "I haven't done anything."

"Well, that's certainly obvious." Peeling off her gloves, she tested the soil. "How often have you been watering?"

He blinked. "That one? As often as I can. At least once a week, sometimes twice, if I can get out here."

She propped her hands on her hips. "Good heavens. Cypress trees require deep watering. If you don't provide enough water, you leave them open to all kinds of pests. Cypress tip moth, cypress canker, oak root fungus. What were you thinking?"

For the sake of his trees, he ignored her tone. "How often do they need watering?"

"At least once a day. Twice if they're struggling."

"I can't get out here every day."

"Then you have no business trying to raise cypresses."

He took a breath. "What about the maples?"

She scanned his collection, zeroing in on his Japanese maple. "This one doesn't look too bad. You just need to protect it from the afternoon sun. I'd move it over there, on the east side."

She continued her diagnosis of each tree, imparting advice, testing the soil, touching the bark, rotating a pot here and there before finally stopping at a double-trunked tree. "What's this?"

"A California buckeye. They grow all up and down the coast."

"Why, it's completely leafed out already."

"Yes, but the ones I've seen in the ground drop their leaves by July. I assume due to the lack of rain during those summer months."

Fingering a group of leaflets, she grilled him about its growth rate, light needs, and flowering potential. He offered all he could think of for the sheer pleasure of watching her coddle and caress the plant.

Her long, graceful fingers had accumulated a goodly portion of dirt and sticky residue.

He exhausted his store of information, and she brushed her hands together, cringing as sediment drifted to the floor. Her blisters were no doubt still a bit sensitive.

"What are you going to do with all these?" she asked.

He pushed himself up off the entry's frame. "Why don't we get the lunch basket and walk over to the pond. I can tell you there and it'll be more comfortable."

"I don't mind it here." She slipped a hanky from her cuff and dabbed at the moisture collecting against her hairline. "I love the smell and feel of a hothouse."

"Even so." He held the door, and she reluctantly preceded him through it.

The crunch of the lupine beneath their feet offered the only sound. The pond came into view, rather forlorn looking without a single tree to offer shade of any kind.

Rachel didn't seem to notice, though, heading straight for its banks and squatting down once she reached them.

He flipped the cloth open and settled it onto the ground, dropping the basket in its center. His stomach growled. Looking over at Rachel, he frowned.

Arms hiked above her head, she removed her hatpin and hat with exaggerated slowness. The very stillness of her body gave him pause. Ever so carefully, she set the hat beside her, poised the pin just above the brush on her right, then jabbed.

A glorious smile spread across her face as she held the pin up in front of her, examining what could only be a bug skewered to the bit of feminine frippery.

Her chocolate-colored hair sagged around the edges, tendrils loosening in the cooling breeze. She examined her catch from all angles, then looked up. "Come see. It's a *Phoetaliotes nebrascensis.* I've never seen a real one. Are they common here?"

Slipping a hand into his pocket, he drummed his leg before making his way to her side. "Looks like a plain old grasshopper to me."

She sent him a puzzled glance. "This isn't just some *plain old* grasshopper; it's a *largeheaded* grasshopper. See how big his head is? I can't believe I was able to actually catch it. It was basking."

"Basking?"

"Yes. Some will bask for as long as two hours in the afternoon. This one was basking vertically right there. That's why I had such an easy time catching it."

Removing his hand from his pocket, he knelt beside her and acquired the pin from her grasp. He flipped it over and frowned. "Male or female?"

She peeked around his fingers. "Oh, it's a female. They weigh almost twice as much as the male."

"You saw a male?" He pulled back some lupine to better see the ground she sat in.

"Oh no. You hardly ever catch two largeheads together. As a matter of fact, there have been no observations of largehead courtship at all."

"No?"

She shook her head, clasping her hands in her lap and tilting her head as she scrutinized the insect. "One mating pair was seen in some mixed-grass prairie once. They were basking head up vertically in the usual mating position of grasshoppers. The male's head rested immediately behind and above the female's. Because of the smaller size of the male, the female had to curve up to meet the male, which was curving down."

He had no idea what to say to that.

She glanced up, red flooding her face. "Oh. Oh my goodness. Please forgive me. I get carried away sometimes. I wasn't thinking. I can't imagine—"

She started to get up. He placed his hand over both of her clasped ones, halting her ascent.

"Michael told me about your interest in insects."

"He did?"

"Hmmm. He said you had to leave your collection behind."

She pulled the sides of her mouth down and looked out over the pond. He hadn't realized before what an incredibly long neck she had. Graceful, white, and very inviting.

No tasting, Parker. Absolutely no tasting.

"What did you do with your collection?" he asked.

"I donated it to Amherst Academy. Though I'm not sure they understood the full value of it."

"Most likely not. You are extremely well versed in the habits and identification of largeheads. Do you know all insects so well?"

She pulled her hands out from under his. He withdrew and handed her the hatpin, grasshopper and all.

"Thank you, and no. Grasshoppers are my passion. I had collected a good many of them. But I'd never seen a largehead. Only drawings."

He couldn't hold back the smile that pushed its way out. Standing, he extended a hand. "Well, Miss Van Buren, you may come out to my place and kabob as many grasshoppers as you like. Anytime. With or without me."

She answered with a smile of her own and took his hand. "I'm not going to eat them, Mr. Parker."

His grin widened. "Well, what a relief. I was beginning to fear what exactly might be hiding in yonder food basket."

She was up. He should release her. He did not.

Her smile fading, she retracted her hand and headed to the blanket.

The lupine was so tall that the frayed brown blanket rested like an inverted canopy several inches above the ground, anchored in the center by the basket. She had to lift her skirts to step onto the cloth, then bend over to press it more firmly to the earth.

He took a moment to admire the view before retrieving the bonnet she'd left behind. Finally, she settled down, removed the checkered fabric covering the food, and wiped her hands clean with it. From inside, she pulled forth cheese and some potpies.

Inhaling deeply, he could hardly remember when he'd last had potpie. Or gone on a picnic.

He stepped onto the blanket. "How are your hands?"

She shaded her eyes and looked up. "Much, much better. Thank you."

"Let me see."

She held her palms out. Only one spot still looked fairly raw.

"You have continued with the witch hazel?" he asked.

She nodded.

He sat across from her, stretching one leg out and pulling the other up next to him. Enticing as the food was, he couldn't quite release her bonnet without lingering a bit.

It was a useless thing, really. Nothing like the homemade ones his late wife had worn to protect her from the sun. Instead, this narrow-rimmed bit of fluff trimmed in ribbon, flowers, and berries offered ornamentation only.

The rays of the hot California sun penetrated his consciousness. It would eat her alive if she didn't start wearing something more practical.

He set the hat aside and reached for a potpie. Its flaky, crisp crust and savory creamy stuffing were the closest he'd come to having a religious experience in years.

He glanced up. A bit of filling slipped from the corner of her mouth. Her tongue darted out to capture it and bring it back into the fold.

"Ummm," she said. "I didn't realize how hungry I was." She placed the tip of each finger in her mouth, licking them one by one.

His stomach clenched. *Concentrate on the food, Parker. The food.* "Did you make these potpies?"

"Yes, though Lissa makes them better."

He couldn't imagine that. Breaking off a corner of crust, he popped it into his mouth, but the flavor was lost on him. He wanted something else for lunch. Something he could not, would not, have. Ever.

"So, what are you planning to do with those trees once they are well, Mr. Parker?"

"I am performing a grand horticulture experiment."

That caught her attention. She paused in the eating of some cheese. "Are you, now?"

"Indeed. I intend to turn this landscape of sand, marshes, and scrub brush into forest and glade."

She set her cloth down. "How exactly do you plan to do that?"

"Well, I served as field engineer for the Corps of Engineers, have surveyed and conducted detailed topographical mapping, and have extensively studied European sand-dune reclamation. That has allowed me to complete phase one of my plan already. Thus the ground cover you are now sitting upon."

She scanned the area. "This used to be nothing but sand and brush?"

"It did."

"My. I'm impressed. You've completely tamed the entire area. And the pond?"

"Man-made."

"Good heavens."

He finished off the last potpie. "Yes. I'm well pleased with the reclamation phase. I'm not having as much luck with phase two, though."

"And what is phase two?"

"Planting decorative grounds."

She frowned. "I've not seen a full grown tree in all of San Francisco. Surely you do not think to duplicate the green pastoral landscapes that the big cities have back home?"

He wiped his mouth. "I don't see why not. I've been studying the work and writings of landscape theorists and have come to the conclusion that the good arable land here can be converted into picturesque parks."

Gathering up their lunch, she began to pack the remains in her basket. "Arable land? This?"

"I think so."

"And you plan on using those trees in your greenhouse?"

"To start with."

She nibbled on her lip. "Most of those are deciduous. If you threw in a few conifers, then you would add wild, bold drama to your grounds."

Leaning back on his elbows, he crossed his legs at his ankles. "If I don't kill the blasted things first."

She smiled. "Have you a design drawn up, then?"

"Nothing formal. Just ideas."

"You'll need to plant your trees close together so they will support each other against the buffeting winds."

"My studies indicate a need for space between each tree for root expansion."

She shook her head even before he'd finished his sentence. "You can thin them out later as they mature. They'll never make it otherwise. You'll also need to do something to remove the moisture from the lower stratum of air that the fog creates. Evergreen conifers should do nicely for that."

A couple of hours later, the lazy glow of the sun moving across the sky caught Johnnie unawares. They'd talked endlessly about his vision, giving birth to new ideas while discarding old ones. She'd proven herself to be extremely knowledgeable.

He'd never known a woman so book smart yet so naïve. A bit intimidating her knowledge was at first, but she spouted advice so casually that at some point his discomfort had been replaced by interest. But the naïveté, now that had captured his imagination from the start.

He lay on his side stretched out beside her, head propped in his hand. A good two feet away, she lay on her stomach, her torso held up by her elbows, while her hands were occupied with her hatpin—skewered largehead and all.

"I think if you replace your one-gallon containers," she was saying, "with tall, slender tree pots, then you'll find your plants will develop deeper root systems."

She glanced at him and paused. "What?"

Her hairpins had long since lost their battle against the breeze, and rich brown tendrils lay haphazardly against her neck like a silky sunbonnet curtain.

He brushed the ones closest to her face back against her shoulder. "It's getting late."

"It is?"

He hooked some tresses behind her ear. "Um."

She moved nary a muscle.

"You have the most magnificent eyes I've ever seen. Did you know they change when you speak of things you feel passionately about?"

The toe of one calfskin boot peeking from beneath her hem

pressed against the toe of its mate. She shook her head.

"It's as if someone is holding a gas lamp behind them, lighting them from within." He lifted the basket sitting between the two of them and placed it behind him.

Her gaze tracked the removal of their only barrier. She slowly lay the grasshopper down. "What are you doing?"

"Having some very foolish thoughts."

She pushed herself up to a sitting position and tucked her feet completely beneath her skirts. "Perhaps we should go."

He took his time answering. "Will you help me build my pleasure grounds, Rachel?"

"I'm not sure that would be a good idea."

"Are you afraid of me?"

"Only some of the time."

"Like now?"

"Like now."

"Why?"

She glanced at his lips and moistened her own. "I'm not exactly sure."

Gathering a half dozen hairpins littering the blanket, he handed them to her. She took them and began to repair her hair. He said nothing, just enjoyed watching her do such a trivial thing.

"Will you?" he asked again.

"What?"

"Help me cultivate my grounds. I'll pay you for your time."

"You'll pay me?" She gently removed the grasshopper from her pin and wrapped it in the food cloth.

"Of course. You obviously know more than I do about it, and your time is worth paying for. Will you?"

She picked up her bonnet and secured it onto her head. "Well, I suppose I could. After I'm finished with my chores at the hotel."

He sat up. "Excellent. I'll tell Adams down at the livery that you are to have Sweet Lips anytime you need her."

She removed her gloves from the basket and began to pull them on. "I guess it's settled, then."

Standing, he helped her to her feet. "Thank you."

She looked up. All neat and prim. One hundred percent lady. Except for the endearing sunburn pinking her nose and cheeks.

chapter 7

*I*t had been Rachel's most pleasant afternoon since arriving in the California territory. And now Johnnie had offered to pay her for the care of his trees. *Pay her.*

And there was no question of respectability here. Between this and the money she earned at the hotel and the odd jobs Michael picked up, they would have quite the nest egg when it was time to go home.

Leaning forward, she spoke soft words of encouragement to the sorrel beneath her, for they were still a good distance from town. With a tap of her heel, she followed Johnnie to the top of a rather steep hill, then paused.

In the desert-like valley below, hundreds upon hundreds of men scrambled in every direction, like a colony of ants whose anthill had been disrupted. In the center of the activity sat a crude arena bordered with a fence of tall stakes.

Frowning, she squinted her eyes but could not make out what was inside the ring nor what had caused such turmoil in the crowd. She urged her mount forward.

Bleak hills surrounded them on every side, forming a bowl with the arena at its core. The excited shouts of men encroached on their solitude.

"What's happening?" she asked.

Johnnie adjusted his hat. "Looks like a fight of some kind."

She snapped her gaze to him. "A fight? Between who?"

He pursed his lips. "Well, it's not a who so much as a what."

"I don't understand."

He studied her, as if gauging how much to tell her. "Well, the boys can get a little bored on an occasional Sunday afternoon."

"And?"

"And so they organize a fight of some kind. Used to be just a traditional bullfight put on by the Mexicans."

She sucked in her breath. "Oh, Johnnie, no. You don't really mean that."

He offered her a sad smile. "I'm afraid I do."

"Oh no." An abrupt outcry in the distance grabbed her attention. "What would happen then?"

His chuckle held no humor. "The boys would cheer for the bull."

Sweep Lips whinnied and yanked her head forward. Rachel quickly loosened the pressure she'd inadvertently applied to the reins. "Is that what's happening, then? A bullfight?"

He shook his head. "No. The boys prefer something with a little more variety." He took a deep breath. "So they pit bulls against grizzly bears."

She touched a hand to her throat. "They wouldn't."

"They would and they have. Bear catching is big business now. Promoters will pay upwards of two thousand dollars for a bear."

"That's deplorable. Hideous. I simply have no words."

He sidled J.B. up next to her. "I'm sorry, Rachel. I'd forgotten they scheduled one for today or I'd have taken you the long way around. Give me your reins and stay close. No need to get too near the fracas."

She shook her head. "I'd rather be in control of my own mount."

He didn't look too pleased but didn't press the issue. The closer they got, the more the excitement and bloodthirst of the men conveyed itself to her through the tension in their shouts and catcalls.

It wasn't long before she could see inside the ring. "Johnnie. The bear is chained and there are *three* bulls, not one."

"Just don't look. Now, come on."

Horrid fascination held her transfixed. The bear was giving its three competitors quite a time of it. Indeed, the bulls appeared to be downright frightened by the snarling beast.

Dark-skinned men entered the ring as a unit, lassoed the bulls, and carted them off.

She released a long breath. "It's over, then?"

"Will you *come on?*"

She frowned at his manner but urged Sweet Lips to follow. The mare sidestepped with displeasure, nostrils flared, before finally obeying.

The crowd roared. Rachel swiveled around in time to see a huge, proud black bull enter the arena and paw the dirt furiously. She yanked Sweet Lips to a halt. The mare danced.

"Oh, Johnnie, can't we do something?"

"We aren't doing anything but going home."

"Please."

"No. We're not going anywhere near that crowd."

The bull bellowed fiercely and lunged. The bear caught the attacker's thigh within his teeth.

The bull's howl of agony coincided with the crowd's shout and Rachel's shriek as the animal whipped around, caught his adversary with his tremendous horns and flung him clear up off the ground. The bear somersaulted in the air, interrupted by the length of his chain, and prematurely dropped to the ground with enough force to surely break every bone in his body.

Yet in a flash, he surged toward the bull, teeth bared, and wounded him heavily in the haunches.

Tears poured down Rachel's cheeks as she struggled to breathe.

Winded, the bull moved out of harm's reach before launching a second attack, goring the bear, only to be driven off once again by the grizzly's teeth.

Four times the bull attacked, and though the bear was frightfully wounded, the bull always seemed to come out worse for the wear. Finally, the bear caught him by the head.

The bull desperately fought his way free, ran from the bear, and with a Herculean effort, jumped over the palisade wall—right into the crowd. Men fled in all directions, like corn popping right out of the kettle.

Rachel screamed. Sweet Lips reared up. Johnnie let out a slew of curses.

Holding tight to the reins, Rachel managed to subdue her horse, though she almost lost her seat before accomplishing the task.

Johnnie grabbed for her reins, but she kept them out of his reach.

"*Hold still!*" he cried. "The last thing we need is for that blasted bull to chase you down."

She immediately saw what a terrible possibility that was. For the blood-soaked bull had at that very moment looked around frantically with terror-stricken eyes.

Its attention zeroed in on them, or maybe their horses, then swiveled away before taking to the hills in the opposite direction. Men on horseback followed in hot pursuit.

Bile rose to Rachel's throat. She slid from the sorrel and fell to her knees. Another screech from the crowd brought her head up.

A Spanish cowboy had entered the ring to cart off the bear, but when he got close, the grizzly jumped up and grabbed him. In an instant, the bear was scored with bullets, coming from a host of revolvers carried by members of the crowd. Its body jerked and contorted with each hit.

A man on the uppermost bench fired over the heads of two or three hundred people and hit the grizzly right between the eyes.

Rachel leaned over and cast up her accounts. She became aware of Johnnie's presence beside her and drew comfort from it.

When she was through, she removed the hanky from her cuff and wiped her mouth.

Johnnie helped her to her feet, but she got no more than a few yards before collapsing to the ground again. He squatted down, pulled her onto his lap, and wrapped his arms about her. He held the reins of both animals in one hand. With the other, he pressed her head against his shoulder and rocked her like a babe.

She buried her face in his neck and sobbed.

Johnnie called himself six-half-dozen-and-another kinds of a fool. He'd known what it was the minute they'd crested that hill. He should have turned them both around and circled all the way back.

But it had been late and he needed to get to the saloon before dark. Well, it was nigh on dark now and here they still sat.

Laying his cheek against hers to hold her still, he extracted her hatpin, slipped off her bonnet, and tunneled his fingers into her hair.

She nestled closer. He reached down and hauled her up higher onto his lap.

The gut-wrenching sobs had ceased and were now replaced with hiccups, heavy sniffs, and indecipherable mumblings. His legs had long since fallen asleep and the crowd was no more.

I'll be hanged, but her hair is pure heaven, he thought.

Its silky fineness combined with the pressure of his fingers was too much for the hairpins. They slid from her twist like foliage in the fall, spilling long tresses into his hands and releasing a sudden burst of vanilla.

He combed his fingers through it, sending the remaining pins flying. Over and over he stroked her hair until the rhythm of her breathing grew steady and slow.

"I need to get you home. It's late," he said.

She shifted positions, then relaxed once more against him.

He nuzzled her neck. "Open your eyes, Rachel. Your sister's bound to be frantic with worry."

She opened her eyes and gave him a lazy look. Desire sluiced through him.

He ran his hand down her arm to the curve of her waist. Heaven help him, she was putty in his hands. His for the taking. He gently squeezed her. "Do you think you can stand?"

Rousing a bit, she straightened, allowing some space where before there had been none. The coolness of the night immediately rushed over him.

She shivered. "My hair."

"Is glorious." It fell clear to her waist. He lifted a strand to his mouth, inhaling deeply.

She wrapped her arms around herself. "I'm cold."

He released her hair. The woman had no idea how much jeopardy she was in. He could warm her. Like she'd never been warmed before. But he had no intention of marrying her. He'd been married once before, and he had no wish to duplicate that sad state of affairs.

He shrugged off his jacket and helped her feed her arms into its sleeves. "You'd best get up, love. Or the consequences might be more than you bargained for."

He'd expected her to scramble off him in a hurry, but she moved nary a muscle. His heart began to pound. Then she slowly unfolded herself and stood beside him. Willowy. Young. And incredibly vulnerable.

The horses waited listlessly at the bottom of the hill. No grass to feed on. Just sand.

He scooped her hand into his and headed toward Sweet Lips.

"My bonnet."

"I'll get it in a minute."

"My hairpins."

"It's too dark. You'll have to do without them."

"But I need them. I only have a few as it is."

"I'll get them for you tomorrow. Do you need to ride double with me or are you all right?"

"I'm all right."

He helped her mount but took the lead in his hands.

"I can do it, Johnnie."

Swinging a leg over J.B., he retained control of her horse. "Just hold on. I'll do the rest."

———

A gritty residue caked Rachel's eyes, making them painful to open, yet open them she did. Lying still on the bed, she listened to the shouts, oaths, and threats of shooting that characterized the menagerie of the Plaza at night. Judging from the level of these disturbances and the sparseness of music, the night was winding down and morning would soon be calling.

Weariness consumed her, yet she knew sleep would not rescue her from its clutches. Images of the gruesome dream that had jerked her awake flashed through her mind.

She squeezed her eyes shut but could not hold it at bay. Sweet Lips screeching in pain as a grossly oversized grizzly with horns growing from its head snapped the sorrel in half with its jaws, then gored her with its horns and trampled her with cloven hooves.

Rachel curled up into a ball. She'd returned home last night only to discover Michael had attended the fight. The aftermath of the thrill consuming him, he had described the event in graphic detail to Lissa, who had listened raptly with an unhealthy glow in her eyes.

Rachel pressed a fist to her mouth. For she was no better. Hadn't Johnnie tried to take her away? But the very grotesqueness of the display had held her transfixed.

She covered her face with her hands. This town was just one big trapdoor spider—lurking in its camouflaged lair waiting to pounce on any insect that strayed too close. And when that victim passed by, the spider would rush out and plunge its fangs into it. Paralyzing it and eating it alive.

She swallowed. What was to become of her? Of Lissa? Of Michael? *O Lord. Help me be strong. Help me be wise. Protect me from the spider's lair.*

Conviction over her behavior with Johnnie washed through her. She could not believe she had actually sat in the man's lap, allowing him liberties no lady ought.

Still, she couldn't deny the pleasure and comfort his embrace had provided. *"And in the shadow of Your wings I will make my refuge, until these calamities have passed by."*

That's what it was like, Lord, she thought. *It was as if he took me into the shelter of his wings and gave me refuge until the calamity had passed.*

Yet she knew she had no business finding sanctuary in the arms of a gambler.

But where were you, Lord? Where were you?

She untied the ribbon at the tail of her braid, then unraveled it, pondering the delicious feeling he had induced when he hand-combed her hair.

Lissa's eyes had been wide with curiosity at Rachel's disheveled state last night, but she had stopped just short of asking.

Michael was not so gracious. Scowling, he'd squared up and demanded an explanation. She'd hedged, saying the mad scramble after the fight had frightened the horses, her bonnet had fallen off, and her hair hadn't held up like it should.

He was still young enough to accept her account at face value. Lissa was not. The girl had eyed Rachel the rest of the evening, fraught with speculation.

Rachel brushed her lips with the ends of her hair. Just last year she had clandestinely read one of her father's medical books written by a New York physician of wide experience where he most decidedly stated that the full force of sexual desire is seldom known in a virtuous woman; that nature had provided a more susceptible organization in males than in females.

The entire discourse seemed to suggest that some nameless and horrid immorality would result if the two parties, even in a legal union, were equally passionate.

And that was why it was the female's responsibility to set the moral climate within the family and society.

Tears welled in her eyes. Was her purity nothing but superficial? Something so easily dissolved that she would fall from virtue at the mere touch of a man?

She glanced at Lissa sleeping soundly beside her. And Michael, curled up by the fireplace. They were dependent upon her not only for their basic needs but also for their moral needs.

Slipping from the bed, she stoked the fire and then lit a lamp, turning low the flame before retrieving her Bible from the table. Crawling back beneath the covers, she turned to Proverbs and started with chapter two. The chapter on avoiding adulteresses. She did not stop until she'd read through chapter five, "Forsaking Lust."

Rachel set boiled ham, potatoes, and onions on the table. Johnnie had left right after breakfast saying he wouldn't be back for the noon meal. He hadn't said where he was going, but he took her list of groceries with him. She hoped he picked some of them up today. There were only so many ways to cook pork.

Michael and Lissa filed into the kitchen and the three of them sat down at the table. Soda had eaten earlier, then opened the hotel for business as soon as Rachel and Lissa had finished their chores. He'd eyed the Mexican blanket she had draped over the statue but said nothing about it. Nor did he remove it.

But the men were not so discreet. Of course, they had no way of knowing the ladies sat on the other side of the wall with nothing but a curtained doorway separating them.

"Looks like the missy done covered up Johnnie's naked ladykin again."

"Hoo, I cain't wait to see his expression. He shore is sensitive about that there statue."

"I'm bettin' that's one piece a furniture in this hotel that won't never get scrubbed."

The men exchanged hearty laughs.

Rachel cut a bite of meat and jabbed it with her fork. "What are your plans for the rest of the day, Michael?"

"Well, I heard you could earn as much as twenty dollars for digging a grave," he said. "So I was going to head over to Cemetery Hill and see if they needed an extra hand."

She nodded and took a sip of tea. Grave digging was a worthy occupation and would perhaps give Michael firsthand knowledge of the consequences caused by hard drinking and hard living.

"What about you, Lissa?"

"All this cleaning has simply ruined my hands and feet. I'm going to brew up some very strong peppermint tea to soak them in and then take a nice long nap."

Rachel sighed. "I'm afraid our days of soft hands and feet are long over. Are you sure you wouldn't like to ride out to Mr. Parker's property with me today?"

"And dig around in the dirt? No, thank you."

Before Rachel could respond, a woman in a white, blousy scoop-necked bodice and full colorful skirt entered in the back door of the kitchen.

"I sorry I late." She smiled and pulled a plate from the shelf.

Michael jumped to his feet and gave up his chair.

"Gracias, *señor*."

Rachel stiffened. "What are you doing?"

"I am Carmelita." She sat down, spooned ham and potatoes onto her plate, then began to eat. "I work tables for Mr. Johnnie. I live in room above hotel. He say *la comida* is ready at noon."

"You live here?" Rachel put down her knife and fork.

"Sí."

"And Mr. Parker told you to take your meals here with us?"

"Sí."

Rachel dabbed her mouth with her napkin. "Then where were you at breakfast? Why have I not seen you before?"

"I sleep in morning and now I eat noontime with you, sí?"

Rachel glanced at Lissa. The girl had her gaze pinned to the large expanse of bare flesh exposed above Carmelita's low-cut bodice. Michael's attention had been snared by the same.

Rachel knew what she was supposed to do. Knew what society dictated she do. But never had she been required to perform such an unpleasant task. How could this girl not know it was highly improper for her to sit at the same table as ladies?

"You work in the hotel?" Lissa asked.

"Sí. The men, they like the women. So they play at Carmelita's table and they pay no attention to cards. They pay attention to Carmelita. So Carmelita win much gold."

Whatever reservations Rachel had before, they vanished with this bit of table conversation.

She would not, could not, expose her young and impressionable siblings to the kind of decadence Carmelita would introduce into their everyday lives. No, it was best to nip this in the bud right this very moment.

"Carmelita, I'm sure you would understand if I were to ask you to no longer take your meals with us."

Carmelita paused, spoon halfway to her mouth.

"Don't," Lissa said. "Don't you do this, Rachel. How could you?"

"I'm sorry," Rachel continued, ignoring Lissa's appeal. "But if I am to instill piety and virtue in my sister and brother, then I must do so with a clear conscience."

She quickly shied away from thoughts of her less than virtuous behavior yesterday—and on a Sunday, no less.

Carmelita's gaze bore into Rachel, then without another word, she stood and stepped away from the table.

Lissa jumped to her feet. "Carmelita! Wait."

Carmelita swept through the curtain and into the hotel.

Lissa leveled a glare at her sister before slamming out the back door.

The enthusiastic shouts of men greeting Carmelita easily reached the ears of the two still in the kitchen.

"Was that really necessary?" Michael asked softly.

"Yes," she answered, "but I didn't like doing it."

"I didn't like you doing it, either."

He, too, left without finishing his meal.

Rachel forced herself to stay at the table until she'd eaten everything on her plate. Then she rose and cleared the dishes. But the entire time, her anger at Johnnie for putting her in this position simmered.

Just wait until she got ahold of him.

he door to the shanty was propped open, giving Johnnie a clear view inside. But instead of finding Rachel, he found Merle Sumner. Sitting in a chair, his tight checkered pants peeking out from a sheet, his head thrown back, his face lathered up, and Lissa hovering above him, giving him a shave.

"Is your neck getting tired?" she asked, her soft voice pouring out like liquid honey, the razor poised above Sumner's jaw.

He opened his eyes. "No, my dear. I do not believe I have ever felt so fine as I do at this moment."

Johnnie watched her soften at the man's words, having no idea she had an audience of two instead of one. How could she not have heard him come in? There was no question in his mind that Sumner had heard him, though. The man missed nothing. Had extremely keen senses. Most seasoned sharks did.

She placed her free hand beneath Sumner's head, her fingers spreading through his black hair. "I just wish I could make you a bit more comfortable."

Sumner's hand snaked out from beneath the sheet, touching Lissa's elbow.

Johnnie narrowed his eyes. "Where's Michael?" he asked.

Lissa gasped. Sumner didn't so much as flinch. Just loosely grabbed her wrist to keep her from slicing him accidentally.

"Oh, Mr. Parker. You gave me a fright." She disengaged herself from Sumner then smoothed a hand down the front of her apron.

"Where's Michael?" he repeated.

"A new ship full of gold seekers came in today. It also carried the post, so Mr. Sumner here paid Michael to wait in line and pick up his mail for him."

"Where's your sister?"

"She's at your place. Said you were paying her to water your trees."

He hesitated. "What are you doing, Lissa?"

Sumner slowly raised his head. "I believe she is Miss Van Buren to you, is she not?"

Johnnie didn't so much as acknowledge him. Kept his gaze pinned to *Miss Van Buren.*

She smiled, a little too brightly. "I'm giving Mr. Sumner a shave. Three dollars. Would you like one?"

"I thought you worked with your sister."

"I do, I do. But as you know, we finish up every day at noon."

Johnnie moved his attention to Sumner. The man offered him a slow grin beneath the lather on his face. "You may have a turn with her, Parker. As soon as I am done."

Johnnie tightened his jaw. "Does your sister know about this, Miss Van Buren?"

Lissa pulled herself straight. "Would you or would you not like a shave, Mr. Parker?"

"Depends. Where did you learn to shave a man's face?"

"Your neck is safe with me, sir. I've been shaving my father's for years."

Johnnie pulled out a chair. "In that case, don't mind if I do."

Sumner hooked another chair with his boot, pulled it toward him, and propped his feet up onto it. Flicking the sheet so that his belly gun was visible and within easy reach, he closed his eyes and presented his face to Lissa.

The girl became all business, holding Sumner's jaw with one finger while pulling her strap across his face with the other hand. And in between each stroke Sumner found some reason to touch her.

Nothing overt, but enough that by the time she had finished and her subject pulled the sheet from his neck, Johnnie's unease had risen to volatile levels.

Defend the poor and fatherless; Do justice to the afflicted and needy.

He might not be a Bible-thumping churchgoing man anymore, but some habits died hard.

Sumner measured out three dollars in dust and strolled to the door. Johnnie rose to his feet.

"Enjoy yourself, Parker. I know I did."

Johnnie waited until Romeo had cleared out before turning to Lissa. She busied herself shaking out the sheet, wiping down her instruments, and warming more water. She stirred up the shaving cream, releasing a burst of mint into the air.

Finally, she faced him. "Please, have a seat."

"This is a very dangerous game you play, Lissa."

Her lips puckered. "I don't know what mean."

Johnnie advanced toward her. "Oh, I think you do. No sunbonnet has any business whatsoever attending to a man's toilet, particularly without a chaperone. What will your sister say?"

"My sister is not my keeper."

He stopped before her. "No? In whose shelter do you reside?"

She lifted her chin. "I help with the work, so this shanty is just as much mine as it is hers. Besides, you are not my father, uncle, or brother. No relation at all. I will not discuss matters of such a personal nature with you."

"I see. You're too pure to have a conversation but not too pure to perform a man's toilet."

Grabbing two corners of the cloth, she snapped it into the air, billowing it out like a flag. "Sit down, Mr. Parker. I haven't all day."

He gently took the sheet from her and proceeded to fold it. "Merle Sumner is a card shark and a womanizer. If I catch you alone with him again, I will tell your sister. In the meanwhile, you are to stick to the duties your sister assigns you. Have I made myself clear?"

He handed her the folded cloth.

She snatched it from him. "Get out."

Nodding once, he left the shanty and headed to the livery.

———

He hadn't planned to make another trip out to his property so soon, but as long as Rachel was out there, he'd decided to hitch up a wagon and take the new trees that had arrived on this morning's ship.

He could not believe she had turned Carmelita away. That woman had some kind of nerve. What a sanctimonious prig. He knew full well he could have had her at the blink of an eye yesterday.

So the reality of it was, Rachel was no better than Carmelita. But she obviously thought she was.

He slapped the reins a bit harder than he meant to. J.B. lurched forward, causing the potted plants to teeter before settling back down.

She must have heard him coming, because she was waiting for him at the front stoop of the greenhouse. Her hand shaded her eyes, though the bonnet she had on today was more serviceable than the piece of fluff she had worn yesterday.

He pulled J.B. to a stop. "Whoa there, fella."

"I wasn't expecting to see you." She moved to the wagon. "Where did all those come from?"

Jumping from his perch, he rounded the wagon and yanked the dowels out of their housing. The hatch fell open.

"Why, what are they?" she asked. "They smell wonderful."

He began to loosen the ropes that secured the saplings to the bed. He knew he was being rude, but he didn't trust himself to speak yet. He shouldn't have come.

"Johnnie?"

He released the square knot, then pulled the rope hand over hand.

She stepped closer. "I need to speak to you about something."

He flung the rope down. "You have anything against Mexicans?"

Her hand flew to her throat. "Of course not."

"Then you care to explain to me why you tossed Carmelita out of my kitchen today?"

Jerking her hand down, she whipped her spine up so straight she gained a whole inch in height. "I had no choice."

"Yes you did."

Her shoulders sagged a bit. "I really didn't, Johnnie. What would people think if I allowed a fallen woman to break bread with my family three times a day?"

"I see." He turned back to the wagon bed and grabbed the tree he'd freed. "You're worried about what people would think. Well, that's very *Christian* of you."

"No! I mean, well, it wasn't just that."

Lifting the pot off the planks, he strode around her and into the hothouse.

She scrambled after him. "I have a responsibility, Johnnie. To my family. To the community. If I associate with her, it would look as if I was condoning her behavior."

He slammed the tree down onto a shelf. The exotic fragrance of the new eucalyptus permeated the glass structure.

"And just what kind of behavior are you referring to?"

"You know perfectly well what I mean. She works in a saloon."

"So do you."

"I most certainly do not. I clean a hotel during its nonoperating hours."

"A hotel that doubles as a saloon."

"Quit splitting hairs with me, Johnnie." She propped her fists on her waist. "If it were just me, that would be one thing. But it's not. I have Lissa and Michael to think about. Don't you see?"

"Prove it."

"What do you mean?"

"I'll send Michael and Lissa on an errand. And while they are gone, you, Carmelita, and I can sit down and share a meal."

She clasped her hands. "But I can't. Lissa and Michael might catch us or hear about it later, and then I wouldn't have a leg to stand on."

"Sounds like a bunch of excuses to me."

"My family comes first, Johnnie. And there are rules of society that govern what is acceptable behavior for a lady and what is not. That town at the bottom of the hill may think it doesn't have to follow the edicts of society, but it does. And it's going to start at my dinner table."

"Is that a fact?"

"Yes, it is."

"Well guess what? It just so happens that it is *my* dinner table we eat at. And because of that, I get to choose who sits at it and who doesn't. So let me make this perfectly clear." He pointed a finger at her. "Carmelita can sit, eat, drink, and cavort at my table all the day long if she wants to. You got that?"

Rachel stood in the middle of the aisle, sickly trees on both sides, righteous indignation coming off her in waves. "Then Michael, Lissa, and I will take our meals in the shanty."

So. She wanted to fight dirty, did she? "What? You think you can single-handedly reform me or Carmelita or all of San-Fran-cisco, Miss Van Buren?"

She said nothing.

He slowly closed the gap between them. "Because if you do, you might want to start in your own backyard, so to speak."

Her lips thinned. "Just what is that supposed to mean?"

He slid his gaze down one side of her frame and up the other, making a point to pause at the most inappropriate places. "Well, there's the little matter of your, shall we say, *loose* behavior yesterday, not to mention the fact that your sister runs a shaving salon right inside the hallowed walls of your shanty."

Innocent confusion fanned across her face before she frowned. "What are you talking about?"

He gave her a heated look. "Well, my dear, it is my understanding that unmarried respectable girls do not wallow about in men's laps, giving them free access to their pure, chaste bodies."

The slap was quick, hard, and painful. He didn't so much as flinch.

"I needn't any reminders of my own wayward behavior, Mr. Parker. I was asking for clarification on the shaving-salon issue."

He drew a finger down her jaw. She swatted it away.

"I'm not a teller of tales, Rachel. Which, I would think, you'd find very reassuring. If you want your questions answered, you'll have to ask your sister."

She frowned then looked out the greenhouse windows. "Is she yours?"

He blinked. "Who?"

"Carmelita."

Well, well, well. "No. Carmelita and I do not have that, uh, kind of arrangement. She rents a table from me. If she meets any of her customers after work hours, it's not something I am privy to. Nor do I profit by it."

She returned her attention to him. "Why?"

"Why do I not profit by it?"

"Why would you let her rent out a table in a gaming hall?"

Ah. He knew where this was going. What she really wanted to know was why he would perpetuate the ruining of a woman. Which would then segue into how he needed Jesus Christ as his Lord and Savior.

Well, he'd been down that particular path before. And he'd decided he preferred the wide one over the narrow one, thank you very much.

"A female dealer draws customers," he said, then headed back out to the wagon, forestalling her salvation speech.

She stayed put, quiet and subdued, while he carted tree after tree inside. Their pungent spicy smell overpowered all else.

After depositing the last tree on the shelf, he wiped his hands on his trousers. "Well, that's all of them."

She said nothing. Just stood in the corner looking uncomfortable and confused.

He rubbed his mouth. They were going to be working in close quarters for who knew how long. And he did enjoy those meals. Not just the food, but the company. Perhaps he should try to put them back on even footing. If he could.

"They're eucalyptus trees," he said. "Came all the way from Australia. I've read that they grow extremely fast."

She reached out to finger a leaf on one of the new plants.

"I know they look kind of puny, but they supposedly get root bound, so it's best to get them established in the ground as soon as possible. Won't that be something? To be able to actually start on the planting?"

Her gaze returned to his, distress pouring from those big brown windows into her soul.

He sighed. "I'm sorry, Rachel. For what I said earlier, about, you know, yesterday. I was angry and, well, I'm sorry."

"Me, too," she whispered, then tucked her chin down. He held out for as long as he could before approaching.

The sting from that slap still lingered, and though she had apologized, he had no desire to receive another one, so he kept his hands to himself. When she refused to look at him, he bent down and peeked up under her bonnet.

"I have your hairpins for you," he offered.

She covered her mouth with the back of her hand. Straightening, he reached into his jacket pocket and held out a box of brand new store-bought pins.

A muffled groan escaped from behind her hand, but she made no move to take the pins. Shifting his weight, he kept the pins out there. Waiting.

Finally, she lifted her distraught face. "I can't accept those, Johnnie. You know I can't."

"Women in the camps do it all the time. The respectable ones, I mean. It's not the same. There's so few of you, the fellas just buy all kinds of stuff for the sheer pleasure of it. No one will think a thing. No one will even know."

"I'll know. You'll know. I've already compromised myself far beyond the pale as it is."

He slowly lowered his hand. "I thought you had a forgiving God."

Pulling a hanky out from her cuff, she rubbed dirt stains from her fingers. "I do."

"So did you talk to Him about what happened between us yesterday?"

Trapping her bottom lip between her teeth, she nodded.

"Then you're white as snow. So what's the problem?"

The sad smile that started to form never quite made it to completion. "I'm supposed to go and sin no more."

He tapped his hand against his leg. "Is there some Bible verse that says taking hairpins from a man is a sin? Especially when he's just replacing the ones he disposed of?"

"I'm not accepting the pins, Johnnie. But I do appreciate your going to such trouble over them. It really wasn't necessary."

He crammed them back into his pocket, his irritation rekindled. "You covered up my Lorenzo Bartolini again. I distinctly remember telling you not to do that anymore."

She moistened her lips. "You said not to cover it with a flour sack. And I didn't."

"Now who's splitting hairs?"

"It's highly offensive to me, Johnnie. Please do not ask me to work in that room while that whatever-you-call-it stares at me bold as she pleases."

"I'm not asking. I'm telling. That whatever-you-call-it is a classic, exquisite, *tasteful* piece of art. If she's staring at you, ignore her. But do *not* cover her up. Understood?"

She said nothing.

"Answer me, Rachel."

"I heard you, Mr. Parker."

Mr. Parker? Were they back to that now?

He glanced around the hothouse, satisfied his trees would be fine for the moment. "You about ready to go?"

"Yes. I think so."

"Well, come on with me, then."

After holding open the door, he followed her to the wagon and helped her up. When she was situated, he corralled Sweet Lips, tied her to the back, and proceeded to take *Miss Van Buren* home.

chapter 9

The next two months brought sunshine to the California coast but rain to Rachel's spirit. For as the mud dried up, so did her sister. Each passing day Lissa's complaints and insubordination increased.

She'd adamantly denied any knowledge of a shaving salon and threatened to eat with Johnnie and Carmelita if Rachel didn't believe her.

She resented performing what she considered menial tasks in the hotel, when in fact everything she did was nothing more than an honest woman's work. Why, women had been doing such chores for centuries before and would continue doing so for many centuries to come. Still, if there was an easy way out, Lissa would take it.

Rachel had caught men hauling the water for her. Beating the ticks for her. Preparing the fire pit for her. Purchasing trinkets for her. Just yesterday Rachel had come upon a large, burly man up to his elbows scrubbing one of Michael's shirts with such violence the suds flew and the buttons popped off, and with Lissa lounging at his side not the least bit remorseful.

O Lord. When will you send us a vessel that will take us safely home?

Trudging her way from the livery back to the shanty, Rachel turned her thoughts to the progress she and Johnnie had made with his property. The eucalyptus trees had been planted according to a well-thought-out design strategy they had come up with. And the unending arrival of ships brought new trees and shrubs, many of which would be ready for planting next spring.

Like clockwork, she would head to his land as soon as lunch was over and stay the rest of the day, enjoying the solitude and peace it offered. Enjoying the new variety of insects she'd discovered. But most of all, enjoying the lazy Sunday afternoons there with Johnnie.

Another ship had been docked and abandoned this morning, so Rachel had headed back early to see if its cargo included any wash buckets. She approached the hotel and quickly realized a few of the old timers had dusted the streets with gold, for a crowd of newcomers crawled on their knees in the middle of the Plaza to "strike it rich."

They dug up the soil with knives, crumbled it to dust in their hands, blew on it, and picked out shiny little fragments that they carefully wrapped in bits of paper.

The pursuit of commerce continued to keep the square busy and loud, with new buildings thrown up nearly every day. The hammering of nails, the delivery of planks, and the sawing of wood forced the men to shout above the din.

She noted that the corner lot across from the hotel was being leveled. She also noted that Mr. Johnnie Parker stood on its border discussing architectural drawings with a man whom she recognized as the surveyor.

A movement down Washington Street caught her attention. The young man pushing a cart up the steep hill moved much in the way Michael did.

She squinted. It *was* Michael and his face had turned lobster red from his effort. Whatever was in the cart must weigh a great deal.

He stopped in front of Johnnie. They exchanged words, and then Johnnie pointed to his hotel and clapped Michael on the back.

She had already changed directions before she realized her intent to intercept her brother. Waving, she caught his attention. He came up short, forcing her to close the distance between them.

One look in the cart and she knew why he'd stopped. Crate after crate of liquor filled its bed.

"You're delivering *alcohol*?"

"It's a job. And a good paying one, at that. It's not like I'm drinking it."

She pulled her lips down. "I don't like it, Michael. Not one bit. There's bound to be something else you can do."

"Well, Rachel, you're back from the hothouse a bit earlier than usual, aren't you?"

She turned to see Johnnie approaching. Michael wasted no time in grasping the handles of his cart and continuing on his delivery.

"Wait, Michael."

He paused and twisted around.

"Would you tell Lissa to come here, please?" she asked. "I need her to come with me in case I find a laundry tub down by the Presidio."

He darted a quick glance at Johnnie before returning his attention to her. "I, um, I'm not really sure she can come right this minute."

Where before his face had been red from exertion, this surge of color originated from an entirely different source.

"Whyever not?"

He shifted his feet. "This is heavy as a box stove, Rache, and I'm on a schedule. Isn't that right, Mr. Parker?"

"It certainly is, son. You go on now and finish your work. I'll see if I can be of assistance to your sister."

"Don't you even think about taking another step, Michael, until you tell me what is going on."

Her brother once again directed his focus to Johnnie, who gave him a slight nod. With that, Michael turned his back and continued on his way.

Nonplussed, she whirled to face Johnnie. "Just what was that all about?"

"A boat came in today, and I have a large order on it. It will take Michael every bit of what daylight's left to tote it all up here."

"I meant about Lissa. Where is she?"

"I don't think he knows, does he?"

Rachel narrowed her eyes. "I'm not sure. Do you?"

"Know if he knows? No."

"Don't play word games with me, Johnnie." She crossed her arms. "Where is Lissa?"

"I couldn't exactly tell you."

"Can't tell me or won't tell me?"

"Is there something wrong?"

She uncrossed her arms and clenched her fists. "There is going to be something terribly wrong in a minute if you do not quit running me around the mulberry bush. Now, where is she?"

He said nothing.

A ripple of unease began in the core of her being. She unfurled her hands. "What is it, Johnnie? What has happened?"

The blue of his eyes was a perfect match for the clear sky behind him. "I'm not sure anything has happened."

"But you expect something to happen?"

He pulled a handkerchief out of his pocket and wiped his forehead. "I think, perhaps, you'd best go on home. If I'm not mistaken, Lissa is in the shanty. She usually is this time of the day."

Rachel entered the open door of her shanty and found a shaving salon instead. In one quick sweep she discovered a man in green checkered pants and a crisp white shirt with his back turned while he poured water from a kettle into a bowl. A man with a potbelly and wide backside stroked an orange cat asleep in his lap. Another handful of men lounged about the floor reading the paper, swapping stories and, for the most part, watching Lissa.

And a more fetching sight they'd be hard pressed to find. The crisp white apron hugging her waist culminated at the back with a big stiff bow. Leaning over a drowsy miner, she gathered the lather from his face with a steaming cloth and gave it to the man in checkered pants.

Shock and disbelief held Rachel motionless.

Lissa inspected her customer's face for stubble in a slow methodical manner, her finger and thumb wandering about like a gleaner after the harvest.

Her "assistant" then handed her a cup of lather, which she brushed on for the second shave. The helper held out a razor, and

Rachel did not miss the intimate look that passed between them when Lissa took it.

He glanced up and froze. Then, with an insolent smirk, rested a proprietary hand below Lissa's big bow and just above the curve of her buttocks.

As the other men in the room discovered Rachel's presence, they slowly rose to their feet. While she waited for the razor to be safely removed from the customer's neck, she tried to recall where she had seen the offensive man staring her down.

And then she remembered. It was the same man who had been eyeing Lissa that very first week they arrived. When Lissa had made a spectacle of herself in front of the crowd for a hat full of gold. He'd been on the periphery of the crowd, with a predatory gleam even then.

"Get your hands off my sister and get out of my home."

Lissa jumped. The man in the shaving chair jerked open his eyes. The cat meowed and did a figure eight between a pair of booted feet.

"Rachel. What are you doing home so soon?"

Rachel held fast her gaze to what she considered the biggest threat in the room. "I said get out and I meant it."

The other men came out of their trance. "Come on, Sumner. You heard the lady. Shop's closed."

Sumner whispered something in Lissa's ear, and gave her back end a pat. Rachel walked to the fireplace, picked up a poker, and grasped it firmly in her right hand.

"We're goin', Miss Van Buren, we're goin'," the man in the chair said. He whipped the bed sheet from around his neck, wiped off his face, and stood. "Come on, boys."

They headed to the door, then paused. "You, too, Sumner. We won't be havin' you give the missy a hard time."

Sumner picked his jacket up off the bed and gave a slight bow to Rachel. "It's been a pleasure, I'm sure."

He closed the door behind him.

"Have you completely lost your mind?" Rachel asked.

Lissa began to clean up the mess. "I enjoy giving the men a shave, and they enjoy receiving it. I'm very good at it, you know, and I've earned us quite a bit of money."

"How on earth do you expect to marry a decent man, let alone a gentleman, when you refuse to behave as a lady ought?"

Lissa paused. "Don't worry, Rachel. When we return home, no one will know that I tended to men's toilets and you worked in a saloon." She smiled without humor. "It will be our little secret, won't it?"

Rachel narrowed her eyes. "Who was that man?"

"Which one?"

"You know which one."

"His name is Merle Sumner."

"And what has he to do with you?"

"Absolutely nothing."

"I'm not an idiot, Lissa."

"And I'm through discussing it."

Rachel leaned the poker against the hearth. "You will be going with me to the property every afternoon from now on."

"No, thank you."

"You haven't a choice."

Lissa lifted a brow. "You think not?"

"I know not."

Picking up the bowl of dirty water, Lissa opened the door. "We shall see."

Rachel woke with a start and turned her head but could not see Lissa sleeping next to her in the dark. The evening had been a disaster. Lissa had taken that bowl of dirty water out the door and not come back for hours. Where the girl had gone, Rachel couldn't imagine, but she hadn't returned until well after supper.

Then she prepared for bed, brushed that long blond hair until it shone, braided it, and crawled into bed. All without a word. No greeting. No apology. No explanation.

Rachel was at a total loss as to what to do. She couldn't bodily force the girl to do her bidding, but clearly, she must do something and she must do it quickly.

Please, Lord, please. Send us a ship. And in the meanwhile, show me what to do.

She nibbled on her lip. Working in the hotel was obviously a stumbling block for Lissa. Perhaps they could open up a restaurant of their own. Something completely separate from Johnnie and his saloon.

Heaven knew the men would pay a fortune for a home-cooked meal. But that would require a building and a kitchen and supplies and a piece of property to put it on.

It would require someone more reliable than Lissa to help her cook and clean and tote supplies from the docks or from the mercantile.

And it would require money. Quite a bit of money. Every cent they earned had been safely deposited in the customhouse, where neither Lissa nor Michael could get to it. Then, when it was time to go home, the funds for starting over would be available.

If she was to use that to open up a restaurant here, they would not be able to leave at a moment's notice. They'd have to wait until they had paid off their debts and made some profit.

With a prayer on her heart, Rachel slid a hand across the bed, wanting only to touch Lissa while she prayed.

Heavens, this bed was big. She scooted over, reaching, reaching. Nothing.

Abandoning all pretense, she sat up. "Lissa?" she whispered.

No answer.

She ran her hands all over the bed. Her heart began to pound. Perhaps she'd gone to the privy.

Placing her feet on the floor, she felt around for the lamp. "Michael?"

No answer. But that wasn't so unusual. Sometimes the odd jobs he picked up kept him out well after dark.

She hurried to the fireplace, stirred up the embers, and lit the lamp. The shanty was empty.

Rachel quickly dressed and checked the privy, then hurried down the alley. Staying in the shadows, she leaned against the side of the hotel. The Plaza took on such a dreamlike appearance at night. There were no public lamps, of course, but none were needed.

The slight construction of the frame buildings allowed lamplight from within to shine out through innumerable chinks, cracks, and knotholes, producing a most fantastic effect. The muslin walls of the

numerous tents became wholly luminous, casting up gigantic silhou-
ettes of grotesque figures.

Rachel scanned the crowds looking for some sign of Lissa, but with
no luck. The daytime noise of saw and hammer had been replaced with
loud talking, laughter, and music. Singing, dancing, and quarreling.

Yet something was different. Men normally swarmed around the
glitter and music of the saloons, as a *Plodia interpunctella* to a flame.

But tonight they walked past tent after tent. All headed for the newly
constructed two-story house on the north side of the Plaza. She'd heard
it was to be the establishment of a noted courtesan. Yet it looked as
respectable as any residence one might find back in New Jersey.

And, truly, she couldn't quite reconcile herself to that beautiful
structure being used for such decadent purposes. And right on the
town square. No, she had dismissed it as nothing more than rumor.

Now she wasn't so sure. The house was ablaze with light and
activity. A line had begun to form at the door. And a lively waltz
flowed through its windows.

Laughing, a group of men crossed right in front of her. She
jumped back, but not quickly enough.

As one, they stopped. "Miss Van Buren. How are you this evening?"

So many of the men in town knew her name, yet she knew hardly
any of theirs. She squinted, realizing they were in costume. There
were bandits, gypsies, and kings. There was even a "female" with
nothing more than a crinoline fastened over his miner's garb.

"I'm fine, thank you," she answered. "Where are you off to this
evening?"

Paper crowns, calico bonnets, and simple scarves were swiped off
of heads.

A large, scruffy pirate spit a wad of tobacco to the side. "A costume ball, miss."

"Oh? Who's giving it?"

The men shifted, each looking to the other.

A "French count" swept into a low bow before her. "A false visage is
all that is required, mademoiselle, for entry into the soiree. If you deign
to grace us with your presence, I pray you will save me a dance. *Oui?*"

Good heavens. He had the accent down perfectly. Mayhap he was a *real* French count. One could never be sure of anything in this town.

"Thank you, sir, but I'm afraid I have no plans to attend."

With as much grace as she could manage, she stepped back into the shadows, and the men continued on their way.

She pressed herself against the wooden siding of the hotel, covering her mouth. *O Lord. Let Lissa return and squelch this awful premonition I am having. Please, Lord. Please.*

But Lissa did not come home and Rachel's distress escalated. What if the masquerade ball really was put on by a lady of easy virtue? And what if Lissa was there?

Rachel had discovered that the ladies of the night advertised for customers by throwing parties and by daily promenading about the Plaza. And she had caught Lissa avidly watching those promenades from the window of the hotel when she was supposed to be cleaning.

Instead of displaying repentance, the girl would ooh and aah over their fine silks and high-society fashions.

Rachel hugged her waist. She should have long ago put a stop to Lissa's preoccupation with these women.

She moved back to the opening of the alleyway. The line in front of the house in question extended down Washington Street and beyond. She worried her lip. What to do? What to do?

She could wait on Michael, but sometimes he didn't get home until well after the noon of night.

She peeked down the platform fronting the hotel. Lamps shone and music played, but no one loitered on the veranda.

Had Johnnie gone to the party? Surely not. He'd likely have customers, though few they might be.

But if Rachel was honest with herself, she knew, in her heart of hearts, that her sister had gone. And was most likely, at this very moment, dancing in the arms of a stranger . . . inside a brothel.

That thought alone provided her with the impetus she needed to lurch into the Plaza and stride to the brightly lit house. She didn't even bother with waiting in line but went directly to the front door.

A large, burly sultan blocked her entrance. The red sash wrapped around his muscular waist held not only a sword but a pistol, as well. "You have an invitation?"

She hesitated. "I don't need one. Women are granted entry for free."

He smirked. "Not sunbonnets. Your kind aren't allowed. You'd best go on home now, miss."

"I'm, um, only dressed as a sunbonnet woman. This is a masquerade ball, isn't it?"

He took her by the shoulders, spun her around, and gave her a gentle push. "Good night, miss."

She turned back to him. "Please. I think my sister is in there, and I need to speak to her at once."

The man scowled. "I'm sorry, but you cannot come in."

"I'll only be a minute."

"No."

She swallowed. "Then will you get her for me and bring her to me?"

"No."

She glanced at the men crowding the door but did not see the French count and his companions.

"Will you help me, sir?" she asked the musketeer standing closest to her. "Do you know my sister?"

The musketeer did not answer and would not meet her gaze.

"Look, miss," the sultan growled, "you are making my customers uncomfortable. Now, this is the last time I'm going to ask you to leave. After that, I'll personally escort you home, if you get my meaning."

She squared her shoulders. "These gentlemen would not let you touch a hair on my head."

He narrowed his eyes. "Try me."

Glancing up his huge frame, she experienced her first bit of unease. He was a giant of a man, and he most likely knew exactly how to wield the weapons he wore. She had no wish to start a brawl. But there was more than one way to skin a cat.

She presented her back to him and made her way to the City Hotel.

The place was practically deserted. Soda laughed with a man at the plank bar and poured him a drink while that awful, awful statue proudly reigned over the room.

A group of men rolled some dice.

Carmelita sat skimpily dressed on the piano bench singing "Mr.

O'Reilly" while a clean-shaven man Rachel had never seen banged out the notes.

Johnnie was nowhere in sight.

She quickly approached Carmelita. "Have you seen Lissa?"

Carmelita stopped singing, reached over to take the cigarette out of the piano player's mouth, and deeply inhaled.

Rachel swallowed her reaction. The girl had outlined her eyes with kohl. It looked positively wretched. A slow stream of smoke came from her puckered lips, interrupted by smoke swirling out her nostrils. "She no is here."

"Do you know where she is?"

The spangled camisole Carmelita wore hid nothing, revealing her entire upper body through its transparent film. "Same as everybody. She at the fiesta."

Rachel placed a hand against her stomach. She'd suspected, of course, but having those suspicions confirmed took the very breath from her body.

She looked to the window, then back at Carmelita. "I have a favor to ask you."

Carmelita flicked ashes from the cigarette.

"I need to attend the party. But ..." She moistened her lips. "I have nothing to wear. Might I borrow something of yours? I'll pay you."

"How much?"

Rachel took a very deep breath. "Name your price."

The piano man started up on a new tune, eyeing them but saying nothing.

Carmelita crushed the cigarette tip into the bench. "I no can help."

"Please. She's just a child. I must bring her home, and I haven't a moment to lose."

Carmelita rose. The two women stood face-to-face, each taking the measure of the other.

Finally, Carmelita sighed. "Come. I help you."

Thank you. Rachel followed her to the back, through the tiny kitchen, and out the door. Carmelita sailed past the shack and rounded the corner to a set of narrow stairs tucked into the side of the building. Rachel lifted her skirt and jogged up the steps.

Carmelita opened a door at the top and quickly lit a lantern. The room was shabby but clean, though a stale, closed-up smell pervaded the little cubicle. The orange cat lay curled up on a cot with a bunched up Mexican sarape at its side.

A battered chair and pork barrel sat tucked in one corner. Old calendars, gaudy hangings of silk and fancy cotton together with brightly colored flags decorated the coarse plank walls.

She wondered if this was where Carmelita entertained her customers, then dismissed it from her mind. This was Carmelita's home. The place she lived.

A clothesline tied at eye level from one wall to the next held Carmelita's wardrobe. A mélange of colors and spangles had been draped over it, causing the line to sag heavily in the middle.

The girl quickly flipped through the clothing, obviously looking for something in particular. Finding it, she shoved the clothes on top to the side and tugged a red skirt and bolero off the line.

"Thank you. How much do I owe you?"

"I no take your money, *señorita*."

Rachel frowned. "But you must."

"No. No money. Now quick," she said. "Off with *las ropas*."

Rachel blinked. "I'm sorry?"

"Your clothes, your clothes. You must take off."

"Oh, that's quite all right. If you'll simply give those to me, I'll pay you and take them to my shack and put them on there."

"Is too hard by yourself." Carmelita pushed Rachel's hands aside and with quick dexterity unfastened her dress. It crumpled to the floor. Rachel had not even bothered with a corset during her rush to find Lissa. Still, in fact, wore her nightgown in place of a chemise and petticoat. What would the woman think?

Carmelita tugged on the ties at Rachel's neck.

Rachel captured the girl's hands, holding them still. "What are you doing?"

"Is no good, *señorita*." And with that, Carmelita disposed of the garment.

Standing in nothing but drawers, she crossed her arms over her bosom.

Carmelita lifted her brows. *"Es muy bonita, sí?"*

Rachel felt heat rush up her neck and into her cheeks. "I'm going to need a mask of some sort."

"No worry. We cover your face. No one know is you." Turning, she yanked a gossamer chemise from the line and tossed it to Rachel. "Put this on."

She caught the garment one-handed. It was like holding a film of cobwebs. "No, Carmelita. Absolutely not. I'll go get a chemise of my own."

"Is no time." She flipped back through her clothing. "Try this."

It was a cotton shift. Once she had it on, she realized it had an off-the-shoulder style and the neckline plunged daringly low. But with the bolero, her shoulders and torso would be covered.

Biting her lip, she secured the buttons along the front. Oh, but she was going to strangle Lissa when she got ahold of that girl.

Carmelita strapped an exquisitely made red corset—*red*—about Rachel's midriff and helped her with petticoats and the red silk skirt, then rummaged through an old trunk hidden behind her clothing.

"If you're looking for a crinoline, no need to bother. I don't wear them."

Rachel picked up the jacket and put it on. Land sakes. It was cropped off just below the bosom, calling attention to her exposed neckline above the chemise and the red corset hugging her waist. She tried to pull the edges together, but they would not meet. Clearly, the braided black frog closures were for decoration only.

"I can't wear this. It's too small and my corset is showing." She started to take it off but couldn't get it past her elbows.

Carmelita surfaced with a black feathered domino. "Corset is supposed to show. That's why is red."

"No. I will not wear it. Now help me get this off."

A string of Spanish poured from Carmelita's lips. Rachel had no knowledge of the language but was able to make a fairly good guess at the content.

"No more time, señorita. Señor Parker no is happy when Carmelita no work. We must go. Hold this." She placed the mask over Rachel's eyes.

Out of reflex, Rachel reached up to hold it on. Carmelita tugged the bolero back up over Rachel's shoulders and tied the mask on.

"Ah, is Señorita of Mystery, yes?"

Shooing Rachel out the door, Carmelita handed her a black fan and blew out the lantern.

The mask limited Rachel's range of vision. She could only see what was directly in front of her. Disguising herself had seemed like such a good idea. Now she was not so sure. Perhaps she should simply wait.

Rachel tightened her lips. Of course, she couldn't wait. She had to fetch Lissa. But, oh, was that girl going to get an earful once they returned home safe and sound.

And please, Lord. Please don't let anyone recognize me.

chapter 10

$\mathcal{R}$achel hovered in the archway of the largest and noisiest parlor she'd ever seen, her black-feathered fan open and fluttering in double time. She had been given entrance by a different doorman. No sultan in sight.

The house reeked of smoke, perfume, sweat, and alcohol. Yet its interior decor smacked of wealth and affluence. White lace curtains, damask drapes, elegant fixtures, and luxurious furniture—though all furniture had been consigned to the perimeters of the vast room.

Along one wall, linen-covered tables held hundreds of bottles and decanters, manned by well turned-out butlers. Opposite the beverage tables was a full band and on the third side an ornately carved coffee-and-cake stand.

The centerpiece and focus of the room, however, were the dancers in a sea of motion. All conducted themselves with extreme decorum. The reception could be described as nothing other than tasteful, dignified, and very correct. Except, of course, that men with red bandannas tied to their arms assumed the female position in the waltz now taking place.

Only four women were in attendance. Women of unquestionable elegance. Women who wore the exquisite, intoxicating costumes of

— 115 —

such characters as Cleopatra and Diana. Women who daily prome-
naded the Plaza.

No sign of Lissa.

A disturbance at the far corner diverted all attention. She caught
a glimpse of three new women shepherding in a tall, gangly girl in a
lavishly hooped dress with matching shawl. They introduced her as a
visiting sister from the East.

The girl blushed, simpered and fiddled with her fan. The band
struck up a rendition of "Polly Wolly Doodle." The men crowded
around her, vying for a dance and giving Rachel a better view.

Her breath caught. Beside this new guest stood Lissa, in a provoc-
ative gown and a diamond tiara.

Before Rachel could make a move, the French count bowed
before her. "May I have this dance, *mademoiselle?*"

Without waiting for an answer, he swept her into his embrace and
onto the parlor floor. The placement of their hands made it impossible for her to shield herself with the fan. Worse, it caused her bolero
to gape open.

She tried to pull away.

He drew her closer. "Hush, my pet. I will not tread upon your
slippered feet like so many of my compatriots."

Rather than make a scene and call attention to herself, she acquiesced to the flow of the dance, hoping it would bring her closer to
Lissa.

"And where has the countess been hiding you? For your beauty
and grace surpass any woman present."

She dared not say a word for fear her voice would be recognizable.
She tucked her chin, pretending shyness, which wasn't far from the
truth.

The man's soft chuckle was deep, suggesting intimacy. "Ah, the
countess misses nothing, I see. A bashful *fille de pave.*"

The song came to an end. Rachel stepped quickly from his arms.

He bowed. "I look forward to furthering our acquaintance when,
perhaps, so many are not around."

Rachel shivered. She spun to look for Lissa only to be caught up into the arms of the man who ran the printing press for the local newspaper. He'd dressed as a knight of old, though she supposed his sword had been confiscated, along with all the other weapons, at the door.

"You are a matador, I see," he said. "Your red gown and bolero enflame me as much as any hot-blooded bull. Might I have permission to enter the ring with you later this evening, my dear?"

Shock held her tongue still.

He increased the pressure at the small of her back, pulling her against his chest.

She jerked back.

He lifted a corner of his mouth. "Do you toy with me? Or perhaps you merely want to wound me like the *vaqueros* before going in for the kill?"

His eyes darkened, and he blew a steady stream of warm, mealy air across her chest. She broke from his hold and would have slapped him if a pilgrim hadn't grabbed her hand and swung her into his clutches for a gallopade.

She searched the room for Lissa and found her across the room laughing at the antics of a would-be sheriff as he whirled the girl about the parlor floor. Lissa's flushed face radiated with pleasure and delight.

Rachel endured two more waltzes and a mazurka before managing to break away with an excuse of exhaustion. Heading to the beverage table, she passed a knot of men making fools over themselves in front of the new girl.

Her unladylike high-pitched trilling laugh chafed Rachel's ears. She glanced over at her and ground to a halt.

It couldn't be. Oh, surely not. Lord, please, let it not be so.

But it was. There was no mistaking it. The "sister from the East" was none other than Michael Van Buren, having a grand laugh at the expense of every man in the room.

The memory of his being introduced by a bevy of fallen women, Lissa at his side, made her stomach roll. How in all that was holy had the two of them made the acquaintance of these women?

Michael's glance touched her for the briefest of moments before ricocheting back. His eyes widened, face paled.

A hand touched her elbow.

"I don't believe we've had the pleasure of meeting."

Rachel turned to the sultry voice and confronted a handsome woman dressed like Queen Elizabeth, complete with a high Elizabethan collar and a cinched bodice, less the chemise. The superfluous overflow of her décolletage so overpowered all else that Rachel could not but gawk. It was then that she noticed the soft white cuddly poodle the woman clutched to her bosom.

With long fingernails, the woman scratched the dog between its ears. "I am the countess. And you are?"

Rachel snapped her attention to the owner's face. "I am the elder sister of Lissa and Michael Van Buren, and I want to know what they are doing here."

The countess made a brief motion with her hand, as if she were indeed a queen summoning a servant. "This is an invitation-only affair. I must confess, I don't recall extending one to you."

The sultan appeared at the woman's right hand, a scowl on his face.

"I don't care whether you are a countess, a queen, or the first lady of our esteemed president," Rachel said. "I'm taking my sister and brother out of this house. Now."

The woman's smile bespoke of smug satisfaction. "Oh, I hate to disappoint you, kitten, but I believe that you are in no position to make demands of any kind." She turned to the sultan and in the mildest of voices said, "Get rid of her."

"Oh, there you are. I've been looking for you everywhere." Johnnie, dressed in a plaid tartan, white shirt, red vest, and black tie, stepped between Rachel and the sultan. If looks could kill, she'd be with the Lord at this very moment.

Grasping her elbow, Johnnie turned his attention to the countess. "I see you have met my companion. I do apologize for not introducing you earlier, but the men, of course, have kept her on the dance floor all evening."

The countess gave Johnnie a long, penetrating look. "I believe she looks a bit peaked. Perhaps she needs to go home."

"Of course."

Hoisting up her poodle, she moved around the two of them, motioning for the sultan to follow.

Johnnie propelled Rachel toward the door.

She wrenched her elbow from his grasp. "I have to get Michael and Lissa first."

He made to grab her again. She jumped out of reach and into the Viking behind her. The man, all too happy to accommodate her, wrapped his arms about her waist, pulling her flush against him.

Rachel gasped and stomped on his boot.

Johnnie bodily removed the man's hands from her waist. "She's mine," he growled.

The Viking puffed out his chest. "Says who?"

Rachel stepped close to Johnnie. "Says I." She kept her voice soft and unthreatening.

Johnnie rested a possessive hand at the small of her back.

The Viking looked between the two of them, huffed, and strode away.

The music shifted to a waltz. Keeping his hand at her back, Johnnie moved her onto the parlor floor. "What the devil's the matter with you? And what the blue blazes were you thinking to come over here?" He pulled her into waltz position. "And dressed in that, that . . . where did you *get* that?"

He glided her across the room keeping perfect rhythm to the one-two-three beat.

"I came to retrieve my siblings," she said. "What did *you* come here for?"

He negotiated their way around the other dancers. "Well, it certainly wasn't to look after you."

Before she had a chance to relieve him of any misplaced responsibility, they stopped where Michael was holding court.

He took one look at her, excused himself from his adoring fans, and moved to where she and Johnnie stood. "Rachel, I—"

"We'll discuss it at home. Go. Now."

Grabbing both her hands in his, he took on an affected expression. "Oh, come on, Rache. I was just having some fun with the fellas. I'm not hurting anybody."

She leaned close. "Do you have any idea what this place is?"

He set his jaw. "Do *you*?"

She squeezed his hands with as much strength as she could manage. "Do you have on a *crinoline*?"

The utter disbelief and distress in her tone sobered his expression instantly. "I ... it ..." He sighed. "I didn't mean nothing by it, Rachel."

"You didn't mean anything by it?" She threw down his hands. "You didn't *mean* anything by it? How could you even think to do such a thing?"

He wrinkled his brows. "I didn't think. I'm sorry. I said I didn't mean nothing and I didn't."

She tapped her finger against his chest. "Well, you will take yourself home and you will do so this instant."

Sighing, he nodded and with his boyish gait strode across the floor straight-arming the men who tried to intercept him.

She scanned the crowd for Lissa.

"You were a little tough on him concerning the crinoline, don't you think? He was just having a bit of sport."

"You know nothing about it. There she is." Pointing with her head, she assumed waltz position. "Let's go get her."

Johnnie stepped into her waiting arms, but Lissa was not so easy to chase down. The Robin Hood who spun the girl around the room moved quickly and held her much too close. He leaned in and whispered something into her ear.

Lissa giggled, swatting his shoulder and giving him a wicked look.

"Who is she dancing with?" Rachel asked.

"Merle Sumner."

She tightened her lips. "What do you know of him?"

"Not much. He's a river gambler from Mississippi."

It took the conclusion of the dance and half of another one before Johnnie pulled up beside them. "Shall we switch?" he asked.

"Not on your life," Sumner answered.

But Johnnie had already released Rachel and captured Lissa and was moving to the edge of the floor before Sumner had time to finish his refusal.

"Hey!" Sumner yelled.

Fortunately, the front door lay straight ahead. Rachel trod on Johnnie's heels. Sumner on hers. The four of them were outside in less than a minute.

"What are you doing, Mr. Parker?" Lissa asked.

"Thank you, Johnnie. Lissa, say good-night. It's time to go home."

"What is going on here?" Sumner shouted.

Lissa pulled out of Johnnie's grip. "What are you doing here?" she asked her sister.

"Going to a great deal of trouble to fetch you home."

"Well, you've wasted your time."

Sumner stepped beside Lissa.

She threaded her hand through his arm. "I'm not going anywhere."

Rachel narrowed her eyes. "Oh, yes you are." She turned to the man next to Lissa. "Mr. Sumner, is it? Are you aware that my sister is only ten and five?"

He took Lissa's hand up to his lips. "And a very beautiful ten and five she is."

His lips lingered, nipping the side of Lissa's palm.

Rachel sucked in a quick breath. "Release her, sir. Lissa, come. This instant."

Lissa leaned more heavily into Mr. Sumner. "I'm not a dog, Rachel. I don't come on command. If you want to go home, then you just run along. I'm staying."

"You cannot. I won't allow it."

Lissa smirked.

Mr. Sumner wrapped an arm around her waist. "Good night, Miss Van Buren."

The two of them, cozier than ham and cheese, proceeded back into the brightly lit house.

Rachel sputtered then charged after them.

Johnnie grabbed her arm. "Whoa, girl. I think you've been officially thrown out of the party by the countess herself. Besides, that gown you are wearing is indecent, and it won't be long before some-body either recognizes you or, worse, thinks you're one of the girls."

"I don't care. I can't leave her in there."

She broke free and came face-to-face with the sultan.

"I told you my sister was in there. Now, step aside."

He looked at Johnnie. "Either you get rid of her or I will."

Rachel propped her hands on her hips. "I thought you said no sunbonnets were allowed at this soiree."

"They aren't," the sultan answered.

"Well, my sister is a sunbonnet. So throw her out."

"Your sister is an invited guest. You aren't."

Rachel frowned. "You are mistaken, sir. She could not possibly have been invited."

He said nothing.

"Step aside."

He looked at Johnnie.

"Rachel." He touched her elbow.

She jerked away. "I won't leave her in there, Johnnie. I won't." Her eyes filled. "Don't you see? I *can't.*"

Heaving a great sigh, he ran his fingers through his thick brown hair. "I'll watch her."

She bit her cheek, helplessness encompassing her. "Perhaps you could go tell her I am waiting for her?"

"She already knows that, and she made it quite clear she wasn't leaving. Not yet, anyway."

Rachel hugged her stomach.

"I won't let her out of my sight."

She perused the house's facade. "You tell her I'm going to stand right here until she leaves."

The sultan growled.

Johnnie leaned close to her ear. "If you loiter at the door of this house dressed like you are, the men will mistake you for something you are not. And they are not so easy to handle after an evening of revelry. I'm taking you home."

Grabbing her elbow, he steered her toward the hotel.

"Fine. I'll go home, change into my calico and then come back to wait for her."

He tightened his grip. "So help me, Rachel, I will leave Lissa to her own devices if you do not stay where I put you."

"Why? The men would not dare mistreat a lady."

"Not normally. But they are unpredictable when they are intoxicated. It is simply too dangerous."

She tried to stop.

He increased the pressure. "I will drag you if I must."

"But, Lissa."

"I will bring her home as soon as I can do so without endangering her."

She looked up, tears spilling onto her cheeks. "You will?"

"Yes."

"Why?" She couldn't quite catch the expression in his eyes.

"I have no idea," he sighed.

c h a p t e r **11**

*R*achel was waiting the moment Lissa walked through the door. Michael had retreated to his pallet by the fireplace after receiving the dressing down of his life.

Helping him remove all of the feminine paraphernalia he wore had been embarrassing for them both—particularly when wads of handkerchiefs fell out of his bodice. She used his discomfort to her full advantage, shaming him at every turn.

Removing the crinoline had been the worst, of course. Their beloved mother had died when her crinoline became entangled in the steps of a carriage from which she was alighting. The commotion had spooked the horses, and with her mother's head and shoulders dragging upon the ground, the animals had run quite a distance before anyone could stop them.

To this day Rachel refused to wear a crinoline and wasn't much for carriages, either. She certainly hadn't allowed Lissa to wear the loathsome undergarment, though clearly the girl wore one tonight.

Lissa threw her reticule onto the table and began to remove the white gloves that ran all the way up her arms. She said not a word, but the look in her eyes as she glared at her sister said it all.

Rachel could not care less. "Do you have any idea what kind of place that was?"

Lissa laid one glove over the back of a chair and started on the other. "I believe they call it a parlor house. And only the cream of the crop are allowed to work there."

"Cream of the crop? Cream of the crop! There is no such thing for women of their kind. They are at the very bottom of the rung. The scourge of society. A woman can go no lower than that."

Lissa paused, studying her sister. "You know, Rachel, I don't think it's as bad a life as we've been led to believe."

Where before Rachel's blood had been pumping through her like a river busting through a dam, it now crashed to an abrupt halt, leaving a backwash of panic. "Oh, Lissa. I don't know what kind of tales those women have been feeding you, but their lives are nothing short of pathetic."

"And just what, exactly, do you know of their lives?"

"I know they are morally weak. I know they are everything a proper woman is not. They are not pure, virtuous, tender, delicate, or fragile."

"Good heavens, Rachel. And you believe we are?"

"I believe we strive to be."

Sighing, Lissa removed the pins holding her tiara in place. "Well, I'm not so sure being a proper woman is the be-all and end-all."

Rachel grabbed onto the back of a chair. "How can you even say such a thing?"

Lissa set her crown on the table and proceeded to remove the rest of the pins from her loosely twisted blond hair. "Well, think about it. We live in a shack. We never have time for the finer things. We work ourselves to the bone. And for what? So we can marry some man who will run off chasing after gold that may or may not be there? Only to then come home, get us with child, and gamble away all of our treasure, forcing him to go back and do it all over again?"

Rachel didn't know which issue to address first. Or even how to respond. Her face warmed at such casual mention of procreation, though what Lissa said was certainly true.

She sighed. Never had the two of them needed a mother more

than this night. *Help me, Lord.* "Everything will change when we return home."

Scooping her hair to one side, Lissa presented her back to her sister in a silent request for help.

Rachel automatically began to unfasten the girl's gown.

"Yet the women over at the parlor house," Lissa continued, "don't have to cook, clean, wash their clothes—nothing. They dress in the height of fashion. They are as close to each other as any group of women I've ever known. And no one shuns them on the street except you. The men treat them as if they were royalty. Did you see who was there tonight?"

She didn't answer. For she had recognized a few of them. And, truthfully, had been sorely distressed at her realization that the town's businessmen frequented such places.

Lissa lifted up her fist, ticking her fingers one-by-one. "Why, Mr. Schermerhorn from the mercantile was there. Mr. Beekman from the newspaper. Mr. Wingate from the surveyor's office. Mr. Kirk from the customhouse and even Mr. Livingston. Do you know who he is?"

Rachel shook her head.

"He's a farmer from Kansas here in California with his wife and eight children. He leaves them up in the mining camp and comes to San Francisco under the pretense of picking up supplies."

Lissa stepped out of her gown. The two of them carefully folded it seam-to-seam. "He visits the girls that work for the countess every time he comes to town. *Every* time. And him married. With his wife waiting. And all those children."

Rachel had read about such appetites in married men. But there was a world of difference between reading it and seeing it with her own eyes. Still, perhaps she should try to explain what she had learned to her sister.

She said nothing about the crinoline as Lissa untied it and allowed it to collapse onto the floor.

After shooting a quick glance across the room at Michael to ensure his back was still to them while he huddled on his pallet, Rachel lowered her voice to a whisper. "Perhaps you're not aware, dear, but I happen to have learned that a proper wife only submits to her husband out of duty. So men like Mr. Livingston, not wanting to cause their wives any unhappiness, evidently seek relief at the kinds of places the countess runs."

Lissa froze. "Are you justifying him?"

"No! No, of course not. He's clearly of a weak nature."

The girl propped a hand against her waist, but its impact was a bit lost when she stood in nothing but drawers and corset. "Seems every man in town is of a weak nature."

Rachel shook out her sister's flannel nightdress and slipped it over Lissa's head. "It's because they have nothing else to occupy themselves with. There are no churches to speak of, no lending libraries, no ice parlors, no theatres, no parks, no nothing. And perhaps it is time to do something about it. What would you think about opening a restaurant?"

Lissa's elbows and hands poked against the fabric as she removed her undergarments beneath the shelter of her nightdress. "There, you see. That's just what I'm talking about. You want to work us to the bone, while all of *them* kick up their heels."

Lissa's movements stopped, a dreamy look transforming her face. "Oh, Rache, they give all kinds of fancy parties and balls. And you should see their wardrobes. It's like a museum of Godey's fashion plates. With no expense spared. And their food. Why, they have a cook that makes meals you couldn't buy anywhere in town."

As soon as Lissa threaded her hands through her sleeves, Rachel grasped them. "You mustn't glamorize them, Lissa. For at the dark of night, they debase themselves in unnatural and unwholesome ways."

The girl looked down at their clasped hands. "You want to know a secret?" she whispered.

Alarm bells clamored inside Rachel. *No. No, I do not.*

"I think I might be suited to be one of them."

Rachel gasped.

Lissa squeezed her hands, swallowing but refusing to look up. "I know this shocks you, but try to understand, Rache. I . . . I like the attention the men give me. I like it when they touch me. I *especially* like it when they touch me in places they oughtn't."

This last was said in such a hushed tone, Rachel could hardly hear it. But hear it she did. And with it came the horror of realization that she had experienced those self-same pangs in the arms of a saloon owner.

Rachel wrenched her hands free and grabbed Lissa, hugging her tightly, the smell of smoke clinging to her hair. "It's only because it's forbidden that you feel that way. Eve felt the same thing about the apple, and look what happened to her. You must turn away from it. Stuff it down into a deep hidden place within and never let it out."

Lissa gently withdrew from her sister's embrace, a wry expression on her face. "Perhaps Dr. Everett has some tonic I could take. He should know. He was there tonight."

Rachel groaned. "Oh, Lissa, please. These . . . these *feelings* you have. Are they for someone in particular?"

Moistening her lips, Lissa nodded.

"Well, what happens when the next man wants a turn? Women of that sort have to go the whole hog. Don't you see what I'm saying? They lose the right to say no. They have to accept the touch of *any* man who wants one." She swallowed, apprehension shuddering through her body. "Think, child. Envision some of the filthy pug-uglies in this town. I cannot even stand to smell them. Those poor women have to accept touches of the most intimate nature from them."

Lissa cocked her head. "How do you know all this?"

Rachel took a deep breath. "I've read most every book in Father's library. You would be shocked to your very toes were you to have an inkling of what I've learned."

"Tell me."

"Certainly not. I had no business reading them. I'm not going to compound my sin by repeating their contents to you."

"Did you read about kept women?" Lissa asked.

"Kept women?"

"Yes. Women who are kept, or supported, by one man. He lavishes her with gifts, flowers, poetry, fancy clothes. Everything."

"In exchange for her favors."

"But she doesn't mind sharing her favors with him. She loves him."

"Then why doesn't she marry him?"

"Not all men are the marrying kind."

"The respectable ones are."

"Like the respectable ones that came to the party tonight?"

Rachel had no answer for that. "Kept women aren't loved, Lissa. They are like animals. Petted, offered a few treats, and caged. What woman wants that?"

"What woman wants to kill herself providing for a husband who saves all the sweet stuff for his moonlight lady?"

Rachel wrung her hands. "Not all of them have moonlight ladies." Lissa raised an eyebrow.

"They don't. And you'll just have to take my word for it. Now, we'll hear no more of this foolish talk, and we'll no longer fraternize with women of ill repute. Do you understand?"

"Where did you get your costume?"

O, Lord. "Where did you get yours?"

"From Carmelita," Lissa answered.

"Me, too," Rachel replied softly.

"Well, give it to me, and I'll return it to her tomorrow when you go water the trees."

Rachel was already shaking her head. "No, Lissa. You must stay away from those women."

Smoothing the folded gown on the table, Lissa sighed. "Good night, Rachel."

A lump as hard and heavy as a flat iron settled in Rachel's stomach as Lissa pulled back the blanket and cozied into bed.

Try as she might, Rachel could not get Lissa to accompany her. The girl outright refused. So, leaving her sister under Michael's watchful eye, Rachel dressed in her Sunday best and made her way to the surveyor's office on the corner of Sacramento and Stockton streets.

The smell of fresh wood permeated the newly constructed one-room building. Architectural drawings, plot maps, and assorted papers covered every available surface. Surveying instruments and compasses leaned against the plank walls.

In the center, a man in tattered flannel, dirt, and buckskin sat huddled over his scarred desk, scribbling notes. "Be with you in a moment, boys."

Rachel's stillness must have struck him as unusual, for he looked up and jumped to his feet. "Oh. Pardon me, Miss Van Buren. I didn't realize it was you."

"Good afternoon, sir."

Rachel scrutinized him, trying to remember if he was one of the men who had attended the ball but could not tell for certain.

"If I may say so, miss, you look lovely today. Quite lovely. Is there something I can assist you with?"

"I'd like to open a restaurant, sir. You are the Mr. Wingate that is on the town council, are you not?"

"Yes, yes. I certainly am, and this is wonderful news. I know the boys would love to sample some of those dinners they've been smelling over at Johnnie's place. What did you have in mind?"

"I'd like a sound structure with a kitchen, at a good location, and for a reasonable price, please."

He chuckled. "You and everybody else, miss."

She folded her gloved hands in front of her and his expression sobered.

"Oh, well." He shuffled through some papers on his desk. "Ah, here we are."

He withdrew a large diagram of the city showing a grid of streets. Instead of forming them around the hills, the men had graded the thoroughfares to run north and south or east and west without regard for the difficulty the people would have traversing up and down the steep inclines.

"Here's one a little distance from the business portion of the city that's twenty-one feet by a hundred twenty. It's going for seven to eight hundred dollars."

"Per year?"

"Per month, miss."

Rachel swallowed. "I think that particular location might be better suited for a residence. Have you anything else not quite so costly?"

He slowly straightened. "That was for the lot alone. Without a building."

"I see." Rachel glanced at the plot map. They had saved somewhere in the neighborhood of two thousand dollars. A fortune back home, mere pocket change here.

"Are there any lots with buildings on them?" she asked. "Wooden ones, of course, not canvas."

"Oh, sure, sure. But those run about eighteen hundred a month."

Good heavens. "Mr. Wingate, I cannot afford such sums. Is there anyone you know that is looking to transfer their holdings? Perhaps while they go up to the diggings?"

He unhooked the glasses that perched on his nose. "I'm sorry."

Frowning, Rachel bit her lip. "I've noticed that the building next to the City Hotel has been boarded up since my arrival two months ago. Whom does that belong to?"

"I'm afraid that's proprietary information. All transactions go through the council, but if you'd like, I can look that piece of property up."

He replaced his glasses, pulled a ledger out from beneath a slew of papers, and flipped it open, running his finger down each page. "Ah, here we are. Yes, that lot is eighty by eighty, and with the building, the asking price is fifteen thousand."

"Fifteen thousand! But it's been sitting there empty for two months."

"I'm just going by what it says here, Miss Van Buren."

"Perhaps you could speak to the owner on my behalf? I would be glad to exchange my services for rent. Why, he could receive all his meals for free, or I could take in his washing, or any number of things."

He slowly closed the book. "I will ask. Could you come back in a couple of days?"

"Yes, of course. And thank you."

———————

"But I don't want to," Lissa whined. She fell into one of their chairs, shoulders slumped. "I soak my hands every day at this time in peppermint tea. Besides, the men will be coming soon for their shaves."

Rachel squatted down at her sister's feet, taking hold of her hands. The peppermint tea soaks had not done much to slow the callouses that had formed on Lissa's pretty white palms and fingers. "Your shaving-salon days are over. And my saloon-cleaning days are over. We both need a switch."

"We're not working in the hotel anymore?"

"Only for as long as it takes us to get the restaurant open and running. Then no more cleaning up after all those men."

Lissa stared at Rachel, her expression inscrutable.

"Come on, let's go see what our new home looks like."

She tugged Lissa to her feet and grabbed a lantern, and then the two of them walked over to the abandoned building next door.

The proprietor must have been convinced by Mr. Wingate of Rachel's potential for success, because the rent he negotiated on her behalf would start out ridiculously low and move up on a graduated scale. Lord willing, this would give her time to establish her business and turn a bit of a profit before being expected to pay the inflated prices that currently pervaded the market.

It took her three tries to make the key turn within the rusted lock on the front door. The sound of scurrying rodents reached her ears as she slowly pushed the door open and sunlight spilled into the large spacious room.

The girls stood side-by-side in the doorway, trying to see beyond the path of light and into the gloomy darkness. Rachel lit the lantern and held it high. Whoever had lived in the house before had been in a great hurry to leave.

A rough plank table, three times the size of an ordinary one, afforded ample room for an entire family plus a number of guests. Long benches lined both sides of the table. Dishes and doilies coated in dust lay eerily in place, as if the family would be called to dinner at any moment. No time had been taken to cover the furniture with cloths or stack the dishes on a shelf.

A huge boarded-up window with real leaded glass was to the immediate left of the door. The daubing that filled the cracks in the plank walls had long since disintegrated and crumbled, allowing shafts of light to pierce through the darkness from all sides.

Some broken bamboo fishing rods made frames for two screens covered in cream material and painted with sprays of wild roses. This token attempt at domesticity looked rather pathetic hanging at odd angles from two rusted nails along the otherwise bare wall of the building.

"It has a wooden floor," Lissa said.

And so it did, filthy though it was. They stepped inside, a closed up musty smell dominating the room.

Lissa caught the door. "Don't close it. This place gives me the collywobbles."

Rachel left the door open and they walked across the room to an archway that separated them from the remainder of the house. Their high-heeled slippers echoed within the room, bouncing off every corner, their skirts setting off a whirlwind of dust.

Lissa sneezed. Rachel pulled a cobweb from her nose and mouth.

The other side of the archway held a kitchen with everything in its proper place. Three pairs of work boots were neatly lined up by the back door, a set of stockings slung over the edge of one boot. They had clearly once been wet but were now as dry as a sand bed and hard as tack.

A table covering, which had formerly been flour sacks, had taken on the appearance of a mop cloth and was neatly folded atop a pastry table. A muddy pair of well-worn pantaloons lay across the back of a spindly chair that, along with three other chairs, surrounded a second table.

A broom, dishcloth, and face towel each occupied a nail in the wall. A frying pan, with marks of grease, sat ready and waiting atop a wood-burning stove.

Rachel moved to examine the stove more closely. Every part of it showed signs of gross neglect, but with a bit of attention, perseverance, and hard work, she just might be able to make it work again.

"Would you look at this, Lissa? It's a Leamington. Why on earth would someone leave such a thing behind?"

But Rachel received the sound of hollow footsteps as a response.

She turned in time to catch the back of Lissa's skirts heading up a set of stairs tucked into the opposite wall.

A bubble of excitement began to percolate inside Rachel. How precious of the Lord to provide her with a home already furnished. She had expected to find a vacant building and instead had been blessed with a structure that would require very little investment indeed.

Lissa clunked back down the stairs. "It would be easier to knock the whole thing down and start over than to try and clean this place."

Rachel smiled. "What's upstairs?"

"Besides rats?"

"Besides rats."

"Two rooms. Two cots. One stove."

Warmth at God's generosity swept through her. "Well, I suppose we should start at the top and work our way down. You ready?"

"No, I'm not ready. I want nothing to do with it. This is your idea, not mine. If you want to work yourself to an early grave, you go right ahead, but leave me out of it."

Even angry, the girl was a sight to behold. The red scarf wrapped about her head would not quite hold the profusion of blond hair within its confines. Her green eyes snapped with anger and life. Her pretty jaw jutted out in stubbornness.

Rachel could love no babe born from her own body more fiercely than she loved this sister of hers. "Come now, it won't be as bad as all that. A little scrubbing never hurt anybody."

Lissa burst into tears. Not little tears. Not quiet tears. Big, bold, dramatic tears. She flung herself into a chair, sending up a poof of dust around her, and covered her face with both hands.

Honestly. It was a shame that acting was such an immoral occupation. For Lissa certainly had a flare for it. Rachel moved to her and pulled her up into her arms, holding her while the girl spent out her sorrow.

She patted Lissa's back. "We shall make a list of all that has to be done. I will let you choose which tasks you find least offensive and you can start with those. Agreed?"

"I'll find them all offensive."

Her muffled reply caused Rachel to give her a tight squeeze. "It will be fun. We shall sing while we work, and when we are through, we will have a place all our own." She pushed Lissa back a ways so she could see her face. "And we will buy you some pretty fabric for a new dress that you can wear on opening day."

Lissa wrinkled her nose. "Nothing calico."

"Very well, dear. We shall buy you something frivolous indeed."

Rachel wasn't going to buy that girl anything. Not at this rate. Every job Lissa did she left half done. Every job she did took three times the amount of time it should. Every job she did was accompanied by incessant complaining.

What should have taken the two of them three weeks at most was stretching into more than a month, and they were still far from done.

Michael could not help much, what with all the jobs he held during the day and on into the night. And the girls only had the afternoons to work due to their obligations at the hotel and greenhouse.

Still, enough was enough. There was nothing hard about weaving a chair seat, but there were certain steps to follow, and if you skipped any steps, it would show.

Rachel looked at the ladder-back chair and its freshly woven seat, sagging in the middle and fracturing along the sides. Clearly, Lissa had not soaked the splits in water before starting. If she had, they would have tightened on the chair frame as they dried, produced a good firm seat, and not cracked along the edges when she nailed them down.

Rachel tossed down her mop cloth and burst through the back door. Lissa was not in the yard.

Rachel checked upstairs, downstairs, inside the scullery, inside the pantry. Where in the world had that child run off to now? There was nothing to do but carry on until her sister returned. But when she did, there would be a reckoning like never before.

Not even a full hour had passed when Rachel had given up all pretense of anger, overcome instead with concern, and went to find

Michael. The two of them combed the town but had no luck in finding Lissa.

Darkness fell, so she and Michael decided one of them should stay home so that when her sister returned it would not be to an empty shanty. The obvious choice for staying behind had been Rachel, but she didn't like it. Not one bit.

She locked up their soon-to-be restaurant and, instead of going to their shack, hid in the shadows of the alleyway watching for any sign of the girl. Friday nights were always bad, but tonight the Plaza was even louder than usual, filled as it was with recent arrivals.

On all sides of the square, throngs of men hurried about. The tangle-bearded long-haired miner just in from the diggings counted his dollars by the thousands while the cleanly shaven easterner had expended his last cent in getting here.

A shot rang out, its bullet whistling over the heads of those in the street. The newcomers ducked instinctively. Those who had been here a month or more paid no more attention to such trifles than they would to the hum of a mosquito.

An argument in front of the El Dorado captured Rachel's attention.

"Why, we haven't had a good hangin' here for months." The miner spat a wad of tobacco into the square.

"Wall, that last hangin' was a few pence short in the shilling. The most brummish pardner in town is always the first to holler, 'Hang him.'"

"Tain't so. Only them that deserves it swing from the noose."

"All my eye and my grandmother. Why, the fellers pullin' on the rope might just as well be on the other end of it. It's all a matter of who hollers first." The man pressed a fat finger against one nostril then bent over and blew out a wad of phlegm from the open nostril. "Why, a'one of us could start running after Dick here, hollerin', 'Hang him! Hang him!' and these loafers would pour out of the tents and string him up without givin' him a chance to speak fer himself."

Scratching his belly, his friend pursed his lips. "Well, I say we test yer theory, Tedder." He turned to the boy beside him. "What do say, Dick? You wanna play hare to us hounds for, oh, fifty apiece, boys?"

While the youth named Dick took another swig of whiskey, his companions measured out their dust and poured it into the boy's pouch. He handed over his liquor and started across the Plaza at a lively pace. His friends followed, shouting, "Hang him! Hang him!"

No fire bell could have cleared the bars more effectively as every tent and shack emptied at once. Covering her mouth, Rachel watched the boy race up Washington Street and disappear from her view as he cut across Dupont, only to reappear at Clay when a group of revelers captured him and slipped a rope about his neck.

Had Tedder not caught up with them and interfered, Rachel knew beyond a shadow of a doubt that that boy would never have seen the dawn. She sagged against the wall.

Where is Lissa, Lord?

The temporary excitement created a reckless atmosphere as the drunken, yelling, pistol-firing men celebrated their brush with blood-letting.

Afraid to linger in the alley when the mob's lust for violence reached such dangerous heights, she returned to the shanty.

Sitting at the table, she rested her head in her hands and prayed without ceasing. Before the hour was up Michael came through the door, his cheek swollen, nose bloodied, and lip cracked.

"Michael! Oh heavens. What happened?"

He looked at her, tears pouring from the eye that wasn't swollen shut. "It's Lissa. Sumner has made her his without marrying her first."

Rachel gasped. "By force?"

"No," Michael choked.

Rachel shook her head. "No, Michael, no. You must be mistaken."

Anger contorted his face. He picked up a chair and threw it across the room. It crashed into the wall before splintering and falling to the floor. Grabbing another, he raised it above his head.

"*Michael!* Stop!"

He didn't stop, but with tears pouring down his cheek, he threw the table, the ewer, the bowl.

Pressing her back against the wall, she covered her mouth. "Please," she whimpered.

The front door banged open. Johnnie bounded in, wrenching the trunk from Michael's grip. Michael whirled around and, shoulder down, barreled into Johnnie, carrying him to the wall and pinning him there.

Johnnie tossed the trunk in his hands out of harm's way. Michael swung at him aimlessly.

"*Nooooo!*" Rachel screamed.

She ran to Michael and tried to grab his arm. Instead, his elbow caught her in the collarbone, knocking her to the floor.

The men froze.

Johnnie dropped beside her. "Are you hurt?"

She raised herself up on her elbows. He helped her sit up. Michael crumpled to the floor, cradling his head in his hands.

Getting onto all fours, Rachel crawled to him, wrapped her arms around him, and cried. For him. For her. For Lissa.

"What happened?" Johnnie asked.

She could only shake her head.

"Where's Lissa?"

She laid her cheek against Michael's bowed head. "I don't know. Michael said . . ." She sucked in a shaky breath.

"Michael said what?"

Raising her gaze to his, she tried to focus, but tears washed her vision. "He said Mr. Sumner has turned Lissa into his kept woman. I have to find her, Johnnie. I have to bring her home. Tonight."

"No," Michael croaked. "I don't want you out there."

She stroked his hair. "Do you know where they are, love?"

"No." His reply was muffled and strained. "I don't know where. But the man who told me said terrible things about Lissa." He looked up then. "I knocked the words right down his throat, Rache. I did."

"Shhh. Shhh." She smoothed his cheek with the back of her hand.

"You were right," he said. "I am a lousy protector." Tucking himself up into a ball, he rolled to the floor and covered his head with his arms.

"No, Michael, no. You are a wonderful brother and provider and protector. It is not your fault." She stroked his arm, his side, his leg.

Eventually, his body relaxed as heartbreak and exhaustion rendered him oblivious to the fact that he had fallen asleep, boots and all.

"I must go and find her," she whispered.

Johnnie bent down on one knee. "You cannot. Where would you go?"

She closed her lids for a moment but received no relief from the ache in her eyes. They felt as if they'd been scraped with sandpaper. "I will start at the countess's."

He gave her elbow a gentle squeeze. "Under no circumstances will you go there again, Rachel. I mean it."

She could not believe her body had any more tears to produce, but evidently it did. "I must. She is my responsibility."

He was shaking his head before she'd even finished her sentence. "No. Let me go. I will find her."

"She is my sister."

"And you are my friend. What kind of man would I be to let you do such a thing? It isn't safe. It isn't practical. It simply isn't an option. And besides that, Michael needs you."

She struggled to her feet and retrieved a blanket from the bed, then draped it over Michael, tucking it securely around him.

"You will go tonight?" she asked.

"Yes."

"This very minute?"

He touched her chin. "This very minute."

Johnnie had heard Sumner had built a house that morning. It was one of those prefabricated iron ones purported to be grooved in such a manner that all parts of the house, roof, and sides, slid together, making it possible to assemble in a day's time.

He stood in front of the twenty-by-fifteen-foot structure on a lot elevated well above the business part of town. It was supposedly a prime piece of real estate, free from dust and overlooking the harbor. But darkness swallowed any view other than the twinkling tents blanketing the hills below. Looking at them, he hadn't realized until now how much the city had grown.

Taking a deep breath, he approached the door and hammered his fist against it. "Sumner? It's Parker. Open up."

No response. He hoped in spades this was the right house. He banged against the door once more. The windows shook, the metal clanged.

"I'm coming. Don't knock the thing down."

The door swung open, and muted light from some distant spot in the house outlined Sumner. Mussed from sleep—or something else—the card shark stood before him in trousers, bare feet spread. "What do you want, Parker?"

"Where's Lissa?"

He blinked a moment before a knowing grin curved across his face. "Jealous?"

Johnnie curled his fists but kept them at his side. "Tell her to collect her things. I'm taking her home."

Sumner propped a shoulder against the doorframe and crossed one foot over the other. "This is her home."

"You married her, then?"

He harrumphed. "Not likely."

"Then she's leaving."

Sumner cocked his head, scrutinizing Parker. "I might be willing to share her after a time. But for now, I think I'll keep her to myself. When I'm ready to spread the love a little, I'll be sure to give you first dibs."

Rage churned inside Johnnie. A noise sounded down the hall. A moment later the door widened to reveal a thoroughly tousled Lissa wrapped in a filmy silk robe.

Johnnie pinned his gaze to Sumner's. "I'm here on behalf of her sister. I don't want to fight you. But I'm taking her home."

"I'll not go with you, Mr. Parker," she said. "So don't waste your time. If you take me by force, I'll simply come right back."

Sumner slid an arm about Lissa's waist and cinched her up against him. His hand rode up, down, and around the girl's side.

Johnnie studied her face for signs of distress or regret. It may have been dark, but anybody would be able to tell she exhibited neither. Just the opposite, in fact. The poor disillusioned thing was clearly in love with Sumner.

"Rachel's beside herself," Johnnie said. "She wants you home."

"It's too late," she replied. "The deed's been done."

O Lord. "If you come with me now, we can shove all this under the rug. So get your things and let's go."

She didn't so much as twitch. "Tell Rachel we're going to be married."

"Is that so?" Johnnie quirked a brow at Sumner. "And when might that be?"

"As soon as Merle can arrange it."

Johnnie returned his attention to her. "He's lying."

Her only response was a patronizing smile, as if he were some slow-witted child who had no power within his brain.

"If it's to be a speedy marriage," he said, "then why don't you come on home tonight and marry him tomorrow?"

Sumner and Lissa exchanged an intimate look. "Actually, we've already spoken our vows to each other and to God," she said. "Saying them to the preacher is really nothing more than a formality."

"It's a lot more than a formality."

She shook her head. "Not to me, it's not."

Sumner gave Johnnie a knowing smile.

"What am I supposed to tell Rachel?" Johnnie asked.

"Tell her to come by for tea. I'd love to show her my new house."

"You know she can't do that. Not unless you have a marriage certificate."

Sumner patted Lissa on the hip. "Well, we'll just have to make it all nice and official, then. Won't we, love?"

She smiled.

"Someone beat Michael up."

Lissa sucked in her breath. Johnnie knew it was a sorry thing to do, but he could think of nothing else to jar her out of this fairy-tale world she had manufactured.

Concern filled her eyes. "What happened?"

"Somebody said something ugly about you." He let the impact settle for a mere second. "You can't ask Rachel to worry about you and play nursemaid to Michael both at the same time. She needs you. Michael needs you. Now, get your things."

She bit her lip. He could see she was vacillating. She looked up at Sumner.

He kept his pose casual and his touch gentle but narrowed his eyes. "It's our wedding night, Lissa. You walk out of here and all bets are off. Not only that, but I'll make sure what's left of your reputation is in shreds by this time tomorrow. You're mine now. You're not going anywhere."

That's it, Sumner, let her see your true colors. Johnnie glanced to see her reaction, but instead of anger, the girl's face softened and filled with pleasure. What a naïve, stupid, empty-headed chit.

She snuggled closer to Sumner and turned back to Johnnie. "Please tell Michael I'm sorry and I hope he feels better."

With that, Sumner pushed away from the doorframe. "Night, Parker." He pulled Lissa back into the entry and softly closed the door.

———

Rachel slipped into bed beside Michael.

"Lissa?" he croaked. "Rachel?"

"It's me," Rachel whispered.

"Did Johnnie find her?"

"Yes."

"Did he bring her home?"

"No." She felt around the bed with her hand until she found his. She entwined her fingers with his.

"Are you all right?" she asked.

A long pause. "No," he whispered.

Tears slipped from the corners of her eyes. "Me neither, love. Me neither."

———

Rachel slammed the door behind her and leaned against its wooden bulk, clutching the brown parcel to her chest. Dust motes swirled in the empty shanty.

Marriage. Johnnie said that scoundrel had promised Lissa marriage. Rachel pushed herself up off the door. And if that's what he'd promised her sister, then that's what her sister was going to get.

Moving to the bed, she dropped the parcel on top of it and stared. She had fired question after question last night when Johnnie had returned. He'd answered all but one.

Under no circumstances would he reveal the location of Lissa and Sumner's love nest.

Too dangerous, he'd said.

Nothing you can do, he'd said.

She grabbed a knife, sliced the twine encircling the package, and carefully folded back layers of brown paper until the contents spilled forth. She picked each one up and spread it across the coverlet.

Head scarf. Felt hat. Cloth purse. Red flannel shirt. Corduroy pants. Under waistcoat. Underdrawers. Revolver pistol.

A fortune. It had cost her a fortune, but where one's treasure lies, so lies one's heart. And what greater treasure than her precious sister?

So she'd spent a huge chunk of the gold she had been saving so painstakingly. And she'd have spent twice as much if it meant saving Lissa.

She wasn't exactly sure when the idea had come to her. Sometime between the church service this morning, the Sunday promenade of the fancy women, and the cleaning up of the shanty.

Michael would not talk, nor would he let Rachel coddle him. He had attended church—swollen eye and all—helped her restore their shanty to a semblance of order, then left to haul goods from the wharf to whatever establishment was paying him.

Johnnie had headed out to his property, and for the first Sunday since arriving in San Francisco, she would not accompany him. Not unless he told her where Lissa was. He refused.

She carefully refolded, restacked, and rewrapped her purchases, tying them off with the twine, then slipped them under the bed. She'd wait until Michael had left for the evening and until the men of this town had imbibed a little too heavily before carrying out her plan.

———

Work boots slapping against the dirt, hair hidden inside a head scarf, and hat pulled down to her brow, Rachel wended her way from the wharf to the plaza. The smell of fish and filth clung to her and her newly purchased clothes. She hoped she hadn't overdone it.

Hitching up her trousers, she readjusted the pistol strapped to her waist. The weapon and her purse of gold were the only clean things on her entire body.

She'd expected the pants to feel restrictive and clinging, but they were surprisingly accommodating, allowing a freedom of motion that actually inspired her to add a bit of swagger to her step.

Rubbing shoulders with men of every color, size, condition, and strength, she labored to keep all expression from her face as depraved curses and ribald jokes hounded her ears.

Noises from the direction of the plaza beckoned with tricksters at every bend now, plying their trades.

"Here's the place to git your money back," shouted one. "The veritable string game. Here it goes. Three, six, twelve ounces no one can put his finger in the loop."

Afraid to make eye contact, she shouldered by without finding out exactly what "the loop" was.

Newspapers from two months before were selling for a dollar apiece. A lariat-swinging vaquero performed for a drunken audience.

She rode the wave of those around her into the El Dorado. The large tent housed a massive bar with four young men in shirtsleeves and collars dealing out drinks to thirsty customers lined up three deep.

The men may as well have been a swarming mass of ladybugs migrating to their annual clustering spot, so tightly were they packed into this pit. She could not obtain so much as a glimpse of the gamblers sitting around tables or the cards that held them enthralled.

Glasses jingled, curses abounded, and in a distant corner, two violinists scraped furiously on their instruments. How on earth would she ever discover the whereabouts of Lissa's lover in this mess? Inch by inch, the pack with which she moved made its way to a large table covered with a stained blue cloth.

A demure, well-dressed man looking every inch a respectable banker faced a group of dirty, drinking, smoking miners shouting out their bets between swills of spirits.

"I won two ounces on the deuce. Take off two o' them air buttons," roared a thin-faced watery-eyed man.

The dealer shuffled.

"Hold on!"

Rachel heard the shrill voice but could not locate its owner until a curly-haired boy whose chin barely cleared the tabletop plopped a weighty buckskin bag on a card.

"Six ounces on the ace," he cried.

She quickly looked around to see if the boy had any relatives or friends in the crowd, but it appeared that no one even knew the lad.

Play began and the ace must have won, because the men closest to the boy banged him on the shoulder and offered congratulatory words.

The boy pocketed his original bag but placed his winnings on yet another card. "Bar the port."

She had no idea what that meant, but cards were brushed aside and others took their place. Over and over the boy won until grown men were placing their bets according to what the boy did.

Having worked his way through one entire deck of cards, the dealer chose another pack, shuffled, cut, and made a layout. The jack and queen graced the tablecloth, and for the first time she saw the boy hesitate, as if he could not quite decide which was the most worthy.

"Twenty-five ounces on the queen," he said, gathering the whole of his winnings and placing them on her royal majesty. Few others bet, but it was of no consequence, for the little urchin won yet again, turning his twenty-five ounces into fifty.

Then fifty became a hundred. A hundred became two hundred, and the table in front of the lad was completely covered with gold.

"I'll break that bank or it'll break me," he cried. "How much you have?"

"Bank's at two hundred fifty ounces," the dealer replied.

"I tap the bank upon the tray."

The crowd stilled and Rachel could not help but recall this very scenario occurring that first day in Johnnie's hotel, except this was worse. Much worse. Johnnie had fleeced an adolescent. This boy could not have seen more than six summers.

She still had no inkling as to how the game worked, but without hurry the dealer turned the cards over one by one until he stopped, hesitated, then calmly leaned over and scooped all the gold onto his own side of the table.

Dizzy and sick, she looked to the boy, taking comfort in the fact that his original buckskin bag rested safely intact about his waist.

With a stiff lip and an air of defiance, the boy plopped that self-same bag back up on the table.

And lost it in the very next round of play.

She barely suppressed a groan. *O Lord. What will he do? Does he have anything to eat?*

Whistling "Oh Californy," the child turned his back and strutted out as proud as any dandy that ever lived. The men parted way for him, and she slipped silently behind him.

Before she could lose him amidst the crowd, she caught up to him in the street. "Oh, son, whatever were you thinking? Where are your parents?"

He scrutinized her without ever ceasing to whistle.

Taking his arm, she led him into an alley between two tents. "You must tell me how much you lost. Do you have any money on which to come and go?"

Still he did not answer. Just sized her up and whistled.

She quickly untied the purse at her belt. "How much do you need?"

The whistling immediately ceased. He chanced a quick glance into the street. "I believe you're a good egg," he said. "So mum's the word?"

She found herself nodding.

"You want to know how much was in that bag?" A delightful grin spread across his face. "Wall, I'll tell you. Just four pounds of duck-shot mixed and nothing more."

He slapped both hands against his thighs as laughter overtook him. "What a swar'rin' and a cussin' they'll be doin' when they open it up."

She could not decide if she was relieved or angry or just plain saddened. But she definitely was not amused. At all.

He didn't seem to notice.

But maybe he could help her. "Do you know of a Mr. Merle Sumner? I believe he's a professional gambler."

All mirth fell from his expression like a curtain dropping after the final call. "What bus'ness ya have with 'im?"

"I, uh, I owe him something and I'd like to pay him."

The boy's smile held no humor. "Wall, ya needn't worry, then. He'll find you. Them blacklegs always collect. The cause of all our troubles, they is. Murderin', thievin' rascals, ev'ry last one of 'em."

She sucked in a breath. "Are you speaking of Mr. Sumner in particular? Do you know him?"

"Know who he is. Wears them green-checkered pants like one of them rangers wears a badge." He narrowed his eyes. "He threatenin' you, miss?"

She raised a brow and leaned in closer. "Now, I'm going to tell you something. . . . Mum's the word?"

He nodded.

"*I'm* going to threaten *him*."

The boys eyes widened. "Ya need any help? Ya know, somebody to watch yer back while ya do yer deed?"

Land sakes. She couldn't decide whether to feel warmed or horrified by his offer.

She shook her head. "Best not. This is my fight, not yours. Now, do you know where he lives?"

"Shore. Just built hisself a metal house up on Telegraph Hill."

She listened carefully to the directions, committing them to memory, before giving him a bit of dust for his help. It wasn't until she was well on her way that she realized he'd called her "miss."

Pulling her hat low, she tried to swagger while simultaneously keeping her pantaloon-covered hips from giving her away.

ohnnie watched Michael collect their winnings and
pay out their losses from the Chinese box at his
side. The boy had a way with figures and was easily one of the best
croupiers he'd ever had.

The fellas were getting restless, though. He caught Soda's attention
and the barkeep hastened over.

"What will you gentlemen take to drink?" Johnnie asked.

The men called out their preferences to Soda, who promptly filled
the order and returned, remembering exactly what each of the twenty
or so men had requested. A break in the play ensued while each
lushed it up.

He turned at the grazing of his elbow. "Well, there, Cotton. How's
the evening treating you?" He shook hands with Marty Shine's boy,
whose curly hair was so blond it looked almost white.

"I done struck hardpan and pay dirt over in the Dorado, then lost
it all on the tray."

"Did you now? Well, that's a shame. A shame, indeed. What
brings you here? You know I won't let you play."

"I know." The boy looked about the group of men, but no one

paid the two of them any heed. He leaned close. "It's about yer spare rib. I think she might be in a fix."

He tensed, knowing immediately the boy was speaking of Rachel and not wasting any time pretending she wasn't his woman. Cotton wouldn't believe him.

"What's happened?" he asked.

"Fer as I can tell, nothin' yet. The trouble is, I give her my word. So what's a fella to do when you give a bonnet yer word but you have a pardner who you've swarn to stick to through thick and thin, heat and cold, thaw and freeze?"

He gave the boy his full attention. "You swear your partner to secrecy."

Cotton pinned him with his gaze. "Mum's the word?"

"Mum's the word."

"She's all git up like a feller and askin' where to find the Weasel."

It took every bit of control he had not to react in front of the men. Any sudden movement and the boys became skittish real fast. Too many guns and drunks to risk that kind of foolishness.

"Where is she?"

"Last I saw her, she was headed toward the Hill."

He swore. "How long ago was that?"

"Maybe an hour."

"Why didn't you come to me sooner?"

"Been playin' follow my leader."

He frowned. "Don't tell me you have a gun now?"

The boy puffed out his chest. "Got me a Colt."

Pushing his chair back, he motioned to Carmelita. "Boys, I'm going to give you into the hands of the lovely Carmelita. Be respectful now, or you'll find yourselves on the wrong side of my door."

He put a hand on Cotton's shoulder and guided the boy to the bar. "You have something my partner can do to earn some poke, Soda?"

"Shore 'nough I do."

"Well, he's packing now, so don't make him mad."

Soda lifted his brows. "Wall, I don't have no work o' no kind for fellas who pack a pistol."

Cotton immediately pulled his gun from his belt and handed it to Soda. "You put it where you likes, Soder. Jis' tell me what to do."

With controlled haste, Johnnie left through the back entrance and checked his own revolver before heading to the livery for J.B.

The hustle and bustle of town fell behind Rachel as she hiked up Kearny to Telegraph Hill. Outlined at the top was the telegraph station Misters Sweeny and Baugh had built. From the observation deck on its roof, she had heard the two men would constantly scan the Golden Gate for incoming ships, then announce impending arrivals by semaphore.

The Hill wasn't as close to the Plaza as it appeared. And the degree of the slope was steeper than she'd expected, as well. Winded, she stopped a moment and held the stitch in her side.

The treeless settlement below looked almost pretty from this vantage point, with its luminary tents clustered about the bay. And so big. She'd had no idea it now spread out so far. She marveled at the number of wooden buildings. When had those been erected?

Taking a deep breath, she pressed forward. If the directions the boy had given her were correct, the house should be just around the next curve.

None of the light that filled the streets and Plaza reached this far out, and the quiet darkness both soothed and unnerved at the same time. Ocean waves thrumming against the shore offered a false sense of serenity, while the brisk breeze whipped about her, bringing with it whiffs of salt and fish. Or maybe it was herself she smelled.

In the distance a faint outline of a box house began to take shape, and within moments she stood in its yard. She wished she could see it better. Light glowed through the curtainless window, making it easy to see the barren parlor within. No furniture, no rug, no Lissa.

Was the seducer home or had he left her sister alone while he pursued the pleasures town had to offer? If Lissa was alone, perhaps she could be talked into returning home.

Yet nothing would ever be the same. There were only two kinds of women. The chaste kind and the other kind. No, Lissa had no choice in the matter. She must enter into holy wedlock with this despoiler.

But what if he beat her? Rachel narrowed her eyes. If he so much as harmed a hair on Lissa's head, Rachel would personally wait until he entered the Plaza, then chase after him, screaming, "Hang him!"

What if he refused to marry? Rachel carefully removed the revolver from her waistband. She would persuade him otherwise.

What if they were . . . busy? *O Lord. Please don't let them be busy.*

Stepping to the door, she struck it with the butt of her pistol, then lowered her voice an octave. "Open up."

She heard some shuffling, then silence. She pounded on the door again. Almost immediately it swung open.

She leveled her gun at the man before her.

He slowly raised his hands up and out, ballooning the sides of his shirt.

She kept her voice low and gruff. "Get your woman. We're going to the preacher."

"Lissa?" he called over his shoulder.

She heard a scrambling, then her sister's voice. "Who is it?"

"Just come here a minute, love. Would you?"

Rachel could not quite decipher the look in his eyes. But she knew he took her seriously. Very seriously.

The door widened. "Rachel! Oh, Rachel! In heaven's name, put that thing down!"

So much for her disguise. Then, to her distress, Lissa threw herself between the gun and the man.

Without taking her gaze off Mr. Sumner, Rachel raised the gun. Now it pointed at his forehead. "Sir, do not move a muscle. Lissa, step to the side."

Sumner stayed as he was.

So did Lissa. "What is the matter with you? Are you crazy?"

"Are you married?"

"Sort of," Lissa screeched. "Now stop it. This instant."

Rachel closed one eye and looked down the sight of her gun. "Either you are or you aren't."

"Rachel, so help me if you shoot him I will never in all my born days forgive you. I love him. And he loves me. *Please.*"

She kept him pinned in her sight. "Do you love her, sir?"

He didn't so much as flinch. "I do."

"Then why isn't her last name Sumner?"

"I will see to it."

She opened the eye she had closed. "Good. Lissa, if you don't want to get married in that calico, then you need to change. We are going to 'see to it.'"

"Absolutely not. I won't have Merle forced by gunpoint down that hill. You might stumble and blow his head off by accident. He said he would marry me and he will. Now, if you don't put that thing away, I'll take it from you."

"You try and you'll be a widow before you're a bride."

The pounding of a horse's hooves sounded from the hill. Barely had they come to a stop when they were replaced by human footfalls.

Rachel's focus remained on Mr. Sumner and vice versa. Her arms began to fatigue, but she continued to hold them straight and steady.

Lissa left her post and raced into the yard. "Oh, thank heavens. Mr. Parker. You must do something. Rachel is threatening to shoot Merle."

My stars and garters, what is he doing here?

"Put the gun down, Rachel."

"This is none of your affair, Mr. Parker. Go away. Lissa, either you, Mr. Sumner, and I all go down that hill and find a preacher or you and I go down to the shanty alone. But you are not living in sin one more minute."

Lissa groaned. "Ooooh. This cannot be."

The girl moved back to the doorway, hands on her hips. She, thankfully, did not return to her position as human shield for this rapscallion.

"You know, Merle," she said, "I'm not even sure Rachel knows how to use that thing. Never in my entire life have I ever seen her harm any living creature in such a violent manner. Suffocating in jars. Yes. Annihilating with a revolver. No."

No snake could have struck faster. Of course he *was* a snake, so that explained why in one fluid motion he knocked the pistol from her grip, grabbed her wrists, and twisted them around and up her back.

She would not cry out, no matter how much it hurt.

Then to her everlasting pleasure, her dear Johnnie Parker ever so casually palmed a very handsome Colt and held it loosely at his side. "Release her. Immediately."

He did. She scrambled to pick up her gun, but Johnnie got to it first and placed a boot on it. She looked up.

"You will leave it."

Oh my, but he was furious. Well, so what? She hadn't asked for his assistance. Still, she stood, leaving the pistol, and turned back to Lissa. "You're going with me."

"I'm not. I love him. Not that you'd understand. But it doesn't matter whether you do or don't. Nobody but you and Mr. Parker are taking a trip down that hill. Merle and I are staying here."

Panic began to nibble at her insides. "Lissa, you are too young to discriminate between the respectful homage of a sensible gentleman and the self-serving lies which flow so smoothly from the mouths of vanity-puffed shallow-brained men."

Lissa stiffened. "How dare you."

A mixture of grief and despair overcame Rachel. "Think, dear. Please. He's not just some adventurer looking for a buried treasure, he's a *professional* gambler. Nightly he pursues his soul-killing avocation, little caring for the mental agony of his victims. And he's not content with ruining only those of his own sex. By his very nature, he's on the alert for young, beautiful victims of the opposite sex. And you are far too captivating to go unnoticed—for now. But without a wedding ring, what is to keep him from luring the next young innocent when you are beyond the blush of youth?"

The more she spoke, the more hostile Lissa became. The girl clenched and unclenched her fists, squinted her eyes, locked her jaw. Why could her sister not perceive what a sham this man was?

Lissa jabbed a finger into Rachel's chest. "Well, that's certainly the pot calling the kettle black when your beau is a saloon owner. Talk about a soul-killing avocation. Talk about taking advantage of the childlike."

"He's not my beau."

"Oh no? Have you let him touch you?"

Try as she might, she could not stop the rush of blood to her face.

Lissa crossed her arms. "Well, well, well." She looked at Johnnie. "Do I need to send Merle after his pistol, Mr. Parker?"

How on earth had this conversation run amuck? "Lissa, I am not living in sin with Mr. Parker."

Leaning back a bit, the girl cocked her head. "No. I'm sure you aren't. There's no need to, is there? For Mr. Parker owns a facility that allows lovers to meet with minimal fear of detection. He's quite discreet, I hear."

Suddenly Johnnie loomed over the two of them. "You will keep a civil tongue in your head when you speak of your sister. She's done nothing, and I'll not have you slandering her."

Lissa lifted her brows. "'The gentleman doth protest too much, methinks.'"

He narrowed his eyes.

Rachel took a fortifying breath. "Lissa, enough of this. It is time to come home. Clearly, the man is not going to marry you."

"Good night, sister," Lissa said.

Rachel looked then to Mr. Sumner. But she would receive no help from that quarter. She'd just called him a shallow, brainless deflowerer of innocents. And he looked none too happy about it.

Still, she could try. "You will marry her?"

He nodded once. "I will."

"When?"

His gaze shifted to Lissa's. "When I can pull myself away from her long enough to fetch the preacher." His expression was nothing short of lecherous. "So far, I've not been able to let her out of my sight for even a moment."

Rachel swallowed, and her sister moved into an intimate torso-to-torso embrace with him. Hooking his wrists together, he settled them at the curve of her buttocks and leaned down to give her a lusty kiss.

Good thing Johnnie had her pistol. Turning, she headed back down the hill, tears stinging her eyes.

Shaking with fury, Johnnie had yet to come to a point where he could so much as utter a word to her. Dragging J.B. by the reins, he watched Rachel pound down the hill, slipping and sliding, spine as straight as a streetlamp. The breeches clinging to those swinging hips had his imagination doing double time and his temper even worse.

What had she been thinking to hold a gun on a no-good like Sumner who'd just as soon shoot her as look at her? Anger rushed through him all over again.

About halfway down, she stopped and whirled around. He nearly ran her over.

"I want you to quit following me," she snapped. "What are you even doing here?"

"As it happens, we live on the same piece of property. So if it looks like I'm following you, it's only because I'm going the same place you are."

"I meant what were you doing up at Lissa's place?"

"Coming after you."

"Why?"

"I don't trust Sumner."

"I'm not your responsibility."

"Well, praise the Lord for that, anyway."

She shoved him, hard, and he wasn't expecting it.

Before he could secure his footing on the steep slope, he dropped the reins, fell down, then sprang back up. "What did you do that for?"

"I did it out of sheer meanness. And if you don't leave me alone, I'll do it again."

"What the fiery furnace were you thinking back there to hold a gun on Sumner? Have you lost your mind? Do you have any idea whatsoever how dangerous he is? He'd kill you without a moment's hesitation."

"It wasn't loaded."

"What wasn't loaded? Your gun? Your gun wasn't loaded! Woman, do you have nothing but space in between those ears of yours? Never, ever aim an unloaded gun at somebody!"

She had the nerve to look at him as if *he* were the stupid one.

"Are you trying to tell me it's safer to point a *loaded* gun at somebody?"

"Of course it's safer. My sainted aunt, but you are the most troublesome apron on the face of this earth."

"Well, who asked you? Did I ask you to be my keeper? No. No, I did not. So in case you're wondering, you're dismissed."

"From what?"

"From being my keeper."

She spun back around, but he grabbed her by the waist of her breeches before she took so much as a step. "And that's another thing. What the blazes do you think you are doing parading around town in trousers?"

She swatted his hand away. "It's a disguise. Nobody recognized me."

"No? Then how did I find out what you were up to?"

That shut her up for a moment. Not long enough, though. "How did you find out?"

He leaned close. "You are a sunbonnet woman. Every man and boy in the territory knows who you are. And now they are going to think you are just like the rest of the janes that live in this town. Loose and free with their morals. Who ever heard of a sunbonnet traipsing around in pants? Even the whores wear skirts."

She raised her hand to slap him, but he grabbed her arms and jerked her against him. Mistake. Big mistake.

Her chin lifted. Her eyes widened.

A conscience he hadn't heard from in a long, long time started hammering like a woodpecker against his insides, causing him to question what he was about to do.

And as he had since the day his late wife walked out on him, he slammed a lid on the scruples and moved his lips to the ones waiting for him.

Oh, but they were sweet. And pliant. And warm.

The absence of light and the remoteness of their location enveloped them in intimacy. The woodpecker made itself known again.

Rachel squirmed and shoved and stomped on his toe. He pulled back, loosening his grip.

Her flattened chest heaved. He frowned. Where was the rest of her? Had she wrapped herself, then?

Tears sprang to her eyes.

"What's the matter?" he asked.

"Lissa's right. I'm no better than she is. The only difference between her and me is she's more open about what she's doing. I only sin under the cover of darkness."

He scowled. "You are nothing like her. Nothing. She is choosing to live an unchaste life. You aren't."

"Then would you please explain to me why it is that I am in your arms and have no desire whatsoever to make you stop kissing me?"

All traces of anger left him in a whoosh, only to be replaced with intense male satisfaction. She'd liked their kiss. Wanted, in fact, more of them. Well, that made two of them.

"You don't want me to stop kissing you any more than I want you to stop kissing me. There's no sin in that."

"'Do not stir up nor awaken love until it pleases.'"

Contentment sluiced through him. "Have I awakened the love in you, Rachel?"

"Yes," she whispered.

He grazed her chin with his finger. "I've never kissed a girl in pants before, nor one that stinks to high heaven. What kind of fragrance are you wearing, woman?"

She humphed.

He kissed her again. This time she didn't struggle.

"Go riding with me tomorrow," he said.

"I can't."

"Can't or won't?"

She didn't answer.

"I want to show you something," he urged.

"What is it?"

"Some trees."

"What about Lissa?"

"There's nothing you can do, Rachel. You're going to have to let her go."

She shook her head. "I can't."

"Then pray for her. But in the meanwhile, you can't just quit doing normal everyday things."

She blew a bit of hair from her face, but the wilted tendril returned to drape across her vision. "Oh, I don't know, Johnnie."

"You have to come with me. Please?"

She stayed silent so long he was sure she'd refuse him. "What kind of trees are they again?"

He let out the breath he'd been holding. "The kind you have to see to believe."

She nibbled her lower lip.

"We'll leave at first light," he said.

"But, I have to clean the hotel in the morning."

"One day won't hurt, Rachel. Say yes. Just this once."

She stepped back, fingering the waistband of her britches. "Just this once?"

"Just this once."

*O*n a typical morning, the fog would crash over the mountaintops like a tidal wave and pour down the sides of the slopes before spreading across the top of the sea and town, obliterating everything in sight. This morning, though, the fog was conspicuously absent, giving way to glistening sunshine sparkling so brightly atop the blue water that it hurt Rachel's eyes to look at it. But then, her eyes had been hurting for a while, as she had spent the whole night long mourning over Lissa.

She shoved those thoughts aside, determined to take solace in the feel of her horse and the scenic beauty of the California territory.

Bit by bit they left behind the hilly tip of the peninsula holding boisterous, frenetic San Francisco along with its bay of deserted windjammers bobbing in the tide. Gradually the horses made their way onto a coastline with a succession of heavily-wooded ridges on one side and a shimmering sea on the other.

No visible signs of human habitation presented themselves, but the shoreline was busy with activity. Wild geese flying high in a V, pelicans cruising just above the water's surface, wings flapping—one flying this way, one that, each with an urgent destination in mind. Waves slapped against the sand; wind whistled loudly past her ears.

Evidence of dying fish along with barnacles on rotted wood reached her nose. Sweet Lips jerked her chin up, and Rachel acquiesced, allowing for a little more freedom in the length of the reins.

She surveyed the seascape, but the view was illusive, making it difficult to tell the islands from the mustard-colored mountain ranges, so smoothly did they blend together. The water surrounding them changed from olive to green to blue depending upon its depth.

A loud honking quickly pulled her attention up the shoreline, but she could spot no boat. The sound swelled into a chorus of not barks exactly, but more like extraordinarily loud consecutive belches, each on top of the other.

She frowned. Johnnie pointed. Following the direction of his finger, she spotted a group of rocks up ahead that swayed like wheat. Squinting, she gently tugged on her right rein, leading Sweet Lips to the water's edge.

In a few moments, she could see they were not rocks at all. Her eyes widened.

"Sea lions," Johnnie said.

She resisted the urge to trot, not wanting to frighten the huge almost black animals jumping, swimming and, well, playing amongst a group of boulders several yards into the sea. And, my, but they were noisy. Just like true Californians.

Sweet Lips whinnied.

"Shhhh. It's all right, girl." She moved the horse back up onto shore, reined her in, and slid from the saddle. In a moment, Johnnie stood beside her.

She gasped and pointed. "Look. A baby one."

"Yes. They give birth to the pups in June and July. Pretty big for a newborn, huh?"

She handed him her reins and walked closer. He followed, pulling the horses behind him. Several mothers and pups lounged against the rocks soaking up the sweet heat of the sun's rays.

"Good heavens. Look at that one. Why, it must be upwards of eight hundred pounds," she said.

"That's a male. See that bump on his head? They get those when they're around five."

"The smaller ones are females, then."

He huffed. "If you can call three hundred pounds small."

Smiling, she once again followed the direction of his finger to a couple of lions cavorting about the water. Clearly, it was a male and female and they were ... kissing. Necking. Wrapping their massive bodies around each other and swirling round and round in a graceful, amorous ballet.

He chased her. She chased him. Then they twisted themselves together like rope and spun beneath the surface, disappearing as water rippled in their wake.

Goose bumps broke out across her skin. Never in all her born days had she seen anything so sensual. Not even with her insects. And certainly not while standing isolated and alone next to a man of whom she was growing more and more fond.

She peeked up at him, then lost herself within the depths of his blue gaze. For he had not been watching the lovers but had, instead, watched her watch them. And the sensations she'd been feeling before increased tenfold.

The barking receded. The breeze died. The smell of salt and horse metamorphosed into the smell of Johnnie Parker.

Was this how it had been for Lissa? If so, Rachel could certainly understand how effortless it would be to succumb to such feelings. Feelings so tempting, so strong it was as if she fought the gravitational pull of the very earth.

Even knowing her own principles were as firm as the rocks of these native hills, knowing her faith was deep enough to rely on the strength of almighty God, she stood before this man vacillating between giving in and holding fast.

And why not? She lived in a town where virtue was regarded by the mass as only a name. Where the females numbered perhaps a hundred, yet from that number she could not have selected but one with whom she could have associated. And that one had just crossed the line of demarcation.

She took a deep breath. "I don't think this is a good idea, Johnnie. What we're doing. I'd like to go back now."

There was no question he understood her meaning. The currents between them were as real as the ones in the ocean.

His face softened. "We can't turn back now. We're almost to the turnoff. And the best is yet to come."

That's precisely what she was afraid of. But truth be told, she didn't want to go back. Going back meant facing all the emotions she had shoved into the little box she kept deep inside her. And this time, she'd had to shove them down, cram the lid on, and sit atop it to keep its contents muzzled.

She'd rather go see some trees. For where there were trees, there were insects. *Help me be strong, Lord.*

Johnnie must have sensed how little it would take for her to bolt, because he didn't lift her into the saddle but chose instead to lock his fingers together and give her foot a boost.

Casting one last glance at the sea lions and another at the town well behind her, she allowed herself to be drawn into the wilds of uncharted territory.

———

They'd spoken hardly at all. The silence between them comfortable. Peaceful.

The forest of redwoods was just ahead, but Johnnie had no wish to rush Rachel and cut short her delight in the vast carpet of green they wove through nor the theatrics the fruit trees performed for her. Apricot, almond, pear, and plum all burst forth with showy leaves. And as much as Johnnie enjoyed these rolling hills, he found this time it was not nature's display that drew his admiration but the woman beside him.

She wore a brown work dress and a serviceable bonnet whose wide brim protected her from the sun and, often, from his gaze. And in this field of flowers, with her calico bonnet and silky tendrils of hair that refused to stay caged, she looked every bit the young innocent she was. Only the puffiness around her eyes hinted at the weight she carried on those delicate shoulders.

Reaching the edge of the clearing, they left the field behind and entered the perimeter of the forest. Within moments they moved into a world like none other.

Rachel pulled her sorrel to a stop. He followed suit. Clusters of giant, perfectly straight majestic redwoods of an age that harkened back to the creation of time filled the quiet, shady glade in which they sat.

Sliding off her horse, she dropped the reins and craned her neck back. Up and up and up the huge trees rose, dwarfing them, humbling them. Mere mortals in a universe so vast, so old that troubles shrank into tiny grains of sand.

Dappled light poured through the lacy canopy, splashing across her face like dew.

"I feel like we're in a cathedral," she whispered.

He smiled at her reluctance to speak in a normal voice. But he understood, for the stately columns formed a chapel of sorts with high windows rising up to the sky. And as much as he liked to pretend otherwise, anyone who stood on such hallowed ground could not question the presence of God in this place.

A stream gurgled across rocks playing leapfrog along its bank. Delicate ferns congregated about its edge in deeply shaded shallows. Leaves whispered in the cool breeze.

"Are you cold?" he asked.

She shook her head and moved deeper into the forest, approaching a tree bigger around than the two of them put together and every bit of two hundred feet in height.

"How old do you suppose these are?" she asked, placing her palms against the bark spiraling up the tree.

"I don't know. A thousand years? Two thousand?"

"I've read about them, but never did I dream . . ."

She ran her hands up and down the trunk, learning its texture, caressing its length. Leaning in, she pressed her face against its bark.

His mouth went dry and he swung off his horse.

She pulled back and looked at him, wonder filling her eyes.

He quirked a brow. "If you'd like to kiss something, Rachel, I can think of an alternative that would be much more satisfying."

A giggle spilled from her lips, bouncing from tree to tree and transforming her face as her cheeks mushroomed and her eyes sparkled. "I was *smelling* it. You know, seeing if it had a fragrance, like a cedar or something."

He felt a smile of his own answer hers. "Well, it doesn't." *I do, though.* But he kept the thought to himself.

Dragonflies, gnats, and butterflies zipped around the water. A spider's web stretching between two trees shimmered in the light.

"Have you noticed they all seem to be bunched together in groups?" She stood with her head cocked, fists resting against her waist as she studied a cluster of redwoods.

"I have."

"Must have something to do with the way they pollinate."

O Lord. I will not be able to survive another discussion on mating rituals—of trees or anything else. If you want me to behave, then you'd better knock some sense into that girl.

"Oh, look at that one. It has a cavelike alcove carved out of its base." She ran over to it and stepped within. "Look. It's huge. I can stand up in it. So could you. Come over, Johnnie, and let's see."

She proceeded to explore the scar in the tree, picking at its edges and debating with herself on what might cause such a phenomenon.

He stepped inside. She whirled around, crashing into his chest. He grasped her arms, then lightly slid his hands down their length before releasing her.

Her eyes grew wide and wary.

Better, Lord. That's better.

Still, he did not withdraw. But she did, then skirted around him and back out onto a winding path.

Johnnie followed her past huckleberry bushes, through shady corridors, and across glistening pools. He'd grabbed their lunch but tied the horses back a ways, as this particular section of the redwood thicket was like a forest of poles, one after another, after another.

"This is what I imagined the forests in all those fairy tales to look like," she said, weaving through the trunks as if practicing the choreographed steps of some fancy ballroom dance.

She picked up her skirts and flitted to one of the giants that had fallen and lay sprawled across the earth from which it had sprung. It was clear she wanted to climb atop it, but its circumference was huge and there was no ladylike way in which to manage the feat.

Finally, she squatted and carefully began to pick at the dead tree. He moved up behind her, casting a shadow across both her and the trunk. She peeled back a large section of bark, unearthing countless bugs of every sort.

"Ohhhhh," she sighed. "Would you look at all those?"

He swiped a hand across his mouth.

"Look in the lunch basket, would you, Johnnie? And see if there is something I can put these in."

He didn't move and she twisted around to look up at him.

"I didn't bring any empty jars," he said. "Just food."

Puckering her lips, she stood and brushed her hands against her skirt. "Let's eat then, and clean some of those jars out."

He lifted a corner of his mouth. "You misunderstand. I don't have any jars at all, only food. But I am hungry. Would you like to go ahead and eat anyway?"

"Of course."

He'd forgotten to grab the blanket when he tied the horses, but she didn't seem to mind and plopped right onto the dirt, hands folded primly in her lap.

He smiled. A child waiting to eat her meal so she could move on to dessert. Or in this case, bugs.

He unpacked biscuits, bacon, and boiled eggs, as well as some elderberries he'd picked while she was exploring.

Peeling the shell off an egg, she glanced at the bugs she'd uncovered. "Mayflies can't eat during their adult life."

He paused. "Not at all?"

"Not at all."

He looked at the tree. "Are there any in there?"

"Oh no. But just one little section like this can turn up beetles, millipedes, and all kinds of worms."

Breaking open his biscuit, he sandwiched slices of bacon inside. "How did you get so interested in bugs?"

"Insects." She shrugged. "Mother let me have a flower bed when I was little, but my favorite part was seeing what lived in the soil and on the leaves of the flowers. So Mother took my shovel away."

"That, apparently, didn't stop you, though."

"Heavens, no. I simply dug a secret garden behind the shed then cultivated poison ivy around it so everyone would leave it alone."

He hesitated before taking a bite of biscuit. "Didn't it get in your way?"

"What? The poison ivy?" She shook her head. "No, I'm immune to it. Doesn't bother me in the least."

He lifted his brows.

"After that, I spent hours outside, checking on bird's nests, collecting insects, studying leaves. One time when Mother had a tea party, she grabbed a china pitcher I'd been using and poured water filled with tadpoles right into the cups. She was soooo angry."

He settled back against the tree trunk and stretched out one leg. Gone was the prim-and-proper Rachel, and in her place was a rebellious little minx full of life and mischief.

A breeze ruffled her bonnet's brim. "Even Michael didn't know I used to slip out of my window at bedtime. I'd shinny down the porch posts so I could run to the pond, and oh, you've never heard anything so lovely as a pond at night. Crickets, cicadas, frogs. It was heavenly."

He wondered if she and Lissa had shared a room. If Lissa knew she'd snuck out. But he didn't ask. Didn't want to make her think anything she'd done might have influenced her sister. Though he couldn't help but wonder if it had.

"By the time I was eight, I had confiscated six of Mother's hatboxes. I filled them with insects, and hid them under our bed." She dabbed the sides of her mouth with her hanky. "But the little insect guide I had didn't identify all of my specimens. Only some."

Pulling out a huge cluster of elderberries the size of a dinner plate, he shared the tart treat with her. She popped several in her mouth, pursing her lips and batting her eyes as she chewed the sour berries.

"What did you do about the insects you couldn't classify?" he asked.

"Asked for divine intervention, mostly. Then, when I was thirteen, Papa took me to the dentist, and on the way home we stopped at the Natural History Museum." Her face lit up. "Oh, it was something to see, Johnnie. Row after row after row of insects. All labeled with their Latin names."

Her hands stilled; her eyes grew distant. He stayed silent, leaving her back in that museum.

After a moment, she smiled and gave a short little huff. "The next day I locked myself in the water closet, jabbed my gums with a pencil, and told Papa my mouth hurt." She gave him a knowing look. "The second he saw those swollen red gums he took me straightaway to the dentist."

He grinned and felt his chest tighten when she smiled back.

Then her smile turned into snickers and her snickers into suppressed laughter. "You know what?"

He shook his head, amused simply because she was.

"I had to visit the dentist so many times that Papa became disgusted with the man for not doing his job and ended up becoming one himself." She doubled over, grabbing her waist, laughter filling the glade as his joined hers.

"Your father was a dentist, then?" he asked.

"Toward the latter part of his life," she said, sitting up and swiping the water from her eyes.

"What did he do before that?"

She shrugged. "A little of this A little of that. My earliest recollections place him clerking in a general store—that went bust. Then he was a minister who, after Mama's death, lost the faith. Before finally becoming a dentist . . . whose debts exceeded his income."

Faint sunlight broke through the gathering clouds, glazing the bark of a nearby redwood. Its branches cascaded down one side of the tree like a woman's unbound hair flowing across one shoulder.

"I suppose it was the lure of pocketing a fortune in gold," Johnnie said, "that incited him to drag you and your family here?"

"That about sums it up." She brushed some crumbs from her skirt. "So, Mr. Parker, I've told you a secret or two about me. Now you must tell me one about you."

Without giving himself a moment to consider the consequences, he gave her a whopper. "I used to be a missionary."

Her jaw dropped. Literally. He could see a streak of purple elderberry stain running down the center of her tongue before she snapped her mouth shut. "You don't say so. Do tell."

He regretted his revelation immediately, but it was too late now. So he mentally shrugged and decided to give her the short and sweet version.

"I had long yearned to share the holiness of saving heathen souls, so I signed up with the Commissioners for Foreign Missions out of Connecticut. And though they desperately needed engineers, they liked their missionaries to be tempered with the wisdom and tolerance of marriage—and I was but an adventure-seeking bachelor."

He offered her more berries. She waved her hand no.

"So what did you do?" she asked.

"As it happens, an unmarried woman with a passion for planting the vine of Christianity in faraway lands had applied to them the day before. So the board did a bit of divine appointing, informed me of what God had ordained, and prepared Gwendolyn to enter into marital bliss and sanctification."

He smiled a humorless smile. "We met in Westport on February 19, married on February 26, and immediately thereafter headed with three other couples to the Oregon region. When we arrived, we found out the Indians were perfectly happy as they were and had no interest whatsoever in converting."

Her face had completely paled. "You are married?"

"No." He heaved a great sigh. "My wife is dead."

"Oh. I'm so very sorry."

"Don't be. I'm not."

Her eyes widened, and he, once again, wished he could call back his words. The breeze had picked up and the sky had suddenly darkened, though noon had passed less than two hours earlier.

"Perhaps we should think about heading back," he said. "Looks like we might be caught in a shower otherwise."

But she didn't move. "Johnnie, you cannot just say something like that and then leave it."

"Yes, yes, you can." He gathered up the remains of their lunch and returned them to the basket. Thunder cracked above their heads. "Come."

They made it only halfway to the horses when the deluge began. Grabbing her hand, he pulled her to a group of redwoods gathered about in a circle and ducked inside one whose base had a scar big enough for four people to stand. A curtain of water separated them from the outside, adding intimacy and solitude to their hiding place.

"Where are the horses?" she asked, shaking the water off her skirts.

"They'll be fine. Wet, but fine."

The silence between them stretched into subtle awareness. She untied and removed her saturated bonnet, then wrung it out. "How long do these usually last?"

He squinted. "They vary. Maybe this will be a quick one."

Bending down, she tested the dirt with her hand then sat down and leaned against the tree wall. "You may as well sit. It's not wet right now and we might be here a while."

He hesitated, then sat down beside her. "I'm sorry you didn't get to capture any bugs."

"Insects. And it's okay. I've had a marvelous time. Truly, I have. I wouldn't even mind riding home in the rain if we must."

He looked at her, realizing from what she'd revealed earlier that she was most likely very serious. "No, let's give it a chance to settle down first."

But she wasn't listening to him. She was searching his eyes as if trying to plumb into the depths of his soul and see what was buried there.

"What happened on your mission journey?" she asked.

He tightened his lips. "I don't want to talk about it."

"Have you ever talked about it? With anyone?"

He didn't answer.

She covered his hand with hers. "Tell me, Johnnie. I want to understand how a missionary could end up running a saloon."

"Ah, Rachel. It's a cautionary tale and not even a good one at that."

"Please?"

Resting his head back against the tree, he surveyed the intricacies of the inner bark patterns, trying to focus on that rather than the warmth coming from her palm. "The whole thing was a disaster. We started out so full of ourselves and our mission, recharging every night with a prayer meeting, and if the train stopped long enough, we'd hold one by day."

"Then what went wrong?"

"Eventually our piousness so consumed us that we became patronizing and haughty toward each other." He sighed and looked down. "We argued all the way from Westport to Columbia. Mile by mile."

"Who? You and your new wife?"

He shook his head. "The couples. Two against two. Unless, of course, the enemy wasn't at hand, at which time we'd turn on each other. And over the most asinine topics. A calf would be wounded by a wolf pack and we'd bicker over whether it was a sign of provision and we should eat it or God was testing our mercy and we should save it."

He spread his fingers wide, allowing hers to drop between them, fitting within his as smoothly as cogs on a wheel. He grazed their length. So long. So graceful.

"With the forced companionship of the trail," he said, "and our intolerance for the others, it wasn't long before the fragile relationship between Gwendolyn and me started to corrode."

He listened to the water pound outside their shelter. "It was a dismal trip. Cold, rainy, exhausting. We hadn't even reached Missouri before Gwendolyn was crying because her father's hogs were more comfortable than she was."

Rachel straightened her legs, crossing them at the ankles as she flicked her skirt down. "Go on."

"Some wayfarers and free trappers overtook us and rode with us a while. One man in particular had traveled a good deal and held the women mesmerized with his tales of Switzerland and Italy and some country where dogs dug men out of the snow."

He looked down at her.

"Did you like him?"

He offered her a sad smile. "Actually, I did. I liked him very much. He visited our caravan often, even after we had reached Popo Agie. Over the course of the next year he would breeze through and entertain the ladies with his fine manners, his buffalo robes, and tales of his military past."

"So what happened?"

"We needed ministers, teachers, doctors, machinists, supplies, and funds. We had none. Not only that, but the Indians just were not interested in the gospel of Jesus Christ. The whole time we were there, we only converted one. And he ended up being disowned by his tribe and simultaneously rejected by white society."

Rachel moved onto her hip, facing him. "What of Gwendolyn?"

He sat a long time before answering. "The truth is, she could barely endure my company. And the Indians—whose souls we were supposed to be saving—frightened her. As it happens, the last time our trapper friend came through for a visit, he brought us olives, potted meat, candies, and fruit pastes. Then he left . . . with my wife."

He heard her quick intake of breath.

"I received word later that year that Gwendolyn had died in child-birth." He brushed some dirt off his pant leg. "Because of the timing, I never did know whose child she'd birthed. His or mine."

"And the child?" she whispered.

"Stillborn."

"Oh, Johnnie."

He shrugged. "So I joined the Missouri Mounted Volunteers and marched three thousand miles from Fort Leavenworth to the mouth of the Rio Grande. No commissary, no uniforms, no pay, and no discipline." He smiled. "Fought two battles, lived off the land, and when our one-year stint was over, none of us reenlisted. Been in California ever since."

Dampness had begun to infiltrate their dirt floor, loamy smells filling the cavern.

"That is a cautionary tale," she said softly.

He looked down at her. She shivered.

"Are you cold?" he asked.

"I'm all right."

But the temperature had dropped and all she had on was that brown work dress, wet from being caught in the rain. He shrugged off his jacket and, taking it by the collar, draped it around her shoulders.

Yet after he had it securely about her, he did not relinquish his hold of the lapels. Her thick hair strained against the pins within it. Several tendrils had escaped to tickle her face and coil down her back.

He explored the delicate lines of that face, the pinkish hue the sun had painted onto her cheeks this day, the long, thick lashes framing her rich brown eyes.

She moistened her lips.

He brushed a lock of hair from her cheek. "I'm going to kiss you now, Rachel."

Her eyes widened slightly, but she didn't pull away.

He applied some pressure to his jacket, drawing her closer. "Have you ever been kissed?"

She slowly nodded her head. "By you. Last night."

"That's not the kind of kiss I mean."

She frowned in sweet confusion.

He slipped an arm about her waist. "If you want me to stop, you just say stop."

"I want you to stop," she whispered.

But her eyes said something much, much different.

He lifted one corner of his mouth. "That's cheating. I haven't started yet. You have to wait until I start. Those are the rules."

And with that, he leaned into her and captured her lips with his. They were soft and smooth and very still. He gathered her nearer, trying to coax a response from her. But she moved nary a muscle, like a doe that senses danger.

He followed the line of her jaw with his lips, then nipped the lobe of her ear. "Kiss me back, love. Kiss me back."

He felt her exhale-inhale in quick succession.

Touching her chin with the crook of his finger, he stroked her lips with his thumb. "You might ought to breathe, as well."

He bent his head and this time she relaxed a bit. Need flooded him, but he held it in check. He just wanted a little taste. Well, that wasn't exactly true. But it was all he would allow himself.

Kissing her sealed lips, he slid his hands through her hair, down her back, and underneath to scoop her up onto his lap.

Raising his knees to better hold her, he felt her hands flutter about his shoulders before finally resting against his chest. He angled his head, deepening the kiss.

Her lips gently parted beneath his. Euphoria shot through him. By jingo, but she was sweet.

A soft sigh came from the back of her throat as her hands landed on his cheeks, where she held him securely in place.

But she needn't have bothered. He wasn't going anywhere.

She gently pushed him back, breaking their seal.

"Oh," she gasped, eyes round and filled with passion.

He quickly swooped back down, not wanting to give her an opportunity to question herself.

She squirmed.

Not yet. Not yet, Lord. Just a little more. Please?

But she wasn't trying to escape. She was trying to free her hands, and when she did, they were everywhere at once—racing along his arms, grazing his neck, stroking his hair.

Groaning in frustration, he knew he should keep his own hands firmly planted at the small of her back, but they would not obey. He kneaded her back, her shoulder blades, her waist.

Then slowly, ever so slowly, they crept up her sides and around until he held her within his palms.

She squeezed his shoulders. "Oh, oh. We should stop."

He froze but did not pull away.

She covered his hands with hers. Whether to restrain him or hold him in place wasn't clear. And then he knew. Knew that she wanted to stop but did not know how. And much as he'd like to go on, the damage afterward would be much worse than any pleasure they might derive—delectable though it might be.

Slipping his hands back down to the small of her back, he drew her close and simply held her, resting his lips against her hair. They stayed as such, allowing the tumultuous feelings rocking through their bodies to settle. And though he couldn't speak for hers, his never completely stilled.

He wanted this woman. Oh, how he wanted her.

He felt her take a shaky breath. "Poor Lissa. No wonder she surrendered. And he offered her marriage? In the midst of all this, he offered her marriage?"

Not exactly what he wanted to discuss at the moment. "Most likely," he replied.

He couldn't quite catch the title she assigned to Lissa's lover, but surely she didn't say what he thought she did.

He hugged her tight and smoothed her hair. "Hush. Don't think of it."

But he wondered if Rachel would've complied if he'd offered her marriage. No, she would not because he wouldn't ask it of her. Nor would he offer for her. He had no interest in entering into matrimony with anyone. No matter had badly he wanted her.

"I'm sorry," she mumbled against his shoulder. "I'm so sorry."

"You've nothing to be sorry for, love."

She shook her head. "I wasn't talking to you."

He absorbed the implication of that for a moment, then gave her backside a gentle pat. "Up you go. The rain has stopped."

She twisted around to see for herself and immediately became all atwitter—jumping from his lap, shaking out her skirt, cramming pins more securely into her hair, and reaching for her bonnet.

He got to it first. She paused.

"Don't," he said.

She looked up at him, and he hooked some hair behind her ear.

"We've both been wondering and now we know." He handed her the wet bonnet. "I'll not pressure you again. Okay? The next time, you will have to start it."

"I won't start it, Johnnie. I shouldn't have allowed it this time. Moral weakness is not to be tolerated. I'm supposed to be an example to the rest of society. How will Lissa ever see the light if I fornicate? How will the men of our town see the light?"

He grimaced. "Take the deuce, but I hate that word. We were not fornicating. We were merely kissing."

She shook her head. "Not in my mind, Johnnie. In my mind, I did much more than kiss you. And the leap from thought and word to something actually happening is very short indeed."

Heat rushed through him. She had fantasies about him? Was that what she was saying? Sweet merciful heavens. What was she thinking to reveal such a thing to him? Hadn't her mother taught her anything?

"How old were you when your mother died?"

She looked away for a moment. "Thirteen. Lissa was nine."

Well, that certainly explained a lot. "Who said you were responsible for all of society? Or for anyone other than yourself?"

She blinked. "Why, everyone. I can't think of one matron in our entire church back home who didn't stress such sentiments. Even my etiquette books gave instructions on such things. A woman's public image must be flawless. Any departure from propriety is a sign of vulgarity."

Coming from a woman who collected bugs and wore breeches. "Have you committed your Bible to memory the way you have these etiquette books?"

"I haven't memorized the whole thing, if that's what you mean. But I know I'm not to make anyone stumble. I know I have a responsibility to my weaker brothers and sisters."

"Seems to me like you've sure taken on an awful lot. I thought that's what your God was for. Why not give all this to Him and quit worrying about it?"

She fingered the wet bonnet in her hand. "Like you?"

He stiffened. "Who said anything about me?"

She closed the distance between them. "That's not how it works, you know. You can't just throw the obligations you have toward others and society at His feet in order to free yourself up to do whatever you please without any regard for your conscience."

How in the blazes had they gotten from fornication to theology? Well, however it happened, he wanted nothing to do with it.

He gently tugged her against him. "I'm just saying that stealing a kiss now and then isn't some mortal sin."

"And I'm just saying I want to stay within the boundaries God has set for me. Not only that, but it is my moral obligation to be an example to the men and women of this town. And do you know what I think? I think a great many of them are possessed of good principles. I think that by constantly interacting with those who are less stringent morally, they imbibe in customs that back home would have been quite revolting to their natures."

"What a great bunch of foolishness."

"What they need is somewhere they can go. A place that offers something other than drinking and gambling. Like my restaurant."

This was even worse than talking theology.

She skimmed the stubble on his jaw with her knuckles. "I'm leaving you, Johnnie."

He tensed. "What do you mean?"

"I'm moving into my restaurant tomorrow. I hope to open it in another couple of weeks, and when I do, it will be an alcohol-free place where the men can come for a home-cooked meal."

"Tomorrow? You're moving out tomorrow? What about my hotel?"

"I guess it's time to hire someone else to clean it."

"No one will clean it the way you do."

She offered him a slight smile. "That's probably true."

"Why can't you still live in the shanty?"

She didn't answer.

He splayed his hands and increased the pressure at her waist. "I like having you in the shanty."

She tucked her chin. "I like being there."

"Then stay."

"I'm sorry."

He knew she'd been working hard on her new place, yet this decision to move tomorrow had come out of nowhere and he'd not been at all prepared for it. But what could he do? Nothing. Not one blasted thing.

"Is that place even habitable?" he asked.

He felt her huff. "By San Francisco standards, anything with four sides and a roof is more than habitable."

He moved his lips to her hair and inhaled. So sweet.

"My trees?" he asked.

"I'll only be serving lunch at first, so if you'd like, I can still tend to your trees in the late afternoon."

He didn't examine too closely the bit of relief that statement invoked. He could attribute it to concern for his trees, but he knew better. And it was a Pandora's box he had no wish to open.

She took a step back. He released her and watched as she pulled on her bonnet. Its wet rim drooped in front of her eyes.

He lifted it up with a finger and peeked beneath. "I don't think it's going to do you much good. Why don't you wait and put it back on just before we get to town?"

Biting her lip, she slipped it off. "All right," she whispered.

Threading his fingers with hers, he led her from their hideaway and back to the horses.

chapter 15

The shock of Rachel leaving him high and dry with no one to cook and no one to clean had finally worn off. And in its place had come hurt, then anger. He'd been doing fine without those things before she arrived in San Francisco, but now the boys had gotten used to clean bedding and he had gotten used to her cooking. To her very presence.

The least she could have done was give him a little notice. But she hadn't so much as darkened his door since she left two weeks ago. He knew she had been going out to his property to care for the plants, but it hadn't been with him.

Johnnie shuffled, cut, and reshuffled the deck of cards. "Your cut," he said to the man named Isaac in a red cap and scarlet flannel shirt.

Isaac cut the cards and Johnnie whisked them up. Maybe it was for the best that she had taken her pure-as-snow, tightly corseted, buttoned-to-the-neck self somewhere else.

He flipped over the first two cards. "Jack and deuce. Make your bets."

He'd been married once already to the holier-than-thou type and found their expectations were hard to live up to. Not only that, but when push came to shove, it turned out their kind wasn't so holy after all. They were nothing but hypocrites.

The players relaxing around the table staked ounce after ounce upon the jack.

Rachel was a sunbonnet woman, and he hadn't seen one in a while. So long, in fact, he'd forgotten what a trial they were. Well, no more.

He tried to push her from his thoughts, but his patrons wouldn't allow it. Expounding on her activities had even taken precedence over talk of making California a state.

He threw out two more cards.

"She still at it, Clyde?" Jonah asked.

Clyde, choosing to watch Rachel from his vantage point at the front window rather than play a round of monte, dug inside his nose with a fat stubby finger. "She's still at it. That gal shore is somethin'."

"I done told her I'd hammer those boards back in place, but she ran me right off the place."

Clyde wiped his finger on his backside. "Oh, I'm a thinkin' that I'm the one what could help her with a thing or two."

Johnnie glared at the circle of dirty, unshaven men and checked his irritation. Why should he care what they said about her?

He could see that Geoffrey didn't feel the same, though. The man may have been dressed in miner's garb like the rest, but he used to be a fancy lawyer out east somewhere.

"You shouldn't speak of a lady in such a way," Geoffrey interjected. "She deserves our utmost respect, even if she is not within hearing distance."

The men looked at each other sheepishly and Clyde turned downright red.

Johnnie rapped his knuckles on the table. "All down, gents?"

"Hold onto yer hats, boys," Clyde cried, whipping *his* hat off and smoothing his hair back. "Here she comes."

The entire table threw their cards face down and crowded around the window. The men fell silent as each jockeyed for a position in front of the window. Johnnie tightened his lips. They were in the middle of a game, for crying out loud.

"Oh. She's comin' this way."

"Shhh. Here she is."

Johnnie threw his cards down, as well, furious at his body's reaction to their words. His heart was beating, his hands were sweating, and his stomach clinched into a knot.

Rachel stopped in his doorway.

He rose to his feet. "You shouldn't be here."

Her gaze swept the room, snagging on his statue. The men had taken great delight in covering it up for her once Soda told them she wasn't allowed to.

Every day it had worn something different—calicos one day and flannels the next. Since she'd left, they continued their tradition but didn't worry so much about which parts were exposed and which weren't. Today, his Lorenzo Bartolini wore a set of suspenders. Nothing else.

A hint of humor touched her face. She curtsied to the clump of men packed beside the window. They made a spectacle of themselves whipping off their hats, elbows flying, while trying to bow when they were so congested.

She turned back to Johnnie. "Excuse me for interrupting. I was just wondering if Michael was here?"

"No."

She hesitated. "Oh. Well, if you see him, would you send him home please?"

"Is there something you needed, Miss Van Buren?" Isaac asked.

"Oh no. It can wait."

"You need us to tote somethin' fer ya?"

"Actually, I was trying to move my new stove to the opposite wall, but—"

An army of volunteers offered to help.

She glanced from Johnnie to the table of cards to the group of men.

"I would appreciate it very much. Thank you."

The entire roomful poured out the door to personally help her with her stove.

Disgusted, Johnnie stepped out onto the verandah. "Boys! You walk away from a game and you'll forfeit your gold, you will."

"Go ahead, Johnnie. You take it. We're gonna help Miss Van Buren."

Johnnie narrowed his eyes. That dad-blamed female just walked off with a whole hour's worth of business. The men disappeared inside her place.

His memory chose that moment to remind him Rachel had only been thirteen when her mother had died. And it was highly likely she'd not been told that God engineered her body to want and accept what a man had to offer. That there were good and excellent reasons a woman shouldn't allow certain liberties. Liberties similar to the ones she'd already allowed him.

He kept his eyes trained on the door. He knew she was fine. That particular group of rowdies would rather die than harm a hair on her head. But she was a sitting duck if somebody like Sumner got a hold of her. And there were plenty of them in this town.

Before long, the boys stumbled out her front door, talking all at once and heading toward the wharf, anxious he was sure, to spread the tale of how they had helped the sunbonnet with her new restaurant.

He strode to her property and through her door, which was set to the right of a huge bay window fronting her shop. He paused and closed the door softly behind him. The muffled noises of the Plaza soaked through the walls. The smell of lye and lime mixed with yeast and molasses. The plank floor running between him and the entry to the kitchen housed two long tables with benches on either side.

He frowned. All was quiet and still within the building. Perhaps she'd stepped out back. He skirted the tables and made his way to the archway that separated the serving room from the kitchen.

Rachel stood inside, back turned, admiring her stove. The apron bow tied at her waist drooped, its strings trailing over the curve of her skirts.

And that's all it took. Memories of her companionship and sweet kisses obliterated whatever notions he'd had of forgetting about her.

He studied the laboratory in which her very livelihood rested. Numerous sconces would provide excellent light. Narrow windows running along the upper edge of her east and west walls took advantage of the ocean breeze, which combined with the height of the ceiling, would provide maximum ventilation.

A door leading to the outside offered access without having to traipse through the dining area. And an alcove jutting off the back most likely held the scullery, pantry, and storeroom. Tucked into the opposite wall were a narrow set of stairs.

The piece of furniture holding court in the center of the west wall, however, was what held her rapt attention.

Rachel brushed her hands across the Leamington kitchener stove as if she were smoothing wrinkles from a tablecloth. It was said to surpass any other range in use for easy cooking by one fire.

And she could see why. It had a hot plate that would keep her vessels boiling without injuring their contents. The wrought-iron roaster had movable shelves, a draw-out stand, a double dripping pan, and a meat stand.

The roaster could also be converted into an oven by closing the valves, allowing her to bake breads and pastries in a superior manner.

Whoever owned the building must be working the gold mines. She could think of no other reason for leaving such a valuable piece behind, not to mention the rest of the furnishings.

She polished the large iron boiler with her apron skirt, running it over the brass tap and steam pipe, the round and square gridirons, and a set of ornamental covings with a plate warmer attached.

She had taken the stove apart piece-by-piece, cleaning, scrubbing, and oiling it until it worked and looked as good as new.

"You walked off with my customers."

She squealed and whirled around. How could she not have heard him enter? "Mercy, Johnnie, you scared me to death."

He said nothing.

"How long have you been standing there?"

He kicked up one corner of his mouth. "Long enough to wish I were that stove."

She shook out her apron. He'd said he wouldn't try to steal any more kisses, but he didn't have to. He could call them to her mind with a whispered word or a heated look.

Even now, the very picture he made looming in her doorway with one hip cocked, sleeves rolled up, and hat in hand upstaged even the stove.

And he was doing it again. Giving her one of his sleepy looks.

"Did you need something?" she asked.

He sucked in his breath. She tilted her head, trying to puzzle out why *he* looked so discomfited but could come up with no reasonable explanation.

He tossed his hat onto the pastry table. "Why have you been ignoring me?"

"Why are you building another saloon?"

"What? You mean the Parker House?"

"Is that what you are calling it?"

"The one on the corner?"

She propped her hands on her waist. "Exactly how many saloons are you in the process of building?"

He drew his brows down. "Just the one."

"Then obviously that's the one I'm talking about. That one on the corner." She pointed toward the northeast. "That metal two-story imitation of a country mansion."

"That's why you're ignoring me?"

"What do you think?"

He rubbed his lower lip with his hand. "You know, Rachel, it isn't a sin to run a gambling house or even to serve liquor."

"Not a sin? *Not a sin!*" She placed both hands on top of her head. "Gambling is an insidious art. And the drinking. The drinking is even worse."

"Get your Bible."

She lowered her hands. "What?"

"Go ahead. Go get your Bible. You show me where it says drinking and gambling are sins. You show me where it says that, and I'll shut her down today. This minute."

"Ephesians 5:18: 'Do not be drunk with wine.'"

"You ever seen me drunk?"

She moistened her lips. "No."

He nodded, as if accepting a compliment.

"You're serving it, Johnnie."

"Exactly. I'm serving it. You got any verses in that pretty little head of yours that say anything about serving it?"

"The very fact that you serve it encourages others to drunkenness."

Spinning toward the pastry table, he landed both hands on it and hung his head. He stayed there for several minutes before looking over at her. "I have absolutely no control over what the men of this town choose to do with their liquor."

She clasped her hands together.

He stood and leaned a hip against the table. "Listen, if you want to be this town's Holy Spirit, you go right ahead. But don't expect me to do the same."

She stiffened. "I am not trying to be anyone's Holy Spirit."

"Oh no?"

"No."

"Okay. Conscience. You trying to be anybody's conscience?"

Her mother's words whisked through her mind as surely as if that blessed woman were standing right there in the kitchen.

"The measure of a lady is determined by the success or failure of her husband and by her ability to encourage others to greatness."

"Only through encouragement."

"Ah, Rachel. It's an impossible task what you've set yourself up to do. Even God gives His people free will choice."

"Well, He doesn't serve temptation up to them on a silver platter."

He raised his brows. "Now you really do need to go get your Bible. I suggest starting with Genesis 3: Temptation of Man."

"Anyone can justify anything if they twist up their Scriptures enough."

He lifted a corner of his mouth. "Yes. They certainly can."

She tightened her lips. "If you don't mind, I need to go to the mercantile. We open tomorrow, and I have some supplies I need to pick up."

He drummed his fingers against his leg. "I came to get my storeroom key back."

She hesitated, then drew the key up through the neck of her dress before pulling it over her head.

His fidgeting stopped. His body straightened. His eyes darkened. Neither of them moved, then he took a step toward her.

She held out her hand, palm up, in the universal signal for stop. "No. No more of that. I'll be your friend, Johnnie, but nothing more."

"Because I run a gambling house that serves liquor?"

"Among other things."

"What other things?"

He knows you, Lord. And you know him. And you want him back, don't you?

She lowered her hand. "You've forsaken your greatest friend of all, Johnnie. How can I, knowing that, feel secure in a serious relationship with you?"

He winced. "One has nothing to do with the other."

"It has everything to do with everything."

He held out his palm.

She took a step, and then another, until she was close enough to place the key in his hand.

He closed his fist over it. "I miss you."

Her mouth relaxed. Whatever she'd imagined him saying, it wasn't that.

"Do you miss me?" he asked.

You have no idea.

"Answer me," he said.

She slowly nodded her head.

"The city's first concert is tomorrow night at the schoolhouse."

"I saw that. In the paper. An evening of song, piano music, and 'comic recitations,' it said."

"Go with me?"

Her heart flip-flopped. *O Lord. Why couldn't he still be a missionary?*

"I'm sorry, but thank you."

His gaze never wavered from hers. "Scared?"

"Out of my wits," she whispered.

He brought the key to his mouth and kissed it.

Feeling an impact she dared not acknowledge, she took a deep breath. "We'll be serving our first meal tomorrow when I ring my bell at noon. Will you be coming?"

He put the key around his neck, letting it drop underneath his shirt. "Probably not, love."

"I'll not charge you. Seeing as we're neighbors and all."

He stood for long, tense moments staring. Delving into her very soul with his penetrating gaze. "I think I'm falling in love with you, Rachel."

And then he turned and left.

———

Rachel and Michael filled the tables with platters of beefsteaks, hash, potatoes, bread, biscuits, and griddle cakes, along with tea and coffee, then rang a loud, heavy bell that Michael had found on an abandoned ship.

Men poured in from all quarters, each measuring out three dollars in dust as if it were no more than five pennies. When all were settled about the table, Michael offered a prayer, the conclusion of which signaled a scramble of hands, arms, and elbows.

Dishes flashed by in a blur, foodstuffs slid from platters to plates, crisp commands punctuated the air.

"Taters."

"Bread."

"Steak."

"Coffee."

On it went until all were served and shoveling food into their mouths. The cacophony of sounds from moments before dissolved into slurping, chomping, and burping.

Michael and Rachel stood unmoving, then slowly turned to each other.

"Looks like we're in business, Miss Van Buren."

She allowed a smile to stretch across her face. "So it does, Mr. Van Buren."

"Who's gonna wash all those dishes?"

Her smile broadened. "You and me, sir. You and me."

"What do you think about hiring on some help?"

"I think at three dollars a plate, we could hire the Queen of England if we wanted to."

————

Rachel turned her head to the side, trying to see her coif in the tiny looking glass hanging above her toilet table. Oh, what she would give for the full-length mirror that had graced her dressing room back home.

And she desperately missed the big feather bed she'd had when renting Johnnie's shack. But such lavishness was no longer to be had, for she now made do with a cot and a blanket.

The toilet table before her was no more than a trunk elevated by two claret cases and draped with neatly fringed blue linen. Across its top she had placed a rosewood workbox, two Chinese ornaments of exquisitely carved ivory, and a Bohemian glass cologne stand—all token items she'd brought with her from New Jersey.

She smoothed her hand along the twist of hair pinned tightly to the back of her scalp, then reached for her made-over bonnet. She had covered it with green taffeta ribbon and a garland of cherries.

Carefully fitting it on her head, she tied a large bow beneath her chin, dipping and turning to see how she looked in her reseda-green cambric dress. She'd not worn it since arriving but had saved it for a special occasion.

Tonight's concert at the schoolhouse and the grand opening of the Cottage Café certainly warranted a bit of extravagance.

Moving to a little pine table beside her bed, she briefly scrutinized the oilcloth she had tacked over its top, pleased once again with its result. Pine had such a dreary look about it that she'd not only wrapped her table but also a wide bench that stood at the foot of her bed. Its neat plaid covering gave it an almost sofalike look.

Cupping the lantern on the table, she blew out its flame. Then did the same with the sconces on either side of her looking glass. The warming stove in the corner, with braided rug at its feet, held no fire as of yet, and she paused one last time before leaving the sanctuary of her very own room.

Michael had installed windows that could be rolled open, inviting the ocean's breeze right into her chamber. The calico curtains draped along the window's edges waved as if shooing her out the door.

Turning down the wick, she extinguished a genuine gas fixture mounted alongside her door and hurried down the hall to tap on Michael's door. "Are you coming?"

"Be right there," he answered.

Lifting her skirts, she negotiated the narrow stairs leading to the kitchen. All stood clean and quiet after their noonday meal.

It didn't seem quite right. This peacefulness. The world should have stopped and shared in her mourning of Lissa. Not a day went by that Rachel didn't think about her. Wonder about her.

Was she happy "playing house" up on that hill? Pretending she was married to that man? Cooking for him. Darning for him. Sharing with him something he had no right to receive?

But the world offered no answers, nor had it stopped spinning. Hadn't so much as hiccupped. Just kept gambling, drinking, and searching for gold.

Straightening a stack of plates, Rachel sighed and moved into the dining area.

The second pine-board table was the only piece of furniture she'd had to purchase. Oh, how she wished she could have decorated it with some daylilies or buttercups, but of course, there were none to be had.

Biting her lip, she took a seat, folded her hands, and examined the room. The barren walls with two lonely screens of painted roses looked stark and uninviting, but the room had come alive as soon as the men entered it.

She had calculated what she must charge for each meal based on the cost of its ingredients plus profit. The resulting figure bordered on the indecent, so expensive it was. Yet, with eggs costing three dollars each, sugar, tea, and coffee at four dollars per pound, and meat priced up through the roof, she'd really had no choice.

She'd hinted to Michael that they were quite comfortable financially, but the truth of it was they'd have to be very, very frugal in order to pay their rent, pay for their supplies and sundries, and hire some help.

Which meant Michael still needed to find odd jobs and she still needed to work on Johnnie's property. She'd best not do it on Sundays when he was there. As close as he had come to a declaration yesterday and as close as she'd come to admitting the same, it would not be at all wise.

She gripped her hands together. Just thinking of the way he looked and of the words he'd said created a flurry of activity inside her stomach.

"Rachel?"

Yelping, she spun around, nearly unseating herself in the process. Johnnie had poked his head and shoulders inside the front door.

"What are you doing?" He stepped in, a baffled look in his eyes.

She quickly stood, smoothing her skirts. "I was, um, praying."

"She was daydreaming," Michael said, coming through the back entryway. "I'd bet my boots we'd have opened two days earlier if we could get back the hours she's spent ruminating over who knows what."

"*Michael!*" She seared him with a look so intense, even he received the silent message and held his tongue. For all the good it did her.

Stiff with humiliation, she could not bring herself to look at Johnnie. And what was he doing here anyway? She'd already told him she wouldn't allow him to escort her to the concert.

And if he thought to casually walk over to the schoolhouse with her and Michael, then he had another think coming. Even though the three of them would know he wasn't her escort, no one else would.

She heard Michael walk past and open the door. "I'll see you there."

"Wait," Johnnie said. "I need you to wait on the porch. Your sister will need an escort."

"Aren't you taking her?"

"Not this time."

"Then who are those flowers for?"

Flowers? she thought. Had he brought her some lupine? But the sting of embarrassment kept her from looking up to see.

"Just wait on the porch, Michael. She'll be out in a minute."

The door closed, then silence.

Johnnie moved into her line of vision several steps back from the table that she hovered behind. Still, she kept her chin tucked.

That didn't keep her from admiring the tight-fitting gray kersey-mere trousers he wore, though. They must have been new. She'd never seen them before. The legs of the pants covered his boots, strapping under the heels to hold them down.

She watched his knees bend as he lowered himself to the point where he could look back up into her face. "I came to congratulate you on your day's success. The boys have done nothing but talk about it all afternoon. They especially enjoyed the mince pie you served for dessert."

He straightened, and she could not keep from following his progress. The jacket he wore was no ill-fitting ready-made coat of cheap material and cut. Clearly, the wool frock had been custom made by a gifted tailor.

His tucked linen shirt held tiny single pleats running from neck to waist with a cravat of the same fine linen at his throat.

This was no gambler's garb he wore, but something any gentle-man back home would be proud to own. She continued her trek up, finally resting in the solace of his gaze.

O Lord. He's absolutely beautiful.

"I wondered if there were any leftovers." His attention moved to her lips. "Have you a sweet for me?"

"Yes, actually, I do," she answered.

He moved toward her, bringing out the hand he had hidden behind his back, a huge cluster of delicate cream-colored syringas in his grasp. "Congratulations."

Her gaze flew to his even as she moved around the table to accept his offering. "Oh. Wherever did you find them?"

The most penetrating and unique fragrance wafted about her. Closing her eyes, she held them against her nose.

"They are as common as dandelions in the mining camps upriver," he answered. "A couple of men by the names of Audubon and Crocker brought these in with them today."

"Audubon the naturalist?"

He shrugged.

"Well, they're beautiful, Johnnie. Thank you ever so much." She brushed a bloom with her knuckle. "I'm going to go put these in a pitcher of water, then I'll be right back with that piece of pie."

"No. No pie. You'll be late for the concert. I'll get it later."

When she returned to the dining area, he was nowhere in sight.

She stepped out onto the platform. "Where's Johnnie?"

Michael pulled his pacing up short. "He's already left. Come on, the place is filling up fast."

Taking her brother's arm, she glanced at the schoolhouse. A mass of flanneled backs crisscrossed by suspenders crowded the door. When the two of them arrived, however, the men immediately doffed their hats, parted like the Red Sea, and allowed them to enter.

chapter 16

*R*achel pressed a handkerchief to her nose upon crossing the threshold of the packed-to-capacity schoolhouse. A nauseating perfume of sweaty, unwashed, alcohol-ridden men pervaded the room.

She waited until Michael paid a man at the entrance for admittance to the event. Seats were five dollars, standing room three dollars, women free of charge. She heard the doorman inform her brother that every seat had been taken except those on the front row, left side of the aisle, which had been reserved for women.

She scanned the room looking for Johnnie but could not locate him among the masses, for the entire populace had come to their feet upon her entering. Michael took her arm, led her to the front, and faltered when she came to a standstill.

On the left side of the front row sat four women. All extravagantly, yet tastefully, dressed. All women of fair but frail natures. She could not, would not, sit side-by-side with them.

A handsome, even dashing, gentleman on the first row, right hand side, quickly swooped into a bow. "If it pleases you, miss, I would be honored to offer you a seat."

Every tongue stilled and every eye in the place focused upon the unfolding scene. Troubled, she looked earnestly at the man before her.

Large disheveled curls framed a fine clean-shaven face with a patrician nose and a kind mouth.

"But, sir," she said, "you must have surely come at the earliest of hours to acquire a seat in such a coveted location."

"I insist."

She smoothed the concern from her face and curtsied. "Then I insist you visit my café for a free meal. Our grand opening was this very day."

He extended a hand to help her rise from her curtsy. "You are the proprietress of the new Cottage Café, then?"

"I am." She placed her hand in his and glanced at Michael.

He stepped forward. "May I present to you my sister, Miss Rachel Van Buren?"

The gentleman brought her fingertips to his lips, brushing them as quickly and lightly as a delicate butterfly. "Enchanted."

He then held his hand out to Michael. "Henry Crocker of Minisink, New York."

"Michael Van Buren of Elizabeth, New Jersey. Rachel? Mr. Crocker."

She lifted her brows. "Are you, sir, by any chance, working with the naturalist John Audubon?"

A glorious smile broke wide across his face. "I'm working with his son, Woody."

She crinkled the handkerchief she still held in her hand. "Good heavens. Do you share his enthusiasm for flora and fauna?"

"I am but a student to his master, but yes. I have trunks full of painted specimens of the most fascinating nature that I stumbled upon during my crossing here from New York."

"Oh. I would love to see them."

His eyes lit up. "It would be my honor to share them with you." His gaze moved to something behind her, and he bowed.

She turned and sucked in her breath. There on the arm of Mr. Sumner stood her sister in an exquisite gown of silk so full from the crinoline beneath, it brushed both sides of the aisle. Her left finger remained glaringly ringless.

"Good evening, Rachel," Lissa said. "Your bonnet is a lovely accent for the green. Hello, Michael."

Michael leaned over and kissed her cheek yet cut her escort cold, allowing not even a flicker of acknowledgment to cross his face. Rachel had no notion what to do. She realized now that she had unwittingly become the before-show entertainment and paled.

Michael quickly grasped her elbow and lowered her into the seat Mr. Crocker had vacated.

Sumner moved past them and seated Lissa next to the Cyprians on the left. Immediately, the five women greeted one another as if long lost friends. The men in the rest of the room lowered themselves back into their chairs.

Rachel felt as if she had been sucked into a vacuum so deep and so dark never would she ascend. Closing her eyes, she tried to quell the nausea in her stomach. She dabbed her handkerchief along her hairline, then against her lips.

The distinctly feminine whispered exchanges from across the aisle assailed her ears, though she could not ascertain their actual words.

Something cold tickled her hand. She opened her eyes. Johnnie stood before her pressing a tin cup of cooled water against her fingers.

Greedily she took it in her grasp and sipped from it, allowing it to soothe her throat, her stomach, her hurt. She gave it back to him, conveying a very private thank-you with her eyes. One meant only for him.

He unobtrusively squeezed the fingers she held the cup with, then strode down the aisle and out of her view. She fixed her attention on the upright piano protruding at a right angle from the wall. A teacher's desk had been shoved against the west wall and held three men atop it.

Mr. Massett, in a fine frock coat and dark wool trousers, entered with a flourish and introduced himself as a gentleman from New York City who now resided in a shack along the road leading to Washerman's Lagoon.

Flipping his jacket tails behind him, he took a seat in front of the piano and performed many of his own ballads, applying gusto and drama to his melodious voice. The miners gestured, whistled, and stopped just short of firing their pistols in an uproarious show of approval.

For his recitations, Mr. Massett delighted the company with a comedic imitation of an elderly woman and a German girl applying for positions of soprano and alto singers in a Massachusetts church choir. His audience injected shouts and encouragement throughout.

The finale consisted of a full rendition of "Yankee Town Meeting," in which Mr. Massett most effectively played all seven parts.

As the audience leapt to their feet for a resounding ovation, Rachel politely joined them. The evening should have been one of the highest points since her arrival, but the presence of her sister mere feet away aligning herself openly and publicly with used women obliterated any pleasure the evening had to offer.

She had spent every moment in prayer—beseeching, interceding, grieving. She could not wait to escape the suffocating sensation the closed-in room impressed upon her.

As soon as decently possible, she turned and scurried down the aisle and out the door, not pausing for even a moment to locate Michael. She all but ran across the Plaza and into the café.

As soon as she crossed the threshold and closed the door, she fell to her knees and covered her face with her hands, keening with deep anguished cries. She felt a quick breeze as the door opened, then quickly shut. The bolt clicked loudly into place.

Then Johnnie was there, holding her, rocking her. Did his intuitiveness have no bounds? How had he known that it had taken every bit of strength in her body to sit through that concert while seeing Lissa from the corner of her eye? Watching her laugh, sway to the music, even put two fingers in her mouth and whistle with the best of them?

Moaning, she pulled away from him and rose to her feet.

"Are you all right?" he asked.

"No. If you'll excuse me?"

"Rachel."

"Good night, Johnnie. And . . . thank you."

She left him standing in the dining room and strode straight to her room, as sure as a cicada nymph in its totally black underground chamber, for she had nary a light to guide her.

Falling onto her cot—bonnet, shoes, and all—she grabbed the ends of the coverlet and flipped it over her like a fruit tart, then curled into a ball and pleaded with the Lord to hear her cries, to intervene in Lissa's life, and to destroy her enemy.

———

Rachel woke in the wee hours of the morning listening to the revelers outside her window. Oh, how she longed for just one night of normalcy. A night with sounds of crickets and frogs and nocturnal animals. A gentle breeze with the smell of fresh sweet corn on its wings. A garden in the back with tomatoes, snap beans, and cucumbers. An innocent and guileless sister whose worst sin was to curl up in the window seat reading Shakespeare by candlelight when she was supposed to be sleeping.

Sitting up, Rachel shuffled to the toilet table and retrieved her buttonhook. She allowed her shoes and clothing to drop to the floor in a heap, leaving them there while she slipped on her nightdress and crawled back into bed—this time underneath the covers.

She took out every action and reaction she'd had since arriving in California, trying to discover what she should have done differently. Where she went wrong. What she needed to do now to resolve the situation with Lissa.

"Fornication and all uncleanness or covetousness, let it not even be named among you.... The wrath of God comes upon the sons of disobedience.... Let no one deceive you with empty words.... Do not be partakers with them.... Not to keep company with anyone who is sexually immoral ... not even to eat with such a person."

Bits and pieces of Scripture pelted like rain, until together they formed a dense, murky puddle. Exhaustion tugged at her lids, promising relief from worry, release from guilt. And before she succumbed to its narcosis, the thought of what she must do came to her.

———

Rachel stared at the back of the "No Prostitutes" sign she had propped in the storefront window, then returned her attention to the couple who had inquired about work. They were cousins and had journeyed from Texas to a mining camp near Sacramento, where the woman's husband had died of exposure.

They sipped their coffee, and Rachel, having made her decision, outlined her new employees' duties. Frank was a tall, muscular man with a long face and long teeth. His eyes drooped—at the top, eyelids hid a third of his dull brown irises, while at the bottom they revealed nothing but the whites—giving him the impression of a sad hound dog. Rachel judged him to be in his late twenties.

The newly widowed cousin, Selma, was a shy girl with soft hazel eyes, light curly hair, and a solemn mouth.

Rachel set down her cup. "Well, then, when can you start?"

Frank lifted his brows. "How does right now sound?"

"Marvelous." She stood, escorted them to the kitchen, and put them to work.

Though Frank's main chore would be to manage rowdy customers, in the meanwhile, he took care of toting, scrubbing, and chopping. Rachel concentrated on food preparation, and Selma proved to be extremely adept at the cooking. Michael did, more or less, whatever he was asked by whomever needed him most.

"Hullo?"

The call came from the front room. Rachel glanced at the others.

"Would you like me to chase whoever it is out?" Michael asked.

"No, I'll take care it." She wiped her hands on a damp towel, then moved to the dining area.

"Mr. Crocker."

He stood just inside the door jacketless, hatless, and hopelessly stiff. His curly hair fell across his forehead in several different directions. A large flat leather satchel hung from his fist.

"Come in, come in," she said. "It's so good of you to stop by."

His shoulders relaxed. "Am I interrupting? I was going to wait until you opened, but then I wanted to show you my paintings and thought you would be too busy to look at them during the meal."

"Yes, you are quite right. And I would have been dreadfully disappointed. Those are your paintings?" She indicated his satchel with a nod of her head.

He hesitated. "How familiar are you with Audubon's paintings?"

"Very."

"Mine don't compare."

She patted the table with her hand. "Show me."

He laid his portfolio down and opened it to reveal an intricate painting of two birds, one a deep, rich brown, the other a lighter version of the first.

"Flycatchers," he said. "This dark one is the male."

"Oh look. It's like they have whiskers. This is the female, then?"

"Yes. They have a habit of wagging their tails and singing: *phé-be, phé-be, phé-be.*"

His soft, reedy rendition filled the room, the sound coating her with thoughts of trees and forests and home.

"Do you know more bird calls?"

"Many." He flipped the paper over, revealing beneath it an olive bird whose bright red eye zeroed in on a spider spinning its web.

She leaned close, squinting.

"It's a red-eyed vireo," he said.

"I was looking at the spider. It looks a bit like a black-and-yellow garden spider with those markings, but I can't be certain."

At his silence, she looked up, then felt her face heat. His eyes had grown wide.

"Excuse me," she said. "Please continue."

"How is it that you can identify a spider with one glance?"

She twirled her hand round. "Oh, I'm sure I'm mistaken. It was just a guess."

"On the contrary, you are quite right. Are you a naturalist?"

"Mercy, no. My penmanship is horrid. I've never even attempted to draw. I cannot imagine." She tightened the bow at the back of her apron. "Besides, I'm not a bird watcher so much as an . . ."

A smile played at his lips. "As an . . . ?"

Oh heavens. She couldn't very well say *an insect watcher.* "Nothing. Really. What's next?"

Thankfully, he was too polite to press her and showed her the rest of his paintings without incident.

"They are beautiful," she breathed. "And you are right, your style is a bit different from the Audubons', but I wouldn't say inferior. I would say yours are more vibrant." She traced the edges of the paper. "More lively. Why, just look at these barn swallows. This one is practically squashing the other one."

His face turned a deep shade of red.

She suppressed a smile at his show of modesty. "Can you chirp the way they do?"

"Their calls vary depending on their purpose."

"What would these two sound like?"

He emitted a very satisfied sounding chirp.

"Oh my. They must be pleased with themselves."

"Yes, well." He cleared his throat.

"I confess, though," she said, "I've never been too terribly fond of swallows."

"No? Why is that?"

"Because they have to catch tens of thousands of insects to feed their young. Why, they can clean out a garden of its insects in a day's time."

He folded his portfolio and tied it closed. "Most people appreciate that."

She shrugged. "Not me."

"Well, then, that could only mean one thing."

"And what would that be?"

"You are a watcher of insects?"

She studied her fingernails, noticing the remnants of flour beneath them. "Do you think me silly?"

"I think you are most charming. So charming, in fact, I would like to know whom I must ask permission of to see you socially."

Oh dear. She hadn't expected that. He was handsome, certainly, and interesting. But she, well, just wasn't prepared for such a question.

"I spoke too soon."

"No, no," she said. "I, well, I had to think a moment of the person with whom you must speak. My brother, I suppose. He is my closest male relative."

"The one I met last night?"

"The same."

He bowed. "I will see to it, then."

"Oh. I didn't even offer you a single thing to eat or drink."

A grin spread across his face. "Then I suppose I'll just have to come back again, won't I?"

She offered him her hand. "I suppose you will. Good day, Mr. Crocker."

He kissed her fingertips. "Miss Van Buren."

———————

"Henry Crocker came by and asked me if he could court Rachel."

Johnnie paused in the polishing of glassware he and Soda had washed. "What did you tell him?"

Michael shrugged. "I said sure. I mean, why not?"

"Why not, indeed? Where is he taking her?"

"I don't know, but she told me to pick up a bottle of whiskey for her."

"A bottle of whiskey? For cooking purposes?"

"No. She has some kind of temper-thing that keeps her from cooking with any spirits."

"Temperance."

"That's right."

"Then does she need it for medicinal purposes?"

"No. She's as healthy as a horse."

Johnnie grabbed the edge of the bar and leaned forward. "Then what does she need whiskey for?"

"I don't know. Didn't ask."

"Don't you think you should? As her brother?"

Michael frowned. "Well, I don't usually do the asking around there. I usually do the answering."

"Does this whiskey have anything to do with Crocker?"

Scrunching up his lips, Michael took his time in answering. "I don't really know. He's picking her up after dark tonight, and she told me she needed it today. But that doesn't make any sense. Why would Crocker need Rachel to buy his whiskey for him? No, one probably has nothing to do with the other."

"And just where does he think he's taking her at such a late hour?"

"I don't know. She didn't say."

Johnnie threw down his rag. "Well, don't you think you should find out?"

"What's got you fired up all of a sudden? I've never asked you where you take her. So why would I ask Crocker?"

"Because Crocker has made his intentions clear."

"Well, that's a sight more than you've done. Maybe you ought to make your intentions clear. Just what are they, anyway?"

He stood stock still then pushed off the bar and started polishing again. Soda, he noted, had placed an unwarranted amount of attention onto his polishing.

"I haven't decided for certain," he said finally.

"Well, then, let Crocker have her. Seems like a nice enough chap to me. He goes to Sunday services, shaves, and is interested in all that nature stuff. That's bound to be better for her than some saloon owner."

"A virtual match made in heaven," he growled.

"Exactly."

"They still require a chaperone. You need to go with them."

Michael wrinkled his nose. "Tonight? I don't want to go tonight. Rachel gave me the day off. It's the first one I've had free since we opened."

"It's your duty. As her closest relative."

"Well, I'm not going. If you're so worried about it, you go."

Johnnie carefully placed the glass on the shelf behind the bar, then picked up another one. "Are you asking me to be your representative?"

"Now, don't start talking fancy. I'm not asking you anything. I'm just saying if you think it's so important that her and Crocker have a chaperone, then you go right ahead and chaperone."

Johnnie plucked a bottle of whiskey from below the counter and handed it to Michael. "Don't mind if I do."

Michael took the liquor and headed out the door.

"That whiskey's for your sister," Johnnie shouted after him.

Michael gave him a half-hearted wave before the door closed behind him.

c h a p t e r **17**

$\mathcal{I}$t had only been dark for about twenty minutes when Crocker arrived in front of her café with an open-top carriage. After jumping to the ground, he tapped on her door and was granted entry almost immediately.

Johnnie blew a stream of smoke from his cigar then sauntered over, stopping to stroke the muzzle of the horse harnessed to the hired conveyance.

He clamped his teeth around the cigar. The man had some nerve carting Rachel off after dark—alone—in a carriage. Just where were they going that they needed a carriage?

The door opened, and Rachel bounced out chattering without restraint. With one quick glance he noted she wore an old calico frayed along the edges. The kind she usually wore gardening.

Crocker's clothing was every bit as serviceable if not a bit more crisp. He closed the door, and they both came up short at seeing Johnnie.

"Evening." Johnnie bowed.

Rachel looked as if she'd been caught sneaking out her bedroom window. She hastily adjusted a checkered cloth covering the large basket slung over her elbow. But he could still see the outline of a whiskey bottle tenting the cloth.

"Why, Johnnie," she said. "I'm sorry, but we're closed."

"I know." He formed a series of smoke rings, each traveling through the other. "Your brother's otherwise occupied, so as your closest neighbor and trusted friend, he has asked me to chaperone."

"He *what?*" Indignation poured from her like champagne at a hurdy-gurdy show.

Crocker immediately stepped forward. "Good evening, Parker. I appreciate your willingness to join us. I confess, I had worried a bit over Miss Van Buren's reputation, so I am vastly relieved to have you along."

"No trouble whatsoever. Glad to be of service. Shall we?" Johnnie offered his hand to Rachel, not even trying to hide his smile. What could she do? With Crocker's endorsement, it would be nothing short of scandalous for her to rebuke him.

She eyed the horse, the carriage wheel, and his hand. "Could you hold the horse while I step up, please?"

"I have it," Crocker answered.

As soon as the man's back turned, she narrowed her eyes. "Don't you have a saloon to run?" she hissed under her breath.

He said nothing, just kept his hand out, palm up.

She slammed the basket into it and grabbed a huge amount of skirt into her grip, treating him to a view of serviceable boots and a good portion of calf. Placing a death clasp on the handhold, she all but hurtled herself up and onto the landing in front of the seat.

The horse whinnied and sidestepped. Rachel squealed, plopped onto the seat, and frantically gathered her skirt around her.

Crocker used both hands and soft words to soothe the horse.

Frowning, Johnnie snuffed his cigar with his boot and climbed in beside her. "What's the matter with you?"

"I hate carriages and I hate you," she quipped under her breath.

She hated carriages? What was wrong with carriages? But Crocker mounted from the other side, sandwiching Rachel between them and keeping Johnnie from questioning her further.

He relaxed, stretching his arm along the seat back behind both her and Crocker, and allowed his legs to fall open, his left thigh bumping intimately against her right.

She grabbed the basket from his lap and in the process unobtrusively shoved his leg away from hers. He allowed it to fall back, this time exerting enough pressure to let her know he wasn't going anywhere.

Crocker unwrapped the reins and gave the horse a quick slap. They lurched forward. With her hands full of basket, Rachel had no way to steady herself. Johnnie grabbed her shoulder and pulled her up against him until the horse settled into a steady trot.

She dug her elbow into his side.

He blew in her ear.

She whipped her head around to sear him with a look so full of antipathy it would've killed a lesser man.

He squeezed her shoulder, gave her a slow wink, and mouthed a kiss before releasing her. She immediately tried to scoot away from him. He casually placed one finger against her shoulder.

She glanced at him.

Keeping his attention on the road, he gave her a slight negative shake of his head, then removed his finger from her shoulder. She might be as rigid as a fence post, but it was his side she stayed plastered against. Not Crocker's.

"So, tell me about your trip over, Henry," Johnnie said. And for the rest of the ride Johnnie plied the man with question after question, giving Rachel no chance to participate.

In the meanwhile, Johnnie used every opportunity to steady her when they hit a bump, lean into her when making a point with Crocker, caress her when her companion wasn't looking.

She stiffened. She squirmed. She caught her breath.

At one point, Crocker interrupted his discourse. "Would you like to stop and rest for a bit, Miss Van Buren?"

"No." She swallowed. "No, thank you. I'm fine."

Johnnie leaned slightly across her. "She's not much for carriages," he confided, grazing her neck with his thumb. "Are you, my dear?"

His face was a mere inch from hers. She tightened her lips.

"Oh, I had no idea," Crocker said. "You must forgive me."

"It's quite all right," she said. "We're almost there."

And over the next rise, Johnnie's very own property loomed. He frowned. Just what were they coming out here for? It was way too dark to show Crocker the trees.

When they pulled up, Crocker and Johnnie both vaulted to the ground. Rachel immediately shifted over toward Crocker's side of the seat, so Johnnie grabbed the horse and watched her escort gallantly offer her a hand.

It was just as well. Had Johnnie been assisting her, he'd have hauled her down by the waist, and the temptation to pull her against him on her way to the ground would have been too much. His game would have been up for certain.

As Crocker kept up an entertaining dialogue, Johnnie found himself liking the man more and more. Had the circumstances been different, they might have been friends. But Crocker posed the first real threat yet.

All the other men coming through town were too rough, too reckless, or already married to women back home. Crocker was educated, a naturalist, and quite debonair.

He wasn't coming to find gold but to record for posterity paintings of birds and wild animals. A life that would very much suit Miss Rachel Van Buren.

So why was he trying to sabotage her chances with such a perfect find?

Crocker retrieved a lantern from underneath the seat, then followed Rachel to whatever destination she had in mind. The full moon offered just enough light to see by.

Johnnie, content for now to watch and listen from here, scratched the horse's chin. But if they ventured much further, he'd move in.

They stopped and set down their supplies.

"Shall I light the lantern?" Crocker asked.

"Not yet," she whispered, their voices carrying across the meadow to Johnnie's ears with no trouble.

Crocker uncorked the whiskey. Johnnie frowned. Rachel held a jar up to him, and when Crocker poured a small bit for her, Johnnie's feet moved of their own volition.

But she didn't drink any. Instead, she took a square of cloth and dropped it into the jar. He hesitated.

She relinquished the jar to Crocker, then pulled from her basket a *petticoat?* Johnnie surged forward.

No sooner had he reached them than she thrust the undergarment into Johnnie's arms.

"Here," she said. "Hold this a minute, would you?"

A strong fragrance of vanilla wrapped about him like a boa constrictor, having much the same effect. He couldn't breathe, couldn't move, couldn't think.

Only feel. The supple fabric caressed his arms. The knowledge that this intimate garment once sheltered her long limbs played havoc with his body. His fingers rubbed the edges of the hem, snagging his calluses.

Crocker took no particular notice of the garment at all. How could he not notice? How could he stand there unaffected?

And why did that make Johnnie angry and relieved all at the same time?

Because I'm in love with her. And have been for some time.

He held himself perfectly still. Maybe it was just lust. Heaven knew the woman drove him mad with wanting. But he'd wanted women before. Yet he'd had no desire to protect them, to share confidences with them, to grow old with them.

What made this one different? He scrutinized her. She was lovely, yes, but beauty faded over time. Why didn't that matter to him? Perhaps it was because she was so alone. So needy.

But most every woman he'd met since his wife's death had been alone in the world. So what was it? It couldn't be her deep faith. That was a negative, not a positive.

The last thing he wanted was to be strapped to a God-fearing woman. They were nothing but hypocrites bound by rules that no human could possibly adhere to.

Yet that wasn't true with Rachel. Not entirely. He saw how she hated the choices her sister had made, but still loved the girl. How she'd risked her own reputation to save her sister's. How she'd built an alcohol-free establishment that would offer future families a respectable place to go. How she'd fought the desires she felt toward him simply because she wanted to do what was right.

Yet never once had she blamed him for the feelings he stirred in her. She placed all responsibility at her own doorstep. What a cad he was to push her and take advantage of her weakness.

Crocker said something and she laughed. Johnnie squeezed his fists, crinkling the petticoat. He wanted to wrap his hands around Crocker's neck and rail at the man to leave her alone.

She belonged to him and nobody else. Nobody else. And for better or worse, that's the way it was going to be from now on.

He thought about his saloon. She'd want him to give it up. Well, she'd just have to get over that. He wouldn't ask her to give up her café. Why should he have to give up his place of business?

She'd want him to be a man of God. He took a deep breath. Going to Sunday services again wouldn't kill him. He'd do that much for her. He'd seen the way other women used to pity the matrons back home when their men refused to attend church.

Well, he wouldn't do that to Rachel. He'd go with her. Every single Sunday for the rest of his days. But he knew there was a world of difference between going to church and being a man of God.

A man of God, most likely, wouldn't run a gaming hall. But what would happen to Soda if he shut things down? To Carmelita? She'd have to go back to prostitution for certain. And Soda had nowhere to go. What kind of Christian would he be to turn them out on the street? Why, none at all.

Rachel materialized before him, tugging on her petticoat. In his mind, it was done. He wanted to shake on it—so to speak. He bent toward her.

She dug her nails into his arms. "Johnnie!" she hissed.

He blinked.

"Let go."

No. He'd never let her go. Never again. He shook his head.

She yanked on the petticoat. "*Let go.*"

His mind cleared. Crocker. He couldn't explain things to Rachel as long as Crocker was there.

Still, he didn't release her underskirt. "I will not," he whispered. "He'll see it."

She looked at him as if he'd lost his senses. "See what? Whatever are you talking about?"

"Your intimate wear. As your chaperone, I cannot allow such a thing. What do you need it for?"

"To catch insects. What do you think I need it for?"

Her answer so confounded him, he loosened his hold. She whipped the garment from him and strode back to Crocker.

"Light the lantern," she commanded.

Johnnie furrowed his brows. Crocker lit the lantern and placed the globe over the flame.

She started to hand the man her petticoat.

"Stop right there," Johnnie shouted.

The two jumped apart. Johnnie grabbed it from her.

"Oh, for heaven's sake," she said. "You hold it then." She spread her arms out wide. "Like this."

He wadded it up. "I will not."

"You are wasting our light. Now quit being such a ninny and hold it open. What on earth is the matter with you?"

"No man will lay his eyes on this garment." He looked at Crocker. "I will not allow it."

Crocker still held the lantern, and Johnnie could see comprehension dawn. He knew. He knew exactly why Johnnie was objecting so strenuously.

A slow smile spread across Crocker's face. "Would it help if I turned my back?" He didn't wait for an answer but simply turned around.

Rachel wrenched the petticoat from Johnnie. "There. Now hold your hands out wide."

Never had he wanted to kiss a woman so bad in his life. He glanced at Crocker's back but decided against it. He spread his arms wide.

Shaking out the garment, she turned it upside down and grasped its hem. She placed one end in his left hand. When she stretched to place the other end in his right, he closed both arms about her, petticoat and all.

She gasped. He gave her a quick, hard squeeze before releasing her.

She stood for a moment, thoroughly befuddled. "I need you to stand back-to-back with Mr. Crocker, please."

He complied, holding the petticoat wide.

"Can you move the lantern to your right, Mr. Crocker, so your body doesn't block the light?"

He did so.

Bugs swarmed against the white undergarment. She looked around, locating the whiskey jar. The piece of fabric had completely absorbed the liquid, but Johnnie could smell the fumes from here. She began flicking insects from her petticoat into the jar.

"I do believe, Miss Van Buren, you are getting those bugs drunk," Johnnie said.

"Insects," she corrected.

He smiled. "Why do you want inebriated bugs?"

"Insects. Because they'll be whole when they die and I won't damage anything with a pin."

His arms began to ache, but he held steady. Finally she stood, then looked at him, wary. Curious.

He winked.

She backed up, hit the basket with her heel, and would have lost her balance and her bugs, but he lurched forward and yanked her against him.

He pressed the petticoat to her waist. "Gather your things. It's time to go home."

———

Opening on Sundays had been a huge temptation. Especially since the men flocked to the saloons immediately after church.

Still, Rachel could not reconcile herself to working on the holy day. And this Sunday was no different. Pulling on her bonnet, she moved down the stairs and into the dining room.

She stopped short. Johnnie sat at one of her tables drinking coffee and reading the newspaper.

"What are you doing here?" she asked.

He drained his cup, folded his paper, and stood. "I'm escorting you to church."

"But I already have an escort."

He pulled on his jacket. "Don't you want me to go to church?"

She clasped her hands. "Well, of course I do."

"All by myself?"

She bit her lip. "No. It's just, well, Mr. Crocker is to escort me to church this morning."

Johnnie's shoulders relaxed. "Oh, is that all? Well, he won't be able to. He sent his profound regrets. Sorry if I can't remember the exact words he used."

She narrowed her eyes. "What happened between last night and this morning to change his mind?"

Flipping his hands palm up, Johnnie lifted his shoulders in a shrug.

"You said something to discourage him, didn't you?"

He glanced toward the kitchen. "Ah, Michael, there you are. Shall we, then?" He held out his arm.

"What did you say to him?"

Johnnie took hold of her hand and placed it in the crook of his elbow, holding it there while he all but dragged her to the door. "I have no idea what you are talking about."

Pulling at her hand, she freed herself. "I'll not go to church with you, Johnnie. He'll think I prefer your company over his."

He gave her a look that could melt butter. "You do, love. You do."

Michael opened the door. Both men stared at her expectantly.

"I'm not going with you, Johnnie. I mean it."

He studied her for a moment. "As you wish."

She waited until he crossed the Plaza and strode into the school-house before allowing Michael to escort her over.

The men jumped to their feet upon her arrival. Michael walked her down the center aisle to three open seats beside Selma and Frank. Johnnie stood next to one of them.

He smiled and held a chair for her. She had no choice but to sit down or make a scene. Fortunately, Mr. Crocker was nowhere in sight.

The sermon was excellent. She hoped Johnnie was paying attention.

After the service, he secured her to his side and expressed his appreciation to the minister, inquiring about the man's family. Supposedly, the preacher's wife was due to arrive in a few months. Johnnie suggested the four of them get together for dinner as soon as that momentous occasion occurred.

It seemed to Rachel that Johnnie knew every man in the room, and he took great pains to speak to each one of them. With the proprietary way in which he introduced her, it looked—and felt—as if they were a couple.

But they weren't. And she had no idea how to correct the impression. Well, she'd make sure it didn't happen again. As soon as she got him alone, she'd give him a piece of her mind.

And not just about this morning. About last night. The very idea of him acting as chaperone was absurd and manipulative. What did he think he was doing?

Yet when they left the schoolhouse, he didn't walk her to the café; he steered her toward the Parker House.

She tried to dig in her heels. "What are you doing?"

"I want to show you my new place. It opens tonight."

"You're opening on the Lord's Day?"

He said nothing, just continued steady on their course.

"I can't go in there," she said.

"Of course you can."

"I can't. It's a saloon."

"It's my home."

"What about your cabin behind the hotel?"

"It's still there."

And then they arrived. On his porch.

He held the door. "It hasn't opened, so it isn't officially a saloon yet."

She hesitated, then walked in totally unprepared for the tasteful and handsome interior. Gas chandeliers hung from the ceiling. An even wood floor gleamed from a recent polishing. Mirrors hung along the walls. A long L-shaped bar stretched along the side and back with an assortment of glassware, wine, whiskey, and she didn't know what all lining the shelves behind it.

Green felt tables occupied the open area of the vast room. Fresh flowers in a china vase graced a sideboard.

"This must have cost you a fortune," she murmured.

Disappointment washed over her upon spying his statue. It stood upon a raised platform in the corner, shamelessly and unrepentantly displaying its attributes.

Placing a hand against her waist, Johnnie guided her to his kitchen off the back. Larger than hers, it held a stove, a scullery, a storeroom, and work tables. A pot of coffee sat on a hot plate.

He poured them each a cup, then leaned his hip against a table. She collected her cup and took a sip.

"I love you," he said.

She swallowed down the wrong pipe, choking, coughing, spilling the brew she held in her hand.

He gave her a slight smile. "I see your cup overfloweth."

She set the drink down, pulled a handkerchief from her sleeve, and held it to her mouth. Sweet merciful heavens.

Braving a look, she froze. The man was dead serious.

He took another swallow. "Will you marry me?"

She didn't know what to do. What to say. The truth was, she loved him, too. She could admit that to herself now. But never would she act upon it. Not unless he was willing to make some major changes.

And from the looks of that gambling house they'd just walked through, he wasn't.

"Johnnie, I . . . I . . ."

He set his coffee down and pushed himself away from the counter. She took a step back, but he had a very long reach and easily captured her waist.

He pulled her ever so gently against him. "Say yes."

"No," she whispered, but her answer did not stop his descent, nor his kiss. And this kiss was the sweetest one yet. Slow, tender, and exquisitely sensual.

Oh, how she would love to learn the secrets of the marriage bed with him. He was such a good man. Deep down. But he was selling his soul for worldly things. And at some point, that would erode any respect she held for him. Any love she held for him.

She broke their kiss and took a step back but allowed his hands to rest against the curve of her waist.

Tears filled her eyes. "I'm sorry."

His hands tightened. "No. You can't just ignore what we have. I know you feel it. I know you do."

She nodded her head. "Yes, I do. I do. But I won't marry you, Johnnie. I can't."

His hands ran up and down her sides. "Things are different in California. What is a mite questionable in the East is perfectly respectable here."

She let the tears fall, not bothering to swipe them away. "God is still God in California. The Bible is still the Bible. And I am still me. I cannot do what you are asking me to do. I cannot be the wife of a man who nightly robs the last ounce of dust from men who've been accumulating it for months with the intention of sending it to their wives and children." The tears streamed, over her cheeks, around her jaw, down her neck, and into her ruffled collar. "I could never live on the profits of such a thing. It would kill me."

His Adam's apple bobbed. "It is my livelihood," he pleaded.

"I know," she blubbered.

"If I don't run this saloon, someone else will."

She nodded. "I know. I know."

He cinched her to him while she sobbed over the loss of something they both wanted so very, very much.

"I'll not take no for an answer," he said.

"I'll never say yes. Please don't tempt me beyond what I can bear."

"I will pressure you every waking moment. I will haunt your dreams. I will slay every competitor."

She pulled back, crinkling his lapels in her hands. "Oh, Johnnie. If you would only take all that stubbornness and channel it for the good. Then you and I both could have what we want."

"I just spent a fortune building that saloon."

"Who cares about that when it's eternity you should be investing in?"

He swooped down so fast she had no time to prepare. Never had a kiss been so fierce, so possessive, so all consuming. She tried to pull away, but he held her fast. And, truth be told, she wanted this kiss. Wanted something to remember, to take to bed with her at night.

So she answered him with an intensity of her own. But when his hands ventured where they oughtn't, she knew who must be the strong one.

Help me, Lord.

Get out of there. The thought was so strong, so powerful, she could not ignore it.

Yes. Yes. She wrenched herself from Johnnie's hold, spun around, and raced out the door.

The miners passing by stopped short. Without pause, she wove through the tangle of men congesting the square. Johnnie shouted her name.

But she didn't stop. Not until she was through the café door, up the stairs, and in the sanctuary of her room.

Throwing herself onto her cot, she hugged a pillow, pressing her face into it. The downy lump was a paltry replacement for what she really wanted.

chapter 18

Rachel didn't hear from Mr. Crocker for two weeks. When he finally ventured into the café, he told her he'd been out on an expedition and had several new paintings. She had agreed to look at them the following Sunday.

Which was tomorrow. Already. And still she could not work up any real enthusiasm for their appointment.

Johnnie had been by for coffee every morning since declaring his feelings. Bolting the door did no good; he'd come in the back. Refusing to sit with him did no good; he'd follow her around. Withholding conversation did no good; he'd talk enough for the both of them.

This morning was no different. So she just capitulated, poured herself a cup of coffee from the stove, and entered her dining area to find him reading his paper.

"Morning," he said.

"Good morning."

"What's the matter?"

She sat down. How could he tell from those two simple words that something was the matter?

"There's a ship leaving for New York this week," she said.

He folded the paper and laid it on the table. "Are you leaving?"

She stared out the window, unseeing. "No."

"Why not?"

Scraping a loose splinter of pine with her fingernail, she sighed. "I have a prodigal that needs a place to come home to. To leave her would be unthinkable."

He covered her hand with his. "I'm sorry, love."

Swallowing, she nodded and extracted her hand.

"I have something for you," he said.

She blew on her coffee.

Reaching under his chair, he brought out a glass jar with a whiskey-saturated cloth inside and slid it toward her. Setting her cup down, she lifted the jar, eyes widening.

"Oh, Johnnie." Standing, she quickly removed her apron, smoothed it out onto the table, and then popped the lid off the jar. The smell of whiskey burned her nose.

With gentle motions, she gave the jar a series of slight shakes until a dead bee with a bright, shiny green head and thorax tumbled out. "You brought me a green *Halictidae*."

He scratched his chin. "I did?"

"Yes, I'm not sure what species, of course, for we have nothing like this at home. I'm confident it's in the *Halictidae* family, though." Slowly sinking into her chair, she clasped her hands in her lap. "I can't accept it."

"You can't?"

"Heavens, no. I'm trying not to encourage you."

She leaned close and examined the black and yellow striped abdomen. Yet it was the sparkly, jolly green shade of the rest of its body that near took her breath away.

"Rachel?"

"Hmmm?"

"I risked life and limb to catch that pesky thing instead of squashing it dead."

She looked up.

"If you don't take it," he said, voice low, eyes dark, "I'll pitch it back in that jar and carry it up to your private room myself. And that, my dear, would be much more titillating than if you simply accepted this green hali-whatever-you-call-it."

She nibbled on the inside of her cheek. "That's blackmail."

His eyes didn't so much as flicker.

She turned the bee over with the tip of her finger. "Well, perhaps. Just this once. But no more. It simply wouldn't be right."

He offered her a noncommittal smile.

———————

Rachel laid the individual pudding molds upside down, thinking of all the specimens Johnnie had brought to her these last several weeks. He evidently had half the population in the mines collecting insects for her. Each time she tried to reject an offering, he threatened to carry it personally up to her room.

So she accepted them. And took great care to dry them, label them, and pin them to a board.

"They're ready for dessert," Frank said, hands full of soiled serving platters.

Quickly tapping the small almond puddings out of their molds and onto a large plate, she tried to suppress her irritation. Selma was doing nothing other than wiping down the stove, yet she would not pause long enough to help with the customers.

Certainly, she was a shy, quiet girl. But she wasn't timid. Still, nothing could convince her to work the front room. To make matters worse, Saturdays were their busiest and Michael had yet to make an appearance.

Taking the dessert platters, she entered the dining room. Her feet slowed as the men at the end of the table gave up their seats for some late arrivals.

She delivered the puddings, then wavered in indecision. Her "No Prostitutes" sign was quite prominently displayed, so she'd never been put in a position to serve these women before.

She moved not an inch as she stood between the devil and the deep blue sea trying not to notice the women's full-sleeved form-fitting jackets spreading out over their waists. Nor their bonnetless, half-shingle coiffures that framed their faces with curls while leaving the rest of their manes hanging loose and long.

Was this to be a new form of advertising for them? For they could not, of course, take out ads in the newspapers. Yet that did not keep them from promenading on Sundays, from throwing lavish soirees, from attending public events, nor even from handing out cards printed in fancy script with the location of their rooms. Why, just last week she'd heard of a café owner hiring women to pose without clothing on a special platform in his dining room.

She shuddered. This was to be an establishment run by the respectable for the respectable. To allow these moonlight women to sit at one of her tables enticing men into sin was simply not to be tolerated.

Her clientele quieted as she approached the foursome.

A woman with coal black hair and faintly painted lips removed a glove. "We're here for dessert only, though we'll gladly pay the full three dollars, won't we, Mollie?"

"Sure will."

The other two looked at Rachel expectantly.

"I'm sorry," she said. "This café is a family establishment. It does not serve fallen women. I'm afraid I'm going to have to ask you to leave."

The women scoffed in obvious amusement. Silence descended like a guillotine.

Leaning back, the woman with black hair raised a skeptical brow. "You're going to toss us out?"

"I'm sure it will not come to that. You'll not be served, so there is no reason for you to stay."

Black Hair's gaze roamed throughout the room, pausing to touch on customer after customer. A smile revealing straight but smoke-stained teeth spread across her face. "On the contrary, my dear, I see about fifty or so reasons to stay."

A muffled, deep-throated chuckle sounded from a corner of the room followed by a shushing.

The woman named Mollie captured Rachel's attention then freed the top buttons of her jacket, producing a profusion of cleavage from the stranglehold of her corset. "My, but it's warm in here," she said.

Rachel swallowed her shock. The woman wore no chemise.

"That's enough, ladies," Frank said.

Rachel let out a slow breath, relief pouring through her. He must have sensed something was afoot when the room quieted. He moved beside her and stood, legs spread wide.

Black Hair cocked her head. "Surely you're not suggesting you would actually manhandle us, are you, Frankie?" She ran her tongue across the edge of her lips.

"I said that's enough. If Miss Rachel says you leave, then you leave."

"Well, the girls back at the Empire are going to be plenty amused when they hear *Frankie* threw us out in a bid to keep this place respectable." She snorted.

He took hold of Mollie's elbow and forcibly brought her to her feet. "Have a good afternoon, ladies."

Black Hair hesitated, then must have concluded Frank was serious. She rose. "My afternoon will be fine. I'm wondering how very lonely your afternoons are going to be when word goes around."

"I'll get along just fine."

She pulled on her gloves. "Ah, that's right. You work here with your *cousin*, don't you? So nice to have family in times of trouble. Come along, girls."

After they left, Rachel returned to the kitchen, her customers avoiding her gaze. Word must have spread like fire, for Johnnie walked through the back door within the hour.

"You all right?" he asked.

She scrubbed a pan in a large tub of suds. "Yes. I'm fine. Do you know where Michael is? He never showed up for work."

"He told me you gave him the day off."

"On a Saturday? He knows that's my busiest day. Why would he think that?"

Selma slipped between them with a stack of newly dried plates. "Howdy, Mr. Parker."

"Hello, Selma." Johnnie stepped out of her way. "Well, I'll send him over."

Rachel looked up. "He's at your place?"

"Now, don't get in an uproar. I said I'd send him home."

"What's he doing over there?"

Johnnie tugged at his earlobe. "He said he told you."

"Told me what?"

"That he's renting a table from me."

"He's what? You mean to tell me he is *dealing?*"

He held up both hands and backed out the door. "Listen, I have to go. I'll send him right over. Okay?"

But Michael never made it home. Not even by nightfall.

———

Rachel lifted her head from the pastry table, where she had dozed off in the crook of her arm. Michael stood in the open doorway, his youthfulness accentuated by the oversized man's shirt divided into sections by suspenders that held up his loose-fitting pantaloons.

"Have you been at Johnnie's?" she asked.

He closed the door. "Yes."

"Dealing?"

"Yes."

"Why?"

"I'm good at it, it's a lot more fun than scrubbing dishes, and I can make a month's salary in one night."

She turned up the lamp then patted the spot across the table from her in invitation.

He shook his head. "I'm tired. We can talk about it in the morning."

"I could have marched over there and dragged you home by your ear, but I chose not to embarrass you in that way. In return, I expect you to do me the courtesy of answering a few questions. Right now."

He took a deep breath. "I said we'd talk about it in the morning, and that's what we'll do."

He strode past her and to the stairs.

Jumping up from the table, she grabbed the lantern and followed. "I'll not make the same mistake twice, Michael. I'll not let you be lured into a life of sin, too."

He said nothing.

"I mean it."

He paused at his bedroom door. "I'm a man now, Rachel. You need to leave me be."

"A man? You are a child."

"I'm the only man this family has. It's time I started acting like it."

"By dealing cards?"

"By cutting the apron strings."

He stepped into his room and shut the door firmly behind him.

———————

Rachel gave a brief wave to Mr. Crocker, then stepped into the café.

"Where have you been?" Johnnie barked.

Rachel jumped, then pushed the front door closed. "What are you doing here?"

"Answer my question."

She untied her bonnet and pulled it from her head. Mr. Crocker's "giddy-up" and the jangle of his horse and wagon filtered in from outside as he headed back to the livery.

She smiled to herself. He'd been very careful to come with a wagon instead of a carriage this time. Such a dear man.

She moved to the table beside which Johnnie stood, then sighed and sat down. She'd been looking forward to the sanctuary offered by early Sunday evenings when the café was closed and she had the place all to herself. But that was not to be.

"Where have you been?" he repeated.

"It's none of your business."

"Do not toy with me, Rachel. I went out to my property and you weren't there. Were you with Crocker?"

"It's none of your business."

He slammed both hands onto the table and leaned toward her. "You are the woman I am going to marry. I'd say that makes it my business."

She rubbed her forehead. "My word, but you are stubborn, and I am too tired to argue with you."

"Good. Then get your things and let's go see the preacher."

She rolled her eyes. "You told me you would send Michael home."

"I tried."

"Not very hard, obviously."

Johnnie frowned. "He said if I took away his table he'd go rent one from Ralph at the Dorado. I figured letting him stay at my place was the lesser of two evils."

"Two wrongs don't make a right."

He stepped over the bench and sat down. "There's been a lot of talk about those women who came here yesterday. Talk that kicking them out was sort of harsh."

"I didn't know what else to do."

"They are still people, Rachel. With feelings."

"You dare to lecture me?"

"I'm not lecturing." He drove his fingers through his hair. "I'm trying to help."

"They came to solicit business."

"How do you know? Maybe they just wanted a sweet."

"Then they'll have to make their own."

Her front door opened. A sunbonnet woman stepped in. Her travel dress of dark homespun wool had a high neckline and an unboned bodice that buttoned up the front.

Johnnie and Rachel both stood.

"Please forgive me," the woman said. "I saw that you were closed, but the only places open were, well . . . My husband was supposed to meet me at the docks, but our ship arrived several days late and I don't know how to find him."

A woman. A real live respectable woman. Rachel moved toward her and clasped her hands. "Oh, hello. And don't worry about a thing. Why, Mr. Parker here knows most everyone in town. I'm ever so glad that you stopped in. Please, would you join us for some refreshment?"

"Oh no. I can see you're closed. I wouldn't want to impose."

"It's no trouble." She glanced at the cup sitting in front of Johnnie. "There should be some coffee on the warmer. Won't you be our guest?"

"Oh, that does sounds lovely."

Rachel led her to the table.

"I'll get it," Johnnie said, picking up his mug and heading to the kitchen.

"The town wasn't quite what I was expecting," the woman said.

"No, I imagine not."

Johnnie entered carrying a tray with three steaming cups and a cool, wet cloth neatly folded on a plate.

"Why, thank you so very much." The woman dabbed her delicate porcelain face and pale hands with the towel, then took a sip of coffee.

Closing her eyes, she allowed her shoulders to relax. "You have no idea how wonderful this is."

Rachel and Johnnie exchanged a smile.

The lady took a few more sips before opening her eyes. They were as green as a grasshopper.

"Goodness," she said. "How terribly rude of me. I'm so sorry."

Rachel shook her head. "Nonsense. I understand exactly how you feel. You take all the time you want."

Still, the woman put her cup down and surveyed the shop. "A café. How very delightful."

"Thank you. Allow me to introduce myself. I'm Rachel Van Buren. Proprietress of this restaurant. And this is Mr. Parker. He owns the Parker House on the corner."

"How do you do? I'm Mrs. Merle Sumner."

"Merle Sumner? *Merle* Sumner?" Rachel grabbed the edge of the table, slowly coming to her feet. "You are *wed* to Merle Sumner?"

A brief look of resignation and grief flashed across Mrs. Sumner's face before she carefully smoothed it of all expression. "I am and have been for two years. Do you know him?"

"Sweet merciful heavens." Rachel looked to Johnnie, telegraphing him a silent message. *What do we do?*

"Perhaps if you would just point me in the right direction, I will be on my way," Mrs. Sumner said, standing.

"He knew you were coming?" Johnnie asked.

"Of course."

"I would be happy to escort you to his home."

"No, thank you. I'd prefer to do this alone."

He nodded, walked her to the door, and gave her directions to the little house on the hill. Rachel sank onto the bench, wrapping her arms tightly against her waist.

She heard the door click shut, the bolt slide into place. Johnnie sat next to her, his back to the table, and placed his elbows on his knees.

"He's married," she said. "Married! How could that be? He promised Lissa he would marry her, knowing full well the entire time that he could not. Oh, Johnnie. What will Lissa do? What will happen to her?"

Her heart began to race. Her stomach soured. She dug her nails into her sides. "What a heartless, unconscionable scoundrel. What are we to do?"

"I will see to it."

"How? How will you see to it? The man is *married.* What can you or I possibly do now?"

He swiped his mouth. "I can at least be there to catch her when he throws her out, or when his wife does. I will have her home before the day is done."

He started to stand and she grabbed his hand. He settled back down.

"She's my sister. I will go."

"No. This is going to be devastating enough for Lissa without her having to suffer her humiliation in front of you. Don't do that to her."

"Then Michael. Michael must go. He said he was meeting some friends this afternoon."

"I'll find him."

As soon as he left she allowed her show of bravado to crumble and fell to her knees. *O Lord. O Lord. You must do something. Please.*

he sun had long since disappeared when Michael slogged in the back door, weary, wind burned, and wearing half the dust of California. He flopped into a chair and using his toes, pushed off one boot, then the other. They fell with a *thunk-thunk* onto the plank floor.

"Where's Lissa?" Rachel asked.

Michael didn't answer. Instead, he propped an ankle on his knee and began to massage his foot. A musty, closed-in smell drifted to Rachel's nose.

"What is it, Michael? What's happened?"

"She won't come home."

"You can't mean to tell me she's still at Mr. Sumner's?"

"No. She's definitely not at Sumner's." He switched positions, working the soles of his other foot.

"Is she all right?"

"She's pretty torn up. Wailing and crying and carrying on."

Rachel set her elbows on the table, leaning her mouth into her fists. "Where is she?"

"I've rented a room at the Parker House and have her there for now."

"Why won't she come home?"

He stilled and looked over at her, a flare of resentment flashing in his eyes. "She says there's a sign in your window that warns her kind away."

Rachel sucked in her breath. "I wasn't referring to her."

"Weren't you?" He picked up his boots and stood. "Listen, I don't like her being all by herself. She's awfully upset. I'm gonna stay with her."

Rachel slowly lowered her hands. "For tonight?"

"Well, I was thinking I'd go ahead and move in over there."

She rose to her feet. "Temporarily."

He toyed with his boots. "Permanently."

An ache pressed against her chest, making it hard to breathe. "What if I take the sign down?"

He swiped a hand under his nose. "She said the sign would have to be removed and you'd have to serve those women who you kicked out that time along with any of the others that come in."

"I can't do that, Michael. You know I can't."

Pinning his gaze to hers, he frowned. "I don't know that at all."

"Michael, please. I'm trying so hard to do what's right. If I were to compromise my standards, what kind of witness would I be?"

"What kind of witness throws out sinners?"

"Unrepentant sinners."

"This whole town is nothing but unrepentant sinners." He shook his head. "No, I'm leaving, Rache. I won't be living here and I won't be working here. This place has gotten itself a stench worse than any gambling hall in the whole of San Francisco."

"Miss Rachel? Everything all right in there?"

Rachel squinted against the sun shooting through her window. Her entire body hurt—legs, arms, shoulders, back, neck, everything. She straightened, shoving the covers to the bottom of the bed, and groaned.

The knock came again, more insistent this time.

"Miss Rachel?"

She opened her mouth, but tears collected again and clogged her throat, making her answer an undecipherable jumble.

The door squeaked on its hinges.

Selma stepped in and over to the bed. She laid a hand against Rachel's forehead. "You sick?"

Rachel shook her head, tears spilling from her eyes.

"Mr. Johnnie's beside himself with worry. I swear that man has been here every fifteen minutes since early this morning."

Rachel pushed herself up and swung her legs to the floor. "I'll be fine," she whispered.

"You just take all the time you want. I wouldn't have disturbed ya, but Mr. Johnnie made me come up and check. Wouldn't leave until I did. He's waiting down there right now for a report."

"What time is it?"

"It's only nine. Still early enough."

Rachel ran a hand beneath her eyes. "I'm sorry. I didn't mean to sleep so long. I'll be right down to help with lunch."

"No need. Frankie and I have it under control."

She shook her head. "We'll be shorthanded as it is without Michael. Just give me a minute."

"What do you want me to tell Mr. Johnnie?"

She swallowed. "That I'm fine. I'm . . . fine."

Selma tilted her head. "You don't look fine to me." She pulled a handkerchief from her apron pocket and handed it to Rachel.

"Thank you." She dabbed her eyes and cheeks. "Selma, do you think it's wrong to exclude women of ill repute from my restaurant?"

Selma looked away, considering. "I wouldn't know. I can surely see why you do. I can't help but feel for 'em, though. Not too many of 'em are happy with their lives. Ain't nothin' they'd like better than to walk away and start over."

"Then why don't they?"

"Oh, it's not all that easy, I reckon, when you think about it. They're alone. With no respectability. No money. No place in society. Ain't too many choices open for 'em, really."

Rachel rubbed the handkerchief in her hands. "Well, what do they expect? To play the harlot and then walk away unscathed and play the lady?"

"Ain't nobody can live a life like that and walk away unscathed. The question is, if they walk away, where would they go?"

"Home. To their family."

"Maybe the lucky ones. If they have family. And if their family would take them back. But just 'cause their family takes 'em in doesn't mean society will. And what about those that have no families? Or families who've disowned them? What then?"

"So you think I should allow them in the restaurant?"

"Let me ask you this. If one of 'em walked away from a life of sin, would you accept them like you would some lady who had never crossed the line?"

"You mean like Lissa?"

"I mean like anybody."

"I don't know. I've been taught my whole life there is no going back. But now, with Lissa, I'm not so sure." She moistened her lips. "For now, though, I'm referring to those who are still, uh, practicing their profession. Lissa wants me to serve them. What do you think? If it was your restaurant, would you serve them?"

Selma sighed. "That there's the rub, Miss Rachel. It ain't my café. It's yours. Which means it makes no nevermind what I would do. Only what you would do."

Rachel finished off the sixth square she'd knitted that hour. It was just large enough to hold one dumpling, whose appearance would be very pretty when boiled in the coarse cotton.

Frank hauled in wood for the stove and Selma stirred meat into a pot. The two worked silently, only speaking in muted tones when absolutely necessary, and then only to each other.

The back door banged open. All three of them jumped.

A pale and limp Lissa lay draped across Johnnie's arms. "Where do you want her?"

Rachel lurched to her feet. "What happened?"

"She swallowed a powerful narcotic. She needs a doctor and somebody to watch over her."

He made his way to the stairs. "Which room? Yours or Michael's?" he asked over his shoulder.

Rachel scrambled after him. "Put her in my room for now. It's to the right."

He waited while she opened her door, then preceded her in, gently laying Lissa on top of the cot. Rachel grabbed a buttonhook then began to release the buttons on Lissa's boots.

Johnnie bolstered up her head with a pillow. Her face held no color, not even her lips.

"Is she breathing?"

"Yes." But he placed a hand beneath her nose, checking again for air.

"What happened?" Rachel whispered.

"I'm not completely sure. I do know that Sumner really does seem to have a deep affection for her. Never have I seen him as happy as he's been since she agreed to be his . . ."

Swallowing, Rachel slipped one boot off. "But what actually happened when Mrs. Sumner arrived?"

"I don't know. Michael insisted on going up to the cottage alone. He didn't say anything to you?"

"Not about that."

"Well, Mrs. Sumner has taken up residence with her husband. That's about all I know." Johnnie felt Lissa's forehead. "I sent Michael to find a doctor. Do you have a cool cloth or something?"

Rachel scurried down to the kitchen and back. Folding the cloth in half, then in half again, she laid it across Lissa's forehead. The girl didn't so much as budge.

Rachel touched the back of her hand to her sister's cheek. Her skin felt clammy. "How do you know she swallowed something?"

"The empty vial beside her bed." He reached into his pocket and put a tiny corked bottle on Rachel's bed stand. "Be sure to show this to the doc when he arrives."

Rachel placed a hand over her mouth. "Will she be all right?"

He looked at her. "I don't know."

"You found her?"

"No. Michael."

"Oh, Johnnie. How awful for a young boy to have to see such a thing."

"He's a man now, Rachel. It's time he learned his way."

"He's fourteen."

"In this territory, that's a man and then some."

She fisted her hands. "Oh, how I hate this place."

He averted his gaze, surveying the items on her bed stand and toilet table. The collection of dried insects resting atop the covered bench snagged his attention.

Taking a closer look, he ran his finger along the perimeter of one board. "Well," he said, "would you look at this?"

A disturbance downstairs indicated the arrival of the doctor.

Johnnie took a deep breath and moved toward the door. "I'll send him on up and then I guess I'll be going." He hesitated. "Rachel?"

She looked up, meeting his troubled expression.

"I love you." Then he disappeared.

Rachel had expected someone Papa's age. The young man before her was old enough to grow facial hair, but it looked misplaced on him. Like a schoolboy pasting on a moustache for the school play.

And what a moustache it was. Black and shaped like an A, its eaves hung a good two inches beyond his face.

He removed his hat. "I'm Dr. Chadworth."

"How do you do. I'm Rachel Van Buren and this is my sister, Lissa."

"Your sister?" His gaze darted between them. "I, uh, I hadn't realized."

She suppressed the bit of defensiveness flaring to life at his implied censure.

She handed him the vial. "Michael thinks she drank something harmful."

He uncorked it and ran it under his nose the way she'd seen some of Papa's friends do when judging the quality of a wine. She wondered how any fumes could possibly get past that moustache.

He set a worn leather bag on the bench and moved to her bowl and ewer. "May I?"

She lifted her brows. "Of course."

The next several minutes soothed Rachel's doubts as the man finished washing up and went about examining his patient. He pressed his fingers against Lissa's wrist, checked her eyes, listened to her heartbeat, and looked all around her lips, tongue, and mouth.

After each step he would "hmmm" to himself as if making some evaluation within his mind about her condition. Finally he returned to his bag and withdrew a small bottle of black liquid.

"What's that?"

"Something to absorb the poison. It may or may not work. Only time will tell. Now, if you please, Miss Van Buren, I'm going to have to ask you to step outside."

"Why? Will it hurt her?"

"No, no."

"How will you get her to swallow it?"

"Never fear, Miss Van Buren. Now, please, we haven't a moment to lose." He cupped her elbow, steered her into the hall, and left her facing a closed door.

She paced. She sat on the top stair. She prayed. And still the doctor did not come out.

The noon bell rang. Good heavens. She rushed down the stairs, but Frank, Selma, and Michael had all under control.

Michael. He was here. At work. Right where he belonged.

The next half hour kept her busy filling cups and shuffling platters. She had just picked up another pot of coffee when the doctor entered the kitchen.

Michael came in from the scullery and stopped. Frank set down some dirty platters, and Selma paused in the spooning of pureed raspberries onto some tarts.

The doctor zeroed in on the girl. "Hello, Selma. It's, uh, good to see you."

"Her name is Mrs. Johnson," Frank growled.

Red filled the doctor's face. Selma returned her attention to the raspberries.

Rachel frowned. "Would you care for some refreshment, Dr. Chadworth?"

"I would appreciate that very much. Thank you."

He took a chair at the pastry table, making no effort to hide his regard for Selma. She ignored him completely.

"How is Lissa?" Rachel set a cup of brew in front of him.

He took a sip. "Well, I managed to get a good deal of activated charcoal down her. Lord willing, she'll wake up soon."

"Charcoal? You fed her charcoal?"

"Activated carbon, actually. It has strong absorption qualities. Why, a professor at the French Academy of Medicine drank a lethal dose of strychnine in front of his colleagues and lived to tell the tale because it had been mixed with the carbon black."

"I see. Will she suffer any ill effects from this carbon?"

"She shouldn't."

"What about from the elixir?"

"Depends on how much she ingested, but it's my guess she'll awake soon enough."

Standing, he thanked Rachel for the coffee, tipped his hat at Selma, and left through the back door. Rachel stepped out with him to make payment for his services.

In the dining room a harmonica took up the tune of "Yankee Doodle," and her customers serenaded the place, their unique version of the song coming through the windows loud and clear.

"California's precious earth turns the new world frantic:
Sell your traps and take a berth across the wild Atlantic.
Every one who digs and delves, all whose arms are brawny,
Take a pick and help yourselves—off to Californy.

"How this flush of gold will end, we have statements ample;
Perhaps a few sacks they will send, only for a sample.
But we hope this golden move really is all true, sirs.
Else will Yankee Doodle prove a Yankee doodle doo, sirs."

The jovial mood of the men highlighted her sense of desperation and heartache. Returning to the kitchen, she left instructions for Frank and Selma before making her way up the stairs.

———————

Rachel's body ached from spending the night in a chair and from frequent trips up and down the stairs.

With a start, she opened her eyes. She must have dozed off again. Repositioning herself, she once more drank in the sight of her sister. Oh, how she had missed her.

Rachel peered at Lissa more closely. She didn't look any . . . well, *different*. Didn't look as if she had been ravished. Or mistreated.

She was a bit pale, of course, but other than that the girl looked well fed and as sweet as ever. Color had come back to her lips, and her eyelids quivered upon occasion.

Rachel had placed cool cloths on her head and bits of ice in her mouth but had yet to receive a response. She tried to prepare herself for what she would say when her sister did wake. Surely the girl would now see the error of her ways. Would be ready to reform.

They could take the next ship home and no one would ever be the wiser. But what would happen if some nice young man wanted to marry Lissa? She would, of course, have to tell him of her past. Wouldn't she?

And then what? What man would want used goods?

What if she didn't tell him? What if they left this place and pretended it never happened?

But it had happened. And the girl would be starting off a marriage on a lie.

Lissa stirred. Rachel jumped to her feet.

Her sister opened her eyes, confusion playing across her face.

Oh, thank you, Lord. Thank you.

"I feel funny," Lissa croaked.

Rachel picked up a cup of broth. "Here. Have a sip."

She supported Lissa's head, and the girl took a swallow before closing her eyes and falling back into a slumber.

An hour or so later, she fully awoke and drank deeply from the cup.

"Where am I?" she asked, settling her head back onto the pillow.

Of a sudden, Rachel realized that Lissa had not been inside the café since its completion. "This is my room."

"Has Merle come?"

Rachel slowly nodded. He had come, but she had told Frank to refuse him entry.

"Where is he?"

"I wouldn't know."

"What did he say?"

"I wouldn't know." Rachel swallowed at the pain she saw in Lissa's eyes.

"You sent him away, didn't you?"

"I did."

Lissa pushed the covers down. "I need to find Merle."

Placing a hand on her shoulder, Rachel pressed her back against the mattress. "Not yet, Lissa. When you get a little stronger."

"Don't touch me," she hissed. "I'm leaving. Now. Where is Michael?"

Rachel clasped her hands together. "I'm not sure."

"Well, find him."

Biting her lip, Rachel nodded and left the room.

She sent Frank over to the Parker House to make inquiries, and within moments Michael appeared. She allowed herself to acknowledge that his once boyish features had subtly taken on a more angular appearance, accentuated by his frown. When had that happened?

"She's awake?" he asked.

"Yes, but she won't talk to me. Only to you."

He took the stairs two at a time.

Lissa leaned against the doorframe, her cotton nightdress rumpled, her golden hair disheveled. "Get me out of here."

"What are you doing?" he said. "Get back in that bed."

"I can't stay here, Michael. I'm soiled goods now and must go to live with others of my kind."

His face conveyed nothing but compassion. "You're not a leper, Lissa. It's not as if you have some dread disease that requires you to walk through town shouting, 'Unclean, unclean.'"

She gave him a slight smile and held out her hand. "Please."

He encircled her waist with his arm. "It's too soon. I can't take care of you the way Rachel can. Now, lean on me and let's get you back in that bed."

"I'll ruin her reputation if I stay here. Besides, women like me aren't allowed in her Holy of Holies."

"Did she tell you that?"

"She didn't have to. She has a sign in her window that says it all."

Rachel stood at the landing. Michael looked at her, questioning.

She swallowed. "You are welcome here, Lissa. You will always be welcome here. I will take the sign down."

Lissa teared up. "No, Rache. Don't do that. I'm not worthy of it."

Rachel rushed forward and clasped her sister to her. The coolness of her skin reminded Rachel of Lissa's fragility. A silver hair ornament scratched Rachel's cheek. She wondered if it was a gift from Merle. A gift for services rendered.

"Oh, Lissa, let's get out of this town. Let's get on a ship and go back home and forget any of this ever happened."

Lissa shook her head, sobbing against Rachel's neck. "I can't. I can't."

"Not today, of course. But when you are stronger. I will make the arrangements. I will take care of you. We don't even have to go to Elizabeth. It could be another town that's new to us."

"No. You don't understand. I can't leave him. I love him."

Rachel rocked her sister. "He's married, dear. You must let him go."

"But don't you see? He doesn't love her. He loves me."

"Shhhh. Come, let's get you back to bed."

"No. I can't live without him. I won't live without him. And if I stay here you will not let me see him."

"He's married. And his wife is here, taking her rightful place with him."

"No!" she screeched and shoved Rachel away. "He's mine. She may have possession of his name, but I have possession of his heart."

"For how long, Lissa? For how long?"

"Forever. He swore an oath to me."

She reached up to brush a tendril of hair behind Lissa's ear, but the girl jerked back. Michael grabbed her elbow to keep her from falling.

Sorrow filled Rachel. "He swore an oath to his wife, as well. His word means nothing."

Lissa slapped her. Full across the face, wrenching Rachel's head to the side. Rachel covered the sting with her hand, stuffing tears of pain and rejection down deep inside.

Michael sucked in his breath. "Stop it! Both of you."

He propped Lissa against the doorframe then disappeared inside Rachel's room only to return with a blanket.

The sisters faced one another, separated by a moat of regret, disillusionment, and loss.

Michael draped the covering over Lissa's shoulders.

"I'm taking her with me, Rachel."

Rachel stepped back.

He slipped an arm around Lissa, and together they shuffled to the stairs. It was not wide enough for the both of them.

He moved onto the first step. "Put your hands on my shoulders."

She did. Grasping them, he tugged her against his back and squatted down. "Come on. I'll piggyback you."

"I don't have the strength to hop on. Just move slowly. I'll be right behind you."

A lump the size of a grapefruit lodged in Rachel's throat. At the bottom of the stairs, Michael lifted Lissa into his arms. They left without so much as a good-bye.

Rachel went to the front window and peeked out the curtain. Michael came into view and headed straight for the Parker House. She watched him disappear inside. A young boy burdened with a fallen sister whose depravities had rendered her so weak she could not even walk.

The tears she had held in check rushed in like a tidal wave. She made her way back up to her room and collapsed onto the bed. It smelled of jasmine. It smelled of Lissa.

Rachel rolled over. In her bid to do what was right, she had lost those she held most dear. She pulled her Bible from the table at her side.

"If anyone does not obey our word in this epistle, note that person and do not keep company with him, that he may be ashamed. Yet do not count him as an enemy, but admonish him as a brother."

One by one, she turned the pages of Scripture.

"And why do you look at the speck in your brother's eye, but do not consider the plank in your own eye?"

She sighed. One page said to admonish your brother; the other said to look after your own sins.

Which is it, Lord? she thought. *Do I have a plank in my eye? A plank so big I cannot discern right from wrong when I see it?*

She shook her head. Surely sexual immorality was no speck but a plank. Why then did her spirit feel so troubled? So unsure? What was she missing? What could she not distinguish?

Show me my plank, Lord. Please. Will you show me?

$\mathcal{I}$n the months that followed, Johnnie still brought her insects but no longer came for coffee; Mr. Crocker pressed his attentions; Michael continued to rent a green baize table at the Parker House, accumulating quite a bit of wealth; and Lissa went completely wild.

Her exquisite beauty and untamed course of conduct earned her a widespread reputation. One time she swept through the Plaza in an ornate Turkish costume that shamelessly revealed her tiny delicate feet richly encased in embroidered satin slippers.

Another time she dashed through town dressed to the nines and riding *astride* a glossy lithe-limbed stallion as recklessly as a man. Yet Rachel could not deny the poise with which she held her ribbons and the skill with which she handled her mount.

Rachel wondered where the horse had come from. She'd heard her sister had won thousands racing the animal.

And the last time she saw Lissa, Rachel could not but stare, as captivated as everyone else, when the girl pranced through town atop her dark Thoroughbred. A snug burgundy velvet riding habit with a hundred gold buttons hugged her winsome figure. A magnificent hat of sable plumes perched atop her head and sported a short white lace veil over her face. Her eyes flashed earthy and sensual promises from behind its gossamer screen.

Her musical laugh would ring through the Plaza as if she hadn't a care in the world, but Rachel recognized the sorrow and despair beneath it.

Mrs. Sumner did her share of pretending, as well, but clearly she did not hold her husband's love. Though the Sumners lived in the house on Telegraph Hill, word was that Merle had built a lavish manor on the outskirts of town five times the size of his city home. . . . And that Lissa lived there.

Word also had it that Mr. Sumner spent more time at his manor with Lissa than he did at his house with his wife.

Meanwhile, the population of San Francisco continued to explode. In the month of September alone, six thousand passengers from five different continents landed by sea. And another several thousand arrived by land.

The few women among them went to the mines with their husbands. Just in time for the rainy season, for the next two months had offered nothing but rain. Day after day after day.

Frank stomped in the back, scraping the mud from his boots and announcing that more than twelve inches had fallen last night and the streets were a mess.

Rachel wended her way to the front bay window, pushed back the curtain, and watched the water slide down the panes, dividing into tributaries then surging together again. Oh, how she missed the sun. And the freedom it allowed her.

She hadn't been anywhere for weeks other than church services at the schoolhouse. Trying to make the trek out to Johnnie's property was unthinkable.

She attempted to see through the deluge to the Parker House but could not. Still, she could see the crowds of men darting about the Plaza.

Unable to pan for gold in this mess, the miners had migrated to town, only to be preyed upon by the saloons, much like a giant water bug would grab its backboned prey and suck the life juices out of it.

She sighed. November already. Soon it would be Christmas, and she had no family to celebrate it with. No family to exchange gifts with. Michael had not come home since the day he left with Lissa. And Lissa, of course, was forever lost to her.

She let the curtain fall and with shoulders slumped, made her way back to the kitchen to help with the day's food preparations.

———

Johnnie ambled through his Parker House, weaving his way through the throngs of rowdies congregating around the tables. As the crowds had grown larger, his place of dwelling seemed to grow smaller. What had once been one of the largest public houses on the Plaza no longer had the capacity to hold the masses that congregated at its door.

And with this considerable influx came a boxed-in room so stifled with tobacco smoke, alcohol, unwashed men, and clingy, odiferous mud that Johnnie often found himself slipping out the back just for a breath of air.

But there was no such thing as fresh air in San Francisco. For men covered every square inch of the city—even the alley behind his saloon.

The demeanor of the miners had also changed over the last couple of months as less and less gold was unearthed. The rambunctious, carefree ways of before had been replaced with a miasma of disillusionment and disappointment. Guns and knives appeared on the slightest provocation. Crime escalated in a society that earlier in the year would have left a bag of dust unattended, secure in the knowledge that no one would bother it.

Johnnie examined the rain-soaked, haggard, filthy men, allowing that for the most part they were not ruffians or ne'er-do-wells but honorable husbands, fathers, sons, and uncles. Had they been back home, they most likely would not have dreamed of stepping inside a place such as this.

But they had left their wives and children in order to come to this mecca, expecting to find a fortune in a few short days. Yet the easy gold was gone. Laboring ten hours a day knee deep in freezing water produced only meager rewards, if any.

And now they realized it would take months, maybe even years, to gather up enough gold to justify their journey. Their time away. Their very existence.

Desperation and despair had begun to sink in, reinforced by the discovery they could do nothing but sit until the rainy season had passed.

So they came to town, hoping to make on a turn of a card what a thousand hours of panning might produce. Then they could go home a hero. A debt-free man. A man who didn't rely on the charity of his in-laws or the whims of a mortgage holder.

More often than not, though, between the gambling and the women, the miners lost the little they had accumulated and found themselves wondering how they were going to survive the winter.

The rain pounded on Johnnie's iron gambling den like small shot. Oh, but he rued the day he had ordered this blasted thing. It was too hot during the day, cooled too quickly at night, and offered no warmth in the morning. Its anticorrosive paint emitted a sickening smell in the heat that never completely went away. And when it rained, the sound of each drop magnified itself exponentially.

Maybe he should line the whole thing with wood. But, then, he may as well build a wooden structure and leave off the iron.

He sighed. He'd had this argument with himself many a time. And each time he came to the same conclusion. He was stuck with an iron mansion that he loathed but had invested too much in to tear down.

A crowd began to form around Michael's table, and Johnnie slowed to watch.

"Walk up, chaps," Michael called. "Pungle her down and bet what you please. If anyone goes broke, I'll give him money for a big drink of Parker's finest Monongahela whiskey."

Men plunked down their bags and play began. The boy had a flair for dealing and a persuasive call.

Johnnie had encouraged him to return home, but Michael held no regrets about bidding "toting, scrubbing, and a bossy sister" good-bye. He wanted to make his fortune. Just like Johnnie.

So Johnnie had let him stay. Mainly so he could keep an eye on the boy for Rachel. But he disliked the responsibility of being anyone's idol. He was not something a young impressionable boy should strive to become.

The miners stacked up like cards against Michael's table, exhibiting a degree of conformity that had been forced upon them by the town's limited offerings. High boots, heavy trousers, flannel shirts, suspenders, and slouch hats made up their uniform as surely as if it had been mandatory issue.

And the men embraced their anonymity, enhancing it with beards so heavy even relations were unrecognizable. Johnnie studied the look-alike bunch. The anonymity was one of the main currents his business depended on, for with this loss of identity came a loss of inhibition, allowing doctors, lawyers, preachers, bankers, and teachers to stray from the straight and narrow.

A fierce-looking man with an untrimmed beard and hair that appeared as if it had been cut with a jackknife turned up an eight, placing his winnings of the last few minutes at almost twenty-thousand dollars. His worn, tattered clothing sported patches covered with more patches.

Michael showed no sign of concern or distress—only casual indifference. Johnnie knew, though, only too well, the tightness that surely had a firm hold on the lad's innards.

Walk away, Johnnie silently urged the miner. *Pick up your winnings and go home to your wife in Boston or Philadelphia or New Orleans or wherever it is you hail from. It would be best for you and best for the boy here.*

But the man continued to bet, winning a little here, losing much more there. In less than thirty minutes he'd lost it all.

As promised, Michael sifted out enough gold for the man to purchase a whiskey.

A great unease swept through Johnnie. The man looked near collapse. It appeared he had not come with a friend or partner, but alone. Johnnie watched him make his way to the bar. Past the other tables, past the piano player, past his Lorenzo Bartolini, which today wore a feathered Indian headdress.

The man collected his drink, threw it down with a toss of his head, and walked out the door.

Within seconds the report of a firearm sounded. Johnnie shoved his way through the crowd, threw open the door and there, on his porch, lay the man. Dead. Resting in a pool of his own blood.

After weeks of violent rain, the morning dawned without a cloud in the sky. Rachel tied back the curtains, drinking in the canvas of blue propped behind hills of pale green.

She smiled. Only in California would the hills be brown in the summer and green in the winter.

Not bothering to collect her bonnet, she opened the door and stood on her porch, basking in the mild temperature and the breathtaking panorama. Even the sight of Telegraph Hill did not dampen her sense of elation that rose with the sun.

"Glorious, isn't it?"

Rachel turned to find Mr. Crocker, portfolio and all, stepping up onto her platform.

"Indeed it is," she said.

"Can you come out and play?"

She smiled. "I'd love to, but I'm afraid the mud is so deep we'd not get very far."

"Then perhaps I could come in?"

"Of course."

They entered the dining room and he spread out his paintings while she collected some coffee.

After they combed through the most recent additions to his library of artwork, Crocker put them away and drew forth two brown packages. One large and flat, the other small and rectangular.

"For you," he said.

She didn't move.

He untied the twine securing the large package and opened its wrappings to reveal a stack of drawing paper. He then made short work of the small box, which yielded two slender pieces of charcoal. "I'm going to teach you how to make sketches of your insects."

She dared not touch the paper or she'd be lost. "'Twould be an exercise in futility, I'm afraid."

"I'm a marvelous teacher." The tenor of his voice had dropped to an intimate register.

She raised her gaze and found his look intense and disquieting. Brown eyes. Same as his hair. Funny, she'd never noticed his eyes before.

"I'm sorry," she said. "Though your gift is perfectly appropriate, I have decided that as a woman on my own, it is not wise to accept a gift from a man. Any man."

Except for Johnnie, she thought. *But he's different.*

Mr. Crocker swallowed. "Would you be more apt to take it if you were my betrothed?"

The sounds of industry and morning salutations from out in the Plaza reached her ears but not her mind. Only confusion and distress and near panic over his declaration broke through her intellect.

Oh no. Oh no. Oh no.

"Rachel?" he whispered. "Would you be my wife?"

The sound of her forename rattled like a bell clanger in her head, almost drowning out his proposal. Almost. "Mr. Crocker, I, um, I don't know what to say."

He gripped his knees. "Please, call me Henry. And if you would like some time, that would be—"

"Unnecessary," Johnnie said from the kitchen entryway.

The two of them jumped guiltily to their feet.

"Parker!"

"Johnnie!"

He moved into the room, his attention fixed on Rachel.

Blindly reaching for the table, she found its top and moved to stand behind it. "I wasn't expecting you," she said.

"So I see."

"You've not been over for coffee in weeks."

"My mistake."

Henry frowned. "Miss Van Buren? Have I spoken out of turn? Do you and Parker have an understanding?"

She gave her full attention to Mr. Crocker. "I have not been spoken for, no."

"Not officially," Johnnie said.

"Not at all," she spat back.

"Do you love him, Rachel?" Johnnie asked.

"Parker," Crocker interrupted, "I must protest."

"He makes his living in the out-of-doors," she answered.

"That's not what I asked."

"He's easy to get along with."

"So is a pet."

"He's respectable."

"I take that to mean he hasn't kissed you?"

"Parker!" Crocker exclaimed.

"He has not."

Tension fell from Johnnie's shoulders. "Do you love him?"

"That's none of your affair."

"Do you love me?" Johnnie stood close now. Just on the other side of the table, looking tousled and tired. She wondered if he'd been ill.

"A marriage cannot be based only on feelings," she said. "Feelings come and go. A marriage must be based on a solid foundation of trust and respect and . . ."

"Love," he supplied. "You didn't answer my question."

"You have come at a most inconvenient time, Johnnie."

"Answer me."

"The answer makes no difference."

"It does to me."

"It does to me, too," Henry said.

She sighed. "I'm so sorry about all this, Mr. Crocker, and terribly embarrassed."

"No need for any apology," he said. "I do think, however, that you and Parker have a few things to work out. My offer still stands. But he's right. No matter how much respect and trust you have in a marriage, you also need love. I would, anyway."

He gathered up his portfolio, and Rachel walked him to the door.

"May I stop by tomorrow?" he asked.

"Of course." She shut the door quietly behind him before turning to face Johnnie. "I am very angry with you. You had no right. You are not to come through that back door anymore. Front door only. And if it is locked, then it is because I want some privacy."

"All right."

She blinked at his easy capitulation.

"I came over to see if you wanted to go to the beach."

"Johnnie. The man was proposing marriage to me. I can't just tell him I'll think about it and then go to the beach with you."

"Why not?"

"Because. It would be horribly insensitive."

"Well, then, I'll go get him and bring him back so you can tell him no. After that will you go to the beach with me?"

She rubbed her forehead. "I'll do no such thing."

"But it's the first clear day we've had for over a month. It may be the only one. And I want to spend it on the beach with you."

"The streets are too muddy. We'd never make it down there."

"Is that a yes?"

"No."

"Why?"

"You are being obtuse on purpose."

"I'm not." He glanced out the window. "He already knows you aren't going to marry him."

She propped her hands on her waist. "And how could that be when I myself haven't even decided yet?"

He pushed in the bench. "Because if he thought he had a chance he never would have walked out that door and left you alone with me. You love me and he knows it."

He opened the box of charcoal and rubbed a piece of drawing paper between thumb and forefinger. "What are these?"

She snatched them out of his hand and wrapped them back up. "They are a gift."

Frowning, he put his finger on the cross-section of twine so she could finish the knot. "You probably shouldn't have accepted them."

She jerked the twine tight, but he didn't notice and slipped his finger from the string's hold. But not before she took in the brown-ness of his skin. The slight dusting of hair on his knuckles. The prominent veins on his massive hand.

"I've missed you," he said.

She looked up. Worry lines marked his forehead and the sides of his eyes. "Are you well?"

"Just tired," he said.

"You quit coming for coffee."

"So you've missed me, too?" He hooked a tendril of hair behind her ear.

"Yes," she admitted softly.

"Well then, let's not waste the day. Go put on some old clothes, and I'll get us some donkeys."

"Donkeys?"

"They do much better in this quagmire than the horses."

His eyes were even bluer than this morning's sky. "I must speak with Mr. Crocker first."

She expected him to preen or display a show of male satisfaction. He did neither.

"I'll send him over," he said.

"What if you can't find him?"

"He's at my place."

She started. "How do you know?"

"I watched him out the window when he left."

She turned back to look out the window, but of course, Mr. Crocker was nowhere in sight.

c h a p t e r **21**

$\mathcal{R}$ather than going to the main beach, where hundreds upon hundreds of abandoned ships obstructed the view, they rode all the way down Columbus Street to a quiet little cove that had yet to earn a name.

Upon arriving, the cool breeze roared in Johnnie's ears, but he welcomed nature's assault, glad to be away from the town that had bit-by-bit closed in on him.

He dismounted from his donkey and helped Rachel with hers. He'd been unsure how her burro would react to a sidesaddle, but she'd handled it splendidly.

Barely had her feet touched the ground when she flew to a nearby rock, peeking underneath it like a raccoon looking for food.

He secured the animals to a couple of scrub trees, smiling at the work boots peeking out from beneath Rachel's calico. Her brown dress had seen better days, but it did nothing to diminish her beauty or animation.

She wore a blue slat bonnet that protected her face from the sun instead of the superfluous ones that she normally catered to.

A tiny geyser of water spouted up from the sand beside her and she jumped. Moving to her, Johnnie knelt and without a word started digging around the geyser. After a moment, she joined in. In short order a long cigar-shaped tube revealed itself. They kept digging, front paws paddling like dogs after a bone.

It was slow going with the moist sand wanting to slink back into the burrow they dug, but finally they reached their treasure. Digging more recklessly, they uncovered a large clam, almost a foot in length with a tube clamped tight between its shell.

"What on earth?" she breathed.

Johnnie freed it from its muddy home, holding it aloft. "It sucks water down this tube, siphons out the food, and then spits the water back out."

"Fascinating." She touched the ridges on its shell. "Never in my life have I seen a clam this size. I didn't even know there were such things."

He smiled and put it back in its burrow. They covered it up, careful to leave a bit of its eating cylinder above the surface.

"Do the seagulls ever carry off these tubes?" she asked.

"They do. It's a delicacy for them, and they frequently snatch them right out of the clam's mouth with no regard whatsoever to the requirements of its owner."

Much like I snatch gold from the miners, he thought.

She sat back on her heels. "Well, I'm vastly relieved. I had begun to think that even the gulls in California smoked cigars."

He laughed at her foolishness and pulled her up. They built a sand castle, collected shells with which to decorate its facade, and finally dug a large moat around its circumference.

Rolling up his trousers, Johnnie pulled off his boots, yanked off his socks, and splashed into the water. "Come on. It feels great."

He bent and washed off his hands. He could tell she wanted to come in, but it would require the removal of her boots.

She stood by the castle vacillating. He said nothing. He'd pushed her into enough sin; he would do so no more. After a bit she crept up to the water's edge—closer, closer until the tide unexpectedly rushed at her.

Squealing, she tried to outrun it but could not. It crashed over her skirt, boots and all. She bent over to dip her hands in, but the water receded too quickly.

He heard her mumble in irritation, then watched in amazement as she stomped right to him, her boots slapping with each step.

"You're ruining your work boots," he said, not bothering to disguise his amusement, "and I know how fond of them you are."

"They'll dry."

"True. They'll also be ruined."

They stood calf deep in the frigid ocean, the water lifting her skirt to its surface and entangling it within his legs.

"Did you say no to Crocker?" he asked.

"I did."

When Crocker had left the Parker House, Johnnie had watched Rachel's place from one of his upstairs windows. Her suitor had eventually come out with the returned gifts and a solemn face.

When Johnnie procured the donkeys at the livery, he'd heard Crocker had left town for good.

Waves tumbled one on top of the other, each in a race to reach the shore first. A hungry fish nipped at Johnnie's ankle.

"You gave him his gifts back," he said.

"Yes."

He let the impact of that sink in, knowing she'd kept *his* gifts. Had, in fact, treasured them. Cataloged them. And pinned them to a board. He wondered, not for the first time, exactly what it all meant.

"He's left town," Johnnie said.

"Yes. He told me that's what he would do."

"Oh."

After several moments, she turned and tried to head back but her boots did not follow where she led, and at that very moment a thigh-high wave crashed against them. She gasped and began to topple, arms windmilling.

He reached for her, but instead of pulling her up, in her panic, she brought him down. They both fell into the shallow water, submerging themselves beneath its icy abode for mere seconds before their salty nemesis released them.

She rolled to a sitting position, struggling for breath, arms flailing, bonnet collapsed, hair slick against her face, skirt and petticoat churning about her on the water's surface. "My boots!"

She tried to get her footing, but her skirts thwarted her every attempt. He scrambled to the place they had stood and blindly searched with his hands, but try as he might, he could only come up with one boot.

The thought of arriving in town barefoot must have given her the impetus she needed to conquer the ocean's temperature and tow, for she too was cavorting about on all fours.

"It's gone, Rachel," he said. "You can wear mine."

"Don't be ridiculous. I would walk right out of them. Have you any idea how hard mine were to find? The merchants don't carry small boots like that as a rule. And with the streets getting worse every day, I'll be lost. We must find it. We *must.*"

He stood and hurled the one boot safely to shore, then helped her look for the other. But to no avail. Finally, he gave up and took in the sight of his beloved.

The water had plastered her gown to her, delineating with mouth-watering detail every curve, every limb, every everything. Delicious as the sight was, it was the hilarity of her antics that won his attention.

Her hindquarters stuck high in the air, trailed by a profusion of limp ruffles, while her nose barely cleared the surface of the water as she hunted for her lost treasure.

A wave crashed against her face, bathing her in its lust to reach the shore. Swiping her face with an impatient hand, she continued her quest.

"Johnnie? What is it?" She reared back so quickly he thought sure she'd been stung.

He scurried to her side then relaxed. "It's a midshipman."

"Is it a fish?"

"Yes." The fish was like a floating gaslight, giving off almost enough illumination to read by. "It gets its name from the spots on its body that resemble the brass buttons of a midshipman's uniform."

"But look at it. It's, it's glowing."

The fascination of her voice drew his attention. She stood now, and if he were any kind of gentleman whatsoever, he would turn from the magnificent display she offered.

But the sweetness of Rachel was simply too much to deprive himself of. Besides, she was to be his wife, and everything there before him would one day be his.

Still his conscience prickled.

At least the gown isn't white, he thought, for the brown color of the dress held no translucent qualities, thus providing at least a modicum of modesty.

He perused the outline of her shape, which left little to the imagination. And her legs. Old mother Eve, but her legs went on forever.

"What triggers it to turn up its lights?" she asked.

He took a deep breath, forcing his gaze back to the fish. "No one really knows, but speculation is that it's beckoning one of the opposite persuasion for, uh, romantic reasons."

She looked skeptical. "I don't know. Have you taken a good look at that face? Why, it's about the ugliest thing I've ever seen." She tilted her head. "Maybe that's why it lights up. So its enemy can see the midshipman's face and then swim away in terror."

He smiled.

She looked up.

"I've missed you," he said.

The sun touched her cheeks, her eyelashes, her lips. "Why haven't you come for coffee?"

"I had some things I needed to sort out in my mind."

"And have you sorted them out?"

"Almost." That was as close to the truth as he could come. He'd gone back and forth in his ruminations about her. He knew that to marry her he must give up not just his livelihood but the monstrosity he had paid a fortune to build. Yet the truth was, he didn't want her living in that squalor anyway.

So he'd quit courting her over coffee every morning and instead focused his attention on his business. But with each passing day, the profession he had chosen for himself held less and less attraction. Even the money no longer completely compensated for the dissatisfaction of his work.

And when that man had taken his life's blood on the front door stoop of Parker House, it had shaken Johnnie mightily. Had shaken Michael, as well. The boy had not dealt cards since. Had instead worked in the kitchen washing glasses and running errands.

"We don't even know if he was a Christian," Michael had confessed to Johnnie after the doctor had pronounced him dead and the men in charge of the cemetery carted him off.

And Johnnie had no answer for his protégé.

After that incident, he found himself hoping, no, *praying,* that the men in his saloon would only win and never lose. He shook his head. He was going off his bean.

Still, he had walked down to Mickle's Dry Goods and purchased a Bible. Then he'd started reading it. Again.

And the more he read, the more he realized it wasn't Rachel he should be giving up his business for, but the Lord.

"No one can serve two masters; for either he will hate the one and love the other, or else he will be loyal to the one and despise the other. You cannot serve God and mammon."

Something sharp rubbed against Johnnie's foot. He jerked, then reached down in the water and withdrew the culprit peeking from its muddy burrow.

"A clam," Rachel said.

He shook his head. "An oyster."

She gasped. "Oh. Do you think it might have a pearl inside?"

He rubbed the black shell between his fingers. "Shall we find out?"

Clasping her hand, he led her through the water. A light wind carried the smell of salt to his nose and threw a spray of water onto his pants. Wet sand cushioned his feet when they reached the shore.

Settling onto his knees, he withdrew his jackknife from its scabbard at his waist and introduced its blade into the seam of the oyster's shell.

He worked it all the way around until he could pry open its tightly sealed mouth. Poking around the gooey insides with his knife, he hadn't really expected to find anything.

Yet there in its center was a perfectly round ball. Removing it carefully with forefinger and knife, he dropped it onto his shirt, wiped it clean, and rolled it into the palm of his hand.

"Oh," Rachel breathed. "Look. *'Again,'*" she quoted quietly, "*'the kingdom of heaven is like a merchant seeking beautiful pearls, who, when he had found one pearl of great price, went and sold all that he had and bought it.'*"

Matthew thirteen-something. He'd passed over the verse a million times. He looked at the miracle of the pearl cradled in his hand, then at the miracle of this woman who knelt before him. And with the sea gulls squalling, the waves crashing, the damp sand sucking at his knees, and his heart pounding, he knew what he must do.

All that I have to give, I give to you, Lord, he silently vowed. *My heart, my mind, my soul, my body.* He sighed. *And my business. I am in your hands. Do with me what you think is good and right.*

Rachel took the pearl from his palm and placed it in hers. "It's so perfect. Perfect in color. Perfect in shape. Perfect in beauty."

She transferred the pearl back to him, and he tucked it carefully into the pouch at his belt and sheathed his knife.

She gasped and pointed. The sunset's hint of rose teased the cloudless sky, causing the mountaintops to glow like pieces of coal in an age-old fire.

The phenomenon that had captured Rachel's attention, however, was not the transfiguration of nature's sky but a flight of seventy, maybe even eighty, white pelicans. These regal creatures were not the brown pelicans that were as common as miners. These beauties were as rare as sunbonnets.

With regal dignity, they soared with long necks curved back, yellow bills resting forward and white wings displaying a spread of almost ten feet.

They coasted about the cove without any apparent purpose other than sheer pleasure. Johnnie knew what was coming, but even knowing did not detract from the amazement he felt when without the slightest provocation they all began to turn.

Large arcs. Small arcs. Tightly honed circles. Each creature with a unique dance that made up a whole until the entire flock revolved like the wheel of a wagon.

Ten minutes the performance lasted with the individuals and

groups painting a multitude of patterns against the glowing colors of God's palette.

Then, with no warning, the great white birds rolled into a long V that closed like scissors into a straight line.

Yet even as these exceptional beings rode the air as a unit without hardly moving a wing, they retained their individuality. One dipping. Another swaying. Still another rocking from side to side.

Free, yet carefully staying within the framework of the whole.

c h a p t e r 22

*J*ohnnie was looking to lease the Parker House. In the meanwhile, business carried on. But the taste had become so repellent in his mouth that he had decided, with or without a renter, he was closing the place down. Tomorrow.

He'd find places for Soda and Carmelita to work if he couldn't keep them on himself. The men who rented tables, however, would easily find new posts within a day's time.

A young man sidled up to Johnnie's table and calmly placed a bag of nuggets atop it. Thirty thousand dollars worth of nuggets. Johnnie peered through the smoky haze to take the man's measure.

He was old enough to shave but not old enough to grow a full beard. The fuzz above his lip made it look as if he needed to wipe his nose, and the spotty patches of hair on his cheeks begged for a razor.

"Where are you from, son?" he asked.

"Galveston, Texas."

"You have family there?"

"Have me a wife and two little ones."

Pursing his lips, Johnnie shuffled the cards. "You placing a bet?"

"Sure am. I'm pundling down the whole caboodle."

"I see." Johnnie began to cut the cards over and over with one hand. "Thirty thousand in gold could last a lifetime in Galveston."

The boy grinned. "Yeah. But sixty thousand could last you two."

Johnnie chuckled. "You planning on living two lives?"

"Feels like I already have. One at home and one in Californy."

"What's your name?"

"George William Henry Harrison Jackson the Third."

Johnnie lifted one corner of his mouth. "Well, George William Henry Harrison Jackson the Third, tell me about your family."

George spent the next five minutes extolling the virtues of his wife, his boy, and his new baby girl. "Why, I been gone so long," he continued, "I ain't seen that baby since she was all pruned up from the birthin'."

Johnnie nodded. "I imagine having those little ones is quite a trial for your woman. Having you come home with thirty thousand in gold would impress not just her but her father, too, I'm wagering."

"Hoo, ain't that the truth. Her pa'd strut 'round town like a turkey gobbler in a hen pen."

Johnnie placed the cards face down on the table and looked the boy right in the eye. "You really willing to give all that up for one game of monte?"

George narrowed his eyes. "You scared I'm gonna break the bank?"

"You'd need a thousand times that to break the bank. But if you pick that pouch up and put it in your pocket where it belongs, you could sail out of here on the next ship and go home a hero. And if I were you, that's just what I'd do."

George scratched the back of his head, knocking his hat askew. "If that's what you would do, then why haven't you?"

"I don't have a woman."

"An old man like you? Why, I'd o' thought you done had a whole passel of young'uns by now."

Johnnie shook his head. "Oh, I have somebody I'm sweet on, but she won't have me because I'm a gambler."

"Well, that's a right shame."

Johnnie brightened. "Say, you might could help me out."

"How's that?"

THE MEASURE OF A LADY

"Well, my sunbonnet runs the café right over there on the corner. The noon bell is due to ring any moment now. What would you think if you and I went over there right now and bought a meal from her?"

The boy scratched his chin, clearly skeptical.

"Then," Johnnie continued, "when she serves us up, maybe you could mention to her how I wouldn't let you gamble away your thirty thousand but instead had you take the next ship home?"

Johnnie stood, not giving the boy a chance to consider. "You do this for me, and I'll personally buy your ticket back to Texas. Then this time next month you'll be with that woman of yours and the youngsters, too. What do you say?"

George's eyebrows lifted, and he stuck out his hand. "You got yerself a deal, pardner."

———

Johnnie made sure he knocked on the *front* door the following morning.

Rachel opened it wide and took a step back. "What do you have behind your back?"

He kept himself face forward so she couldn't see. "I can't tell you yet. Now, go get me something to drink, woman. I'm near dying of thirst."

Smiling, she closed the door behind him, bolted it, and went to pour their coffee.

He stuffed the old flour sack underneath his seat, took off his hat, smoothed back his hair, and then rubbed clammy hands against his trousers.

"Good morning," she said softly, coming in with their cups.

"Morning."

They sat, but he could no more take a swallow than play a harp with a hammer.

"Is something wrong?"

"Not a thing," he said.

She leaned back, taking a drink. "That was a wonderful gesture you made yesterday for George William Henry Harrison Jackson the Third."

He humphed. "Anybody with a name like that needs all the help he can get."

She smiled, her gaze never wavering.

"What?" he asked.

"Nothing, really. I'm just wondering what has you tied up in knots this morning."

How could she tell that? "I'm, um, I'm leasing the Parker House."

Her eyes widened. "Leasing it?"

"Yes. I've decided to get out of the saloon business."

She slowly straightened and set her cup on the table. "Oh?"

He nodded.

"What will you do then?"

He again rubbed his hands against his legs and took a deep breath. "Well, actually, I was thinking I'd settle down. You know, with a wife. Maybe have a kid. Or two. Or twelve."

His words lingered, an echo of innuendo reverberating throughout the room. Preparing her. Preparing him. Raindrops began to tap on the big bay window.

"And how are you planning to support your wife and twelve children if you are no longer running a gambling house?"

He rested his forearms on the table. "Well, as it happens, I own a great deal of real estate here in San Francisco. I could support a family and then some on the rents alone."

She stared at her brew as if it held the secrets of the universe. "Rents from people who are running saloons?"

Uh-oh. He slowed down. *Tread carefully, old boy. Tread carefully.*

"I'm not sure what you mean," he said.

She folded her hands and looked him square in the eye. "What I mean, Johnnie, is that if you lease the Parker House, your family will be living off the profits of a gambling den. Furthermore, you could find that your next renter decides to use your property as a brothel. How would you feel about your children having a father who owns a gambling den and bawdy house?"

He swallowed. "I don't think I'd like that very much."

"I don't imagine your wife would, either."

"So what are you saying?"

"I'm not saying a thing."

"I could collect three hundred thousand dollars in rent fees from the Parker House, maybe even five hundred thousand. If I sold it outright, I'd stand to lose millions."

She took a sip of coffee.

"Listen, Rachel. I can see your point about a bawdy house. I'll give you that. But there is nothing in the Bible about gambling dens. Nothing."

She ran her finger along the rim of her cup. "I wish you and your wife well, then."

His stomach tightened. "I won't be running them. I won't be frequenting them. I won't have anything to do with them."

"Other than profiting from them."

He rubbed the back of his neck. "I'm going to build a greenhouse as big as my saloon and become a tree farmer."

Her finger stopped.

"San Francisco isn't some mining camp that's going to fold up overnight," he said. "This town is going to be something. And part of that will include populating it with flora and fauna. I plan to be the major supplier."

"Then what do you need all those properties for?"

"Security. In case we have a bad growing season or something."

"I'd rather go broke."

"Admirable, but not practical."

"I wouldn't be able to sleep at night."

He allowed a slow smile to form. "That'd be all right with me."

Pink filled her cheeks. "I'm being serious."

"You think I'm not?" He grabbed the old sack under his chair and set it on the table between them.

After a moment, she loosened the drawstring and pushed the burlap sides down. A pair of small tan work boots stood inside.

"Oh, Johnnie. They're beautiful. Wherever did you find them?" She stroked the hide of the sturdy leather. "You know I can't possibly accept—"

"Will you be my wife, Rachel?"

Her hand stilled and her eyes lifted, softening to the color of molasses. Several seconds passed before the merest hint of amusement began to play about her lips. "You brought me a pair of men's boots as a token of your favor?"

"It would have been less trouble to move a mountain than to find those boots."

She let out a short laugh. Then her smile faded and she closed up the gunnysack. "I won't marry a man who profits from gambling and drinking."

He found himself having to take deep breaths in order to calm his frustration. "And I won't marry a woman who thinks she can lead me around like a bull with a ring in his nose according to the whims of her conscience."

"Is the money so important to you, then?"

"Don't twist my words around, Rachel. We live in a world of folks who don't believe in Jesus Christ. I'm going to rub shoulders with them, conduct business with them, and debate politics with them."

"We don't have to profit from them."

"You already do."

"I most certainly do not."

"I see. You ask each of your customers if he's been saved by Jesus Christ and if he says no you refuse to feed him?"

"Don't be ugly, Johnnie."

"I'm not being ugly. You are talking out of both sides of your mouth. You have this ridiculous sign up about not serving prostitutes and instead cater to the very men who make use of their services. How is that different from renting my property to someone who runs a gambling hall?"

"It just is."

"No, it's not."

"As a Christian owner of an establishment, I must portray a flawless public image. Not flout the standards society sets down."

"Standards, ha." He stood. "They are nothing but a bunch of tripe that dictate how you women are to dress, walk, talk, laugh, eat, even smell flowers. Did you know there is a right and wrong way to smell flowers?"

"Yes."

"And fainting," he continued, "for the mere purpose of proving you're delicate. How do you even keep up with what occasion constitutes a faint? Do you carry a list around, then consult it and *then* swoon?"

"Well, I can tell you this much," she said, standing. "Serving women of ill repute in my eatery would definitely require a swoon."

He tightened his lips. "What does your rule book say about women who collect bugs? Dig in the dirt? Roll around in the ocean showing off their pantalets?"

She stiffened.

He leaned in toward her. "And what about the claim that proper women have little or no sexual feelings? Because even you cannot deny that female passion exists. And not just in the whores."

Grabbing his hat, he whirled around and slammed out of the room.

Hurt, horror, and guilt competed for dominance within Rachel. Grabbing the sack of boots, she threw it at the door, rattling its hinges.

She knew physical love was acceptable, but it was not to be confused with sexuality. According to what she'd read, most women were not troubled with sexual feelings of any kind. Those whose feelings were excessive and who crossed the moral lines often caused debilitation and ill health not only in themselves but in the men whom they preyed upon.

She swallowed, not able to still the memories of Johnnie's kisses. And touches. And her wish for more. Much more.

But he had twisted everything around in order to justify what he wanted to do. Yet she could not deny some logic behind his statements. She did serve men who had very likely visited *those* women.

Falling to her knees, she rested her forehead against the bench. She knew the Bible said to *"put away from yourselves the evil person."*

Yet a few pages over, it also said, *"This punishment which was inflicted by the majority is sufficient for such a man, so that, on the contrary, you ought rather to forgive and comfort him, lest perhaps such a one be swallowed up with too much sorrow."*

Confused and disheartened, Rachel stayed on her knees, earnestly seeking a revelation.

"Oh, it smells so good," Selma exclaimed, balancing on a chair while tying a ribbon to a branch of the fragrant evergreen. Frank had brought the potted tree into the shop and placed it in front of the bay window.

The grand fir had grown since Rachel had last seen it. She had not been out to the greenhouse in ages due to the rain, nor would she have gone anyway. Not after last month's argument with Johnnie.

She didn't ask how he was, but Frank told her he no longer ran the Parker House or the City Hotel. She didn't ask where he was living, but Frank told her he was still staying in the cabin behind the hotel. She didn't ask how Frank acquired the tree, and he didn't offer the information.

The three of them spent the morning making impromptu decorations. Frank strung a bowl of cranberries. Selma wrote Bible verses on small bits of paper in a lovely script. And Rachel made sachets of cinnamon, cloves, and ginger.

Between those and the ribbons from her sewing basket, they were running out of branches to adorn.

Frank plopped into a chair. "This tree trimming is a lot of work."

"Then play us something, Frankie, while you take a rest," Selma said, spearing one of her verses onto a tree limb.

To Rachel's surprise, Frank pulled a harmonica from his pouch and began to play a medley of Christmas carols. Selma sang along, her voice clear and true. It was a side of the cousins Rachel had never seen.

When Frank began to play "The Cherry Carol," Selma grabbed her skirts and sashayed about the room singing each verse by heart. Rachel kept time for her by clapping to the beat.

"Joseph was an old man and an old man was he,
And he married Mary Queen of Galilee.
When Joseph was married and his cousin Mary got,
Mary proved big with child, by whom Joseph knew not."

The front door banged open. Selma yelped. Frank cut off in mid-note. Rachel whirled around.

On the threshold stood Lissa in an elegant claret-colored walking dress of cashmere. The ermine trimming its high collar matched the rich muff encasing her hands. A single-plumed hat sat at an angle upon her head.

Rachel's heart began to hammer.

Leaving the door open, Lissa stepped inside, taking in the tree and the occupants of the room. "Well, isn't this a festive little scene."

Slipping one hand out of her muff, she pressed down on her skirt, causing it to bell out in the back a bit as she negotiated her way around the fir and over to the front corner of the room.

She snatched the "No Prostitutes" sign from the window and held it up as if she were the teacher and the three of them were her pupils. "This says you do not allow prostitutes."

A tightness formed across Rachel's chest. "That is correct."

Outside, Michael ran by the window, grabbed the doorframe, and swung himself into the shop. "Lissa!" he cried. "Don't!"

She strode directly to Rachel. "I'm tired of every yokel in this town laughing at you behind his hand, including these fine *employees* of yours."

Michael grabbed Lissa's arm. She yanked free of him and slammed the sign down on the table beside her sister.

"If you do not allow prostitutes, Rachel, then you'll need to find someone else to work for you. Because even though Selma is no longer plying her trade, you know what they say: once a whore, always a whore."

Rachel sucked in her breath.

"Furthermore, it might interest you to know that you pay rent to the very woman you threw out earlier this year. She runs a brothel on Dupont Street, and had she been the vindictive type, she could have thrown *you* out on your ear."

Lissa spun around and left the shop as suddenly as she had entered it.

No one said a word. No rebuttal. No excuses. No denial.

Yet, clearly, everyone in the room knew. Except for her.

Michael took a tentative step forward. "She's just upset, Rachel. It's two days before Christmas and Sumner is making merry with his wife. Lissa thought he was going to spend this time with her. You saw her. She was all dressed up and everything."

Rachel didn't know what to do, who to look at, what to think. So she left. She simply wended her way around the table, through the kitchen, up the stairs, and into her room.

She didn't cry. Didn't wail. Didn't anything.

Curling up into a ball on her bed, she closed her eyes.

Please, Lord, please. I want to fall asleep. Then we'll talk. Please?

Michael moved to the front door and carefully closed it. "I'm sorry. I didn't think Lissa would really go through with it."

"It's all right," Frank said. "There was nothing you could do."

Michael looked at Selma. She didn't look young and pretty like she usually did, but old and tired.

In a way, he was relieved the story had finally come out. He'd known, of course. Known since Rachel had hired her.

And so did everyone in town. Word was that Selma had been a music teacher when she and Frank left Texas to come west, that she had been a girl full of zest and adventure. Upon their arrival, Frank had found her a job as a governess for some wealthy Spanish family, then tried his luck at the mines.

But Selma had gotten tired of waiting and had come down to San Francisco looking for something better to do. The El Dorado had offered her forty dollars a night if she would sit at a lansquenet table and deal cards.

Michael had heard a bonnet was to start work there, so he'd made a point of being at the Dorado her first day. Selma had entered the den, her steps slow, her gaze touching the paintings that lined the walls. Before she could even find her table, she'd fainted.

The man behind the bar told Michael that Selma had been taken to her hotel and left there but that the owner had checked up on her the next morning and doubled his offer. She'd accepted.

Night after night, he'd watched Selma resist the pressure the men had constantly applied. But the longer she worked, the more relaxed she seemed to be. With the paintings. With the men. With the offers being cast her way. Until one day, she started dealing out more than just cards.

The night Frank returned to town, he stormed into the Dorado like a bull ready for a fight and dragged Selma out. That was about the same time Rachel had opened her café.

Michael ran a finger inside the collar of his shirt. Didn't seem to matter too much what the fellas did around here, but the women were different. Everybody knew who they were. And exactly what they did.

Selma lifted a tear-filled gaze to him. "I'm so sorry. This will cause more trouble between you. I ..."

"It'll be fine," he replied. "She knows you. It'll be different."

"She knows her sister, too."

He had no reply for that.

Selma began to collect the leavings of their decorating. "I'll just clean up here and then ... go."

"She needs you, Selma," Michael said. "The shop opens in a couple of hours. She can't run it without you. Please don't go."

Selma placed ribbons onto a tray.

Michael glanced at Frank, but the man said nothing.

"I'm going to check on Rachel," Michael said, "then I'll get back with you."

Upon reaching her door, he eased it open. Rachel lay on the bed, knees drawn up to her chin.

He stood in indecision, wondering if he should go to her. And if he did, what he would say. In the end, she took the decision from him by looking back over her shoulder.

"You all right?" he asked.

"I was going to rest for a little while before I opened."

Stepping into the room, he closed the door behind him. "Selma is leaving."

She swallowed and nodded.

"Are you going to let her go?"

"I don't see what choice I have."

He sat down on the edge of the bed. "She's given up her old ways. You gonna force her back to them by taking away her job?"

"Oh, Michael. I'm so confused. I like her so much. I do, but how can I keep her on?"

"It isn't like she works for you and then does, you know, after hours."

"How can you be so sure?"

"I'd have heard."

She laid an arm over her eyes. "I cannot believe this is even happening. Why didn't you tell me?"

He stayed silent.

Moving her arm, she looked at him. "Is that why she refuses to work the front room?"

He studied his nails.

"Did you know that woman owned this building?"

"Yes," he sighed.

Rolling over, she placed her back to him. "Put up the closed sign. I won't be serving lunch today."

chapter 23

The donkey slipped, nearly tossing Johnnie off and into the infernal mud it waded through. Cursing, he shortened the reins, keeping the jackass under tight control.

The town was nothing but one big quagmire. No telling how many bodies they would exhume from this mess come spring. Men who had become drunk, lost their footing, and sunk into the goop with no one the wiser.

Slowing his pace, he eventually allowed his mind to wander. Michael had told him all that had transpired yesterday. Johnnie hurt for Rachel. For Lissa. For Selma.

He wondered what Rachel would do now that she'd discovered her landlady was a prostitute. A prostitute who had let out the place for a sum well below market value.

Johnnie wondered why the woman had done it. But couldn't begin to guess her motives.

Not able to sleep, he'd retreated to his property in the wee hours of the morning. He missed Rachel with an intensity that was palpable, and the land made him feel closer to her somehow.

Over this last month he had spent hours there trying to direct the flow of water. Trying to nurture the trees. Trying to restore his relationship with God.

The peace he had gained this morning, however, evaporated along with the night as dawn brushed the sky and mud suctioned the strength from his donkey. What a way to start Christmas Eve.

A spark on the horizon caused him to yank his animal to a halt. An instant later, a huge flame spiraled up from the center of town.

Dread and fear clamped his chest like the jaws of a vise. Even with the recent rains, San Francisco was nothing but wood and cloth kindling. And it had caught fire, with not one single engine to its name.

It took every bit of self-control he had not to slam his heels into the sides of the donkey. He knew that would only delay him. The mud was close to three feet deep here, and there would be no hurrying through it.

He urged the animal on, speaking to it with a calmness he didn't feel. Shouts of alarm drifted up to him, and he gleaned a bit of comfort from them. If he could hear them, Rachel could hear them.

What would she do? Where would she go?

Black smoke billowed up from the fire as it gained momentum. If it wasn't the actual Plaza that had caught, it was awfully close.

The smell of burnt wood tickled his nose, though there was no wind to speak of. Or rain—now that they actually needed it.

Men scurried up the hills and away from the fire. Some dragging trunks, some shouldering valises, some with no more than their mining gear.

Like a trout swimming upstream, Johnnie pressed ever onward. As the mud became more manageable, the donkey became less so. The screams of the fire and the terror of the men transferred themselves to his mount.

He forced the animal forward. In the twenty minutes it took him to reach the edges of the Plaza, the fire had turned into a roaring wall of destruction, greedily licking up the entire east side of the square.

The donkey refused to go any farther. Johnnie jumped off and plunged into what felt like the insides of an oven. Ashes, cinders, sparks, and smoke consumed any air worth breathing.

Dennison's Exchange, the Parker House, and the El Dorado all wore fiery cloaks. Goods of every description lay piled in the muddy Plaza. Men of all nationalities swarmed like bees through the square, no one making any effort to stop the blaze.

Already the fire teased the Cottage Café. He scanned the crowd to no avail. He shouted out Rachel's name, but a deafening crash shook the Plaza. Dennison's roof collapsed and the walls caved in.

Reason told him Rachel would have long ago left the café and maybe headed to the waterfront. But his gut was not convinced. After a split second of indecision, he ran to the door of the shop.

The lock scorched his fingers. He worked for several more seconds trying to unfasten it but could not.

Why is the door still bolted? Did she go out the back?

Hurrying to the window, he kicked it in and crawled through, shoving the Christmas tree's branches aside. Smoke had already filled the place and more poured in the now exposed window. But the room was still navigable and somewhat breathable.

"Rachel!" he shouted.

Coughing answered him.

O Lord!

He raced through the eatery and kitchen. On the stairs, Selma had Rachel by the waist, trying to help her down.

Johnnie took the steps two at a time and held out his arms. Rachel came to him. Scooping her up, he ran out the back.

"Come on, Selma! Can you follow?" he yelled.

"Yes! Hurry!"

"Grab my shirt so I know I haven't lost you!"

He felt Selma secure a fistful of his flannel, and together they plowed through the mud, down the hill and, finally, to the wharf.

Rachel pressed her face to his shoulder, taking short, quick breaths, interspersed with coughs.

Smoke replaced the morning fog that usually hung over the water. Men crowded the shore and pier, guarding their salvaged belongings.

A violent explosion from the Plaza caused all to cease moving and watch the spectacle on the hill. Johnnie guessed the alcohol within the dens most likely caused the blast.

He splashed into the tide, Selma with him. She swished her hands in the water and wiped Rachel's face.

"Rachel? Are you all right?" Johnnie asked.

"I'm sleepy. And my throat hurts." She coughed and rested her head against him.

"What happened?" he asked Selma.

"I don't know. She was wandering around upstairs, confused. As if she were lost."

"Didn't she hear and smell the fire?"

"Yes, but from what I can gather, by the time she finished dressing, she'd inhaled so much smoke she couldn't remember where the stairs were."

Rachel coughed.

They moved to the pier and Selma sat down. Johnnie settled Rachel next to her, resting her head in Selma's lap.

"I'm going to take a little rest, Johnnie," Rachel said.

"You do that, love. You rest." He brushed the hair back from her face. She closed her eyes.

"She'll be fine," Selma said.

Johnnie swallowed. *Please, Lord, let her be fine.*

"I have to go, Selma. I have to help put out the fire."

"Be careful, then. And don't worry about Rachel. I'll stay with her." He looked at Selma. Soot covered her face, blackened her hair.

"Thank you," he said.

She gave him a slight smile.

"Where's Frank?" he asked.

"Doing what he can to help, I reckon."

Johnnie took Rachel's hand in his, running a thumb over her knuckles. "How did you know she was still in there?"

"I didn't. I was just checking to be sure. Almost turned around when I got to the upper floor. The smoke was much worse up there."

A shiver ran through him. "Well, I better scrounge up a bucket or two and start filling them."

"Go on, Johnnie. She'll be fine. I'll stay right here with her."

He squeezed Selma's arm. "Thank you."

Rachel opened her eyes, trying to assimilate the babble of voices, the sound of the ocean, the smell of something burning, and the pain in her throat. Where was she?

She attempted the question, but only a moan issued forth.

A tender hand stroked her head. "How do you feel?"

It was Selma.

"What's happening?" Rachel whispered.

"The Plaza's on fire."

She struggled to sit up. Selma helped her, supporting her weight by sidling close.

Nothing could have prepared her. Bright red fire consumed what had to be an entire row of buildings up by the Plaza. Timbers crackled. Sparks flew. Jets of fire, steady and intense, shot upward.

"The café!" Rachel exclaimed, coming fully awake.

Selma patted Rachel's arm. "It had already caught when we got you out."

"Got me out?"

"You don't remember?" Selma asked.

"Not really. Bits and pieces, maybe. I remember you being there."

Selma looked away, saying nothing.

Had this girl saved her life? Had this woman, who—according to everything Rachel had been taught—was beyond the pale, risked all to save the very person who had denied her?

Rachel couldn't remember for certain. But she had a feeling that was the case.

She thought of the prostitute in the Bible who had been taken outside the city walls to be stoned. *He who is without sin among you, let him throw a stone at her first.*

In a rush, a multitude of sins that Rachel herself had succumbed to flashed through her mind. In every instance, she had gone before the Lord and begged His forgiveness. Which He had granted. Immediately upon request.

How could she do any less for someone else? Who was she to say one sin was worse than another?

"Have you seen Michael or Lissa?" Rachel asked.

"No."

"Johnnie? Frank?"

"Fighting the fire."

The words caused a commotion in her stomach. *Keep them safe, Lord. Keep all of them safe.*

She watched the conflagration then noticed the bevy of spectators lounging about the pier. Why weren't they helping to put out the fire? Where was the bucket brigade?

The only work being done was by draymen, who emptied their carts of someone's personal belongings before turning back to the city for another load.

She stirred. "We must do something."

"There is nothing to do. We have no red shirts. No hooks and ladders. The men will have to battle it themselves."

"Then we'll haul buckets of water for them."

She pushed herself to her feet, setting off a slight throbbing in her head before she could capture her balance.

Selma quickly steadied her. "I told Johnnie I'd keep you here."

"I'll handle Johnnie. Come on."

With that, they stepped off the pier and began to examine the merchandise stacked along the wharf. Rachel helped herself to a pile of blankets. When she found a barrel of vinegar, she signaled a drayman.

"I need you to place these in your cart and carry them to town."

"I'm not hauling that barrel up this hill."

"Yes you are. We need it for the fire."

He frowned. "Well, it'll cost you ten dollars."

"Ten dollars? I want you to take it up the hill, not to New York City!"

"Ten dollars or you can carry it yerself."

"The town is on fire. Have you no decency?"

"No. None at all."

She narrowed her eyes. "Fine. Ten dollars. Come see me at the Cottage Café when this is over."

"It ain't thar."

"What's not there?"

"The café."

She blinked, dumbstruck, then looked at the flames. An overwhelming sense of loss hit her for the first time. She would have to start all over. The very thought made her want to fall to the ground and shake her fists.

Everything she owned, gone. Just like that.

Her work place. Her supplies. Her Bible. Her green Halictidae. Everything.

She took a choppy breath. She wouldn't be starting off alone. She had a God. And her life. She glanced at Selma. And a friend.

She straightened her spine. "Then meet me at the place the café *used* to be."

He chewed on his cheek. "Did you keep yer dust in the café?"

She placed her hands on her hips. "No. I keep it at the custom-house."

Those must have been the magic words. He hoisted the barrel onto his cart. She and Selma crammed the blankets around it.

With a nod of her head, Rachel indicated the mercenary man and rolled her eyes.

Selma's expression conveyed her understanding.

They followed him up the hill, the hissing and roaring of the flames increasing. Men rushed back and forth. The heat intensified.

They headed down Montgomery Street, where men armed with buckets threw water up as high as their strength would let them in an effort to drench the buildings. The fire had not yet reached this point but would before the day was over.

Rachel had the drayman unload her barrel and blankets. She then opened the barrel's valve and began to saturate the blankets with the vile-smelling vinegar.

Men quickly lined up next to them, and Selma distributed the blankets. The men covered as many roofs as they could.

A rider on a fine black stallion charged down the street as if the mud were of no consequence. Rachel's breath caught in her throat. It was Lissa, riding astride in trousers and a flannel shirt, her hair billowing out behind her.

"Quick," she shouted. "We need men to help pull down some buildings."

Several men stepped forward and she gave them directions.

"Rachel," she yelled.

Rachel straightened.

"I've sent some of the wounded over to my house. It's big and we have plenty of room. But I need someone to see to them until I can get there. Will you go?"

To her house? The place that she lived in . . . with her lover?

"If your enemy hungers, feed him; If he thirsts, give him drink."

Taking a deep breath, Rachel nodded. "I will go, but I don't know where you live."

"I do," Selma said.

Lissa pulled up next to them.

"Where are you off to?" Rachel asked.

"I'm going to use my horse to help pull some buildings down."

"What good will that do?"

An explosion shook the ground. Lissa's horse danced, then stilled under its master's tight control.

"If there are no buildings in the fire's path, it should burn itself out," Lissa explained.

"Will that work?"

"I don't know. I hope so."

"Have you seen Michael?"

"Not yet."

Another explosion rent the air.

Lissa fought again with her mount. "I have to go."

She touched her horse's flanks and started forward.

The verses God had long since planted in Rachel's heart poured forth within her soul, and she could no more ignore them than she could keep herself from breathing.

"If anyone has a complaint against another; even as Christ forgave you, so you also must do."

"Lissa?" Rachel yelled.

Her sister reined in and turned.

"Be careful?"

A bittersweet expression crossed Lissa's face. "I will if you will."

And then she was gone.

chapter 24

$\mathcal{R}$achel had never seen a more curious structure. She was accustomed to straight lines and even surfaces. The columns and alcoves jutting out at various angles from Lissa's house fascinated her.

She'd heard the home had been constructed with timbers of ships that had run aground, but as it was painted in bright yellow, she couldn't tell. The windows, doors, and roof line had been adorned with whimsically carved trim painted in a contrasting blue.

A roomy verandah with an ornate balustrade surrounded the entire manor. Upon it lay a dozen men in various states of distress. She quickened her pace.

"Gentlemen, help is here," she said, climbing the wide plank steps. "I am Miss Van Buren, and this is Miss Johnson."

With a sweep of her gaze, she took in a mélange of singed beards, blistered faces, swollen hands, and horror-stricken eyes. The smell of burnt flesh clogged her nose. Maintaining a calm, ordinary demeanor took some doing.

"Miss Johnson and I will put some poultices together and see if we can make you more comfortable. But first, something to drink."

"Whiskey?"

The pathetically hopeful note in the whispered question tore at her heartstrings. "We will save that for those who need it the most," she offered gently then followed Selma through the door and into the parlor.

Her step faltered. The furniture was richly carved and covered in blue and gold brocatelle. Fabric of the same design framed windows that faced the street, along with an under curtain of richly embroidered lace.

A pier mirror in a gilt frame hung above an impressive fireplace with a white marble mantel. Two chandeliers decorated with cupids hung from the ceiling.

"We'll get the floor filthy," Selma said, lowering her voice to a whisper.

Rachel gave her a little push. "Go on. Let's find the kitchen."

The kitchen was not as grandly furnished as the parlor, but it was big, functional, and well equipped. Herbs and spices contained in bottles and pouches lined a shelf, while others hung drying from the ceiling.

She glanced out the back window. "Oh, Selma, look. A water pump. Right in the yard."

"Praise the heavens, let's go."

Selma pumped and Rachel rotated the buckets until they had four filled. Once inside, Selma set the water to boiling; Rachel raided the storeroom.

"I found lettuce, cucumbers, and potatoes," she said, returning to the kitchen.

"Oh, thank goodness."

Rachel placed them on the table. "As soon as you get the lettuce boiling, would you mind slicing these up? I'll see what I can find for makeshift pallets and bandages."

Lissa's bedroom was even bigger than the parlor and just as ornately decorated. A chaise lounge built for two. A gilded toilet table. Oversized oriental pillows bunched up in an octagonal alcove, their rich fabrics embroidered with fine gold threads.

The focal point, without question, though, was the large bedstead curtained in white linen. The gilded and ornately carved piece spoke of opulence and decadence.

She felt small and intrusive. But the men outside were in a bad way and needed some creature comforts. She would just open the camphor trunk sitting in the corner, grab whatever blankets or calicos lay on top, and leave.

A red satin gown lay on top. She peeked underneath it. Sapphire brocade. Under that, gold silk.

Sumner's things. Lissa's unmentionables. Unmentionables the likes of which were made for tantalizing, not for hiding under. Gossamer. Feathers. Sheer white lace trimmed with red ribbon. *Red.*

At the bottom were the blankets and calicos. She gingerly tried to remove them without displacing the clothing on top.

Then she all but ran back to the sanctuary of the kitchen. Selma had a tray laden with sliced cucumbers, sliced potatoes, a mug, and a bottle of whiskey.

Rachel glanced at her.

"It'll help dull the pain. Now go on."

Laying down the linens and her misgivings, Rachel picked up the tray, moved to the porch, and found two other women quietly conversing with the men.

The first woman straightened. She had short curly black hair and a wide forehead, worry lines marring its surface. "You Miss Van Buren?"

Rachel nodded.

"I'm Josephine, but everyone calls me Jo." She indicated her companion. "This here is Annie."

Annie was a tall woman with hair parted down the middle and slicked back into a bun. "Lissa sent us. She thought you could use some help."

Every lesson, every sermon, every book had drilled into Rachel that these women were the antithesis of all that was good and righteous. That to consort with them would make her one of them.

Yet the tighter she tried to hold on to those teachings, the more troubled her spirit became. Every time she opened her Bible of late, she read about grace, mercy, forgiveness. She read about bringing others to Him through acts of service and kindness and love.

Why, she'd worked with Selma for months and had experienced no ill effects.

And Lissa. Lissa may have been living a life of sin, but she wasn't evil. She was certainly acting outside of God's will, but did that make her irredeemable? Lost forever? And if it did, then what was the point of Christ dying on the cross?

A man moaned, and all thoughts but one left Rachel's mind in an instant. She looked at the two women, both of them clearly torn between concern for the men and apprehension over being tossed off the porch.

"Indeed I do need some help," Rachel said. "Have you been here long enough to examine the patients?"

Their rigid postures relaxed.

"Not all of 'em," Josephine said. "But Bart here is burnt pretty bad."

"Well, I have some cucumbers and raw potatoes. They should feel cool to the skin and help with the swelling."

"Jo? Is that you? You have some whiskey fer me?" The voice came from the opposite end of the porch.

"It's me, Patrick. Just hold on a minute and let me get organized."

"What are your full names?" Rachel asked.

The girls looked at each other.

"I'm Josephine Bellingham."

"And I'm Annie Holmes."

"Gentlemen?" Rachel called. "I will not have these ladies addressed with such familiarity. Josephine's name is Miss Bellingham and Annie's name is Miss Holmes. Do I have your cooperation?"

"Miss Bellingham?" It was the same voice as before. "You have some whiskey fer me?"

Jo smiled. "Yes, Patrick. I have some whiskey. But nobody gets anything unless Miss Van Buren gives the say-so."

The rest of the afternoon passed in a blur. Selma and Annie took over the kitchen, while Rachel and Josephine tended to the men.

All twelve patients were conscious. Those with the most superficial looking burns tended to be more agitated and uncomfortable than the ones with severe burns.

The man that worried Rachel most made no complaints at all. His hands looked as if they'd been shredded. His head was just one big hot air balloon—puffed up and unnaturally round. His singed hair and beard curled up like snakes. His swollen lips had grown to three times their normal size.

Josephine carefully applied lard to his hands, then wrapped them with strips of cotton torn from one of Lissa's calicos. "Now don't you worry about a thing, Bart. I'm gonna have you fixed up good as new."

Dull eyes stared back at her, pupils so big and black his irises could not even be seen.

"What would you think about letting me shave off that ol' beard o' yours?" she asked. "I been secretly wonderin' if you're hiding dimples under there, and now's my chance to find out."

She kept up her monologue, cutting his shirt off his body as she examined him further for burns. The smell must have been choking her, but she gave no indication of such. Just worked and cared for Bart, ministering to his spirit as much as his wounds.

Miss Josephine Bellingham was a good nurse. And nurses were in very short supply in this territory. Very short supply indeed.

An inkling of an idea began to form. Rachel mulled it over as she moved from man to man. She applied poultices of apple slices for headaches, served up onion juice and honey for coughs, and patted lettuce swabs on any skin too bright or too pale.

Before the dinner hour, five more women came to help and dozens more men came for treatment.

The whiskey supply in Lissa's storeroom turned out to be plentiful. Rachel allowed the women to administer it liberally, knowing it would dull the pain and induce amnesia for those who needed it.

Bit by bit the history of the seven girls leaked out. One of them had been raised on a small Missouri farm working from dawn until dusk. She came west seeking a better life.

Another one, a widow, had borrowed capital to set up a millinery shop in Massachusetts. The conditions of the loan were so severe she'd had to mortgage everything, including three dozen pair of underclothes. Her business had failed. So she had come west.

Yet another was a Georgia slave, the daughter of a white man and a Haitian quadroon. She'd come west to escape slavery.

Some had been accompanying loved ones on the trek to California, only to arrive orphaned or widowed. And hungry.

All seeking a better life. All without food, money, and options.

Rachel could not think of them anymore as women of ill repute. They were simply women. With worries and feelings and compassionate hearts.

It was early evening when Lissa slogged up the steps of the verandah covered in mud from head to foot. "The fire is still burning, but it won't spread any further."

"Michael?" Rachel asked.

"Is fine. Now, how are these boys?"

Relief poured through Rachel. She wanted to ask about Johnnie, but if he wasn't here for treatment, then Lord willing, he was all right. Still, she'd ask as soon as she could manage a private word with Lissa.

She watched her sister go from man to man, stopping to say a word, touch an arm, adjust a blanket. She spoke to each, knowing many by name. How could she manage to look elegant wearing trousers and half of the mud in San Francisco?

Poise. Self-confidence. Grace. From where had it come?

Lissa made a full circle before stopping in front of Rachel. "Do I look as bad as I smell?"

Rachel smiled. "Worse. Come on to the back and let's find you something to eat."

"I'm a mess."

"We'll take care of that, too."

They walked through the parlor, only to be waylaid as Lissa made the rounds again, comforting the men strewn about the room.

She didn't so much as blink at the mess they'd made of her home. Rachel had covered the furniture as best she could, but many of the men's wounds had festered, leaking fluids and saturating both the pallets and the rich brocatelle underneath.

Lissa flashed a dimple, thanking a man named Sherman for

inviting people to help themselves to his wine before they blew up his building.

"Mr. O'Farrell took great pride over his selection of claret," she said, "preening over his choice while Misters Hunt and Weston used their best efforts to remove an entire barrel of the cheapest kind."

Whether the men were enlivened by her tale or from her obvious amusement over it, Rachel couldn't surmise. But she marveled that anyone could draw a smile from them.

A bittersweet emotion fell over her as she recognized bits of the old Lissa and bits of a new one.

Young but brave. Brokenhearted but resilient. And filthier than any man in the room.

They stepped into the kitchen, and Rachel carted buckets of water in from the back porch.

"Tell us what has happened," Rachel said.

Lissa scratched her neck. "Everything on the east side of the Plaza is gone except for the Delmonico Restaurant at the corner of Clay. An entire side of Washington Street burnt to the ground, and many halls have been blackened and charred."

All the girls gathered into the kitchen to hear Lissa's news.

"What stopped it?"

"Water-soaked blankets, bucket brigades, and blowing up or pulling down the houses in its path." The dried mud on Lissa's face had cracked around her eyes and forehead.

Annie dragged a copper tub into the center of the room. Rachel began to fill it.

"Some of the merchants on Washington refused to have their buildings blown up," Lissa said.

"What happened?"

She shrugged. "Nobody listened to them and blew their places up anyway."

Selma took some water from the stove and added it to the tub.

Lissa shoved the suspenders off her shoulders, untucked her shirt, and began to disrobe. "At the most critical point, though, hundreds of those rowdies just stood there and refused to so much as pick up a bucket unless they were paid ridiculous wages."

Dropping her clothes in a heap around her ankles, she stepped into the tub and sunk into its heat.

Rachel swallowed her shock. Never had she seen a woman completely unclothed before, but no one else seemed to notice, least of all Lissa.

The girl dunked herself completely under, then after a moment of sloshing came up sputtering and scrubbing. Rachel grabbed some soap.

A lull fell while Lissa rested against the rim of the tub and Rachel lathered her sister's hair.

"Oh," Lissa moaned. "That feels so good. It's been so long since you've done that for me."

Rachel smiled. She'd not done it since Lissa was a child. A lifetime ago.

"Did you see Johnnie?" Rachel asked.

"He's fine. Tired, but fine."

Oh, thank you, Lord. "Did you tell him where I was?"

"I did. I don't think he'll make it by tonight, though. I imagine he'll stay with the fire. Just in case."

A jasmine scent wafted up from the soap. "Lean forward. It's time to rinse."

Lissa complied and Rachel poured fresh water over her. Someone handed Rachel a blanket. Lissa shoved the hair and water from her face, then rose.

Rachel wrapped the blanket around her and helped her step out.

Gripping the blanket, Lissa looked at the bedraggled women in her kitchen. "So, what can we do to make the men more comfortable?"

Josephine shook her head. "Not much, unless they could lay their heads on some of those big pillows of yours."

"My oriental ones?"

"Do you have any others?"

"I don't suppose I do." She paused a moment before padding across the kitchen. "Well, come on then. Follow me to my room and you can get them."

Dr. Chadworth, having first tended to the men on the front lines, finally made his way out to Lissa's place at dusk. Covered with mud and sorrow, he pulled a blanket up over Bart's head. "I'm sorry."

Rachel's body immediately felt so heavy her legs struggled to support it. When had he slipped from sleeping to no longer breathing? She'd checked him less than thirty minutes earlier.

She swallowed, fully aware this land claimed many a life, but it was the first time it had claimed one within her realm. Josephine looked at her, eyes tearing as she blinked rapidly to shoo them away.

Rachel grabbed her hand and squeezed.

The young doctor examined each patient. Rachel made mental notes of which treatment he prescribed, but it was Josephine who asked all the questions.

"What are you doing?" Josephine asked, as the doctor bent over another man.

"Listening to his breathing."

"He's breathing."

"I know, but is it rapid? Shallow? Is it making noises?"

"What kind of noises?"

"Oh, bubbling noises or anything sonorous, musical."

"Is it?"

"No, this fellow sounds good. Very good."

"What if he were making noises? What would it mean?"

"It'd be a sure sign of smoke in the lungs, and that can be much more deadly than even the burns."

And so it went. The doctor checked for weak pulses, clammy skin, drops in body temperatures, blue fingers or toes. Swelling, restlessness, extreme thirst, blank expressions, oozing pores.

For some, he prescribed poultices. For some, he suggested splints of rolled newspapers to hold their limbs immobile while they healed. For most, he recommended whiskey.

Snapping his medical bag closed, he peered at Josephine. "Remember, you're not just treating a wound, you're treating a fellow human being. And he'll need much more than a splint and a bandage. He'll need your attention. Your conversation. Your encouragement."

And encouragement and attention were what the women gave through the night. Taking shifts, they slept in the spare bedrooms, watched the men, and worked in the kitchen.

The hours before dawn found Rachel on kitchen duty and Annie keeping an eye on the men.

Yawning, Rachel spread honey on some sliced turnips. By morning, they would produce a soothing cough syrup.

A soft knock sounded at the back door. She opened it. Johnnie stood leaning a shoulder against the siding, so covered in black soot he was hardly recognizable.

A warm bubble of euphoria burst inside her. Until now, she hadn't realized how tense she'd been, wondering if he was all right.

"Morning," he said, reeking of smoke.

"Good morning."

"Lissa told me I'd find you here."

"And so you have. Is it over?"

"It's over. And we're both homeless. And my Lorenzo Bartolini is gone. Shattered into a million pieces."

"Oh, Johnnie. I'm so sorry."

He sighed.

"Would you like some coffee?"

His eyes drifted closed. "I'm too tired."

"Some breakfast?"

"Too tired."

"A bath?"

He lifted one lid but made no comment.

She touched his hand. "Are you all right?"

"I can't move. I'm just going to sleep right here. 'Night."

She stepped out onto the porch with him. The sun must have started its ascent, for it was a bit lighter outside. But smoke overlaid any yellows and pinks nature's sky had to offer.

"Come on," she said. "I'll pump some water and you can rinse off. That will help."

She tugged on his hand and he followed.

Bending over the handle, she pumped. Her arms and back protested, but she persevered.

He unbuttoned his shirt and let it hang over his hips then stuck his entire head under the spout. He scrubbed his hair and face, then reared back up.

Water ran down his back. He cupped his hands. She pumped some more.

He swiped his neck, splashed his shoulders and chest, then scrubbed his face again. It didn't do much good. He was filthy. But whole. And safe. And sound.

She'd quit pumping, taking her fill of this man she'd come to love. He shivered.

"There are some blankets on the porch," she said.

But the blankets were all gone. She crept into the bedroom and snatched up the one she'd been sleeping under, then took it to him.

He'd secured his shirt, patches of moisture giving evidence to his recent dousing.

Flinging the blanket over himself like a tent, he rubbed his head before pulling it off, then lifted one corner to his nose. "It smells like you."

She smiled. "Come inside and let's warm you up."

He grabbed her hand and drew her against him. "Not yet."

She snuggled close, sharing her heat with him and ignoring the smell of smoke that clung to his shirt, his hair, his skin.

"We're homeless."

She patted his back. "You said that already."

"We'll both have to rebuild."

"I suppose so."

"Seems kind of silly for you to go to all that trouble when you could just share whatever I build."

She smoothed her fingers along a tear in the back of his shirt. "Is that a proposal?"

He brushed a hand down her hair. "Seems to be a habit of mine, proposing to you."

"What are you building?" she asked.

He leaned against the siding, pulling her with him. "A really big hothouse."

She pursed her lips. "With bedrooms?"

"No. I guess I'll have to build a separate house to live in."

"That's good. I'd hate to start my married life sleeping on the floor of a hothouse."

He pushed her back so he could see her. "What are you saying?"

"I'm saying I'll marry you, Johnnie."

"Because I'm not building a saloon?"

"Because I love you."

"What about my rental properties?"

"I'm not quite sure how I'll manage that yet. But I've figured out it's not my job to set the standards. What you do with your business is between you and God. And I trust you both."

In her imaginings, this moment held exclamations of joy, accompanied by warm embraces and inspiring kisses.

Instead, he frowned. "Are you still suffering from the smoke you inhaled.

"No, no. I'm fine."

"Then why this sudden change of heart about who I rent my properties to?"

"Because Jesus didn't withdraw from the world. He ate with sinners. He befriended tax collectors. He let a prostitute anoint his feet with her unbound hair. Maybe in your business dealings with these lessees, you can offer them a hope they wouldn't otherwise know."

"Just like that? You've come to this conclusion just like that?"

"Well, no. I've been praying about it for months. Over and over the Lord would send me to Romans 12, where He talks about His body. And that everyone's function is different. And that one part of the body shouldn't think of itself more highly than another. And if He wants to put you in a position where you can minister to the lost in a way that I'm not particularly fond of, well, who am I to argue?"

"Do you really mean that?"

"I really mean that."

Bending his knees, he yanked her against him and kissed her like he'd never kissed her before. Without breaking their seal, he straightened, lifting her up off the ground and spinning them around.

When he finally released her, they collapsed together against the house.

"Well," she said. "That was even better than I'd imagined."

"Your pardon?"

"Nothing."

He kneaded her back. "You do know I'd never lease our property to someone who sells women, don't you?"

"Yes, I know."

"And for what it's worth, I'm not completely sure anymore about renting to saloon owners. So until I can ascertain a clear answer about that, for now, I'm going to limit my transactions to those merchants who deal in businesses of a less questionable nature."

O Lord. Have I told you recently how precious you are to me?

She relaxed into Johnnie. "Can one of those properties be designated for the rebuilding of the Cottage Café?"

The massage stopped. "Why? You needn't work anymore, Rachel. I'll do the providing from now on."

"Yes. You're quite right. Someone else ought to run it. Soda, perhaps? Or Frank and Selma? The main thing is I need a place for my wards to work. A safe place that can ease them into an honest day's work once they are ready."

"Wards? What wards?"

"The wards from my House of Refuge."

He sighed. "What House of Refuge?"

"The one I'm going to build for girls who don't want to be prostitutes anymore."

She heard his head fall back against the planks of the house. His thumb drew circles at her waist. "So what you're saying is you not only want me to build you a restaurant, you want me to build you a House of Refuge?"

"Yes, please. If you don't mind."

He said nothing.

"You see, I'm going to teach the ones who can't read to read. The ones who can't sew, to sew. The ones who have never learned proper etiquette, proper etiquette."

"What will you teach the ones who know all that but just want out?"

She nestled deeper into his warmth. "I'll teach them about the grace of God."

"Shouldn't you think about this first?"

"I have thought about it."

"Discuss it with me, then?"

"I am discussing it."

He ran his hands along her back. "You're telling me."

"In an ever so polite way."

"Ah, Rachel." He kissed the top of her head.

"Do you object?"

"There will be those who say passive feelings about such things are all that is suitable for elegant ladies."

"Then I guess I'm not elegant."

"There will be those who say that reformed or not, fallen women are not fit for any society but that which lies in the graveyard."

"And that will make me angry. For it is the very men who say such things that frequent the houses of shame."

"Well, that's certainly true."

She nodded. "You'd be amazed to discover the backgrounds of these women. Selma used to be a music teacher. Did you know that?"

"I'd heard it."

"The women here helping me take care of the men? They're not evil, Johnnie. They're just women. Women who have made bad decisions. Like me. Except everyone knows about theirs." She sighed. "Jesus forgave lots of prostitutes."

"Yes, He did."

She heard a bout of coughing from the front of the house. "Will you lose business, do you think, if I do this?"

"I don't think so. But even if I did, it wouldn't matter."

"You don't mind, then?"

"No. I do have a question, though."

"What is it?"

"Who's funding this?"

She smiled. "Worried?"

"Just wondering."

"Well, for starters, I could use the money I have saved up. Then, I thought I would solicit funds through lectures and print tracts. Maybe some of the preachers could do a sermon for me."

He tunneled his fingers into the hair framing her face and tipped her head up. "What if my tree farm gave a percentage of its profits to your cause?"

She squeezed him. "Oh, Johnnie. Would you?"

"Of course."

Raising up on tiptoe, she thanked him in a manner as old as time.

c h a p t e r **25**

$\mathcal{F}$inishing her morning prayers, Rachel rose from her knees and looked at the white organdy dress lying across her cot, with new underclothes and stockings by its side.

This was the day she had been preparing for since the moment of her birth. The day she would become a man's wife. Johnnie's wife.

Less than a month had passed since the fire, but a month in San Francisco was equivalent to a lifetime anywhere else. By the close of Christmas Day, frames of new buildings had begun to change the silhouette of the Plaza, where two million dollars worth of property had burnt to the ground just twenty-four hours earlier. The square had been one ceaseless sound of hammers, axes, and saws ever since.

The town council had offered Rachel use of the schoolhouse until she and Johnnie could be married. So he began immediate work on the House of Refuge. It was to be a two-story affair set on the hillock overlooking his pond.

He'd constructed it so that the living quarters for her wards would be abovestairs, while a couple of cozy little rooms below would serve for the two of them and any future offspring. Though it was not ready to open, it was habitable, and Johnnie insisted they marry right away so she could stay on the property and help him design his greenhouse and orchard.

The thought of planning a wedding without a mother had so daunted Rachel that she had decided to keep the affair simple. With plans for opening the House of Refuge consuming most of her time, she could barely manage to make a bonnet. Sewing a wedding gown would be out of the question. She had intended to simply remake one of her old dresses into something suitable.

But Selma would not hear of it. Quiet, shy Selma had transformed into a military commander. She shooed away Rachel's concerns about the time it would take to sew a gown and the money it would cost and the difficulty they would have in even finding fabric.

Selma scoffed at the idea of doing without a silk bonnet. Frivolous or not, she insisted that Rachel would have one.

For every argument, the girl not only had a ready answer, but she had Johnnie as a staunch supporter.

Rachel had no idea how Selma had managed to procure the luxuries she had in this wild town, but procure them she did. The organdy for her gown, the fine silk for her bonnet, and a pair of the softest, most supple white kid gloves she'd ever beheld in her life.

Selma took her measurements with pieces of twine, and two weeks later Rachel had gone out to Lissa's to check on the handful of men still in recovery. Four of the seven women who had helped out the day of the fire wished to live in the House of Refuge.

Although Lissa expressed no interest in participating herself, she graciously allowed them to stay on while they cared for the men and awaited the opening of Rachel's house.

It was that very day Selma, Lissa, and those four other women presented Rachel with an ivory gown and an exquisite collection of underclothes. Never had she felt so humbled. So undeserving. So touched. And now it was time to wear them.

A soft knock sounded at the door of the schoolhouse, and Selma peeked her head in. "I've come to help you dress. You ready?"

"I'm ready."

"I ain't never seen such gewgaws in all my life," Cotton complained, pulling at the round linen collar fastened to his neck with a large white bow.

Smiling, Johnnie straightened his own cravat before turning to the boy. Squatting down, he began to retie the boy's collar. "Now, Cotton, ring bearers play a very important role in the ceremony. When you give me the ring I'll be placing on my bride's finger, I'm going to need you to look sharp indeed."

Cotton heaved a put-upon sigh. "I'll do right by ya', pardner, but it shore seems like a lot o' magoozlum to go through when you could just sling her over yer shoulder and be done."

"Now, you don't mean that. A man doesn't sling a sunbonnet over his shoulder, and you know it."

"Asa Booker did."

Johnnie chuckled. "Well, that was different. His girl wasn't exactly a sunbonnet."

"He married her, didn't he?"

"He did."

"Then don't that make her a bonnet?"

Johnnie paused. "It does to me, boy. It does to me." Squeezing Cotton's shoulder, Johnnie stood. "Now, try and leave that bow alone, all right?"

Cotton crossed his eyes and wrapped his hands around his neck as if he were choking.

Johnnie slapped him playfully on the back. "Me, too, son. Me, too."

The waiting was going to turn Rachel's brains to crackers. Where in the great horn spoon was Selma? Rachel had insisted that Selma stand up with her. She had asked Lissa, but once again her sister had gently begged off.

After much vacillating and with a great deal of reluctance, Selma had finally agreed. But only if she could wear a simple gown of her choosing. Nothing extravagant. And no fancy bonnet to match the bride's. Rachel had long ago acquiesced and all had been arranged.

Now the day had arrived, and Selma had arrayed Rachel in her finery and then left to prepare herself. She should be here by now.

Rachel could hear the crowd gathering in the Plaza outside and spun at the knock on her door.

"Selma?"

The door opened.

"Michael. Oh, look at you."

Wearing a brown wool suit and shiny new boots, he handed her a thick bouquet of wild pink roses. "These are from Johnnie."

"Good heavens." Their delicate scent floated about her.

"You look beautiful."

The wonder in his voice made her smile. "Thank you. Do you know where Selma is?"

"Frank said she's been casting up her accounts for the last hour and hasn't let up yet. I don't think she's going to be able to stand up with you, Rachel."

A wave of acute disappointment poured through her. "Oh no. Why, she was fine when she left here earlier."

"I think it must be nerves. You know how she is."

"Do you think she's really sick or merely pretending to be so she won't have to stand in front of this crowd?"

He shook his head. "She's sick, Rachel. I heard her myself, and she was retching her guts out."

"Oh, that poor thing."

Rachel blinked rapidly. She had tried so hard not to think about Lissa and had almost managed it. But now she'd have no one. Not her mother, not her sister, not even her dear friend.

Michael stepped forward and gave her an awkward hug. "Now, don't cry. Your eyes get all red and buggy when you cry."

She swallowed and shut her lids until the urge to shed tears passed, even though the grief did not.

"There. That's better," he said. "And I'll stand up with you. The whole time. Seems only right, don't you think?" He stuck out his arm.

She studied her tall, lanky brother in his snappy brown suit and freshly cut hair. He'd recently started working at the mercantile and had come by to see her several times since the fire.

He had no plans to move in with her and Johnnie, but many an evening had found him asking for Johnnie's advice on investing and various other ventures. Maybe they did become men earlier out here in the West.

"Thank you, Michael. I would love for you to stand up with me. That would truly be wonderful."

"You nervous?"

"Terrified." She put her hand in the crook of his elbow.

"Have you told him you snore?"

She gasped. "I do not snore."

He patted her hand and winked. "Yes, you do, Rache. Yes, you do."

Rachel walked out onto the schoolhouse steps blinking at the brightness of the sun and holding tightly to Michael's arm. The men gave out a roar of approval that lasted the whole of five minutes. Even Reverend Taylor's booming voice couldn't settle them down.

They filled the Plaza to capacity, some standing on a temporary dance floor made of loose planks, the rest crowding around in the ankle-deep mud. None but the wedding party had dressed for the affair, but a more appreciative group of guests a couple couldn't have found.

Johnnie took those moments of abandon to behold his bride with her fitted bodice, tiny waist, and fluffy skirt. The wide-brimmed bonnet she wore hid her face from curious eyes. From all, that is, but his.

The men finally settled, and Michael gave her over to him. She moved down one step, and the reverend moved up. Helping her turn her back to the crowd, Johnnie squeezed her hand, then gave his full attention to the preacher, loudly pledging before God and company his love for this woman and his vow to honor, cherish, and keep her.

When it came time for the ring, he took her gloved hand, raising his brows in silent question. She had not made a slit in the fourth finger.

"I couldn't bear to cut it," she whispered.

Nodding, he turned her hand over and released the pearl button at the junction of her wrist, then peeled the glove down, exposing her soft, creamy hand. He brought her palm to his lips, holding it there briefly before sliding the rest of the glove from her fingers.

Cotton yanked on Johnnie's frock coat and gave him a stern look.

Johnnie took the proffered ring from the boy and slid it onto Rachel's finger, repeating the reverend's words. Her eyes widened with wonder, then delight.

He'd had their pearl mounted onto the traditional gold band.

———

Rachel's wedding wasn't exactly the way she had always imagined it, yet she wasn't disappointed. Shortly after the ceremony, the men pulled green baize tables from the saloons and under Selma's direction filled them with a hodgepodge of foodstuffs. The girl appeared to be fully recovered, if a bit pale.

She still wore her work dress, and though the men wanted to dance with her, she insisted her constitution was not up to it. So, instead, she oversaw the refreshments, cornering Frank, Michael, and Soda for help.

Dancing had indeed commenced. Every man present requested a turn with Rachel, but Johnnie would not release her for even one. So the men danced with each other while Johnnie kept her tucked closely at his side.

None of the women from Lissa's were present. If they had attended, the company would have assumed they were "working," and none were willing to do so.

Johnnie introduced Rachel to many more men than she could possibly remember, though a few of his closest friends kept her vastly entertained.

She met Cotton's father. And Levi Strauss, who had a dry wood business. Phillip Armor, a butcher down on Montgomery Street. John Studebaker, a wheelbarrow maker. Samuel Clements, a columnist for the newspaper. Henry Wells and William Fargo, bankers new to town.

The sun was still high in the sky when Reverend Taylor rang the schoolhouse's bell. He called the bride and groom up, and the crowd quieted as they took their place beside the preacher.

"The boys knew if you'd been home," Taylor boomed, "you'd have been showered with everything a young couple needed to get started.

But this bunch is a few pence short of patchwork quilts and pillow sachets."

The crowd chuckled and Rachel glanced at Johnnie. He stood before them in a frock coat of mulberry, a wild rose from her bouquet pinned to his lapel. So handsome was he in his white waistcoat and doeskin trousers, she thought that no magazine could have painted a finer figure than he.

"But there was one thing the fellas here could supply you with that home could not," the reverend continued.

A disturbance from the Delmonico Restaurant captured everyone's attention. Soda, Frank, Michael, and a fourth man struggled to haul a tall shrouded object to the bottom of the schoolhouse steps.

"Allow me to introduce Mr. Thomas Crawford," the reverend said. "Though he hails from New York City, he has come to us most recently from Rome, Italy."

The fourth man who had helped with the carting stepped forward, grabbed a corner of the shroud, and whipped it off. If this Crawford man had sculpted it, he had extraordinary talent.

This female statue held the exact same pose as the one that had broken in the fire, but this one was clothed in a sculpted calico and sunbonnet.

A slow smile split Johnnie's face. "Well, boys, I've mourned the loss of my Lorenzo Bartolini something fierce and wondered how I'd ever persuade my wife to let me have another." He pulled her against his side. "But now, I have something even better. An original Thomas Crawford, handcrafted in the soon-to-be state of California, and a bride who will let me display it in full view. We both thank you!"

The men cheered and whistled and shot their guns. Johnnie drew Rachel down to exchange words with the sculptor. Well-wishers surrounded them.

They slowly made their way to the opposite edge of the Plaza, where Johnnie left Rachel with Selma while he collected Sweet Lips and J.B.

Selma wiped her hands on a cloth.

"You were supposed to be an attendant, not work yourself to the bone," Rachel said. "Why, I never even saw the dress you were going to wear."

"Lands, I had a marvelous time. I'd much rather be doing this than wearing some pretty dress and dancing with all those woman-hungry men."

They hugged.

"Thank you for letting me help," Selma said.

Rachel squeezed her. "Thank *you*, Selma. For everything. I don't know what I would have done without you."

They slipped apart but grabbed hold of each other's hands. The two of them stood there, treasuring the special bond that had formed between them over these last few weeks.

A slow frown crinkled Selma's brows. She darted a quick glance at Johnnie rounding the corner with the horses.

"Oh dear," she whispered. "I probably should have spoken to you about, um, what to expect. Never crossed my mind. I plumb forgot you don't have a mama."

Rachel smiled with a show of confidence she didn't feel. "Don't worry about me," she whispered back. "I read my father's medical books, but don't tell anyone."

"Mercy me. Maybe we better go to the schoolhouse and let me help you out of your wedding finery."

"No!" Rachel swallowed. "I mean, that's quite all right. It's so pretty, after all."

"You ready, Selma?" Frank asked, having returned the last of the tables to their rightful owners.

Johnnie joined them and shook Frank's hand. "Thank you for everything, Frank, Selma. We appreciate all you did. You'll take care of my statue until I can haul her home?"

"We'll put her in the schoolhouse for safekeeping," Frank answered, pulling Selma away from the horses.

Johnnie lifted Rachel into her saddle, raising his brows at the work boots that peeked out from beneath her wedding gown.

"They didn't burn?"

"I had them on the day of the fire."

"Did you? I don't remember."

"Well, they fit perfectly and I never properly thanked you for them."

He grinned. "If I'd known you were going to wear them to our wedding, I'd have looked for something more suitable."

She shook her skirt over them. "You tell anyone and I'll flatly deny it. But this Plaza's a mess and I didn't know what else to do."

Chuckling, he swung up onto J.B.

From the sounds of revelry, it appeared as if the celebration would continue well into the night.

Rachel held Sweet Lips still while she scanned the crowd. "I didn't say good-bye to Michael. Have you seen him?"

"He's here somewhere. You can see him tomorrow."

And with that, they turned their mounts and headed home.

———

Johnnie carried her across the threshold, boots and all, then set her on her feet.

"Are you cold?" he asked.

"A little."

"I've a stove in the back all ready to be lit. It'll be warmer there."

She folded her hands, starting at the feel of her wedding ring. She rubbed it with her fingers, recalling the removal of her gloves. "I love my ring. It's beautiful. The pearl, especially. I shall always treasure it."

"And I shall always treasure you."

She ran her tongue along her lower lip.

"Are you disappointed we aren't taking a wedding trip?" he asked.

"No. Traveling in this mud would be miserable. Besides, I have the House of Refuge to open."

"You're not going to abandon our trees, are you?"

"I wouldn't dream of it." She studied him. "What if you hate it? Tree farming, I mean."

He took her hand and brought it to his lips. "I won't." Keeping his gaze pinned to hers, he turned her hand up and nibbled her fingertips. "I've selected trees known for their rapid growth and hardy disposition."

The ruffled cuff attached to her quarter-length sleeve fell back. "You have?"

"Um." He moved his attentions to her palm. "I'm thinking of bringing in flowers, as well."

She took a shaky breath. "Oh, won't that be lovely?"

"Yes." He tasted the tender part of her wrist.

She slid her eyes closed.

"In three years time I expect our home to be covered with graded drives, grass-covered plateaus, flowers, and young trees."

He had worked his way to her elbow and ran into the sleeve. Then kept going, kissing her right through the fabric and along the rest of her arm.

She turned to look at him, bumping him with the brim of her bonnet. "Oh. I'm sorry."

He placed her hand on his shoulder and made quick work of the bow at her chin, drawing the silken piece off her head. "You are so beautiful."

Encircling her waist, he drew her flush against him, her bonnet still in his hand, and kissed her. Not the chaste kiss he had bestowed after the ceremony, but a real kiss. A deep kiss. A kiss of a man and his wife.

She ran her fingers up into his hair, grabbing handfuls of his thick, black mane. "It's still light outside," she whispered.

He said nothing, yet he must have dropped her silk bonnet because his hands held nothing but her now. He kneaded her waist, her sides, her shoulder blades.

"Johnnie." She tugged. "The book said we must wait until dark."

He leaned just far enough away to look at her, his hands cupping her sides, his thumbs moving restlessly over her rib cage. "The Good Book?"

"No," she said, allowing her lids to close and her head to fall back. "My father's medical book. Written by a doctor. A very renowned doctor."

His thumbs became more bold. A tiny moan escaped before she could stop it.

"Rachel, love, the only book I care about is the Good Book. And if it's not in the Good Book, then I don't care what time of day it is."

She fluttered open her eyes. "You don't think it's a sin, then?"

He wrapped her close, cradling her head against his chest. "I know it's not."

She sagged into him. "Oh, thank heavens."

She felt him smile against her hair before scooping her into his arms and carrying her to their room in the back.

e p i l o g u e

The bell on the Cottage Café door jingled. Rachel looked up. The sunbonnet woman couldn't have been more than fifteen years old and far too pretty for her own good.

Tall, slender, regal, and with a set of magnificent violet eyes, she clutched a valise in one gloved hand and held her wool shawl together with the other. Michael stood beside her, two more valises in his hand.

Silence descended as everyone in the room came to his feet. Rachel immediately moved to them.

"Miss Eldridge," Michael said, "this is my sister Mrs. Parker."

Rachel smiled. "How do you do?"

The girl curtsied. Rachel raised her brows and looked at Michael.

"I found her at the wharf looking kind of lost. She just arrived. Her uncle died on the passage over."

Rachel placed her arm around the girl. "Oh, you poor dear. Are you all alone?"

Miss Eldridge nodded.

Rachel tilted her head. "So, how many marriage proposals did you receive between here and the bay?"

The girl blushed.

Michael scowled. "A hundred, at least. Starting with Harry. I think that old codger lies in wait at the wharf just hoping one of these days some bonnet's going to say yes. You should have seen them. They—"

"Michael?"

He stopped short, realizing his audience. Blood rushed to his cheeks. "I beg your pardon, miss. I meant no disrespect."

Rachel watched in fascination as each of them seemed to turn redder than the other. Michael finally caught himself ogling her and held out a hand—satchel and all—indicating she and Rachel precede him.

Rachel led her to the back. As soon as they crossed into the kitchen, the noise in the dining room rose with excitement.

Michael set the valises down next to the wall and disappeared into the scullery.

Annie wiped her hands on her apron. "Well, who do we have here?"

"This is Miss Eldridge, just off the boat," Rachel said. Josephine set a glass of lemonade on the table. "Here, take a rest now, sugar. You have any family?"

Miss Eldridge shook her head and took the proffered chair.

"Any place to stay?" This from Mary Belle.

Another shake.

Carmelita sank into the chair beside her. "Any dinero? Money?"

Tears filled the girl's eyes.

All productivity in the kitchen came to a halt as the girls surrounded Miss Eldridge and offered words of comfort and support.

Johnnie and Soda came through the back door. Johnnie made immediate eye contact with Rachel.

"A new arrival," she said.

"Ahhh." He set two bottles of milk on the worktable. "And our customers?"

She bit her cheek. "Would most likely appreciate some service."

"Selma?" Johnnie yelled above the commotion the girls were making.

Selma's head popped up like a jack-in-the-box.

"Can't you control these girls any better than this?"

She smiled. "It's a bonnet, Johnnie. And she's all alone."

"Yeah? Well, so are our customers."

"Bonnets?" Selma asked.

He narrowed his eyes. "Alone."

"Oh, all right, then." She clapped her hands. "Come on, girls. Back to work. We have some customers with a hankerin' for some grub."

The door jingled.

"I'll get it," Rachel said.

She swept into the dining room and smiled, moving to give Lissa a hug. "Hello, dear."

Rachel gave a nod to her companion. "Mr. Sumner."

"Mrs. Parker." He removed his hat, greeting several men at the various tables but receiving only grunts in return, if anything.

She hooked elbows with Lissa and pulled her away, saying over her shoulder, "I'm borrowing my sister for a while."

Productivity stopped again as the girls all welcomed Lissa. They introduced her to Miss Eldridge, and Lissa sat down. Faint bluish circles teased the otherwise flawless skin below her eyes.

Pulling off her gloves, Lissa told the girl it would be safest if she stayed in the House of Refuge where she had the protection of the Parkers.

She described the grounds to her. "It's nothing like it is here in town. The House of Refuge sets in the middle of Parker's Tree Farm."

Selma gave Lissa a glass of lemonade.

She took a dainty sip. "There are mounds and hillocks, a huge orchard of baby trees, and a brook winding through the eastern quadrant. But my favorite spot is the pond. Oh, wait until you see it. It is edged with water lilies and filled with swans and ducks."

Johnnie quietly walked to Rachel's side and slipped his arm around her waist, giving her a squeeze of comfort. Lissa loved it out at the House of Refuge, but she would not leave Sumner.

Mrs. Sumner had boarded a boat two months ago to return to the land of her youth. Freeing Sumner to move back in with Lissa.

Rachel ground her teeth together. If there was anyone she wanted to refuse service to, it was Mr. Sumner. A more despicable man she could not imagine. Catching herself, she sighed.

I'm sorry, Lord. I simply do not like him, even though I know him to be knitted together with your very hands. Help me. Help me want to forgive him.

Michael returned to the kitchen and gave Lissa a kiss on the cheek. She noticed his flushed face, guessed at the cause, and proceeded to discomfit him as only a sibling could do.

Rachel had no doubt Lissa understood that any time she wanted, she could walk away from Sumner. And when she did, her family would be there. Waiting.

Rachel looked up.

Johnnie winked, mouthing *I love you.*

She smiled, thanking God again for the man He had given her, for the seed that had just taken root inside her womb, and for showing her that the measure of a lady is determined not by others but by His never-ending mercy and grace.

ecause the city of San Francisco burnt down six times in less than two years (the first time being in December of 1849), much of our gold rush history was lost in those flames—making it exceedingly difficult for the city to preserve original artifacts of the time. Therefore, I had to rely heavily on the personal diaries and journals written by eyewitnesses. Once I had exhausted those sources, I turned to the wonderful compilations historians have made readily available.

I discovered California's history to be so rich it seemed superfluous to make up anecdotes when the real ones were so very colorful. The story about the small boy gambling with duck-shot: true. The bull and bear fight: true. The "hang him" episode: true. The masquerade ball: true. The street sign mentioned at the opening of the novel: true. The name of George Washington's dog: true.

And those were just the tip of the iceberg. I wish I could have incorporated all the tales I unearthed, but there simply wasn't room. It was a fun and entertaining journey, though, and one that my high school American History class skimmed over with alarming brevity.

The City Hotel and the Parker House were both prominent hotels/saloons in San Francisco, but they were owned by Sam Brannan (City Hotel) and Robert Parker (Parker House). I had actually already named my male protagonist Johnnie Parker before discovering there was a Parker House. So it seemed natural to make him the owner of those establishments for the benefit of my story. Johnnie is totally and completely a fictional character, in no way reflecting the actual owners of those establishments.

Blessings,
Deeanne Gist

More Humorous Romance!

Lady Constance Morrow finds herself held against her will aboard a ship bound for the American colonies—a ship filled with "tobacco brides" and felons. Drew O'Connor, a determined Colonial farmer who is nearly as headstrong as Constance, wins her as his bride but soon realizes their marriage of convenience has become most inconvenient.

Gist's witty dialogue and humorous descriptions make this novel compulsively readable.

Ruth Caldwell has always tried to live up to her mother's expectations of what a lady should be...often with less than impressive results. When she's forced to journey west to meet the father she's never seen, Ruth hopes that this might be the place she'll finally fit in. But her arrival brings about more mayhem than even Ruth is used to.

Cathy Marie Hake unites suspense and sweet romance with a generous helping of humor to create an engaging historical novel.